From business to pleasure

"So are you going to tell me what brought you to my door at this ungodly hour?"

Calder didn't raise his head as he answered. "We've had another assassination of a suspect. It was a serial rapist this time. Grady Thompson . . . What kind of world do we live in where children are exposed to this kind of violence?"

Calder put his head in his hands, and Raine watched his thick brown hair fall forward. Raine stood up and walked around the coffee table, sliding next to him on the couch. As she moved to put an arm around his shoulder comfortingly, Calder twisted into her and all thoughts of gentle comfort fled from Raine's mind, pushed away by the smoldering heat she saw in Calder's eyes.

He slid one big hand through her pillow-mussed hair and pulled her toward him. His lips met hers, hard and furious with the force of pent-up fury and eleven months of longing . . .

DANGEROUS CURVES

JACEY FORD

BERKLEY SENSATION, NEW YORK

DANGEROUS CURVES

A Berkley Sensation Book / published by arrangement with the author

PRINTING HISTORY
Berkley Sensation edition / June 2004

ISBN: 0-425-19685-2

BERKLEY SENSATION™
Berkley Sensation Books are published by The Berkley Publishing Group,
a division of Penguin Group (USA) Inc.,
375 Hudson Street, New York, New York 10014.
BERKLEY SENSATION and the "B" design
are trademarks belonging to Penguin Group (USA) Inc.

PRINTED IN THE UNITED STATES OF AMERICA

10 9 8 7 6 5 4 3 2 1

This book is dedicated to

my kickass agent,
Deidre Knight,
who never stops believing in me

Acknowledgments

With special thanks to

Cindy Hwang, my fabulous editor. Thank you for all your support!

My stepdaughter, Dana Brandt—athlete, scholar, and all-around good kid—who was the inspiration for the character of Megan in this book.

Alesia Holliday, a great friend and a great writer. Here's to many happy times ahead.

Katherine Garbera, my newest writer pal. I think I'd go crazy without our monthly lunch/therapy sessions.

The friendly folks at the Cracker Barrel in Seffner, Florida. Thanks for not kicking Kathy and I out even after countless cups of coffee and free refills on our water.

Emily Cotler and her team at WaxCreative design, for caring so much about what you do. Your websites are awesome!

Fellow author Anne Avery. Thank you for all the great information on the Venezuelan jungle. Who knew there were so many things out there that can kill you?!

ONE

COMPUTER hacker Raine Robey was one click away from downloading secure credit information for over one hundred thousand of American Trust Bank's most valued customers when her telephone rang. She ignored the insistent summons, knowing she didn't have much time before AmTrust's automated sweepers detected her presence behind their firewall. It was important that she get in and out without getting caught. The job depended on it.

Her fingers faltered on the keyboard, however, when she heard the voice on the other end of the line after her answering machine picked up. It was a voice she hadn't heard for almost a year—ten months, two weeks, and three days to be exact—a voice she had never expected to hear again.

"Raine, it's Calder. Calder Preston."

Right. Like she wouldn't recognize his voice. Her heart beat faster, thudding against her ribs like a drum gone berserk. While her brain might want to forget him, she feared her heart never would.

"I understand that you're in Atlanta, and that you've started your own business. I think I have an assignment that might interest you."

Raine stared at the computer screen in front of her as AmTrust kicked her off their server with the familiar phrase blinking triumphantly: ACCESS DENIED. She glanced at her watch. It had taken the sweeper almost ten seconds to detect her. In hacker terms, ten seconds was a lifetime. She could have raided their data, sold it to the highest bidder, and booked herself a vacation to China in ten seconds.

Not two days ago, AmTrust's chief technology officer had sat in his twenty-first floor office and bragged about his hacker-proof security.

Hacker-proof, my ASCII, Raine scoffed as she reached across her cluttered desk to pick up the phone. She would prove to the CTO that his system was vulnerable, and she'd convince him that the bank should retain her to fix those vulnerabilities. Unfortunately, she'd have to do it some other time.

"Partners In Crime. This is Raine speaking," she said into the mouthpiece, striving for her best professional voice.

"Oh. You're there."

"Yes, I'm sorry. I couldn't get to the phone before the machine picked up. What can I do for you?" Raine asked, twisting around in her chair to stare at the closed blinds opposite her desk. She had no idea what time it was. She had been determined to break into AmTrust's so-called secure server when she woke up this morning at 2 A.M., her brain buzzing with the problem. Rolling her shoulders, Raine closed her eyes and tried to pretend that she was merely speaking to a business prospect—not the man with whom she had been having regular sex ten months, two weeks, and three days ago.

Calder cleared his throat. "I heard you'd moved back to Atlanta."

"Yes," Raine acknowledged.

"I've been transferred here, myself."

"I know."

There was a long pause before Calder spoke again. "Look, Raine, I know this is awkward—"

Raine opened her eyes, determined to keep the emotion out of her voice as she interrupted, "You mentioned a business proposition that might be of interest to my firm. I don't see anything awkward in that. Why don't you explain the nature of the assignment, and I'll let you know if my partners and I can fit it into our schedules." *Yeah, right. Like that was a problem. Partners In Crime was only six months old and they were struggling to make ends meet. Unless Calder wanted them to run naked along Peachtree-Dunwoody Road, they'd jump on this job like starving Chihuahuas on a pork chop. And they might not even scoff at the streaking job if there was a paycheck involved.*

"All right. If you want to pretend the past never happened, I'll go along with you," Calder said, then added a quiet, "for now."

Raine heard some rustling on the other end of the line and could picture him settling back in his chair, at ease with whatever life was going to throw at him next. She'd always envied his outward sense of calm, maddening as it had sometimes been when all she'd wanted was a down-and-dirty fight and he'd do nothing more than calmly reason with her.

Reminding herself that one didn't fight with one's business prospects, Raine leaned back in her own chair and attempted to mimic Calder's Zen-like air.

"A month ago, I received a crudely written letter from an elderly man," Calder began. "The letter said only, 'Help my daughter.' At first, I just ignored it. I mean, who's got time to deal with vague pleas like this?"

Raine made an appropriately agreeable noise although she had plenty of time to deal with just about anything these days. No errand was too small for her to-do list.

"The letter sat in my inbox for a few weeks, but I couldn't bring myself to throw it away. Finally, a couple days ago, I decided to pay the guy a visit. The thing is, the guy who had written the note was in really bad shape. The nurse taking care of him said it must have taken his patient weeks to write it, and that he probably waited months for the opportunity to slip it into a stack of outgoing mail."

"So why would he have gone to so much trouble?"

"That's exactly what I asked myself. I figured that this poor guy's daughter must need some serious help for him to have expended such an effort to enlist the FBI's aid."

"Why didn't you just ask him for details while you were there?" Raine asked.

"He was recovering from pneumonia. His caretaker said he was difficult to communicate with even when he was well. As it was, he was barely conscious."

"What happened to him in the first place? To make him so sick to begin with, I mean."

"Car accident. Twenty years ago, this guy was at the top of his game. Headed up research and development for Jackson Motor Company here in Atlanta. Then one day, driving the Pronto, one of JMC's very own brand of cars, he gets rear-ended and his car explodes. He's thrown from the vehicle and suffers brain damage and a severed spine. He's needed full-time care ever since."

"That's awful," Raine said, turning to rest her head against her palm, the wrist brace she wore on her right arm rubbing against her cheek.

"Yes, it is. JMC paid for his medical care after the accident, but Mr. Enslar's daughter now foots the majority of the tab for one of the most expensive nursing care providers in the state."

"How did you find that out?"

"I work for the FBI," Calder answered dryly. "I have my sources."

Okay, she'd give him that.

"Besides, while I would never classify myself as being as proficient with a computer as you, I am not without technical skills. Gaining access to the records stored in a local nursing care company's computer didn't present much of a challenge. Even for me."

Raine nodded silently, giving him that point. Calder was definitely not as skilled as she was, but he had not been assigned to the fledgling computer crimes division of the Federal Bureau of Investigation twelve years ago just because he looked good in a dark suit.

"In any event, my research led me to his daughter, one Hope Enslar."

"What kind of trouble is she in? Drugs? Prostitution? Pornography?"

"The answer would be 'D. None of the above.' That's what I can't figure out. Ms. Enslar has a record the Pope would envy. She's never been arrested. Never had so much as a speeding ticket. She attended Georgia Tech on an academic scholarship and graduated with a Master's degree in applied mathematics. After college, she was offered a job at none other than Jackson Motor Company and has been working there ever since. She's been promoted regularly and visits her father often. Hell, she even votes. I can't find anything to indicate that Mr. Enslar's concerns about his daughter have any basis in reality."

"Did you interview her?" Raine asked, and heard the frustration in Calder's voice when he answered.

"No. I'd look like an idiot if I tried to question her. What am I supposed to say? 'We have no victim. We have no crime. But we do have a note from your dad and he's worried about you.'" Calder snorted. "No, I need more to go on than that."

Raine let the information Calder had just relayed sink in for a moment. "What is it that you suspect, then? Is the old guy just trying to get attention? Maybe he's lonely and wants someone other than his daughter to come visit."

"I don't think that's it."

Raine heard more rustling on the other end of the line and guessed that her former lover was now pacing around his small government office like an agitated panther. He'd always hated hunches, preferring cold, hard facts instead. Unfortunately, hunches turned out to be right often enough to make it impossible to just dismiss them out of hand.

"So, what do you want me to do?" Raine asked. "Try to see what dirt I can dig up on Ms. Enslar through less-than-legitimate means?"

"That will do for a start," Calder answered. "Although I doubt you're going to find anything more than what my sources uncovered."

"And if that doesn't work?"

"I want you to go undercover."

Raine jerked upright, almost dumping herself out of her chair and knocking over the Coke that was sitting near her elbow. "Damn," she cursed, lunging for a napkin to stop the river of cola from reaching her keyboard. With that staunched, she turned her attention back to the conversation. "I can't go undercover. I don't work for you anymore, remember?"

"I'm not likely to forget that anytime soon," Calder replied, then added, "much as I might want to."

Raine felt her face go hot with anger. *He* wanted to forget? What about her? It had been she who lost her job when all hell broke loose, not him. It was her reputation that lay in tatters, not his. And her heart that had been broken. Definitely not his.

Taking a deep breath, Raine reminded herself that it was not a good business practice to fight with potential clients. "I can't go undercover," she repeated. "I am a partner in a legitimate corporate services firm. We assist our clients in enhancing their computer security, investigating the backgrounds of their current and prospective employees, and deterring corporate espionage. We don't go around pretending to be people we aren't."

"That's bullshit and you know it, Raine. In order to accomplish your corporate mission, you have to pretend to be someone you're not all the time. When I called just now, you were hacking into somebody's computer system, weren't you?"

Raine leaned back in her chair and repositioned the phone against her ear, the Velcro fasteners of her wrist guard scratching her neck.

"And I'll bet you weren't logged on as <u>rainerobey@partnersincrime.us,</u> were you?"

She frowned. Of course she hadn't been using a legitimate username to break into AmTrust's server. Anonymity was the hackers' friend, the one thing that let them slip undetected—and uncaught if they *were* detected—into one system after another. Only an amateur or an idiot would use her real name while hacking. Still, there was a big difference between posing as someone else while hiding behind a computer screen and doing so in person. It wasn't something Raine had ever balked at doing when she'd worked for the Bureau, but in the time since she'd handed over her proverbial tin star and pistol almost eleven months ago, she'd spent most of her time here in her two-bedroom apartment. Hiding out from the real world, she supposed. In here with her computers, she was safe. The computer world was predictable, without risk. The real world, on the other hand, was full of danger—full of people with questionable motives bent on destroying other people's lives. She wasn't sure she was ready to face that world again.

But starving to death from lack of funds didn't sound like much fun, either. Besides, she had Aimee and Daphne to think about, too. They had signed on with her to form Partners In Crime and had just as much riding on the company's success as Raine did. She couldn't chicken out and let them bear the brunt of the new business development because she was afraid to leave her computer-filled cocoon.

Raine picked up the nearly empty Coke can beside her and drained the last of the lukewarm drink.

"All right," she said finally, "I'll start by seeing what I can dig up electronically. If that doesn't work, I'll go undercover."

"Good. I suppose I don't need to tell you that this is an unofficial investigation?"

"If it were official, you wouldn't have called me," Raine said.

Calder paused before answering, softly, "I called you because you're the best hacker I know. Inside the Bureau or out."

"No," Raine said. "I'm the *second* best hacker you know. The best one framed me for murder ten months, two weeks, and three days ago."

TWO

FIFTEEN-YEAR-OLD Megan Mulroney heard the door locks of her mother's new SUV pop open and resisted coming out of the half-sleep she had lulled herself into. Grumpily, she wished her mom had been gone longer. How could she have caught up on the grocery shopping so quickly? Megan knew they were out of the usual stuff: toilet paper, toothpaste (her seven-year-old brother always used way too much, leaving disgusting globs of white goo all over the bathroom counter when he was done), bread, Shredded Wheat, and probably a dozen other things their family needed to make it through until the next big shopping trip.

Burrowing deeper into her letterman's jacket, Megan stretched out on the backseat of the car, buried her nose into the crook of her elbow, and waited for her mom to tell her to sit up and put on her seat belt. Mom never bent the rules on seat belt–wearing. Ever. No matter how tired Megan was, Mom would wake her up before they hit busy Tremont Street. Until then, though, Megan kept her eyes steadfastly closed, telling herself she'd resist waking up for "just one more second."

Between piano lessons, bassoon lessons, the church retreat, studying for finals, and crew team tryouts, Megan was paying the price for her parentally-endorsed perfectionism by being chronically exhausted. All she wanted to do lately was sleep, but she knew that she'd never get into Harvard or Yale if she didn't keep up her grueling schedule. Like her father said, it was only for two more years. Once she got accepted, she could give herself a bit more breathing room. Until then, she'd continue at this pace, grabbing sleep whenever she could—like during the ten minutes of free time she had after crew practice while her mom was grocery shopping.

With a sigh, Megan felt the heavy SUV turn off the side road that led from the grocery store and onto Tremont. She sat up, grabbing the shoulder strap to her left as she did.

"I know," she grumbled. "Seat belts."

Then she looked up, only it wasn't Mom's familiar brown eyes that met hers in the rearview mirror. Instead, a pair of eerie silver eyes gazed back at her, eyes so cold that Megan felt a shiver creep across her skin.

With barely a hesitation, she lunged for the back door of the SUV. Her mom had only had the car for a few weeks, so Megan fumbled with the unfamiliar catch, just long enough for her to hear the doors lock again.

The man in the front seat gunned the accelerator, sending them speeding through the light at Park Street and making Megan lurch back against the bench seat she had been sleeping on just seconds ago.

She grabbed the seat in front of her and pulled herself upright again, clutching at the back door. She pulled the handle, then tried to dig the lock out of its resting place, all to no avail. The door wouldn't budge. She pushed the lever for the windows, but he'd locked them, too.

"Let me out," Megan ordered, trying not to sound like she was frightened half to death.

The man driving said nothing, just kept looking from the road to the rearview mirror and back again. He had the oddest eyes she had ever seen, and Megan wondered if he was wearing colored contacts. His blond hair was cut short, a bit spiky on top as if he thought that might make him look cool or something.

From where she was sitting, she didn't see a gun or a knife or anything, but she still wasn't sure what her best course of action would be. She could try to attack him from behind, but what if that caused them to crash? Should she try to break one of the windows? Kick open the door? Even those options sounded bad. She'd go flying out of the car and onto the pavement. Or worse, onto another car.

Think, Megan, think, she told herself, looking around the car for something—anything—that might help her escape.

The phrase *What would Charlie's Angels do?* popped unbidden into Megan's mind and she choked down a bubble of hysterical laughter. Some jerk had pasted a WHAT WOULD JESUS DRIVE? sticker on the back of Mom's new SUV last weekend and they'd spent two hours scraping it off the glass with a knife. The saying was a rip-off of the once-popular *What would Jesus do?* slogan that Christians had used a few years ago to get their kids to think about their decisions. Frankly, Megan didn't think Jesus would have any advice for her in this situation. She'd rather rely on the kick-ass women in the Charlie's Angels movies. Those girls would know how to escape from a speeding vehicle that was being driven by a madman, and Megan guessed it wouldn't involve turning the other cheek.

She glanced at her backpack and knew she had her answer. Her trigonometry book alone weighed five pounds. If she threw that at her kidnapper's head, he'd surely stop the car. Megan wasn't exactly sure what she'd do after that, but at least it was better than cowering here on the floor.

Megan threw herself onto the seat, but lurched backward when the driver careened around a corner. Her back slammed against the door and the breath was knocked out of her lungs with an *oomph.* Struggling to breathe, Megan pushed herself up again, only to fall to the carpeted floor when the SUV came to an abrupt stop.

Still, she didn't give up. With a panicked wheeze, she finally managed to pull some air into her lungs as she tried to stand, determined to fight her kidnapper.

But he was already on the move, coming from the driver's seat toward her, his silvery-gray eyes never leaving hers.

"You should always wear your seat belt," he said, his voice calm, as if this sort of thing happened to him every day.

Megan heard the familiar sound of a garage door closing behind her, and the light from the streetlamps quickly disappeared. Crouching, she backed up, her hands feeling along the door for the handle.

"Leave me alone," she said.

"Can't do that, I'm afraid," the man answered.

The door handle was cool and smooth beneath her palms, and the man was so close that she could feel his body heat. She pulled at the handle, squashing herself against the door to get away from him, but the door wouldn't budge.

Megan knew she didn't have any choices left. With a scream, she launched herself at the man.

She was strong. Two years of rowing had left her with muscled thighs and enough upper body strength to beat most guys her age at arm wrestling. She had even beaten her dad a time or two, something she almost hated to do because it left her feeling as if things between them were changing and would never be the same.

She expected to get in at least one good hit. That was all she needed, to get him good on the nose or testicles, just like her mother had taught her. She hadn't expected him to hit her in the stomach so hard that she'd drop to her knees on the floor of the SUV, heaving and retching like her friend Emily after one too many beers at a keg party.

"I was a boxer, honey. If I was you, I wouldn't try that again."

Megan reached out a hand to steady herself on the black leather seat, trying to keep from throwing up. But as another wave of nausea rolled through her, she couldn't stop it from coming.

Mom is going to be so mad at me, she thought as the pepperoni pizza and the salad she'd had for lunch scorched their way up her throat. Tears rolled down her face, and she retched until there was nothing but acid left in her stomach.

The man had taken a step back, and Megan just stayed

there on the floor of the SUV, staring at the faded knees of his blue jeans as the nausea subsided. Every breath she took was agony and she wondered—as if this were happening to someone else—if he had broken one of her ribs.

"I'm going to unlock the doors now. I want you to stand up and walk in front of me until I tell you to stop. You got that?"

Feeling very small all of a sudden, Megan nodded and two tears dribbled off her chin and fell to the now-stained carpet. She heard the doors click open and got slowly to her feet, wincing as pain shot through her chest.

The man put a hand between her shoulder blades and pushed her forward, but it was dark and Megan was afraid she was going to walk into something so she put an arm out in front of her to protect herself. Even that hurt.

Suddenly a light came on, just to the front and right of where Megan was headed. She felt a brief flicker of hope. Maybe whoever was here would help her.

A man who was a few inches shorter than her stepped out of what looked like an office and frowned at them.

"Help me," Megan pleaded, feeling hot, wet tears flooding down her face.

"Be quiet," the man behind her said, not unkindly.

"Please. I haven't done anything wrong. Just let me go. I won't tell anyone anything."

"She was in the Pioneer," the man behind her said, ignoring her plea. "I checked inside before I got in, but I didn't see her."

"That's just fucking great. What do you suggest we do with her? We can't let her go." This man looked much meaner than the man with the silvery eyes, Megan thought. Mr. Silver Eyes seemed calm, not angry at all. Even when he had punched her, he hadn't seemed angry with her.

The other guy—Shorty, Megan labeled him—looked as if he wanted to smack her just for being there. As if it was her fault she was here. There was nothing Megan wanted more than to go home, go up to her room, turn on her computer and her radio, and do her homework while Instant Messaging her best friend, Emily, to tell her about this horrible thing that had happened.

"We've gotta get these cars out to the container tonight," Mr. Silver Eyes was saying.

"Yeah, well, you didn't answer my question. What the hell are we gonna do with her?" Shorty asked, sounding very pissed off.

Megan wished he were closer so she could have bitten off the finger he wagged her way, treating her as if she were some kind of human garbage or something. *Asshole,* she thought. She had no idea what they were talking about, but she knew she had to get out of here. Without moving her head, Megan tried to scope out what appeared to be a three-car garage. She spied a door over to her right, and prayed to both Jesus and the Angels—Charlie's, that is—that it wasn't locked.

When Mr. Silver Eyes turned his attention to Shorty, Megan made a run for it.

One step, then two.

Her hand closed around the silver doorknob.

The knob twisted.

Megan felt herself being yanked off her feet. The zipper of her letterman's jacket dug into the skin at her neck and she started to choke. Frantically, she raised her hands to try to unzip her coat. Her fingers closed around the tab and Megan ignored the pain slicing through her side as she struggled to get free.

The arms of her jacket slipped off once she managed to undo the zipper, and Megan slammed herself against the door, clutching the doorknob.

Then her head exploded. At least, that's what it felt like from the inside as her forehead smacked against the heavy wooden door. Disoriented, she stumbled backward, holding on to the doorknob for support.

Silver Eyes yanked her arm and Megan felt an excruciating pain in her ribs. She let go of the door and heard Shorty say, "Here, tie her up."

Then she was pushed to the ground face first, the heavy weight of Silver Eyes' knee in the middle of her back. When he was done tying her up, he pulled her to her feet and Megan almost tripped. He had tied her feet together and tied her hands together behind her back, and then tied the rope holding her hands to the one holding her feet. She felt all uncoordinated, as if her entire body was in some sort of three-legged race with itself.

Shorty approached, still looking like he wanted to hit her, and Megan shrank back. She could hear the ripping sound of the duct tape in his hand and knew he was going to put it over her mouth. She struggled but Silver Eyes held her arms so tight she was going to have bruises tomorrow. Shorty wasn't satisfied with just putting one piece of tape over her mouth, either. He looped the tape around her head twice, watching her with a smug look on his face the whole time.

Mr. Silver Eyes started pushing her toward the back of her mom's SUV. He put her in the back and made sure the piece that covered the space where you were supposed to put your shopping or your luggage was in place, hiding her from the view of other cars or interested passersby. Megan heard him lock the door—a sound she was beginning to despise—and pressed her ear to the door to hear what the men were saying.

"Relax, Tony, this is not going to be a problem."

Megan couldn't hear what Shorty said back, since his voice didn't carry like Silver's did. Instead, she heard snippets like, "fucked up" and "didn't you look" and the occasional slam of Shorty's fist on another car.

"Yeah, I fucked up," Mr. Silver Eyes said. "I am the first to admit it. But all we have to do is get the vehicles on the container and it will be over. We don't have to worry about killing her—"

Shorty interrupted and Megan wished she could hear him better. It sounded like he said, "Trip'll do that," but she didn't understand what that meant.

Then Silver Eyes continued, "And we won't have a body to deal with on our end."

Although Megan hadn't caught or understood all of what was said, as she lay in the back of her mom's new JMC Pioneer, she started to cry as realization dawned. These men meant to kill her.

She'd never see her mom, or her dad, or Emily, or even her annoying little brother again.

Futilely, she kicked the back door and felt the cord around her wrists tighten. She heard the driver's side door open and close and felt the hum of the motor when the car started. Then they started to move, and Megan lay still and thought about her homework and the dance she was supposed to go to with Emily tomorrow night.

And as the pain from her aching ribs rolled through her, she thought, *I don't want to die.*

THREE

"HEY, you two. We're at a bar, not a funeral. Could you try looking a little less . . . glum? You're scaring off the locals." Aimee Devlin hoisted her pink cosmopolitan and winked at a promising subject across the bar. He winked back and started toward their table, but stopped dead in his tracks when he caught a glimpse of her tablemates. With a weak smile and a shrug of his mighty fine-looking shoulders, he backed away, saving her for a braver man than he.

With a defeated sigh, Aimee turned her attention back to her friends.

Raine Robey and Daphne Donovan. Both ex-FBI special agents like herself, and her closest pals in the world, not to mention her partners in a fledgling new business. Aimee was the mastermind behind Partners In Crime, Inc., a company she hoped was going to make them all rich. God knew the trio had the talent and the brains to make it work. She just wasn't certain her friends were emotionally ready to climb out of the pits of misery they had entrenched themselves in. Of the three, only she had left the Bureau with her psychological well-being intact. And even she was roused at 3 A.M. by the occasional nightmare.

Aimee shuddered and took another sip of her fancy drink. She'd take corporate espionage over serial killers any day.

"I'm sorry, Dev," red-haired Daphne was the first to acknowledge Aimee's plea for a bit of cheer around the table. "I'm just preoccupied."

"Yeah, and I think I've forgotten how to interact with real live human beings," Raine added, taking a healthy swig of her martini. "My conversations lately have mostly consisted of muttering to a bunch of computer screens. Maybe I need to get a cat or something."

Aimee's plea of "please, don't" was seconded by Daphne's horrified "no."

Raine pulled the toothpick with a double-header of olives out of her drink and leveled a narrow-eyed squint at her friends. "I'm not *that* bad."

"You kill everything that crosses your threshold," Daphne said, without malice.

"Even Bentley is afraid of you," Aimee agreed, referring to her youngest sister's forty-five–pound English bulldog who often stayed with Aimee while her supermodel sister was off on photo shoots.

"That's not fair. I just . . . well, I tend to forget about everything else when I'm working."

"We know. That's why you shouldn't get a cat. They need food occasionally."

"And water," Daphne added.

Raine sighed and pulled one bright green olive off the toothpick with her fingers. Then she sucked the pimento out of the middle and swallowed it before popping the olive into her mouth and chewing it. "I suppose you're right. I'm better off with just my computers for company. Relationships with living things are too complicated."

Aimee rolled her eyes heavenward and gestured for the waiter to bring them another round. This much misery could only be drowned with alcohol. Although, she thought, unconsciously rubbing the base of her spine against the back of her chair, the last time they had all drowned their sorrows in booze, they'd each ended up with a lovely Technicolor reminder of that night. She supposed that none of them realized until the next morning how much the intensive, sixteen-week special agent training had impacted their lives. It was there that the three women had met and, despite their different backgrounds and personalities, had bonded—at first because they were the handful of women among so many men, but later because they had come to respect one another's unique abilities. It was also there, in that male-dominated environment, where they had been given the nicknames that were the precursors to their relatively recent body art. Aimee was nicknamed "Dev," Daphne was "Daff," and Raine—by association—was given the moniker of "Bugsy." Aimee smiled to herself. At least Raine hadn't been called "Porky" or "Petunia" after the Looney Tunes pigs. And so it was that they'd decided, after one too many martinis, to have the Tasmanian Devil, Daffy Duck, and Bugs Bunny tattooed on their persons in varying locations.

Despite the circumstances of their tattooing, Aimee didn't regret it. Taz was her little secret, and it always made her smile when she caught a glimpse of him in the mirror. It was something so out of character for her to have done . . . except that it wasn't. Not really.

"Anyway," Raine said after completing her olive-eating ritual on her second victim, "why was it so important for us to meet you here tonight? It's a Thursday night. The only guys here are the corporate-ladder types loading up on a drink or two before heading home to their wives and two-point-five children."

"Actually, I think it's one-point-something," Daphne said.

"Oh, really? Has it come down that much?"

"Yeah. Big families are apparently out of fashion lately."

"Hmm."

Aimee sighed again. "You guys are hopeless. We're young. We're attractive. We're single. You can't tell me there's not one man out there who might be of interest to you."

Raine swigged the last of her drink and turned to face the crowded bar. It was golf shirts and Dockers as far as the eye could see. What did these guys know about child molesters, and serial rapists, and terrorists who would just as soon rip your heart out as drive you to the airport? Nothing. That's what they knew about such things. And up until last July, it had been her job to help keep it so that the average Joe was exposed to as little of that sort of thing as possible.

But now she was on the outside, with a black mark on her Bureau record so dark and deep that she was afraid she'd fall into it and never climb out.

Damn, but she was tired of thinking like this. Why couldn't she be a regular woman like the ones dotting the chic maple bar with its funky art-deco lighting and cute bartenders? She was out of the Bureau now, and she had every right to forget the crimes she had helped solve—and even the ones that had been beyond her abilities to figure out. She should be happy now. Hacking into other people's computer systems promised to be a lot more lucrative than her job with the FBI had been, and she'd most likely never have to witness the horrors she'd seen in her days as a special agent ever again.

So why was she so miserable?

It appeared that Daphne felt much the same way as Raine did, because after her own cursory look around the crowded, noisy hot spot, she turned back to Aimee and said, "You didn't ask us to meet you here to provide girl cover while you scoped out some new prospects. At least not new *personal* prospects."

Aimee tapped one short, neatly manicured nail against the glass-topped table and smiled. "No, I didn't. I was hoping that might be a nice side effect, but I really asked you here for a celebration."

Raine looked over at Daphne, who seemed just as surprised as she was. "A celebration?"

"Yes. I signed our first client today."

Raine took a deep breath and watched Aimee's grin spread over her face. She didn't have the heart to tell her that *she'd* actually signed their first client yesterday morning. Calder had signed and faxed back the paperwork she'd sent him, but Raine decided not say anything. What were the chances that Aimee would check the dates on the contracts anyway?

But it seemed she wasn't the only one who hadn't been

forthcoming with information because Daphne cleared her throat and said glumly, "Actually I signed our first client yesterday afternoon."

Aimee's brown eyes widened and the hand holding her drink stopped just before the rim of the glass touched her lips. "You what? Why didn't you say something?"

Daphne shifted uncomfortably on her chair and started rubbing a chipped spot on their table. "I don't know. I guess I . . . well, I didn't really want to take the job. But I did," she hastened to add, raising her head to look at Aimee and Raine. "I know we need the income, so I took the job."

"Well, what is it?" Aimee asked.

"And why didn't you want to take it?" Raine added.

"I don't know. Just got used to being unemployed, I guess," Daphne answered Raine's question first, sounding as evasive as a cornered drug dealer. "It's an easy job. A bigwig at my brother's publishing house suspects a former employee was embezzling from them. He wants me to track the guy down and see if I can find any evidence of the theft. You know, expensive stereo equipment, matching BMWs, an extra hundred thousand dollars in his bank account. That sort of thing. I guess he figures it's not worth trying to prosecute if the money went up the guy's nose or something."

"That's great." Aimee all but beamed as she raised her glass to toast. "So, here's to Daphne for landing Partners In Crime's first client."

"Um. Wait a second," Raine said, giving Aimee a sheepish smile. Might as well tell the truth now since Aimee didn't seem to mind that she hadn't landed their first job.

"What? Not you, too!" Aimee protested.

"Sorry. I actually agreed to provide services to our own former employer yesterday morning."

This elicited gasps from both women, along with a cacophony of questions.

Raine held up her hand, as if to physically stop the volley of questions being tossed at her. "Yes, the job is really for the FBI, although it's in an unofficial capacity. The checks will not be traceable to our government, nobody inside knows about the job, etcetera, etcetera, etcetera. It's a simple snooping operation, just trying to help my, uh, my contact decide whether to start something official."

"Your contact?" Aimee asked, obviously noticing Raine's hesitation.

Raine closed her eyes, then opened them again and met her friends' gazes. "Yes. It was Calder who called about the job."

Aimee blinked.

Daphne's mouth dropped open.

And silence reigned over the table as the waiter arrived with another tray of drinks.

Daphne closed her mouth, but Aimee continued to blink rapidly, as if that were the only way she could get oxygen to her brain.

"I can't believe he had the nerve to call you," Daphne stated in a tone of voice that probably delayed the effects of global warming by a good three years.

"I know." Raine shrugged and stabbed at the olives in the bottom of her glass. "If we hadn't been so desperate for business, I wouldn't have taken his call."

Aimee reached over and covered Raine's trembling hand with one of her own. "I'm so sorry. We're desperate, but we're not that desperate. I can go to my sisters, ask them for some money."

"And I've always got Brooks to fall back on. What good is it to have a brother on the best-seller list if you can't hit him up for money? Probably gives him material to write about anyway," Daphne said.

Raine shook her head at her friends and business partners. "No. We shouldn't have to borrow money from our families. We're grown-ups, for God's sake. We had successful careers with the goddamn FBI. We were somebody. We should be able to make it on our own."

"But you . . ." Aimee stopped and cleared her throat. "But that means you'll be working for Calder, I presume?"

"Yes. Unofficially." Raine swallowed half of her martini in one gulp.

"Are you sure you can handle this?" Aimee asked.

Raine shrugged. "The job's easy."

"That's not what I'm talking about. Are you sure you can handle working with Calder again?"

With a half-smile, Raine admitted, "No. I'm not sure I can handle it. He nearly broke my heart. I thought I was over it, but when he called—" Rapidly blinking back tears, Raine grabbed the cocktail napkin from under her drink and dabbed at the corner of her eyes. "Shit. I'm sorry. I thought I was past this stage."

Daphne leaned back and picked up her own drink—a hearty dark beer in a chilled glass. She would have been just as happy drinking it straight from the bottle. "I hate this girly crap. Why can't we be more like men and have no emotions besides anger and lust?"

Raine laughed despite her tears, while Aimee just shook her head ruefully at their friend.

Wiping the last of the moisture from her eyes, Raine tossed the napkin to the table. "Well, I kinda like being a woman. We have better choices for footwear. But I do hate crying, it gives me a headache."

"Have another martini," Aimee suggested dryly.

"I plan to. Although they give me headaches, too."

"Yeah, but not till the morning after," Daphne said, raising her own glass.

"Besides," Aimee added, lifting her own glass in salute, "Tonight's a celebration. Here's to us for landing the first three jobs for Partners In Crime. May this be the beginning of a beautiful partnership."

"And the continuation of a beautiful friendship," Raine said, smiling at her cohorts as they touched glasses and toasted one another.

> Am I content to have ruined your career and driven away the man you loved? Have you suffered enough yet for all you've taken from me?
> Only time will tell . . .

Raine looked at the e-mail message again. She had dragged herself to her computer this morning, complete with a one-too-many-martinis hangover, hoping she'd received some information on Mr. Enslar's daughter from one of her sources within the hacker network. She had not expected this chilling message. Even worse, the e-mail had come from her. At least it *appeared* to have come from her, only she was not in the habit of sending vaguely threatening e-mails to herself. Nor to anyone else, for that matter.

She hit "reply" and stared at the return address. Someone had spoofed the Partners In Crime domain name, sending the message from the nonexistent user, gotcha@ partnersincrime.us. It was an easy thing to do, a trick spammers used in the hopes of finding enough gullible souls to buy penis and/or breast enlargers, check out their teen/barnyard animal/celebrity porn sites, or make $100,000 a year working from home. As annoying as these were, however, they were nothing like the message Raine had received.

She shuddered and leaned back in her chair, feeling as if she were being watched.

The person who had framed her for murder eleven months ago wasn't certain if he had sufficiently ruined her life? Raine was tempted to respond, to let the sender know that he had succeeded in his goal of making her life miserable, but knew the message would simply bounce back to her. There was no such user at Partners In Crime, so her response would return to her as undeliverable. And although she could trace the spoofed address, she knew it would end in a dead end. Users sophisticated enough to do this were also sophisticated enough to know how to cover their tracks.

Raine studied the message, trying to find a clue as to the sender's identity. Many hackers had "trademarks" that they liked to leave for other computer whizzes to find. It was a sort of signature or calling card to prove the authenticity of their work, something like having a message or game pop up when the user pressed a certain combination of keystrokes.

There was a small, animated clock after the word "time," its hands moving wildly around the face of the clock as it ticked away. Raine made a note to set her e-mail options to disable these icons. She had only enabled them a few days ago when Daff sent her an amusing set of animated smiley face icons that did everything from argue with each other to turn green and puke. For some reason they made her laugh, so she had willingly turned on a feature that even the most inexperienced hacker knew how to exploit. While the animated icons couldn't do any real damage to her computer, they presented enough of a system vulnerability that Raine didn't typically allow them to run automatically.

The ticking sound was getting louder and Raine was just about to turn down the volume of her speakers when her doorbell rang. The noise so startled her that she nearly knocked over her ever-present soda, making her vow once again to stop leaving open cans near her computers. She must have fried a dozen keyboards that way.

Feeling a bit spooked by the message she had just received, Raine stopped inside her kitchen, just within yelling distance of the door to her apartment, and asked loudly, "Who is it?"

Although she had a peephole that would have let her see the visitor, she knew that if someone wanted to harm her—to shoot her, say—all he'd have to do is knock on her door, wait to see her eye at the peephole, and start shooting. She was so creeped out by the e-mail she'd received that she wasn't going to take any chances.

"It's me. Calder."

The response at the front door was followed by a loud noise back in her computer room—a noise that sounded suspiciously like a gunshot.

Raine gasped and goosebumps rose on her arms like a rash.

Calder pounded on the door. "What the hell was that? Let me in."

There was the sound of another shot from her office, and Raine stood frozen in the kitchen, one hand on the counter to keep herself from crumpling to the floor.

The last time she had heard that sound, she'd ended up being sprayed with someone else's muscle tissue, bone fragments, and warm blood. It had splattered all over her, matting in her hair until she thought she'd never be able to get it clean again.

The last time she had heard that sound had been the night

she had pushed Jeffrey Allen, a suspected child molester, out his front door and to his death.

Raine stood in the kitchen staring at the white and green linoleum, half-expecting blood to start dripping off her again, as it had that night. She didn't look up, even when her ex-lover kicked down her door.

FOUR

CALDER entered Raine's apartment, gun drawn and ready for battle. By rote, he took in the scene, trying to assess the extent of Raine's injuries, as well as the source of the danger.

She stood with her head bowed in the small but tidy kitchen, her hair blonder than he remembered it. She was still in her pajamas—not surprising, she had always been a night owl—her favorite green-and-blue plaid boxers and a Bugs Bunny T-shirt. The hall in front of him was empty, with no shadows to indicate an intruder.

Holding his gun out in front of him, Calder sidestepped into the kitchen in front of Raine and glanced into her living/dining room. There was nothing there except the same furniture she'd owned a year ago.

"Raine, where is he?" Calder asked softly, backing up so that his spine was touching her side. He felt her shudder against him, then heard her take a deep breath.

"It's okay. There's not . . . it's not real," she said, taking a step away from him.

Still suspicious, Calder didn't lower his gun as he turned

slightly toward her. "What do you mean? I heard muffled gunshots."

"It was just an e-mail. Someone sent me a message with an audio clip of a gunshot. That's all."

Calder stepped back and slowly reholstered his gun. He watched as Raine started trembling, wrapping her arms around herself to stop from shaking. He was tempted to take the two steps necessary to close the gap between them and replace her arms with his own, but wasn't sure he'd come away with his balls intact. Instead, he leaned against the opposite counter and gave her some time to calm down, studying her all the while.

He had forgotten how attractive she was, the exact opposite of the hacker stereotype he had expected when he'd first been told she was joining his team in the computer crimes division three years ago. He'd expected a Star Trek fan with bad skin and a rebellious attitude, much like the rest of his team of brilliant computer scientists. Instead, she'd breezed in with her tidy blond hair, athletic body, and no apparent interest in ever becoming a Trekkie, and he'd fallen instantly and desperately in love. Or maybe it had just been lust. Love had come later, but he'd managed to muck that up. Big time.

Which was exactly why he was here today, standing in the kitchen of the only woman he had ever loved but too worried about the fate of his testicles to touch her.

Calder sighed. "So. This e-mail. What did it say? And who was it from?"

Raine rubbed her upper arms and finally looked up at him with faintly bloodshot green eyes. "It was from me," she answered with an inelegant snort. "It doesn't matter. It's just a stupid e-mail."

Calder straightened up, moving away from the counter. "Yes, it does matter. I want to see what it says."

Raine looked at him as if contemplating how much physical harm she could inflict upon him, and Calder resisted the urge to clap his hands around his genitals. He had seen her field record and knew that it would be a mistake to underestimate the amount of strength she packed into her five-foot-six-inch frame. Instead, he held his hands out in a gesture of surrender. "Okay. I'm sorry. I don't need to see it. I was just concerned about you and thought that maybe I could help. But I'll stay out of it." *For now. Until she turns her back and gives me the chance to go snooping, that is.*

Raine nodded and let her hands slip from her arms, but remained where she was. "What are you doing here? I told you I'd send you a written report every week. It's only been two days since you hired me. I don't have anything on Hope Enslar yet."

"I didn't expect that you would. I had the day off and I found out that Jackson Motors gives public tours every Friday morning. I thought that maybe we could go down there and take a look around. You know, just in case we have to send you in undercover."

Calder smiled innocently and hoped Raine hadn't already discovered that this case was nothing but a well-paid wild goose chase. There was a reason that nobody in the Bureau knew anything about Mr. Enslar's letter. If Calder had even mentioned it to his superiors, they would have put him up for a psych eval because they would have insisted that there was nothing to it but a lonely man's sad bid for attention. Hell, that's what Calder believed, too. But Raine didn't need to know that, and she also didn't need to know that the only reason Calder had come to her with this bogus job was because he wanted her back so badly he nearly ached with it. This had been the only plan he'd been able to come up with to get Raine back in his life, and to make it work he had to pretend that he believed Hope Enslar truly needed their help. And he had to make sure Raine never found out that he was the one funding this unofficial investigation—not the U.S. government.

He did his best to look sincere as Raine gave him the once-over, trying to assess if his motives were pure. Which, of course, they weren't. At least not from her perspective.

He must have convinced her, though, because she nodded and said, "All right. I wanted to go take a look at the plant anyway. It might as well be today as any other day. Just let me go get ready. There's soda in the fridge. Help yourself." With that, she turned and walked down the hall.

Calder opened the refrigerator and saw that, as usual, it was well-stocked with bright red Coke cans. He had always been amazed at her diet, which consisted mainly of Coke and french fries. She was like a typical computer geek in that respect. Everything in life was secondary to her computers. If she couldn't eat a meal in front of a keyboard, she'd just as soon skip it.

He pulled a soda out of the fridge and popped open the top, waiting to hear the shower start. When he did, he set the Coke on the counter and peeked out into the hall.

"I don't need to see the e-mail, my ass," he muttered, making his way toward the end of the hall. He poked his head into the only open doorway and found it stuffed full of computer paraphernalia. Same old Raine, he thought, listening with one ear to make sure the shower was still running. He stepped into the room and moved her chair away from the desk.

"You know, that's the oldest trick in the book; waiting for someone to get in the shower to start snooping," Raine said from the doorway.

Calder didn't bother turning around. "I know. But it always works in the movies."

"This isn't the movies, and I'm not some dumb blonde. I didn't for one second believe that you were just going to mind your own business."

Calder moved the mouse in front of him on the desk to wake up the computer screen, only to have a password screen pop up. Damn. He should have known that she would have password-protected her computer.

He turned to face her. "Why won't you let me see it? Maybe I could help."

Raine leaned against the doorjamb and crossed her arms across Bugs Bunny. "I find it ironic that you want to help me now. Where was your 'I've come to save the day' attitude when I really needed it?"

Calder slapped a hand to his heart. "Ouch."

"Yeah. Truth hurts, eh?"

He sat down on the edge of her desk, facing her. If there was ever a time to grovel, now was it. "You're right. I screwed up, and I apologize."

Raine raised her eyebrows at him. "Well, doesn't that just make my little ol' heart go pitty-pat?"

Hmm. This was going to be even tougher than he thought. Maybe it was just too soon. After all, this was the first time they'd seen each other in almost a year. He really couldn't expect to win her forgiveness this easily.

"Look, I'm all out of white flags. I'm sorry for what happened, but that's not why I'm here. I think you're incredibly talented at what you do and I want your help on the Enslar case. That's all. Now, the e-mail you received this morning obviously disturbed you, but as long as it has nothing to do with the case, I'll concede that it's none of my business. But if you want my help, all you have to do is ask."

Raine continued hovering in the doorway, her head cocked as if she were trying to make a decision about something. Whatever it was she was trying to decide, Calder figured he'd come out on the losing end when she shook her head and said, "Fine. I'll keep that in mind. Now, if you'll excuse me, I need to take a shower."

With that, she turned and left him alone with her computers, obviously confident that they were safe from his prying fingers.

RAINE caught Calder's surprised double-take when she stepped into the living room of her apartment half an hour later but she had to give him credit; he didn't say one word about her attire until they were speeding south on I-75 toward Jackson Motors.

"I see you're still driving the boring Buick," she said, breaking the silence that had gone on just a bit too long to be considered comfortable.

"Yeah," Calder responded, with an over-long glance in her direction.

"How are your brothers?" she asked, crossing her knee-high boots at the ankle.

"Fine. What the hell are you wearing?" Calder asked finally, obviously unable to stop himself.

Raine looked down at her very un-FBI-like outfit, complete

with high-heeled boots, short skirt, and floral blouse. "I'm working undercover. As a woman." She turned around and lifted her shirt just enough to let him see the waistband of her skirt . . . and the top of her black thong panties. "Look, no gun."

Calder turned the air conditioner up a notch. "Well, I can't understand why the Bureau doesn't institute that as their new uniform for all female agents. We'd have criminals tripping over each other to surrender."

Raine shrugged. "One advantage of being on the outside, I guess. I don't have to wear slacks and comfortable shoes every day."

"It's definitely a change from the uniform," Calder agreed.

Raine didn't know quite what to say to that, so she let the quiet surround them again. The truth of the matter was, she'd worn this outfit hoping for this exact response from him. Childish as it was, she'd wanted to show off what he was missing. Not that she wanted him back, but still, she wanted him to suffer some of the pain and heartbreak she'd felt when he'd betrayed her, and the best way she knew to do that was to taunt him with something he could never have again.

Not another word was spoken as Calder exited the freeway south of Atlanta and maneuvered the Buick into the far right-hand lane to turn into the Jackson Motors plant. The guard at the gate readily accepted that they were there for the plant tour, giving them a bright yellow visitor's pass and instructions on where to park as he lifted the security gate.

"Nothing remarkable in their security," Raine said as Calder pulled into a parking space in the visitor lot.

"No. He didn't even take down my license plate number."

Raine got out of the car and stood on the warm sidewalk, waiting for Calder to join her. She watched as he exited the car, surprised by her own reaction to him. As much as she wished the attraction between them had died along with whatever love she had felt for him, it hadn't. Her body responded as it always had—with the immediate and almost overwhelming desire to touch him.

It wasn't that he was handsome in a *GQ* sort of way. He

wasn't polished enough for that. If she had to put her finger on what it was that made him so attractive, Raine would have to say that it was because he was just such a "guy." He wasn't overly tall, six-foot-one at the most, but he was muscular with broad shoulders and thick arms and the thighs of a tennis player. He had dark hair, worn just a shade too short for her liking, and greenish-brown eyes and he had, she had to admit, one of the finest asses in the greater Atlanta area, if not the entire state of Georgia.

As they walked toward the entrance to the automobile plant, their arms brushed each other, and Raine felt the heat from their contact slide along her skin like warm silk.

When he opened the door and placed a large, strong hand on the small of her back to usher her inside, Raine felt herself go all goosebumpy and knew, in that instant, that her self-imposed celibacy had made her vulnerable to this man once again.

Reminding herself that thinking this way would only lead to her destruction, Raine purposefully stepped out of Calder's grasp, breaking the contact between them. She was going to call Aimee and Daff as soon as the tour was over and see if they wanted to go out tonight. She needed to get laid soon or she'd never make it through this case without giving in to the temptation to sleep with Calder again, no matter how wrong it was.

Raine took a deep breath and tried to focus on something other than her attraction to her ex-lover. She coughed to cover a snort of laughter when the phrase, "just think about baseball," came to mind. She remembered a late-night conversation with Aimee and Daff when they had howled about sports being all about bats and balls and the sexual symbolism associated with it all. Thinking about baseball was *not* going to take her mind off sex.

"Are you all right?" Calder asked, looking at her strangely.

"Yes, I'm fine. Just had something, uh, stuck in my throat," she answered, trying to clamp down on the hysterical laughter that threatened to choke her. *Must be a delayed reaction to this morning's scare,* she told herself, staring straight ahead as they walked toward a desk near a wall of closed doors. Next to each door handle was a black keypad, obviously some kind of magnetic key reader.

"Can I help you?" a young man with thin glasses and an expensive suit asked from behind the desk.

"Yes," Calder and Raine both said at once. Raine nodded and let Calder go ahead, figuring now was as good a time as any to shift into arm-candy mode. In her days as an agent, she'd learned that living up—or down—to people's expectations often yielded the best results. She'd carefully chosen her outfit today to give people the image that she was the pretty-but-not-too-bright type. That way, any halfway intelligent questions she asked would be answered thoroughly, and, best of all, without suspicion. So, as Calder told the receptionist that they were interested in taking the guided tour, Raine pasted a sunny smile on her face and looped her arm around Calder's elbow.

The receptionist didn't ask for ID, instead indicating a computer where they were to type in their names to get visitor passes and pointing to where they were to wait for the tour guide to appear. Raine typed in a false name and took the badge the receptionist handed her, clipping it to her blouse where it wouldn't obscure her cleavage. Calder took his own badge, then led her to a seating area in the lobby where a dozen others were waiting for the tour to start. He took a seat in one of the round-backed chairs, but Raine remained standing, admiring her new black leather boots. It wasn't long before the door behind her opened and a young woman stepped out. The woman wore a white lab coat over a dove-gray blouse and matching slacks. Raine looked down at the other woman's footwear—always a telltale sign about someone's personality, she thought. Sensible gray flats. Raine had thought so.

Miss No-Nonsense smiled professionally at the small group that had gathered in the lobby. "Good afternoon, everyone," she said. "My name is Heather and I'll be taking you around the plant today."

Raine thought she'd start the tour off right and raised her hand. "Why is it called a plant?" she asked. "I mean, you don't grow things here, do you?"

Heather seemed taken aback. Whether it was because Raine had asked the question without waiting to be called upon or because the question was so inane, Raine wasn't sure.

"Um, 'plant' is short for manufacturing plant. Since we *manufacture* automobiles here, that's what we call it."

"Oh. Thanks." Raine smiled innocently at the other woman while, beside her, Calder bent his head and pinched the bridge of his nose to keep from laughing.

As the group followed Heather through the doorway, Calder took her arm and whispered, "Don't do that again without warning me first."

"Okay, sure," Raine said, with a vacant smile.

As the group moved from one area of the plant to another, Raine kept her dumb questions to a minimum as she memorized the layout of the factory. First, they were given a tour of the engineering offices. "The brains of the company," Heather told them proudly. She merely waved in the direction of the executive offices, which were closed off behind a door similar to the one they had come through at the start of the tour, and then she told them they were about to enter "the heart of the plant." Raine wondered if their last stop would be the "toenails of the organization."

Heather flashed her badge over a magnetic reader and waited for the indicator light to turn green. When it did, she pushed open the door and motioned for the group to precede her onto the catwalk overlooking the crash test area.

Raine looked at the open metal grating on the walkway, then looked down at her boots. "This is going to be hell on my heels," she muttered, gingerly tiptoeing out with the rest of the crowd.

"This is where people's lives are saved," Heather announced grandly, waving her arm over the test track below. "Jackson Motor Company's vehicles are subjected to a rigorous battery of tests: side impact, rear impact, head-on collision, rollover. We simulate virtually every possible type of accident here in the lab so as to ensure the highest quality of safety for our customers."

Raine resisted the urge to roll her eyes at the other woman's brochure-speak.

"We enter our vehicles in all sorts of on and off-road races to test their limits, and our crash test engineers take advantage of this race footage to enhance the safety features on every one of our cars and trucks."

"What about the Pronto?" Raine asked, not exactly sure what she was fishing for, but willing to toss her bait out to see what might bite. "Did the Pronto get put through the same sorts of tests as your other vehicles?"

Heather's smile turned a bit wooden, but she responded professionally, "Yes. Unfortunately, a design flaw was discovered during crash testing, but the management at the time decided to go ahead and release the Pronto into the market. While the defect was significant and the company later recalled the vehicles, the Pronto did meet or exceed all of the government's safety requirements at the time. The recall was purely voluntary on JMC's part, and performed only out of the utmost consideration for the safety of our customers."

It was obvious that the company had anticipated questions about the one and only black mark on their otherwise impeccable record. Unfortunately, Heather's answer didn't help in trying to discover what danger Hope Enslar might be in.

So now what? Raine chewed the inside of her lip as the tour continued. She knew perfectly well that the reason Calder had dropped this "unofficial investigation" in her lap was because he thought there was nothing to Mr. Enslar's concerns. If he had thought there was any real danger, the case would be investigated within the Bureau. But Raine was nothing if not tenacious—a characteristic of every good hacker on the face of the earth—and she wasn't going to stop looking into Hope Enslar's background until she knew everything about the other woman, including her shoe size and what she ate for breakfast. Besides, Raine thought with a smile, she was getting paid by the hour so the more she had to dig to find something on Hope Enslar, the better for her bank account.

"Why are you smiling?" Calder asked, coming up behind her as Heather opened another door with a flourish.

"No reason. Just doing my best to look the part," Raine said, tilting her head and batting her eyelashes at him as she sashayed past him and onto the walkway above the plant's assembly floor.

The noise of the busy machines below was muffled somewhat by the walls of glass lining the grated walkway, but the constant hum and buzz of activity was difficult to get used to. Raine held back and let Heather and the rest of the group get a bit ahead as she studied the floor below.

She had always marveled at the machines that massproduced goods. Each machine performed its tedious task over and over and over again, stopping only when the human responsible for it flipped its OFF switch. Even more amazing was the grace of the robotic creatures as they dipped and swayed from their bases. One machine slid back and forth, leaving a perfect line of bright red paint in its wake. The color looked like a hard candy shell.

The automotive equivalent of an M&M, Raine thought, watching the machine slide back and forth again, this time leaving a coat of paint on the top of the vehicle.

"This is where the rubber hits the road, if you will," Heather said, laughing at her own joke. "Vehicles are built right here on the premises, from start to finish, using parts manufactured all over the world. Now before anyone asks why we don't just use American parts, I'm going to tell you what you'll hear from all the major car manufacturers: Here at Jackson Motors, we believe that it is our duty to our customers, both here in the United States and abroad, to build the very best, most reasonably priced vehicle possible, using all the resources at our disposal. We think that competition only serves to strengthen our economy by keeping wages under control and putting affordable products in the hands of consumers."

There was a general murmuring among the tour group, but no one voiced any dissenting opinions. Instead, they asked questions about the volume of vehicles produced each day, the number of people JMC employed, in what countries the cars were sold, and the like. Not particularly interested in listening to Heather's answers since she'd already done enough research to know all this, Raine drifted away from the group to watch the activity on the assembly floor below.

It seemed very clean and orderly, much more tidy than she would have expected a factory to be. It was also less populated with humans than she had anticipated, cluttered mostly with machines rather than people.

"My kind of place," she muttered under her breath, then squinted at something going on down on the floor below. A man had stopped next to a vehicle and was looking around, as if to see if anyone was watching. Raine turned her head and pretended to be listening raptly to Heather's explanation of the assembly process, still watching the man out of the corner of her eye.

Apparently satisfied that he wasn't being watched, the man pulled something that looked like a coin out of the pocket of his coveralls and slipped it inside the doorframe of an SUV. As Raine watched, the man backed away from the vehicle, seeming to busy himself with the machinery. When the next vehicle pulled into his station, he again looked around suspiciously, dug something out of his pocket, and dropped it into the vehicle.

Moving cautiously so as not to catch the man's attention, Raine took a step closer to Calder, who was standing in front of her, apparently fascinated by whatever it was that Heather was saying. She stood on her tiptoes and whispered, "Take a look down at the floor at the man at your ten o'clock. He's up to something."

But before she could move, Heather broke in with a decidedly cranky, "Do you have a question for the group?"

Startled, Raine came down off her tiptoes and plunged both heels directly into the grating of the catwalk. Off balance, she clutched at Calder to keep from ending up on her rear end in the middle of the walkway and intercepted a look from Heather that told her the other woman was perfectly aware of Raine's predicament.

"Here, hold still while I get you out of those," Calder said, moving her hand off his arm and placing it on the window lining the catwalk. He bent down and unzipped her right boot, gently moving her bare foot to the cold metal grating. Then he did the same with the left, only this time he stopped after removing her foot, holding her by the ankle.

"Let go." Raine tugged on her foot, aware that they were making a scene, and even more aware that the man she had been watching on the plant floor was now studying her intently.

Calder looked up at her dumbly. "You have a tattoo."

Raine tugged again. "I'm aware of that. I *was* there when it happened."

"You have Bugs Bunny tattooed on your ankle," he repeated, still crouching at her feet.

"Yes, and you're the man who put it there," Raine muttered darkly, slapping at his hand, finally getting him to free her foot. Then she yanked her boots out of the grate, gave Heather a chilling glare, and pushed past Calder on her way toward the exit.

FIVE

RAINE leaned against the hood of Calder's Buick and frowned down at her boots. Eleven months out of the Bureau and she was acting like some untrained novice, letting that tour guide get to her. As an agent, she would have been able to stay in character and not risk blowing her cover. Instead, she'd let Heather startle her. So now they had nothing. No leads. No real information. No idea about what sort of trouble Hope Enslar might be in. No clues as to what that employee was dropping into the doors of the vehicles as they sped past him on the assembly line. And it was all her fault for spending the majority of the past year hiding away in her apartment like some coward and allowing her skills to get rusty.

Calder emerged from the glass doors of the Jackson Motors plant, whistling as if she had not just blown their entire operation. Of course, what did it really matter? This was an unofficial investigation that meant nothing to nobody, aside from a lonely old man who was probably just trying to get some attention. It wasn't as if anyone's life was in danger— which was precisely why Raine had agreed to get involved. When she'd worked in the computer crimes division, most of her cases had involved white-collar crimes like embezzlement and fraud. The case that had ended her career had been different from the very beginning. The file that had been dropped on her desk had seemed to be a routine investigation of an Internet porn site, but when Raine had checked out the site, she'd been sickened to see children being molested via a supposedly live webcam. Her initial job was to shut down the site, but she couldn't leave it at that. She'd begged her new boss—she'd asked to be reassigned once she and Calder started dating—to let her trail the child molester and he'd agreed. She'd used clues from the videos themselves as well as spending hours searching the labyrinthine trail of the molester's postings on the Internet to finally locate the house where Jeffrey Allen was abusing his victims.

She gathered evidence about how he lured the children into meeting with him, and also how he scared them into keeping quiet once the abuse had ended. She had meticulously documented every e-mail, every chat room post, every video clip the man posted to the Internet. Still, she was afraid it wasn't enough. She'd seen defense attorneys convince juries that such evidence was easy to manufacture—as if the FBI had a hard-on for some middle-aged schoolteacher from Hartford who had nothing more on his record than a couple of speeding tickets. Why a jury would believe that the Bureau would pick on some innocent man for no reason at all, she would never know. But she had seen it happen on more than one occasion and she had vowed not to let it go that way with Jeffrey Allen.

She'd waited patiently, posing on the Internet as a ten-year-old girl named Ashley Taylor, letting Allen lure her closer and closer to him with promises of horseback rides and puppies—an irresistible duo for virtually every preteen girl in America.

The afternoon that he was going to strike, Raine got her team in place. They had a search warrant, and she had high hopes that they would turn up pornographic videos, filming equipment, and enough incriminating evidence for a judge and jury to be convinced that this sicko should be locked away for life, with no hope of parole.

She had led her team down to Jeffrey Allen's basement, recognizing the stairs from the videos he had filmed, an intricate wrought-iron balustrade with wide hardwood steps leading down into his lair like the staircase of Tara in *Gone With the Wind*. The basement was warm and a bit damp, with colorful posters hung all around the room. In the center was a bed, generously heaped with Beanie Babies. Raine had to fight not to retch at the sight. She'd seen that bed, with Jeffrey Allen's victims lying on the red velvet bedspread, clutching one of the stuffed animals to his or her naked chest. She had seen the fear and bewilderment in the children's eyes as the adult they thought they could trust approached them, stroked them, and then did things to them that would scar them for the rest of their lives.

Watching the videos in her cramped office at the FBI building in DC, Raine had wanted to kill him. The rage building up inside her as this animal used the trust of these children to abuse them had frightened her. The night before, she had confessed to Calder that she was afraid of what she might do to this monster if a jury let him go free.

When she and her team searched his basement and found nothing out of the ordinary, while a smug-looking Jeffrey Allen watched, Raine knew it was likely that he would walk.

She had tried to get him to tell her who had tipped him off, but he just smiled at her, looking as benign as the now-deceased Mr. Rogers.

As Raine handcuffed him—they had a warrant for his arrest based on the circumstantial evidence she had gathered— she knew that Jeffrey Allen was probably not going to be convicted for his crimes. And as she pushed him in front of her out of his front door, she had secretly wished that she could have gotten away with leaving Mr. Allen down in that basement, sprawled across that hideous bed with a bullet hole in the middle of his forehead.

Which was why, she supposed, she didn't react immediately when she heard the gunshot. She had merely thought it was a noise conjured up from her own imagination as she pictured Jeffrey Allen's blood splattering the Beanie Babies and oozing down the red velvet bedspread.

Later, she had been accused of not reacting because she had been expecting Jeffrey Allen to be assassinated as she pushed him out his front door. The truth was, she hadn't re-acted because she had been dreaming about killing him her-self when the sniper pulled the trigger.

"RAINE? Is something wrong?" Calder asked, waving a hand in front of her face as if he'd been trying to get her attention for some time.

Raine blinked, trying to wipe away the past as if it were a speck of dust that had caught in her eye. "I'm fine. I'm sorry I blew it back there." She pulled open the heavy door of Calder's nondescript Buick and slid into the passenger seat while he walked around the front of the car and opened the driver's side door.

"It doesn't matter. I doubt we would have learned any-thing new," he said, getting into the car.

Raine crossed her legs, jiggling her left foot so that the tip of her boot bumped into the upholstered door. She needed a Coke to soothe her nerves. And probably something to eat since it was past noon and she hadn't eaten yet today. Calder pulled out of the parking lot, waving to the gate guard who had turned to watch them leave.

She spied the familiar golden arches a few blocks away and her stomach grumbled. "Would you mind running through that McDonald's drive-thru?" she asked, reaching for her purse.

Calder grimaced. "I thought I'd cured you of your fast-food habit."

"Fortunately, it was just temporary. Believe me, I'll never give up Big Macs for a man ever again."

"Let's go somewhere where you can't get a heart attack just from inhaling the grease in the air."

"We'll go through the drive-thru. Your arteries will be safe."

"Yeah, but will yours?" Calder grumbled, flipping on his turn signal.

"I can take care of my own body, thank you very much," Raine said, snapping her purse closed after extracting a five-dollar bill. She was already salivating over the thought of a bright red carton of greasy french fries.

"Yeah, right. When was the last time you ate a vegetable?" Calder turned down the drive-thru lane behind a green pick-up truck and then raised an eyebrow at her.

"It's really none of your business. But I'll have you know that I ate vegetables for dinner last night." Olives were veggies, weren't they? And she'd dipped the fried mozzarella sticks she, Aimee, and Daff had ordered in marinara sauce. Which was made from tomatoes, right? Hell, that counted as a salad in her book.

Calder looked at her as if he didn't quite believe her, but Raine just ignored him. There was no way she'd be able to convince the man she'd virtually lived with for over a year that she'd changed her atrocious eating habits. When they'd been together, it had been easier to eat healthy. Calder was a great cook, and since he did most of the grocery shopping, she had learned to substitute carrot sticks and celery for the potato chips he refused to buy. If she were being completely honest with herself, she'd admit that she had actually enjoyed Calder's nagging. He had always made sure she ate at least one healthy meal a day. It had been nice to have someone actually care enough about her to force her to get away from her computers long enough to have a meal that didn't come from a sack.

"I'll have the number one meal. With a Coke." She tried to hand Calder her five-dollar bill, but he looked at it as if it were infected with Anthrax and refused to take it.

"Thanks, but I think I can afford this," he said, before giving her order to the speaker box.

The heavy scent of hot, greasy fries filled the car when Calder took the bag the fast-food employee handed him after he'd paid the bill. He slid Raine's enormous Coke into one of the cup holders and put his own moderately sized iced tea in the slot next to it. Then he absently turned up the volume of the radio station as he pulled back into traffic.

Raine rummaged around in the sack and neatly spread two paper napkins over her knees before pulling her hamburger out of the bag. Calder had to admit that the smell made his stomach growl, although he wasn't even hungry.

No wonder the fast-food industry was so successful.

Raine took a bite of her burger and then took a sip of her soda. "So are you going to tell me why you're wasting money on a case we both know is total bullshit?"

Calder glanced her way before turning his attention back toward the street. "I don't think it's *total* bullshit. Maybe just 95 percent bullshit."

Raine grabbed a fry out of the bag and waved it at him. "Look, it doesn't matter to me. I'm happy to rack up billable hours trying to track down whatever you want me to. I just want to be sure I understand why—"

"Wait a sec," Calder interrupted with a frown, turning up the volume of the radio station.

"And in Boston, the search continues for fifteen-year-old Megan Mulroney, who disappeared last night along with her mother's SUV—a black JMC Pioneer with vanity plates SCR MOM. The teen is not considered a runaway and police suspect foul play. If anyone spots this vehicle, please call nine-one-one immediately. Now, stayed tuned for weather on the nines."

Calder turned the volume down and squinted at the windshield while Raine munched on another french fry.

"It's too much of a coincidence," she said after a moment of silence.

"Yeah," Calder agreed.

"Besides, what could a missing car in Boston have to do with Hope Enslar?"

"Nothing, I'm sure."

The paper wrapping around Raine's Big Mac crinkled as she peeled it back so she could take another bite. "Are you going to call the officer in charge of the investigation or shall I?"

Calder was already reaching for his cell phone. "I'm on it."

AFTER trying unsuccessfully for an hour to untie herself, Megan Mulroney had cried herself to sleep in the cramped space behind the second bench seat of her mother's SUV.

Silver Eyes or Shorty—she had stopped referring to them as "Mr." because, in her opinion, they didn't deserve the respect that implied—she wasn't sure which, had driven the car about half an hour away from the garage where she'd tried to escape. Megan had been certain that they were going to kill her when they got to wherever they were going, but instead, after they had driven over a noisy metal grate that sounded like they were going over a bridge, they turned off the engine, and while Megan lay in the back of the car, straining to hear what was going on through her duct-taped ears, it had suddenly gone pitch dark and so quiet that all she could hear was the sound of her own frantic breathing.

And then nothing.

It was as if she had gone blind and deaf in that one instant. *Oh, God, what are they going to do with me now?*

She pushed herself into a sitting position, doing the best she could not to make the ropes around her wrists and ankles any tighter than they already were. With every tug, though, they cut into her skin and Megan was certain that her wrists were already bleeding.

The top of her head hit the thin piece of plastic that covered the back area of the SUV. Megan tried to push it up out of the way, but succeeded only in tightening the ropes even further.

She started crying frustrated, angry tears. She was not going to just sit here and let them kill her without a fight.

Come on, Drew, Lucy, Cameron, she pleaded, *tell me how to get out of this.*

Unfortunately, the Angels didn't respond, so Megan continued trying to get her hands untied. After what seemed like an eternity, she finally slid back to the floor in a defeated heap, exhausted and unable to stop the hiccupping sobs that threatened to suffocate her.

And then, at last, her eyes slid closed, her body forcing her into a deep, dreamless sleep.

When she was jolted awake, it was still pitch dark and eerily quiet, but Megan could feel that they were moving. She rubbed her face against the carpet on the floor of the SUV, trying to remove the crust of dried-up tears from her eyes.

Why don't they just kill me and get it over with? she thought, irritable from being woken from the best sleep she'd had in months.

Then she frowned. Something didn't feel quite right. The vibration from the car's engine didn't jar her as much as this.

Suddenly, the SUV tilted, slamming Megan into the back of the bench seat. Then it moved again, and Megan slid toward the passenger side of the vehicle, her legs crumpling as she rammed into the wall. The ropes around her wrists tightened painfully and Megan screamed through the duct tape, even though she knew nobody could hear her.

The jostling continued and with her hands behind her back she tried to grab onto something so she wouldn't get slammed around every time the SUV moved, but she couldn't find anything to hold on to. Instead, with each roll, she hit the back of the seat or the back door, or had her head bashed into the wall, the ropes digging into her wrists and ankles a little more each time.

And then there was a loud boom and, just as suddenly as it had started, the movement stopped.

Megan lay on the floor of the SUV, staring up into the darkness. She felt like crying again, but forced the tears away. She couldn't think while she was crying. Unfortunately, when she did start to think, it was about how much she wanted to be at home right now, in her own bed with her mom and dad just down the hall in case she got scared. Of course, she was much too mature to go crawling in between them like she used to do when she was Matthew's age. But if she was magically transported to her own bed right now, she knew she'd be awfully tempted to creep down the hall and look into her parents' bedroom and be comforted by the fact that they were there just in case she ever *did* want to come climb into bed with them again.

She closed her eyes, imagining her dad smoothing her hair away from her face like he used to do. The last time she'd slept in between them, Mom had been pregnant with Matthew, her enormous stomach poking into Megan's back when Mom turned toward her in the night. She had felt her little brother's strong kick against her spine and had wondered if he was going to be a soccer player.

She missed Mom and Dad.

As the floor beneath her started to vibrate, Megan felt the hot wet tears start again. She even missed her little brother.

SIX

"I need to do a reconnaissance mission tonight. Are either of you interested in coming along?"

Aimee looked at Raine strangely. "I have a date and so does Daphne."

Raine plopped down in one of the chairs in Aimee's dining room and rested her elbows on the heavy wooden table. Aimee had owned the four-bedroom, three-bath house on the outskirts of downtown Atlanta for as long as Raine had known her. Of the three of them, Aimee was the most financially secure, not because she made more money than Raine or Daphne, but because she had different priorities.

If Raine had an extra hundred bucks, she'd go down to Nordy's and buy a new pair of boots. Or maybe half a pair, if they weren't on sale.

Daff would no doubt go buy a new gun or put a down payment on the latest surveillance equipment.

After researching the market carefully, Aimee would buy stocks or bonds.

Which, Raine figured, was why she lived in a cramped two-bedroom apartment and Daff rented a room from Aimee, while

Aimee owned her house outright and never charged anything she couldn't afford to pay off at the end of the month.

"I'll go," Daphne volunteered, setting the Glock that she'd been cleaning down on the table, the barrel pointed away from the group gathered in the dining room.

"What about your date? You can't cancel on him again," Aimee protested.

Daphne pulled her long, dark red hair into a ponytail and secured it in place with a no-nonsense black band. "Yes, I can. I'll just tell him something's come up. It doesn't matter anyway. I'm leaving for New York in a week and who knows how long I'll be gone. It's not like I'm going to get into a serious relationship with the guy."

"Not if you never go out with him, you won't," Aimee muttered darkly.

Daphne looked over at her friend, her blue eyes listless. "I'm sorry, Dev. I'm just not interested in dating right now."

Aimee's expression softened and she reached out a hand to squeeze Daphne's shoulder. "I know. It's just . . . we all want to see you get on with your life. You can't mourn forever."

Daff squeezed her eyes shut. "Are you sure? Because it feels like I could be carrying this around with me for the rest of my life. That's the part that scares me the most."

Aimee and Raine exchanged glances over Daphne's head.

"Are you sure you should be going back to New York?" Raine asked. "Did you talk to your brother about it? He might not think it's such a great idea."

Daphne opened her eyes and let out a heavy sigh. "Brooks wasn't thrilled that I'm coming back, but he is the one who got me the job. I think he's hoping that, wherever this former publishing employee is, he's not in Manhattan. I would guess that's the most likely scenario, myself. I'll probably only be in the city for a day or two."

Raine was almost afraid to ask the next question, but she knew that if anyone could ask about it, it would be her or Aimee. "You're not planning to go back to Ground Zero, are you?" she asked softly.

Daphne looked down at the well-polished gun on the table in front of her. Raine saw spots of mottled red appear on her friend's cheeks, but wasn't certain if the color was caused by anger or embarrassment. Although why Daff would be embarrassed, Raine didn't know.

When Daphne's brother Brooks had called six months ago to talk to Daff's best friends, he had let them in on his sister's "dirty little secret." After resigning from the FBI the day after the 9/11 terrorist attacks, Daphne had spent the next two years haunting Ground Zero—first as a volunteer helping with the rescue efforts and then as a silent witness watching the open, gaping wound begin to heal.

Raine blinked back tears on behalf of her friend, imagining just what kind of hell Daphne had put herself through day after day.

Daff blamed herself for not being able to convince her superiors that the suspected terrorist she was tracking had plans to attack the United States. They called the threat "credible, but not urgent" and refused to let her take the man into custody. By the time she convinced them to let her go after the man, it was too late. She was on her way to bring him in when all the flights on 9/11/01 were grounded.

She'd been in mourning ever since.

"No, I'm not going to Ground Zero," Daphne said loudly, as if she were trying to assure herself as well as her friends that she was through with that chapter in her life.

"Oh, Daff—" Aimee began, taking a step toward her friend.

Daphne held up a hand to stop her. "No, I'm fine. I mean it. I know that 9/11 wasn't my fault. I know that spending the rest of my life regretting that I wasn't able to prevent it from happening is a mistake. That doesn't mean I'm ready to go on a blind date with a guy who has no idea what it's like to have something like this on his shoulders. I mean, what does this guy do?"

Aimee shrugged. "He's an insurance broker."

"Right. So, if he screws up, the worst that's gonna happen is that some company might go out of business because they get sued and have inadequate coverage. How can he understand what it's like to have something like 9/11 on his conscience?"

"I thought you said you don't blame yourself," Raine said, frustrated that her friend couldn't see how much she still blamed herself for something that had ultimately been out of her control.

Daphne looked at her then, and Raine nearly gasped at the ferocity of the self-hatred she saw in Daff's eyes. "I don't. Why can't you all just leave me alone?"

Aimee pushed her chair back, the legs scraping loudly on the tile floor. "Because we care about you, that's why. And do you know what? If you want to spend the rest of your life watching ghosts at Ground Zero, we'll still care about you. We're not going to go away, so you'd better learn to deal with it."

Daphne slammed her hand down on the Glock on the table, grabbing the gun as she raced from the room.

Raine looked over at Aimee, whose normally tanned skin had gone white with anger. Raine cleared her throat and rubbed the end of her nose with her index finger. "You made her cry," she said mildly.

Aimee shook her head, scowled, and then sighed, releasing the frustration that had built up inside of her. "I know. And I know she hates for us to see her tears. After all, that might convince us that she's a mere mortal like the rest of us."

"Yeah. Super Daff." Raine snorted, remembering the tattoo Daphne had requested be permanently etched on her right butt cheek. Daffy Duck wearing Superman tights and a cape. Super Daff. They had laughed about it that night, too drunk to realize how well their tattoo choices fit their personalities.

Raine pushed her bangs out of her eyes. "Well, when she comes back out will you tell her that I'll pick her up tonight at midnight? At least she won't be spending all night alone."

Aimee speared her with her frank brown eyes. "And neither will you, for a change."

Raine frowned and raised her palms in supplication. "Don't start in on me now. I fully acknowledge my need to get laid, especially after catching myself eyeing Calder's ass this afternoon. Of all the people I should *not* be attracted to, he's at the top of the list."

Aimee's response to that was a cryptic, "Hmm."

With a yawn, Raine slid her chair back and stood up. "I need a nap. Tell Daff I'll be back for her, and you have a good time on your date. Who knows, if it doesn't work out, maybe you can join us."

Aimee smiled, her first of the afternoon. "I wouldn't count on that if I were you."

Raine grinned back. "Well, then I won't wish you luck. Sounds like you don't need it."

"When have *any* of us needed luck to get lucky?" Aimee asked, following Raine outside and bidding her good-bye with a wink and a wave.

I have to pee.

Megan came abruptly awake with the realization that she had to go to the bathroom. Now. Only with her hands tied behind her back and her ankles bound together, the only way to relieve the pressure in her bladder would be to wet herself. Like some . . . some kind of helpless baby.

Suddenly, Megan didn't feel like crying anymore. Instead, she found herself getting pissed off. Really pissed off.

Silver Eyes and Shorty had dumped her in the back of the car as if she were some piece of human garbage. Well, fuck them. She wasn't going to let them treat her like that. She was tired of crying and being a victim. She was not—repeat *not*—going to just give in to them and wet herself.

Megan sat up, feeling the soothing hum of some sort of vibration along the back of the seat in front of her. Her head hit the thin partition that served to hide valuables left in the rear of the SUV from prying eyes.

If she could pop the partition off the makeshift trunk, maybe she could use the edges to cut through the ropes. If nothing else, just getting out of the confined space would be a triumph.

Megan scooted along the floor until her back was up against the driver's side of the Pioneer. She gathered her feet

under her and slid up the wall, bowing her head to let her
shoulders do the work of pushing the tight-fitting plastic out
of place. It took her several tries to maneuver the partition
so it wouldn't fall back into place again, but at last she had it
out of the way and could stand up.

She had hoped that she'd be able to see something out the
windows, something that would give her a clue as to where
she was. But outside the SUV was just more darkness.

Megan shrugged off her disappointment. Once she got
her hands free, she could switch on the dome light. After
that . . . well, after that she'd figure out some way to get free.
But first, she had to get those ropes untied.

And go pee.

The partition covering the back of the SUV had wedged
at an awkward diagonal, with one corner sticking up right
near Megan's face. Unable to use her hands to test the sharp-
ness of the plastic, she used her cheek instead. Beneath the
duct tape covering her mouth, Megan grimaced.

It wasn't rough at all.

Probably so nobody could cut themselves. Or poke an eye
out, Megan thought ruefully as the soft skin of her cheek encountered the slightly rounded edge of the partition. She felt
the tight loop of twine holding her hands together at her back,
trying to ignore the ache of her shoulders after being held in
such an unnatural position for so long. She rested her cheek
against the edge of the plastic for a moment and closed her
eyes. There was no way it was sharp enough to cut through the
rope.

Now what? Megan blinked back tears, reminding herself
that she was done crying.

She scanned the dark interior of the SUV, trying to think
of something she could use to free her hands. She thought
about trying to break a window, but in every movie she'd ever
seen, when the car windows broke, they didn't leave sharp
shards of glass behind, instead shattering into thousands of
useless pieces.

Megan bit the inside of her cheek. Wasn't there anything
dangerous in this car? No sharp edges or potential weapons?

How could car manufacturers make their vehicles so dang safe?

And then it hit her.

How many times had she heard her mom complain about people who threw their burning cigarettes out their car windows? "Doesn't that jerk know he could start a fire? Not to mention that—hello, idiot!—your cigarette butt is litter," her mother would say, glaring at the other driver as she passed.

Yes, cigarettes were litter and they were dangerous. And people used the cigarette lighters in their cars to light them.

Feeling suddenly charitable to all the smokers in the world, Megan shoved the partition out of the way with the side of her arm. Then she leaned over the backseat, pushed herself up on her tiptoes, and wiggled forward, ending up in a face-first heap on the rear bench seat. Carefully, she rolled over, ignoring the edges of the books in the backpack that was still lying on the seat near her head.

She slid off the seat and managed to hop to the front of the SUV where, turning her back to the windshield, she pressed in the cigarette lighter, thanking God that her mother hadn't swapped her lighter for a cell phone charger like Emily's mom had.

The lighter popped after less than a minute and Megan took a deep breath, trying not to think about what could go wrong. The rope could catch on fire and she wouldn't see it before it got out of control. The rope would be made of that nylon stuff that would melt into her skin. Or, even worse, the rope would be made of something that wouldn't burn at all and she'd have to think of another way to get her hands loose.

She shuddered and squeezed her eyes shut, then grabbed hold of the cigarette lighter behind her back. The hot metal burned her fingertips as she tried twisting it into the knot at her wrists and she instinctively loosened her grip. The cigarette lighter fell to the carpeted floor with a soft thud.

Megan opened her eyes and clenched her teeth. The duct tape pulled at the skin of her cheeks as she frowned, rubbing her fingers together behind her back. That had really hurt.

The pressure on her bladder mounted and Megan squeezed her legs together desperately.

I am not *going to wet my pants.*

Frantically, she looked around the SUV for something to help her get the ropes off but, once again, all she could think of was the cigarette lighter. She had one choice. Pee her pants or burn herself getting the ropes off. Megan had the sudden vision of getting rescued, having a cute fireman or two pulling her to safety, and having them suddenly realize that she had wet herself. Or even worse. Because depending on how long she was trapped in here, certain other bodily functions were going to be necessary as well.

Megan swallowed at the vision of herself being let out of wherever she was trapped, grimy and reeking, having the rescue team snicker at her behind her back because she had been so weak. What would people at school think of her then? Even Emily would never look at her the same way if she knew that her best friend had turned into some kind of animal in captivity.

No. She was going to get out of this, no matter how much it hurt.

And then, instead of thinking about the Charlie's Angels girls, with their big hair and tight outfits and Matrix-style Kung Fu antics, she pictured James Bond instead. She thought of Pierce Brosnan at the beginning of *Die Another Day,* being tortured by the North Koreans. They electrocuted him, put him in a pit with stinging scorpions, beat him up. And still he didn't crack under the pressure. Megan slid down the console separating the driver and passenger seats, feeling along the carpet for the cigarette lighter.

I know it's just a stupid movie, but that kind of stuff happens all the time in the real world. People get tortured and beaten. Kids get abused. But they're strong and they survive because they have to. I'm going to be strong, too.

Megan pushed the cigarette lighter back into the heater, forcing herself to slow down her breathing. She pictured Pierce-as-James, watching the bad guys as they approached with their latest pain-inducing device. The cigarette lighter popped.

James knew it was going to hurt, so he separated from himself, his mind retreating to a place where the pain couldn't touch him. The North Koreans approached and he watched dispassionately as they waved the fiery brand in front of him. They touched it to his skin, once and then again. He watched, as if from afar, as his body reacted, futilely trying to avoid the stinging hot pain they inflicted. But it was just his body they were attacking, not his mind. His mind was safely hidden away from them.

And when they were finished, his body lay in a pool of sweat and blood and agony, but his mind had survived unscathed.

"WHAT did you find out from the officer in charge of the Mulroney case?" Raine asked, leaning back in the chair in front of her computer screen.

"Not much more than we learned on the news," Calder answered, sounding as if he were stifling a yawn.

Which he probably was, Raine thought, looking at the bottom right hand of her screen to see that it was just past eleven o'clock at night. Unless Calder had changed his habits in the nearly eleven months since they'd been apart, he had most likely risen early to go to the gym before making it to the office an hour before anyone else showed up. Raine nearly shuddered with distaste. Morning people creeped her out. For one thing, they all seemed so damn self-disciplined. Not to mention self-righteous.

"Sara Mulroney's Pioneer—with her fifteen-year-old daughter in it—disappeared from the parking lot of the grocery store where she'd stopped to pick up a few items. It was a mild night, and she left her daughter, Megan, in the car with all the doors locked and the windows rolled up. Sara estimates that she was gone less than twenty minutes and, when she came out of the grocery store, both Megan and the SUV were gone."

"Maybe the kid went out for a joyride and got into an accident. Have the police checked the local hospitals?"

"Yes. Even though Mrs. Mulroney assured police that

Megan's not the type to do such a thing, the officer in charge wanted to make sure they covered every possibility."

"Besides, no parent ever admits to the cops that their kid is the type to do 'such a thing.'"

"Exactly," Calder agreed. "But in this case, it looks like Megan's parents are right. The problem is, that means that Megan was taken against her will, and the police have no clues as to what might have happened. They took Megan's disappearance seriously from the minute Mrs. Mulroney called from her cell phone in the grocery store parking lot. They alerted the media immediately and had the public searching for a black Pioneer within half an hour."

"Have they gotten any leads?" Raine asked, absently opening an e-mail that had just arrived in her inbox.

"Nothing serious. Pioneers are popular vehicles, so there's been no shortage of reported sightings, but nothing that has panned out."

"Hmm." Raine frowned into the phone and glanced at her computer screen, quickly scanning the incoming message from one of the regulars in her hacker network. KatBrglr, he called himself. Raine smiled and shook her head. She'd be willing to bet that KatBrglr, whoever he was, had no clue how to break into anything without using his computer. She, on the other hand, had been taught by the best.

Fortunately, she'd never been tempted to use the skills her jewel-thieving father had taught her for her own personal gain. She'd seen what a life lived on the edge of the law was like and she wanted none of it. Of course, living on the right side of the law hadn't exactly worked out well for her, either, Raine thought with a snort.

She took a sip of the Coke that was sitting on top of her desk and returned her attention to Calder. "I still think it's highly unlikely that this has anything to do with Hope Enslar, but I'm happy to look into it if it means that Megan will be found. Did you happen to get the VIN of Mrs. Mulroney's Pioneer?" she asked, referring to the seventeen-digit unique identification number associated with every vehicle manufactured in the United States.

It sounded as if Calder was stifling another yawn as he

responded, "No, I didn't think to ask. Do you want me to call Boston P.D. back?"

"No, that's all right. It won't take me more than a few minutes to find it. Besides, it's probably best if we don't let the local police know that we're sticking our noses into their investigation. That way, if we don't find anything, they can't push the blame onto the Bureau."

"Okay. So you're going to see what you can find out about the Mulroney's vehicle—"

"Yes, I'll get the VIN and see if there's any chatter on the Internet about it," Raine interrupted. "I'm also going back to Jackson Motors to see if I can find out what that employee was slipping into the vehicles in the assembly line. There was something very suspicious about the way he was acting, and I want to know why."

"When are you going back?" Calder asked, suddenly sounding very awake.

Raine looked at the clock at the bottom of her computer screen. "Actually, I should leave right now. I told Daphne I'd pick her up around midnight."

"I'm coming with you," Calder said.

Raine stood up and stretched, then tugged up the waist-band of her silky black sweatpants. "You know I don't need your help," she replied conversationally.

"You never have," Calder muttered under his breath.

"That's not true. The one time I did need you, though, you failed me."

She heard his loud sigh all the way from his house in Marietta. "I know, and I'm sorry. I tried all year to apologize, but you wouldn't take my calls. I don't know what more you want me to do, Raine. Should I take out an ad in the *Atlanta Journal-Constitution* and admit to the entire greater Atlanta area that I'm an asshole? Or rent a billboard? Or say it on the radio? I would do all of those things if that's what it would take to make you accept my apology. But you have to admit that there was a part of you that wasn't unhappy to see Jeffrey Allen get blown away that day, so don't try to tell me that my lack of faith in you wasn't just the tiniest bit justified. I know better."

"Calder?" Raine asked, when he finally paused to take a breath.

"What?"

"You suck at apologizing."

He sighed again. Loudly. "I know. I should have stopped after 'I'm sorry.'"

Raine silently nodded her agreement. "Look, I can't do this job if we don't keep things between us on a purely professional level. This case has nothing to do with what happened in the past, so let's just do our best to let it go. You've hired me to look into Mr. Enslar's concerns about his daughter, and my partners and I are fully capable of taking care of it. If there comes a time when I believe we need outside assistance, I'll be sure to let you know. In the meantime, why don't you just leave us to do the job you hired us to do?"

Because I still love you, Calder thought, staring outside the darkened window in his bedroom. *Because every time I hear your voice, I want you back in my life . . . and back in my bed. Because I'm not going to let you go again.* But he didn't say any of that. Instead, he tossed aside the covers and strode to his dresser to grab a pair of jeans. He'd be damned if he was going to let Raine call all the shots. He'd been doing that for too long; he had backed off because he thought that she needed time to get over the hurt from what she saw as his betrayal. But now here it was, almost a year later, and she still wasn't ready to let him back into her life.

Well, ready or not, here I come.

Then, tired of the hangdog role that he'd been playing for far too long, he said, "I'll meet you at Aimee's house in twenty minutes. If you leave without me, you're fired."

Not giving Raine time to respond, Calder hung up the phone, pulled on a black T-shirt, and slid his feet into a pair of tennis shoes. He ignored the insistent summons of the ringing phone as he grabbed his car keys off the dresser.

As the front door closed behind him, he started whistling.

He couldn't wait to see what Raine would do next.

SEVEN

SHE was free.

Megan pried her fingers under the last of the duct tape, wincing when it pulled off the top layer of her skin as it came free. She sucked in the first deep breath she'd taken in who knows how long. Barely able to walk since she was trying so hard to keep from wetting her pants, Megan threw open the door of the Pioneer and hit the headlights. She didn't take time to look around as she made it one step from the SUV, tugged down her sweats and underwear, and crouched to relieve the aching pressure on her bladder.

When she was finished, she grimaced, wishing she had thought to grab a Kleenex out of the glove box. Still, dripdrying was the least of her worries. At least she wouldn't be rescued wearing soiled clothes.

She pulled up her sweats and walked in front of the Pioneer to inspect the mottled skin at her wrists. Besides the welts from where she'd struggled against the ropes, several crescent-shaped burns were etched into her skin. Megan felt oddly proud of those burns. She had done what she had to do in order to survive. She hadn't given up, she hadn't whined and felt sorry for herself and waited for someone to rescue her.

She had rescued herself.

Of course, she thought, peering into the darkness surrounding her, that was just the first step. Now she had to figure out where she was and just what the heck she was going to do to get out of here.

She looked around. The SUV's headlights glowed brightly on a rusted metal wall. Megan pounded on the wall several times, hoping someone would hear the heavy thuds and let her out. As the last thud echoed in the silence, it occurred to her that Silver Eyes and Shorty might be waiting for her outside. If that were the case, she'd be smart to not let them know she'd escaped the Pioneer.

"You've got to start thinking like James Bond," she whispered to herself, her voice raspy after so many hours of disuse.

"Yes, what would James do?" Megan nearly giggled at that, clapping a hand over her mouth to stop any sound from escaping. If James Bond were here, he'd probably slap her across the cheeks and tell her to stop being hysterical.

Megan took a deep breath, trying to calm herself down. Her stomach grumbled, reminding her that she hadn't eaten since lunchtime the day she was kidnapped . . . and she'd ended up throwing that up after Silver Eyes punched her. "Bastard," Megan muttered, remembering the way he'd calmly shoved his fist in her stomach, as if she had been put on this earth to be his punching bag. Boy, did she want to make him pay for that.

For now, though, hunger took the upper hand over revenge. Megan remembered the Pop-tarts she'd slipped into her backpack for a snack and went back into the SUV to retrieve her pack. She flipped the dome light on, ignoring the disgusting stain on the carpet as she leaned over the middle bench seat to get her bag. She took the heavy backpack with her to the passenger seat, rummaging around to find the silver-wrapped treat buried between her books.

She fished the Pop-tarts out of her bag and ripped open the package with her teeth. She was halfway through the second pastry when she stopped, realizing that she had no water to wash down the sugary snack.

Hmm. Now what?

She slowly chewed another bite of the Pop-tart. James Bond wouldn't just go around, eating and drinking and banging on walls without having some sort of plan. That's what she needed—a plan.

Megan looked out the passenger side window of her mother's SUV, but saw only another metal wall. The first thing she needed to find out was what else was in this metal box with her. She forced herself not to shudder as her imagination conjured up snakes and dead bodies.

"Stop that," she scolded herself, popping open the glove compartment to see if she could find water or anything else that might be useful. She pulled out a handful of papers and studied them in the overhead light. Registration. Expired insurance cards. A hairbrush. A set of keys. The owner's manual. Ah, now what was this? Megan pulled a heavy, round object out of the glove compartment and inspected it. A flashlight.

She set that on the dashboard and continued searching through wadded up receipts, sunblock, and a pocket pack of Kleenex. She put the sunblock and the tissues on the dashboard next to the flashlight and went to search the rest of the vehicle. The side storage compartments were filled with maps and some trash, and Megan found herself grumbling over her mother's obsessive cleanliness. Emily's mom's car was a pigsty, overflowing with the junk her three kids routinely left behind—half-eaten bags of potato chips, forgotten cans of soda, comic books and toys. The Mulroney car, on the other hand, was almost spotlessly clean, netting Megan nothing more than a first aid kit, an emergency gallon of water—for which she was thankful—and a blanket stuffed in with the spare tire.

Megan closed the back of the Pioneer and shined the weak flashlight behind her. She knew there was another car there, but she was almost afraid to look in it. What if there was another person in there? What if it was someone bad, like a murderer or something? Almost worse, what if it was a dead body?

Clenching her teeth, Megan sidled along the warm wall and tried to peer into the windows of the car parked behind her mother's SUV. The flashlight's beam was too weak, though, so she had to step closer. And closer. Until, finally, she was standing next to the four-door sedan, holding her breath as she shined the light inside.

The front seats were both empty but the cup holders were full. A brightly colored child's car seat was buckled in the back, partially covered by a blue baby blanket. Megan gingerly lifted the door handle, almost hoping the car would be locked. The door opened easily and Megan wrinkled her nose at the sour smell that wafted out. She leaned one knee on the front seat and peered around the headrest. Then she gasped and leaped back, whacking her head painfully on the doorframe when something in the backseat moved.

"HOW do you plan to gain entry?" Calder asked as Raine took the exit off of I-75 for Jackson Motors. The trip from Aimee's house had been made in virtual silence, with both Raine and her friend Daphne shooting significant looks at one another the entire way.

"I think you should just wait in the car," Raine said, not answering his question. "If Daphne or I get caught, there's no link from us to the Bureau. We can just plead minor breaking and entering and it probably won't get us more than a small fine and a slap on the wrist."

"But, you won't get caught, will you?" Calder asked.

Raine looked at him steadily in the rearview mirror. After a long silence, she said, "This is a pretty easy job. There's no retinal scanning, no fingerprint matching system, just a simple magnetic keycard entry. But that doesn't mean there's no chance of getting caught. That's always a risk, even on the simplest jobs."

"I'm willing to take that risk. Now tell me how you plan to gain entry into the building."

Raine glanced at Daphne, then back at him. "I plan to walk right through the front door."

Calder raised his eyebrows questioningly and Raine

gestured towards a pile of white clothes lying on the seat next to him. "I picked up some cheap lab coats on the way to Aimee's house. They won't be the same quality as the one our tour guide was wearing this afternoon, but they'll do."

"What about security badges? Won't you need those to get in?"

"Gosh, I wonder why we didn't think of that," Daphne said from the front seat, not bothering to so much as turn her head to look at him.

Calder crossed his arms across his chest and met Raine's eyes in the rearview mirror as he shrugged apologetically. "Okay, sorry. You've got it all under control."

Raine nodded. "Could you hand me one of the lab coats? We're almost at the entrance to the plant."

After quickly riffling through the pile to save the largest jacket for himself, Calder passed the other two coats up front. Daphne handed a rectangular badge to him, and Calder spent a moment studying it in the dark. He didn't know where Raine got his mug shot, but it wouldn't have surprised him to find out she'd broken in to the FBI's personnel files and taken the photo from there.

Raine slid on a pair of glasses and tugged her hair up into a quick ponytail before slowing her Volkswagen Golf to a stop beside the small outbuilding that housed Jackson Motor Company's security guard. She pressed the button to lower her window and flashed the guard her badge and a smile.

"Good evening," the guard said pleasantly, bending down to check out the occupants of the vehicle. Then he looked at Raine's card, first studying the front and then turning it over to look at the back. He stepped back inside the guardhouse and swiped the card through a reader, obviously satisfied that Raine was legit when he handed the card back to her. "Late night, huh?" he observed.

"Yes. My colleagues and I were struggling with an issue on the torsion beam on the newest model of the Pioneer and we think we've finally figured it out. We couldn't wait until Monday to see if we're correct."

The guard rolled his eyes good-naturedly. "You engineers are all the same."

Raine nodded sheepishly. "Yeah, we can't help it. By the way, for comparison purposes we'd like to check the suspension of one of our current models. Can you tell me where the vehicles that came off the assembly line today are located? I could go log on to my computer, but we wanted to head out to the lot first."

The guard tapped a few keys on his keyboard and told her, "They'd be out in lot 14B."

"Thank you," Raine said, giving the guy a slight wave as she pulled through the open gate.

"According to this, lot 14B is in the southwest corner of the plant," Daphne said, the plans she'd pulled from the side pocket of the car rustling as she studied them. "The easiest way to get there will be to take the main corridor all the way to the back of the plant and head west. There are security cameras mounted on poles once we get back to the lots, so we'll either need to disable them or find some way to get one of the vehicles out of camera range while we take it apart."

Raine pulled her car into a visitor's spot near the front door, figuring that any employee would do the same at this time of night—even engineers, who were notorious rule-followers. "I'll take care of the cameras once we get there. I brought a laptop and I've already figured out how to tap into the system that controls the security cameras. I'll simply program it to record the first few minutes of our arrival, so the gate guard knows we're there. Then I'll start a loop so the tape will repeat until we're ready to let it start filming us again. All we need to do is be in roughly the same positions when it starts recording again. Otherwise, there will be a jump on the tape that might make the guard suspicious if he's paying attention."

"What is it you expect to find?" Calder asked.

Raine opened the driver's side door and stepped out into the warm spring night. She walked to the hatchback and popped it open, taking a white tote bag out of the back before she answered. "I don't know. I just know that I saw something suspicious going on during that tour today, and if what I saw is even remotely connected to Megan Mulroney's disappearance, I have to know."

Calder and Daphne stepped out of the car at the same time, slamming their doors with the precision of a synchronized swimming team. "Does JMC have audio surveillance as well as video?" Calder asked as they made their way to the entrance of the building.

"Not unless they've added it within the last two years. The plans I was able to find are fairly recent, and I'd be willing to bet that the company wouldn't have bothered. That level of security is just not something most companies feel they need to invest in," Raine answered.

She waved her badge in front of the card reader beside the glass doors that marked the entrance of Jackson Motor Company. The indicator light turned green and the door locks clicked open.

The trio made their way across the now-empty lobby of the manufacturing plant, heading toward the door Heather had taken her tour through that afternoon. Again, Raine waved her card in front of a reader and the light turned green. She pulled the door open and turned back to Daphne and Calder, silently indicating that they should swipe their cards as well. When they'd all been with the FBI, it had been frowned on to let others into the office by "tailgating" on someone else's card. Although many companies didn't punish employees for foolishly holding the door for strangers after using their own cards to gain entry to the building, Raine didn't want to take the chance that the security at JMC was taken a bit more seriously. The indicator light turned green when Daff and Calder passed their badges over the reader and Calder pulled the heavy metal door closed behind him as they made their way down the hall.

It was quiet in the plant, no hum of machinery or chatter of employees passing in the hall. Raine and Daphne walked together in front of Calder, their heads close together while they talked quietly. Daphne took an occasional note on a clipboard Raine had handed her before they entered the building. Raine had changed from her knee-high boots and short skirt to a more demure pair of black slacks and a pair of low-heeled shoes he knew she hated.

Whenever Calder looked at her legs, he couldn't help but

picture the Bugs Bunny tattoo she had on her ankle. He supposed it wasn't so much her choice of subject that surprised him, it was the fact that she'd admitted that he had some part in her decision to do it. For some perverse reason, that made him happy. Every time she looked at Bugs, she would think of him.

Of course, Calder thought with a snort, it could be that she was thinking of how much she detested him.

Daphne handed him the clipboard she'd been scribbling notes on, and Calder realized that even though Raine didn't think the plant was wired for sound, she wasn't taking any chances. Back when she'd been with the Bureau, she'd been commended on her thoroughness. It was one of the reasons she had been suspected of hiring the hit on Jeffrey Allen—it seemed that whoever had done it had covered his or her tracks with the same attention to detail that Raine used when working a case.

Daff had written some automotive catch phrases on the sheet of paper with the words "Just in case" underlined at the top. Calder was grateful that the women were so well prepared, since he had insisted on coming along for no other reason than that he wanted to get back into Raine's life. He knew it was foolish for him to have come along so ill-equipped for the job. Were this a typical case, he would never have inserted himself into the process, leaving that to the agents who were closer to the details and less likely to make mistakes that would blow their cover.

They turned a corner and headed for the door that Daphne had seen on the plans she'd been studying earlier. As they stepped outside, Calder looked over the vast parking lot of newly manufactured vehicles. It was a car thief's wet dream. Row after row after row of shiny automobiles, each one in pristine condition.

"14B is over here," Daphne said, leading the way across the lot.

"How will we know which vehicle to search?" Calder asked as Raine fell into step beside him.

"By the VIN," she answered, as if that explained everything.

"Okay, I know that the VIN uniquely identifies a vehicle, but how is that going to help us narrow our search to cars that were on the assembly line while we were on the tour?"

"VINs do more than uniquely identify a vehicle. They even go so far as to indicate the make, model, engine type, and the plant where the vehicle was manufactured. Part of the VIN is sequential, however, so if we know the range of numbers that were being assembled this afternoon, we should be able to pinpoint it pretty closely."

"I assume you have the VIN range that was manufactured today?" Calder asked.

"Of course. I've even got it down to thirty-minute increments, so it shouldn't be too difficult to find a vehicle that was manufactured while we were standing on that catwalk."

"What are we looking for?" Daphne called out from the middle of a sea of SUVs.

Raine consulted her own pad of notes and read off a series of digits. Since the vehicles had been parked in the order they came off the assembly line, it was almost laughably easy to find their target.

"Now what?" Daphne asked, laying her hand on the hood of the champagne-colored JMC Pioneer and looking at Raine questioningly.

"Now we pretend to be looking at something mechanical," Raine said. "Calder, why don't you slide under the car? Daphne and I will look under the hood."

"You mean you don't know what a torsion beam is?" Calder asked.

"I didn't have time to research *everything*," Raine answered, scowling.

"Do you even know what a transmission is?" Calder asked.

"Do you?" Daphne asked before Raine could respond.

Calder laughed and put his hands up in mock surrender. "I was just asking. But, yes, I do know quite a lot about cars. I have four brothers, after all. If I'd let on that I didn't know a carburetor from a distributor, I'd have never lived it down."

"Good, then why don't you make yourself useful and act like you know what you're doing?" Raine said.

"Okay, I will. But it doesn't make any sense for you and Daphne to open the hood. The suspension system is under the vehicle. You'll only look like you don't know what you're doing if you open that hood."

Raine sighed. "All right. Everybody under the car. I just hope I don't get grease in my hair."

"THIS is like taking candy from the proverbial baby," Daphne said, removing a bolt from the passenger side door of the Pioneer.

"Don't get overconfident," Raine cautioned, holding her hand out for the bolt.

"I'm not. It's just been a long time since I've worked a case that actually went the way it was supposed to," Daff said gloomily.

Calder didn't say anything as he helped Daphne remove the lower panel of the door. Raine felt her heartbeat quicken with anticipation. She had a hunch that whatever that man had been slipping into the vehicles would give them a clue to Megan's disappearance. She had forgotten how much purpose fighting crime gave to her life. It was the main reason she hadn't followed her father on his path to crime. The famous—or infamous, depending on how you looked at it—cat burglar John Robey had taught his daughter all his tricks. Tricks that young Raine adapted for breaking and entering in cyberspace.

In the beginning, it had been exhilarating to crack into supposedly secure systems. But, after awhile, she realized that it wasn't fulfilling. Sure, she could change her best friend's French grade from a B+ to an F as a joke. She could also steal people's bank records, change their criminal histories, and revoke their security clearances. She could wreak havoc with national security, disrupt communications at the White House, and shut down the airline industry, too.

But using her talents to such destructive ends seemed so wrong. Even her father had his own code of honor about his thefts. He never stole from anyone who couldn't afford it. And Raine had known that to be true because when she was a teenager, he'd asked her to provide him with the detailed financial records of several of his potential targets. On several occasions, she'd turned up cases where a target's wealth was all an illusion, and her father had turned his attention to better-heeled victims.

She'd seen it tear her parents' marriage apart, though. Her mother, a wealthy socialite, had initially been attracted to the danger and excitement of being married to a notorious jewel thief, but what she'd ended up wanting was a respectable husband, which John Robey could never be. He wasn't cut out for the corporate world and his illicit activities left little to be discussed at cocktail parties.

Now, as an adult, Raine had a better understanding of how her mother must have felt. While she had adored her father and would always love him, being a jewel thief was hardly the sort of occupation a person could be proud of. But Raine had been proud of her job with the FBI. She had loved solving crimes, bringing embezzlers and child pornographers and other criminals to justice. Perhaps, in some way, she had been trying to atone for her father's choice of profession. Or perhaps she just liked being able to fall asleep at night knowing that what she did made a real difference in the world.

Whatever the reason, as she watched Calder search the door of the Pioneer for the item the JMC employee had dropped inside, she silently admitted that she missed it. She hadn't realized how ready she was to get out of her apartment and get back on with her life until this moment.

"I think I've got it," Calder said, pulling a small silver object out of the doorframe. He sat back on the cool pavement and squinted at the coin-like piece of metal.

"What is it?" Raine asked excitedly, squatting down in the moonlight to get a better view. "Is it a computer chip? Some sort of tracking device?"

Calder slowly turned the disc between his fingers. He frowned as he pulled it closer, trying to make out the words printed in tiny letters on the back. After a moment, he looked up, still frowning.

"What is it?" Raine asked again, her hopes of helping to solve the Mulroney case sinking into the pit of her stomach.

Calder handed her the metal disc, then pushed himself up off the ground, dusting off his rear end. "It's some sort of religious propaganda. Probably put there by some nutcase who thinks he can subliminally convert people over to his side by dropping these stupid things in their cars."

Raine frowned down at the coin before handing it to Daphne, who studied it for a moment before shaking her head with disgust.

"Now what?" Daphne asked.

"Now we put everything back like we found it," Raine answered, narrowing her eyes at the dismantled door of the Pioneer. "And after that, we head to the research and development department. I am *not* leaving here without finding something to help our case."

EIGHT

THE gate guard stifled a yawn and pulled his gaze from the monitor showing the three engineers back in lot 14B when a blue JMC Adventurer rolled to a stop in front of the gate.

"Busy night," the man muttered under his breath as he waited for the driver of the vehicle to roll down his window. Or rather, *her* window, the guard corrected himself as the female driver turned to him and handed over her security card.

"Good morning, Ms. Enslar," he said, swiping her card through his reader.

The woman nodded to acknowledge his greeting, tapping her fingers on the steering wheel without saying a word.

The guard narrowed his eyes just a bit, annoyed that she refused to talk to him. It irked him that some of JMC's employees treated him this way, as if he were no better than the janitors who came to take out their garbage or clean their toilets every day.

Bitch.

He handed the card back to her but didn't raise the security bar, determined to make her say something to him before he let her into the plant. "You engineers sure work some strange hours," he said, leaning his arms on the windowsill as if he had all night to stand there and chat. Which he did.

She looked at him then, her smallish brown eyes meeting his. "What do you mean?" she asked.

"Another group of engineers from R&D came through about an hour ago. Said they had figured something out about the new Pioneer and wanted to test their theory right away. Nice to know that your staff is so dedicated, huh?" *And that not all JMC employees are jerks like you,* he added silently, not willing to risk his job to make a point.

The head of R&D frowned but didn't say anything more, and the guard figured he'd detained her as long as he could without really pissing her off. He pushed the button to open the gate and watched the Adventurer's taillights grow smaller and smaller as Ms. Enslar drove toward the manufacturing plant.

When he turned back to the monitors, he noticed that the engineers who had arrived earlier had finished up with whatever they were doing out in the parking lot and were now headed toward their offices in R&D.

"SHIT," Calder muttered as he felt the vibration of his cell phone from where he'd clipped it on his belt. In his experience, no good news had ever been delivered via phone call after midnight. As a matter of fact, he'd found the cutoff for good news was closer to eleven o'clock. It was all bad news after that.

He reached under his white lab coat, motioning for Raine and Daphne to wait while he read the text message on the small screen. As the meaning of the words soaked into his brain, Calder sucked in a breath between clenched teeth.

"We have to get out of here," he said, reaching out to grab Raine's arm.

"What are you doing?" Raine hissed, digging the heels of her sensible shoes into the worn linoleum.

Calder didn't loosen his grip. "I'm sorry, but I have to go. Now. I need to . . ." He paused, swallowing, not looking at anything in the white hallway as he pushed the words out. "I need to go. There's been a problem with one of my agents."

Raine exchanged puzzled looks with Daphne, then shrugged and allowed Calder to change course. "Okay, we'll go. Daff and I can always . . ."

Raine broke off when a slender woman wearing a lab coat over a pair of worn jeans and a red sweater entered the hallway and headed toward them purposefully. Calder kept walking, his hand still on Raine's arm. Surely, the woman would just keep going. She had no reason to stop them, no reason to suspect that they didn't belong.

Calder remembered Raine's statement earlier that evening. "There's always a chance of getting caught," she'd said. He forced his fingers to relax their grip on Raine's arm. What the hell was he doing here? If they did get caught, his entire career could be on the line. And for what? So he could have the chance to be near Raine again? Yeah, he could just imagine his boss buying that lame excuse.

He forced himself to breathe normally as the woman approached. *She's just another JMC employee working the late shift,* he told himself. Nothing to worry about.

The woman waited until they were almost past her to speak. When she did, Calder closed his eyes, then opened them again almost immediately.

"Just a minute," the woman said, her voice surprisingly commanding for someone of such relatively small stature. "I don't believe I've ever seen you three before. Since you're supposedly engineers in my division, I find that hard to believe. Perhaps you'd care to explain what you're really doing here? I believe our head of security would also like to hear what you have to say."

Calder shook his head almost imperceptibly as a well-muscled man with no shortage of firearms appeared as if out of nowhere, cutting off any possible means of escape.

They were busted. He could almost see his career spinning around as it washed down the toilet. Fifteen years of service to his government, and it was all going down the drain because he had the hots for a blonde with a tattoo of Bugs Bunny on her right ankle.

* * *

"YOU know there's always a risk of getting caught. Even on the simplest jobs," Raine said, her eyes meeting Calder's in the rearview mirror.

He couldn't believe it. They'd gotten caught, and she seemed amused. *Amused!*

"Besides, I don't know why you're so upset. I had a back-up plan in place in case we were confronted. And it worked."

"Yeah, it worked all right," Calder grumbled, watching Raine pull her hair out of the band that held it. It fell in soft blond waves to her shoulders. Beside her, Daphne shoved a baseball cap over her own hair, still bound in its usual ponytail.

He didn't know why he was so agitated. Probably because they'd been caught in the first place. More likely, he admitted to himself, because he'd insinuated himself into this operation with a total lack of preparedness that frightened him. He'd always prided himself on his calm control. He was not the type to go off half-cocked like this.

Only, where Raine was concerned, it seemed that he *was* the type to go off half-cocked like this.

"Would you please stop sighing back there? You're fogging up the windows," Daphne said, her eyes staring fixedly ahead.

Calder clenched his teeth, his molars grinding against each other. "Look, it's easy for you to just shrug this off. You don't have a career to worry about throwing away."

"That's total bull—"

Raine held up a hand, interrupting before Daff could get too far into her rant. "Okay, that's enough. Calder, your career was never in jeopardy. I wouldn't have let you come along with us if I thought it was. This afternoon, I set you up as a consultant for Partners In Crime. If JMC's head of security had wanted to check out my cover story, he would have found everything as I said it was. We're a new company, specializing in corporate security. I felt that JMC's security could be easily breached and the head of security disagreed with me. I told him that we would, at no cost to him, prove him wrong."

"He knew we were coming the whole time," Calder muttered.

"Yes. And despite our surprise run-in with Hope Enslar, everything turned out just fine. I have an appointment—an official appointment, I might add—next month to go over our laughably easy break-in at the JMC plant. So, Partners In Crime has a new client and, while we didn't exactly dig up a wealth of information on Hope Enslar, I don't really think we did any harm, either."

"I suppose you're right," Calder conceded. "Your cover story was a good one."

Raine raised her eyebrows at him in the mirror. "Thanks, although I must admit that I'm disappointed in your lack of faith in me. You know, I was a good agent at the Bureau. I was thorough. And I didn't leave much to chance."

Calder rubbed his forehead with his thumb and index finger. "I know. It's just . . ."

"You don't trust me. I know," Raine said softly, her gaze steady on his.

"That's not true. I'd trust you with my life."

"Yeah, but not with your career."

With that parting shot, Raine broke eye contact, easing her car off the freeway on her way back to Aimee's house.

NINE

WHEN the knock sounded at eight o'clock the next morning, Raine was in the middle of sliding a priceless emerald neck-lace down the tight front of the black leather catsuit she wore. The stone slid between her breasts, cool and hard, the gold chain slipping farther down to tickle her stomach. She smiled and zipped the edges of the leather together to trap the gem against her skin. A breeze blew in from the open window, teasing strands of her hair to dance across her cheeks. She pushed her hair back behind her ears with a gloved hand and turned to leave the room, only to be startled when a black-cloaked fig-ure slithered in from the open window. He crossed to her, his footsteps silent on the ancient carpet beneath their feet.

When he stopped, she could feel the heat radiating out from him in waves.

It was Calder, only he was wearing a policeman's uni-form, which made her frown. Bureau men didn't wear uni-forms. They wore street clothes or suits. Black, blue, or dark gray suits. No pinstripes. And definitely not the poly/cotton short-sleeved number he was wearing now. He had a bright silver star pinned to his chest and a heavy black belt at his waist, with all sorts of handy, cop-looking paraphernalia hanging from it. His polished black shoes glittered green in the suddenly bright bedroom, and Raine glanced up at the ceiling to find that a thousand disco balls were twirling merrily, reflecting the color of the emerald she had stashed between her breasts.

"I knew I couldn't trust you," he said, pulling her zipper down and letting the necklace fall between them. Only, as it lay there at their feet, the emerald changed to a blood red ruby.

And then her father stepped into the room, frowning down at the carpet as the necklace morphed again.

Raine tilted her head, puzzled, and then bent down to pick up the necklace. Only it wasn't a necklace any longer. It was the mouse from her computer. Holding it by the cord, she slipped the mouse inside her catsuit and zipped the front up over the lump between her breasts. The cord dangled outside, but as Raine tried to stash it in her suit, it grew longer and longer, like the beanstalk in Jack's adventure.

Her father watched her silently, disappointment etched across his face.

The pounding got louder. Then her phone rang, and Raine opened her eyes, blinking.

She picked up the phone and, before she could answer, Calder said, "Raine, open your door. I need to talk to you."

"Do you have something against sleep?" she grumbled, hanging the phone up without talking into the receiver. She rubbed her face against her pillow and scooted to the edge of the bed, then slid out from under the covers.

Raine didn't bother trying to smooth her hair or even splash some toothpaste in her mouth. When you'd shared the sort of intimacies she and Calder had shared, attempting to appear civilized in the morning seemed like a moot point. Besides, she was irritated with him for invading her dreams as well as her waking hours. Maybe reminding him that she wasn't exactly a supermodel in the morning would make him give her a wider berth.

Only, when she opened the door, she felt certain that *she* was the more attractive of the two of them.

Calder looked awful. He was still wearing the jeans and

black T-shirt he had worn last night to the JMC plant, only they no longer looked freshly laundered. Instead, there were coppery-brown smears on his jeans and his shirt was rumpled. There were sweat stains under his arms, even though it hadn't been particularly warm last night. But even worse than his clothes was the look in his eyes.

Haunted was the only word Raine could come up with to accurately describe it. With a frown, she opened the door wider and stepped out of the way.

"You look like hell," she said, reaching out to pull him inside her apartment.

Calder rubbed a weary hand across the stubble on his chin and allowed himself to be hauled into her living room. He sank into her couch, resting his head along the back while Raine busied herself in the kitchen making a pot of coffee.

While the auto-drip gurgled away, she leaned against the counter and crossed her arms across her chest. "So are you going to tell me what brought you to my door at this ungodly hour?"

Calder didn't raise his head as he answered. "We've had another assassination of a suspect. It was a serial rapist this time. Grady Thompson."

Raine's arms dropped to her sides as she stood in her tidy kitchen, blinking. "That . . ." She stopped. Swallowed. Started again. "That was one of my cases."

She raised her head to find Calder watching her, his brown eyes steady, observant. "I know," he said. "It was reassigned to Neall after you resigned."

Raine frowned. "Neall? My brother, Neall?"

"Yes. Didn't you know? Neall's in Atlanta."

Shaking her head, Raine pulled a mug out of the cupboard and poured hot, dark coffee to the rim. Then she reached into her fridge and pulled out a Coke for herself and brought both drinks into the living room. She handed Calder the mug and curled her feet under herself as she took a seat across from him in an overstuffed purple chair. "Yes, of course I knew my brother was here. He and I meet every few months for lunch. But he never mentioned that he was working one of my cases."

"You're sure he never said anything to you about Thompson? He didn't mention that he was getting close to an arrest?" Calder took a cautious sip of coffee, still watching her intently over the rim of his mug.

Raine leaned forward and put her soda can down on the coffee table with a bit more force than she had intended. Droplets of caramel colored liquid sloshed down the sides of the can, making a wet ring on the glass tabletop. "Yes, I'm sure. It's not something I'd be likely to forget. Why are you giving me the third degree? I was drummed out of the Bureau, remember? I have had no contact with former colleagues nor have I discussed the cases I was working on at any time during the past eleven months. Not even with my brother."

Calder nodded, setting his own cup on the table and leaning forward to rest his elbows on his knees. "Investigators found an e-mail to Thompson, sent last week. It warned him that 'justice will be served, one way or another.' Neall arrested Thompson at his home early this morning, but as he was handing Thompson over to local law enforcement, a sniper put a bullet in his brain. Thompson's seven-year-old daughter was on the front porch at the time. She watched her father's head get blown off. She ran out into the yard, trying to save him as he fell to the ground. She was . . . she had blood all over her thin little arms and on her pink Barbie nightgown. Jesus Christ. What kind of world do we live in where children are exposed to this kind of violence?"

Calder put his head in his hands, and Raine watched his thick brown hair fall forward. She stood up and walked around the coffee table, sliding next to him on the couch. As she moved to put an arm around his shoulder comfortingly, Calder twisted into her and all thoughts of gentle comfort fled from Raine's mind, pushed away by the smoldering heat she saw in Calder's eyes.

He slid one big hand through her pillow-mussed hair and pulled her toward him. His lips met hers, hard and furious with the force of pent-up fury and eleven months of longing. His tongue thrust into her mouth and she sucked him in, biting him lightly when he tried to pull away.

He tugged at her hair, forcing her head back, and Raine

pulled him down on top of her. His broad chest flattened her back into the cushions, but the contact felt so good that Raine didn't try to wiggle out from under him. Instead, she wrapped her arms around his waist and pulled him even closer.

Calder groaned and broke their kiss, trailing a wet line of kisses from the sensitive skin under her ear down to her collarbone. Then he raised his head and looked at her, his greenish-brown eyes haunted. "I have to get these clothes off," he said in a voice filled with desperation.

Raine closed her eyes, trying to keep her heart from softening toward him. She could handle meaningless sex with her ex-lover as a means to comfort him and to relieve the aching need in her own body. But she couldn't start caring for him again.

This is only about sex, she told herself as she slid out from under Calder and held out her hand.

"Come with me," she said, hating the huskiness in her own voice that she couldn't seem to control.

Calder took her hand, his fingers thick and rough against hers. Silently, she led him down the hall and through her bedroom, stopping when they reached her clean but too-small, cluttered bathroom. With her hands at his waist, Raine slowly slid Calder's blood-spattered T-shirt up over his taut abdomen, past his thick chest covered with a smattering of dark hair, and over his head. He held his arms out like a child, and Raine had to stand on tiptoes to get his shirt off. She tossed it into the hamper beside her, then bent down to pull off his tennis shoes.

When she stood up again, Calder put one broad hand at the nape of her neck to hold her still as he recaptured her lips in a slow, aching kiss. He kissed her as if he were attempting to make up for the nearly eleven months they'd been apart, each stroke of his tongue languorous and held tightly in check. Raine wondered what he was afraid of—that if he let go of his control he'd hurt her or that they'd never get back on safe footing.

Raine ran her hands up his naked chest, teasing his nipples to erection and reveling in the groan that elicited from him. Then she let her hands fall to his waist. Slowly, she unfastened the top button of his jeans, but instead of unzipping them all the way, she reached down to cup him through the warm fabric. He was already hard, his erection straining against her hands as she rubbed her fingers up and then down again on him.

Calder's hips surged forward, seeking more from her. Raine laughed and moved her hands around to squeeze his butt, pressing his hips against her and rubbing back and forth tauntingly.

Calder grabbed her earlobe between his teeth. "Tease," he whispered hotly into her ear.

"Are you complaining?" she asked, pulling him backward with her until her hips were touching the bathroom counter. She pushed herself up to sit on the edge of the counter, spreading her legs so that Calder was nestled between them.

"Not at all," he replied, moving his hands to the insides of her thighs. She had worn a long, white T-shirt to bed last night over a pair of those maddeningly small thong panties, and he longed to slide his fingers along the thin fabric, to make her as crazy and desperate for him as he was for her.

So he did. Nudging her so that her back was resting against the mirror behind her, Calder slipped his thumb under the elastic band of her panties. He slid the pad of his thumb up, parting the already-slick folds of skin surrounding her clitoris. His thumb moved in slow circles, his touch light, and then harder as she let out a soft moan that soon turned to breathy panting as her hips moved forward to press even harder against him.

It was Calder's turn to step back and laugh then. Two could play at this game.

Only, this wasn't a game.

Raine reached between them to unzip his jeans and wiggled them down off his hips. She slid off the counter, grabbed his hand, and virtually shoved him out of the bathroom and down onto her bed. She was on top of him in a second, her wet heat rubbing tantalizingly against his erection.

"I haven't had sex in nearly a year," she whispered into his ear. "If you touch me again, I'm going to explode."

Calder knew exactly how she felt. He rolled over, pinning Raine to the bed as he tried not to rip off her panties. But, damn, those things drove him wild.

"Please tell me you're still on the pill," he said, suddenly realizing that he'd nearly forgotten about birth control.

"Yes, we're safe. I want you inside me *now*." She punctuated her last word with an upward thrust of her hips that nearly sent Calder over the edge.

Raising himself above her, he nudged her knee with his leg and positioned himself to thrust inside her. She lifted her hips and the tip of his cock slid inside her hot wetness.

Calder swallowed and pulled back.

"Why are you still using birth control?" he ground out between clenched teeth, his penis throbbing with a desire he couldn't yet satisfy.

Raine threaded her legs around his hips, locking them together at the ankles and pulling him inside her in one sharp thrust. She threw her head back, her blond hair fanning around her like a golden cloud.

Calder grunted and tried to pull back, but his body had other ideas. His hips were moving, thrusting in small, intense movements, knowing the friction between their bodies was driving Raine closer to climax as she started moaning, "Yes," over and over again, faster and faster, throaty and breathless little noises that sent all his blood to his groin.

"Don't . . . like taking . . . chances," Raine managed to say between yes's.

Neither did he. But every time he was around Raine, that's what he seemed to be doing.

Calder pulled back so that just the tip of his penis was inside her. Then he pulled all the way out and thrust back in again. Then he did it again. And again.

Raine's hands were gripping his shoulders, her fingers kneading in and out like a purring cat. She was moving under him wildly now, and Calder had to grit his teeth to stop himself from coming.

And then it was Raine who was losing control, her muscles clenching and releasing, her heels digging into him as she lay open and vulnerable beneath him. Calder closed his eyes and let himself go, thinking of nothing but Raine's comforting warmth wrapped around him.

After what seemed like hours, but was more likely less than a minute, he pushed himself off of her, sliding an arm under her shoulders to pull her close. They stayed that way, silent, staring up at the ceiling, until Raine finally turned to look at him, rolling over onto her stomach. She laid an arm across his stomach, running her fingers slowly up and down his side. "I'm sorry about Thompson's daughter," she said.

"Yeah, me, too." Calder twirled a length of Raine's hair between his thumb and index finger, studying the subtle shades in each strand as if there were going to be a test later. "I just keep seeing her screaming, 'Daddy, daddy,' over and over again, kneeling in the yard with her nightgown soaked with the bastard's blood."

He felt Raine shudder as he continued toying with her hair.

"He was an animal," she said, recalling the particularly gruesome details of one of Thompson's rapes. He had stalked the woman—a nighttime grocery store clerk who worked two jobs to support herself and her children—to her car after her shift, raped her repeatedly throughout the six hours he held her in captivity, and then left her, naked, in a vacant lot, staked to a fire ant nest. When she'd been discovered at nearly three o' clock the next afternoon, her entire body was covered with welts from being bitten by the ants. Not to mention the damage she'd suffered from the hot sun baking her naked body all day. And the internal injuries caused by being so brutally raped.

"Yes," Calder agreed quietly. "And so was whoever it was who arranged for him to be killed."

Raine's fingers stilled on his skin. "Calder?" she asked, her voice in a near whisper.

"Yes?" He let the strand of hair fall back into place as he cupped a hand around the back of her head.

"That e-mail? The one Thompson received, talking about justice?"

"Yeah?" He looked up at the ceiling, his eyes tracing a crack in the plaster that started at the base of the ceiling fan and wobbled outward like a drunk trying to follow a straight line.

"It was from me, wasn't it?"

Calder's fingers tightened on her skull and the only sound in the room was the soft in and out of their breathing mingled with the hum of the fan. Finally, Calder closed his eyes, blocking out the sight of cracked plaster, and answered. "Yes, Raine. It was."

TEN

RAINE didn't usually watch daytime television, but today she
made an exception. Working hadn't distracted her. Even the
flurry of messages from KatBrglr about a loophole he'd
found in Microsoft's latest security patch didn't hold her interest.

She laid her head down on the pillows in the corner of the
couch and flipped idly from one channel to the next. She
paused briefly on a talk show where a woman with an enormous ass stuffed into a too-short mini and no underwear
shouted at a thinner woman about being "more woman than
you'll ever be, bitch." The slender woman stuck her finger in
the bigger woman's face. Raine thought the gesture was ill-
advised and sure enough, the larger woman body-slammed
her tormentor to the floor while the talk-show host and a man
wearing jeans and a red and black flannel shirt—presumably
the "prize" the two women were fighting over—looked on.
The host pretended to be horrified by the women's behavior,
but Raine could see a gleeful glint in the man's eyes.

Curling her feet up on the couch, Raine clicked the re-
mote control a few more times. She settled on a channel that

was airing back-to-back episodes of "I Love Lucy." That was more her style. She had enough reality in her own life. She didn't need to watch it on TV, too.

Raine closed her eyes, listening to the banter between Lucy and Ethel as Little Ricky wandered onscreen.

God, had life ever really been this innocent? She could just imagine "I Love Lucy" in the twenty-first century, where Lucy discovers that Ricky is really a serial rapist. She's confronted with the truth at 2 A.M. when FBI agents show up at her door and Little Ricky witnesses his father being arrested and then assassinated on the front lawn.

Raine drew in a shaky breath and rubbed her eyes. A wave of weariness washed over her and she curled herself up tighter on the couch. When she'd first started computer hacking, it had been a game to her; a way for her to do something illicit and exciting without really hurting anyone. It hadn't taken her long to figure out that there were two kinds of hackers—those who used their skills to help shine the light on a system's vulnerabilities, and those who used those vulnerabilities for their own gain. Raine had always fallen into the former category, and had joined the FBI to cement her role as one of the good guys.

She didn't enjoy being cast in the opposite role. She had thought that by resigning from the Bureau, she'd be rid of dealing with murderers, rapists, thieves, and child molesters. She'd hoped she could go back to the time where the evildoers she fought had names like PhreakBoy and 2Smart4U, evildoers who spread viruses and disabled networks instead of raping and killing. But someone was trying to pull her back into that world, and she didn't know why. She'd gone from being one of the FBI's top agents to the prime suspect in not one, but two murder cases.

Raine gave a self-deprecating laugh. "Maybe I should have followed in my father's footsteps after all," she muttered. Right now, the thought of being an international jewel thief didn't seem so bad. No, make that an *alleged* international jewel thief, as her father used to say with a wink. Since the police had never gathered enough evidence against her father to arrest him, his true occupation was no more than speculation.

Curling her right hand beneath her head, Raine turned her attention back to the television screen. The black-and-white sitcom faded to a scene of a father and his teenaged son driving down a deserted city street in their new luxury car. Raine closed her eyes, only to open them again when the stereotypical smart-alecky teenager said, "Good going, Dad, we're lost. Again."

The father turned to his son and patted him on the shoulder with a self-mocking smile. "Not to worry, son. With our new JMC, we'll never have to worry about getting lost again."

Then a woman's voice came from off screen. "Good afternoon, Mr. Smith. This is SatTrac, how can I help you?"

The TV dad grinned as the cheery woman told him to turn left at the next light. He did, and they left the dark, foreboding city scene behind them. The teenager in the passenger seat gave his dad two thumbs up as they entered a bright, festival-like area. As Dad parked the car in the middle of the street, the narrator listed the features available on the new JMC, ending with, "And, with the new SatTrac system, you'll never be lost again."

Raine sat up and squinted at the TV screen. If the SatTrac system could pinpoint a vehicle's location in order to give someone directions, why couldn't it tell authorities the location of the Mulroney's SUV? Even if the thieves had disabled the tracking system, the last known location of the vehicle might give them some clue as to Megan's whereabouts. Raine doubted the system was so easy to disable that they would have taken the time to do it in the grocery store parking lot. Calder hadn't mentioned JMC's satellite system after his conversation with the officer in charge of the Mulroney case, but surely the local police had considered this angle. If they had, she'd like to know if they could tell exactly how the thieves had disabled the system. If they had used a computer, Raine was certain she could find out more than the officer in charge had.

She went in search of her cordless phone and found the receiver in the kitchen, but before dialing Calder's number, she paused. He had left her that morning to go back to his place to shower and change before heading back to work.

She knew he was going to be buried in meetings, trying to deal with the fallout of the Grady Thompson assassination. She also knew that he would make certain the e-mail she had supposedly sent to Thompson was thoroughly investigated by whoever was assigned to the case. She only wished she could tell whether his insistence on being thorough was to ensure that she was cleared of any wrongdoing . . . or because he needed more proof to convince *himself* that she had nothing to do with the murder.

Raine nearly dropped the phone when her doorbell buzzed. She looked down at herself, still dressed in the black sweatpants and gray T-shirt she'd pulled on to walk Calder to the door after their incredible hour of sex. Too tired to do anything but sit on the couch and watch mindless television, she hadn't bothered to take a shower or change clothes. Not to mention that she hadn't been expecting company.

"Who is it?" she called, hoping it wasn't the FBI, come to ransack her apartment and take her computers before she had a chance to back them up.

"Thank God you're here, Raine. It's Neall," came the reply through the heavy wood door.

Raine set the phone down on the counter and hurried across the kitchen. She unlocked the triple locks and pulled open the door, opening her home to her brother.

ELEVEN

"I don't believe in coincidences." Alex Jarvis crossed his beefy arms on top of his desk and studied Calder with eyes so dark, they almost looked black.

"I don't either, Alex. That's why I'm suggesting that we look at this from a different angle. Raine's too smart and way too computer savvy to have sent a message to Thompson that could be traced back to her. It's just too damn obvious. Besides, I know Raine and I can tell you that she doesn't have the money to pay hired guns to go around assassinating people."

"Her father was a jewel thief—"

"*Alleged* jewel thief," Calder interrupted his superior, leaning forward to rest his elbows on his knees. "And he never stole more than he needed to survive on. It was his . . . code of honor, I suppose you could say."

Alex raised his thick, dark brows. "He could have left his daughter with a means of income you know nothing about. You can't trust the word of a thief. You know that."

Calder rubbed his forehead with the back of his thumb. He would never be able to convince Alex that John Robey was an honorable thief. Hell, he even had trouble believing it himself. "Okay, I can't argue with you there. But we already know that Raine doesn't have a secret stash of funds. We investigated all her bank records with the Jeffrey Allen case. I think we're focusing our investigation on the wrong person. I think someone's trying to set Raine up and we're playing right into his hands."

"Don't you think you're a little biased? I mean, you were practically living with the woman. Obviously you feel some fondness for her."

Calder glanced at the man he'd known for over five years, then lowered his eyes to stare at the bland gray carpet between his feet. "I love her, Alex. But that's not clouding my judgment. Don't you see? I couldn't love a woman who would take the law into her own hands. I just . . . couldn't. I know that she didn't do it." Calder raised his hands and shrugged helplessly, wishing he knew how to convince his boss to look at this case in a different light.

Alex's chair groaned under his weight as the former college football linebacker leaned back in his seat. "Are you willing to stake your career on it? Because if you continue to see Raine and it turns out that you're wrong . . ." Alex let his voice trail off, his gaze steady and deadly serious.

Calder tried not to flinch under the other man's scrutiny. "Christ, you really know how to put this in terms of black and white, don't you? The woman I love versus the only career I've ever wanted. Nothing like laying everything on the fucking line, eh Alex?"

The corner of Alex's mouth drew up into the barest of grins, then vanished. "Look, I just want you to think about what you're risking with this conspiracy theory of yours. There's gonna be a lot of people who think the obvious answer is also the right answer."

Calder shook his head. "I know. But I can't let them try to ruin her again. I didn't fight for her before and I almost lost her. I can't do it again."

"I don't know what to tell you, then. It seems that the best you can do is to raise your concerns with the team investigating the case and then stand back and let the process work.

If there's no evidence that Raine was involved, you have nothing to worry about."

"What if there is, though? What if whoever it is who's framing her has planted evidence that she hired the killer? I mean, that wouldn't be so hard, right? A few phantom transactions in the bank records. Ten thousand dollars going in and coming right back out. A faked e-mail just happens to wind up in Raine's e-mail account, detailing the terms of the kill. If someone was out to get her, it wouldn't be too difficult."

Across from him, Alex sighed, his shoulders sagging as if he were being crushed by the weight of what he was about to say. "I know you want me to tell you that your career would survive the blow, Calder, but I can't. If we find evidence that Raine has hired assassins to bring down our suspects and you insist on remaining with her, your career in the FBI will be over. You know that as well as I do. Now, if you'll excuse me, I have a conference call scheduled in three minutes and I have to call my wife first to tell her that I'm going to be home late. Again."

Calder stood up and headed toward his boss's door, pausing at the opening. "If it were your wife who was being investigated, Alex, what would you do? Would you just sit back and let the investigative process run its course?"

Alex pressed the last number of his home telephone number and hesitated with the phone halfway to his ear. Then he shot Calder a half-smile. "Hell no. I'd be in the investigators' faces every step of the way. Even if it meant the end of my career."

"That's what I thought you'd say," Calder muttered as he left Alex's office, quietly closing the door behind him.

HOPE Enslar used her key to unlock the front door of her father's two-story house in the stately neighborhood where they both lived. She'd parked her car next door at her own house. It was silly, she knew, for her to live next to her father when they could just as easily have lived together. Two single people living in two four-thousand-square-foot homes seemed a bit ridiculous, but what did it matter? It wasn't like Hope didn't have the money for such things. Indeed, she never worried about the double mortgages or the expensive twenty-four-hour care her father required. Or the car payments for the three cars parked in her garage and the other two parked in her father's.

No, for a girl who had been raised strictly middle class, she had done all right for herself. It was just too bad that the one person she loved more than anything in this world couldn't enjoy the fruits of her success.

"Good evening, Ms. Enslar." Her father's live-in nurse greeted her from where he sat at Norman Enslar's bedside, reading a newspaper.

"Good evening, Randy. I trust that my father is doing all right today?" Hope reached down to smooth an errant lock of gray hair off her father's brow. Her mother had died shortly after Hope had been born and her father had been the only parent she'd ever known. Before his accident, he had been the kindest, most understanding father a daughter could ever hope to have. After the accident, he had become . . . nothing. At two months shy of eighteen, Hope had lost all but the occasional, too-brief glimpse of the man he once was that rose up out of the fog of his usual vacant demeanor.

"He was very well today. We spent some time out in the garden and he seemed to enjoy that. He had his physical therapy session this afternoon. I was just reading him the news. It's too bad about that girl in Boston."

"What girl in Boston?" Hope asked, not really listening to the answer as she rearranged the pillows under her father's head.

"A fifteen-year old in Boston was kidnapped. At least that's what her parents say. Of course, kids run away all the time and the parents always deny it."

"Hmm. Well, look, I'm going to visit with my dad for about an hour. Should I knock on your door before I leave?"

"Actually, if you wouldn't mind, I've got a couple errands I could run. If you'll call me on my cell when you're ready to go, I'll dash back here. I just need to run to Starbucks and pick up coffee, get a prescription refilled at the drug store. That sort of thing."

Hope sat down on the edge of her father's bed and reached for the glass of water on his nightstand. His lips looked a bit dry, and Hope worried that he might be thirsty. "I don't mind at all. I'll give you a call in about an hour."

Randy neatly folded the newspaper and laid it at the foot of the bed. "Great. When I get back we'll finish reading this," he said to Norman, smiling as he thumped the paper with one hand.

After hearing the garage door open and then close again, Hope pushed up the sleeves of her father's loose-fitting pajamas and inspected his arms for bruises. Randy had been her father's nurse for three years and Hope knew she should stop being so suspicious, but she couldn't seem to help herself. One of her father's first nurses had been a seemingly kind middle-aged lady who worked for them for over a year. Hope had been young and not suspicious at all back then. It broke her heart every time she remembered that day she'd come home from school to find her father facedown on the floor. Mrs. Church left around noon to take care of other patients and Father was only alone for a couple of hours before Hope came home, so she had thought he would be okay. The settlement from JMC hadn't come through yet, and, although she had some help from her father's medical plan, it wasn't enough to pay for twenty-four-hour care.

That day, as she'd struggled to help him back into his wheelchair, she'd cried at seeing her once-strong father reduced to this. As she put her arms around his legs to move him, he'd flinched. Hope frowned, but waited until he was all settled in before pushing up his pant leg. That's when she'd seen the line of bruises marching up his thigh.

She had cared for him between the nurses' visits, but hadn't changed her father's clothes, leaving him that dignity, at least. And now she realized that she had naively trusted a perfect stranger to care for her father the way she herself would. The next day, she'd borrowed a video camera from a neighbor and snuck back into her father's room after telling Mrs. Church she was going to school.

When she'd handed the videotape to Mrs. Church's boss showing her employee viciously pinching her patient for coughing or using his colostomy bag, the woman had assured Hope that Mrs. Church would be fired. Hope had vowed then to never let something like this happen again. So now, she checked her father for bruises every time she visited. She'd also installed a video surveillance camera over her father's bed years ago, but had pretty much stopped reviewing the tapes over the past year.

"Still, you can't be too careful," she murmured, covering her father's thin chest with his blanket.

His latest bout with pneumonia had left him even weaker than usual. Where before he had spent the majority of his days in a wheelchair, his illness had him mostly confined to bed.

She sat down in the chair Randy had vacated and told her father about her day, like she always did. It was a comfortable routine, and she hoped he enjoyed their visits as much as she did. Of course, Hope realized that her frequent visits to her father gave her an excuse not to date or go out after work with her coworkers. She also realized her cloistered existence enabled her to be a workaholic. On the bright side, her work paid for the exceptional nursing care she could now provide for her father, not to mention the houses and cars she now owned.

"The annual vehicular crime report came out today, Dad, and do you know what's really funny?" She paused, waiting for a response that he was too weak to give. Even in his normal state, a response might not be forthcoming. On her father's good days, he might be able to signal her with a blink of his eyes or the squeeze of his hand, but on his bad days, it was as if he were nothing but an empty shell. Still, Hope continued talking as if her father were taking an active role in the conversation.

"JMC has four out of the top ten stolen vehicles. Wouldn't you think that would make our cars less popular? I mean, why do people want to own cars that are more likely to get stolen? But, every year, when this report comes out, our sales spike. Isn't that crazy?"

She shook her head, looking out the window across from her father's bed at the trees that flanked the driveway. From here, she could see the corner of her brick house and her own neatly trimmed front yard. "Of course," she continued, still looking out the window, "our vehicles are stolen because they're so well-built, in large part because of the groundwork you laid decades ago. You should be proud of the work you did at JMC, Dad."

Hope turned to smile at her father. "You know, when I started planning my car theft ring, I never imagined it would have this effect. I thought our rising theft rankings would put JMC out of business. In the beginning, that's all I wanted. To punish them for what they did to you.

"Isn't it funny how it's worked out? I got my revenge, but it's so much sweeter than I ever could have planned. My stock is worth millions, I have a salary that's larger than I ever dreamed of, and, to top it all off, I'm making a killing off of each stolen vehicle we sell. Even better, the people who have their JMC vehicles stolen in the first place typically end up taking their insurance settlement and buying from us again. I mean, I don't know why that should surprise me, but it does. I guess they figure that they bought the best in the first place, so why not do it again? After all, what are the chances that they'll have two vehicles stolen? And, of course, with the safeguards I have in place, their logic holds true for the most part.

"In the end, JMC has given me more than I ever expected."

Hope's eyebrows drew together as her father's foot jerked, knocking the newspaper Randy had left on the bed to the floor. She leaned down to pick up the paper, smoothing a hand over the headline on the front page. MANHUNT CONTINUES FOR MISSING BOSTON TEEN. Must be that girl Randy was talking about, Hope mused, placing the paper back at the foot of the bed. Then she rose and gently patted her father's cheek.

"I've got to go, Dad. I love you," she said, turning from the room before the tears slipped out of her father's eyes and slid down his temples and into his faded gray hair.

* * *

"IT'S good to see you, sis," Neall Robey said, making himself comfortable on the couch Raine had just vacated. He was a younger, taller version of his sister, with the same long legs, blond hair, and green eyes. Raine watched as her brother crossed his ankles and leaned back into the sofa as if he hadn't a care in the world.

When their parents had separated, they'd split everything down the middle, including their children. Neall had gone to France to live with their socialite mother in Nice, while Raine had stayed in Texas with their father. During the summer, they'd switch places, crossing somewhere over the Atlantic. It was no surprise that she and Neall weren't close. After all, they'd only spent Neall's first five years together and the occasional week or two overlapping their visits to one parent or another. What was surprising was Neall's decision to follow his big sister into the FBI. Raine didn't profess to know her brother all that well, but law enforcement seemed an unlikely profession for a boy who'd spent all his time with fast cars, rich young women, and gamblers. But who was she to talk? She had been raised by a thief.

"I'm sorry about the Thompson case," Raine said abruptly. "I heard about it this morning."

"Well, word certainly does get around quickly, doesn't it?" Neall didn't sound surprised.

Raine waved a hand dismissively as she perched on the edge of the oversized chair across from the couch. "You know the Bureau. It's a small world."

"Yes, but you're not part of that world anymore. I guess I assumed that it might take more than an hour or two for you to hear that one of my cases had been blown wide open. Literally."

Wrinkling her nose with distaste at Neall's gruesome choice of words, Raine wondered if her brother was really as callous as he seemed. "I'm certain that Thompson's daughter wouldn't appreciate your sense of humor."

Neall sighed loudly and pushed a hand through his thick hair. "I know. I'm sorry. It's just . . . I'm a little on edge after having a man killed right in front of me. I'm sorry," he repeated.

Raine took a deep breath of her own, trying to force the memories of another man, another murder, out of her mind. "I'm sorry, too. I just can't stop thinking about that poor little girl."

"Yes, it was pretty awful." Neall laced his hands together and looked down at them, seeming to study his fingernails. "Look, Raine, I know I wasn't there for you when the Allen thing happened and I wanted to tell you that I'm sorry. I was, um, going through a difficult time with Mom's death. I guess I just distanced myself from it all because I didn't know how to deal with it. And I . . . I wanted you to know that I, um, well, I am not going to desert you this time."

Raine narrowed her eyes on the top of her brother's bowed head. "What do you mean?" she asked cautiously.

Neall looked at her then, his eyes so much like hers that it was almost like looking into a mirror. "I mean, I know about the e-mail you sent to Thompson. The one they *say* you sent to Thompson, that is. But I don't believe it. I just wanted to let you know that you have my support and that if you need my help in any way, all you have to do is ask."

Raine blinked. Opened her mouth. Then closed it again. "I'm . . ." she began, then stopped. "Thank you, Neall. I really appreciate it."

Neall leaned toward her, his hands outstretched. Without thinking, Raine let him take her hands in his. "I mean it. I was questioned this morning and it looks like they're going to put me on administrative leave until I'm cleared of any wrongdoing, but I got the impression that the focus of their investigation is going to be on you. I know you're trying to get your new venture off the ground, but you may be pretty busy defending yourself over the next few months. If you want some cheap labor—hell, I'll even work for free since the government is so generously paying for this forced vacation of mine—I would be happy to help."

"I d-don't know what to say," Raine stuttered, blinking back the tears that threatened to spill down her face. After her father's death, she had been left with a mother who was always slightly disapproving and a brother who was distant, at best. She supposed that's why Calder's lack of trust had hurt her so badly. She had felt she had nobody left to believe in her. Neall's show of support was a welcome surprise.

Raine squeezed her brother's hands. "Thank you. I would be glad to have your help. But only if you're sure you don't mind."

Neall smiled at her then, looking more like their mother now with his perfect smile and easy charm. "I don't mind at all. Isn't that what family is for?"

"Okay, then. Let's get started Monday. Say around noon?"

"Sounds great. Hey, have you got plans for this evening? Maybe we could go grab a bite to eat."

"I'm sorry, I can't," Raine apologized, genuinely disappointed that she had to rebuff her brother's offer. "I'm meeting some friends tonight at Chasey's."

"That's fine. Some other time," Neall said with a rueful smile and a final squeeze of her hands before he released her and stood to leave.

After Neall had gone, Raine sat and stared at the muted television for a long time, surprised—and pleased—that her estranged brother had offered help when she least expected it.

TWELVE

MEGAN rubbed the back of her head as she tried to hold the flashlight steady with her shaking hand. Something had moved in the backseat of the car and she had to find out what it was. After she had slammed the door shut, she stood with her heart pounding as if it were trying to escape from her chest. Finally, though, her heart rate had slowed and she was filled with a sense of calm.

If something was back there, it would be better to face it head-on than to run cowering back to her mother's SUV and wait for it to come get her.

She sucked in a deep breath for courage, and then yanked open the back door of the sedan, half expecting some wild animal to come leaping out at her. Instead, she was greeted with silence and the same sour stench as before.

Cautiously, Megan took a step closer to the car. She knew that she was going to have to lift up that baby blanket, but all she could do was to pray that she wouldn't find a baby under there. She didn't know how long she'd been trapped in this hot metal box, but she did know that it was long enough to cause serious damage to someone who wasn't in good shape like she was. A shiver racked her body as her imagination conjured up a horror movie image.

"Please God, I promise I'll never go see a scary movie again if you just let this be nothing," Megan prayed, briefly closing her eyes. Then she reached out and grabbed the edge of the baby blanket. "Please, please, please," she continued praying. "Let it be nothing."

With a jerk, she pulled the blanket off of the car seat. She let out a huge sigh of relief when she saw the seat was empty except for a bottle half-filled with milk.

Megan gingerly picked up the bottle and sniffed. "This stuff reeks," she muttered, setting the bottle on the floor of the car and turning to finish her inspection. A pile of books lay on the backseat and Megan guessed that they had tipped over when she got into the car. At least, she hoped that's what had happened. She didn't think her heart could take any more surprises.

She piled everything she thought might be useful into the front seat, including the books. She'd never been much of a reader, but she had to find *something* to entertain herself until she figured a way out of this mess.

Her search of the sedan netted her the books, three half-empty bottles of water, two partially drunk sodas—she normally would never have even considered drinking from those but, hey, it was better than dying of thirst—a cache of Cheerios and Cheez-Its that had fallen behind the baby's car seat—same as the sodas, it was amazing how not picky a person became when she was starving—and an apple.

Megan brought her treasures back to the Pioneer and heaped them on the passenger seat. Then, because she needed some time to recharge her courage before exploring any further, she locked herself inside her mother's car and dragged her backpack with her to the driver's seat. She sat, staring straight ahead at the metal wall in front of her, but she couldn't get over the fear that someone was going to creep up behind her. She had seen vague shadows of other cars behind the sedan, other cars that could contain other people.

The hair on the back of her neck stood up and Megan

really, really wished that her parents had never let her watch any of the *Halloween* movies.

"Maybe I could turn the car around so that I'm facing everyone else," Megan said, thinking out loud. Plus, she was hot. The air conditioning would feel good. Maybe she could even get a radio station.

Megan peered up into the darkness, wondering what was on top of her. She couldn't see anything, not even a tiny ray of sunlight. She knew that leaving a car running in a closed space could kill you. *Everybody* knew that. But how long did you have to leave it running for it to hurt? Would five minutes be enough? She could probably get the Pioneer turned around in five minutes, although it would take quite a bit of maneuvering in the tight space.

But what if that five minutes of exhaust fumes killed her? Or alerted Silver Eyes and Shorty that she was still alive?

Megan pulled a mechanical pencil out of the front pocket of her backpack and clicked it absently. A length of lead advanced with each click, but Megan pushed it back. Click. Back. Click. Back. Click. Back.

What should she do? Remain sitting here, afraid someone was going to come up and ambush her, or risk death to turn the car around?

Megan frowned. Fear versus death. Well, that wasn't such a tough choice. She'd just have to take her chances on being surprised. At least she had the keys to her mother's car and could set the alarm system. Someone might be able to sneak up on her in here, but they wouldn't be able to get into the SUV without the alarm going off.

That settled, Megan pulled a notebook from her backpack and opened it to a blank page. At the top of the page, she wrote *Plan* and underlined the word. Twice.

Then she wrote *1*.

Hmm. What *was* she going to do first?

Megan clicked her pencil a few times, then pushed the lead back so it wouldn't break when she started writing. First, she needed to find out what else was here in this metal box with her. If there were other cars, she would search each one and find out if they contained anything she could use. She had no idea how long she was going to be trapped in here, but the remaining Pop-tart and leftover Cheerios and Cheez-Its weren't going to last forever.

Next, she wrote 2. After she found out what she had to work with, she needed to ration herself. She looked at the half-empty bottles of water on the passenger seat. Could she survive on one bottle a day? That was one and a half days, plus whatever was in the jug she'd found in her mom's car and the sodas from the car behind her.

Then she wrote 3. Only, she didn't know what to do next. Try to figure out how to get out of here? That should really be her number one priority, but Megan was almost afraid of what she'd find outside the box. At least in here, she felt relatively safe.

Well, if you didn't count the zombies, wild animals, and murderers that existed in her imagination. . . .

"COULD you hurry this up a bit? I'm going out this evening," Raine announced calmly, taking a sip of the Coke Special Agent Jim Wilkins had brought at her request an hour ago.

"Ms. Robey, you're in no position to be calling the shots here. You're being held on suspicion of murder."

"No, I'm not. I'm being *questioned* about the murder of Grady Thompson, a suspected serial rapist whose file was among the number of cases I handled during my career with the FBI. If I were being held as a suspect, you would have read me my rights. Now, I've already been here for over four hours. I've answered the same questions three times and if we're going to go for round number four, I've got to phone my friends and tell them I'll be late."

"She's a cool one, isn't she?" Wilkins's partner, currently playing invisible cop, said, turning to Calder in the observation room.

Calder didn't even bother to glance at the younger man, watching Raine through the two-way mirror. She *was* cool. Unlike the last time this had happened, when she'd been upset after having another human being shot right in front of her. Yeah, agents were tough. Yeah, they saw a lot of sick shit. But that didn't mean they could just laugh off having some asshole's brains splattered all over them.

"She didn't do it," Calder said. "She's calm because whatever she does, you guys are going to twist it so you can use it against her. If she gets angry, you'll say it's because she hated what that creep did to all those women and that's why she had him killed. If she gets upset, you'll ask if she's sorry that she had Thompson killed in front of his little girl. There's no way she can play this but cool."

"We're just doing our job, sir," Wilkins's partner said.

Calder looked at the man then. "Yeah, I know. And so does she. That doesn't make this any easier."

"Nothing's ever easy in this game."

Calder felt an ache in his jaw from clenching his teeth. "This isn't a game. It's somebody's life. Have Wilkins call me when Ms. Robey is released, would you?"

"Looks like he's letting her go now, sir," the junior agent said, gesturing through the glass where Raine was in the process of standing up. Wilkins held the door open, his face impassive as only someone who knows *he's* not going to end the day in jail can be.

Calder stepped out into the hall at the same time as Raine. She walked past him as if he were some stranger she was passing on the street. Wilkins continued escorting her down the hall, his sidelong glance at Calder the only thing that revealed his surprise at Raine's brush-off.

He knew what she was doing. She was distancing herself from him. That way, if the investigation turned bad—as the last one had for a short time—it wouldn't reflect badly on him. Only, the last time, it had been he who distanced himself, both physically and emotionally, from the woman he claimed to love. He had let her down, and then come crawling back into her life when he thought it was safe.

Only, damn it, it wasn't safe. She wasn't safe. And if he got involved in this, he wouldn't be safe, either.

All he'd ever wanted was to be a lawman, like his father and his father's father, and his grandfather's father before him. That's what Preston men were raised to be. Hell, if he had a daughter, he'd want her to be a lawman, too.

But at the same time he thought it, he wondered if it were really true. Did he really want his loved ones living this life? Dealing with violence and evil every day like he did? Knowing he couldn't protect them?

He thought of a daughter—his daughter—dark-haired like him but with Raine's pretty green eyes. He saw her dressed in a no-nonsense blue suit, her eyes flat and impassive, giving nothing away. Or worse, in a bullet-proof vest, ready to go in and take down some vicious bastard who wouldn't think twice before killing an agent. He saw her opening a door, then a flash. The yelling, the instant rush of activity as the good guys fought to control the situation. Then someone shouting, "Officer down." Only it wasn't an officer. It was his daughter lying dead on the floor of some shithole apartment. Dead. Her eyes still flat and impassive as her blood drained out of her body, dripping onto the cracked and dirty linoleum.

Him, rushing in now. Too late to save her. Dropping down on the floor next to her, cradling her head in his lap. Knowing it was too late. Knowing he hadn't kept her safe. Knowing it was all his fault for not keeping her out of this business of crime and punishment and death.

Calder's stomach clenched at the thought and he nearly doubled over. He put a hand on the wall to steady himself.

"Hey, man. You okay?" Wilkins's partner asked, frowning with concern.

Calder sucked in a breath, trying to dispel the images in his mind. "Yeah, I'm fine. Must be my ulcer."

He straightened up, away from the wall, and looked back down the now-empty hallway.

While Calder was busy wrestling with himself, Raine had walked away.

"WE'RE not going to end up getting tattoos again, are we?" Daphne asked, resting her cheek on the arm she'd propped up on the table.

Raine noisily sucked the pimento out of her olive. "I don't think I could ever drink that much again. Besides, I'm not as upset this time. I suppose once the man you love leaves you for the first time, it gets easier. It's like . . . you're expecting it to happen again, so it isn't as much of a surprise."

"It sure didn't take him long to get you back into bed," Daphne observed glumly.

Raine grimaced.

"Daff, she hasn't had sex in almost a year," Aimee protested, then turned to Raine. "Have you? I mean, I guess we really wouldn't know, would we?"

Raine sighed and bit her olive in half. "Jeez, you're nosy." The she raised her right hand and put her left hand on the table. "I swear, your honor. I have not had sex with another person in the room since my ex-lover admitted that he thought I was capable of murder. No, your honor. The definition of 'person' does not include anything that requires plugging in or blowing up."

Aimee laughed. "All right. The witness may be dismissed."

"Thanks, your honor." Raine raised her martini glass mockingly. "All right. So I did fall right back into bed with him." They all knew who *him* was. "I couldn't help myself. He looked so vulnerable that I found myself wanting to comfort him. The next thing I knew, Bugs was having intimate contact with Calder's ass."

"It *is* a nice ass," Aimee conceded with a sip of her cosmopolitan.

"What I want to know is why it is that we can't see through these law enforcement guys. I mean, we know what they're like. Most of them joined the FBI because they thought it would help them get laid," Daphne said.

Raine twirled the stem of her now-empty glass between her thumb and forefinger. "They're heroes," she said, clearing her throat as she felt the blush race up her neck. She looked from Daphne to Aimee and then back down at the table that separated them. "We don't see through them because we know, more than anybody, what it's like to go out there every day and face the fear. To go knocking on some crackhead's door, knowing today may be your day to be unlucky. Or to go up against some jury who believes that the government is just out to get some poor schoolteacher who insists he's not a child

molester, knowing that what you say and how you present
your case could mean the difference between some kid's life
or death. Or to follow a suspected terrorist and snare him before he's able to buy a Stinger missile that will bring down a
747 loaded with innocent people, knowing that if you don't
stop him in time, the unthinkable could happen. They're heroes. And we were heroes, too, once."

"I'm no fu—" Daphne began angrily.

"We're not the bad guys, Raine," Aimee interrupted before
Daff could launch a full-scale attack. "Just because we're not
agents anymore doesn't mean we can't make a difference."

Raine snorted. "Right. Like me trailing after the head of
R&D for some damn auto company is really going to change
anyone's life. That is, if I can remain out of the FBI's custody long enough to finish the job."

"Hello, ladies. My friends and I were wondering if we
could buy y'all a round of drinks."

Raine looked at the well dressed, perfectly nice-looking
man who had approached their table and wondered if he was
stupid. Couldn't he feel the tension at this table? Daff looked
like she was about to toss her beer across the table and walk
out, probably because she took offense to Raine's suggestion
that she might actually meet someone's definition of a hero.
Raine knew she herself probably looked like Eeyore. Only
Aimee had managed to settle her face into a mask of polite
interest. Aimee was good at that. The woman with a thousand faces.

"We'd be delighted. Would you care to join us?" Aimee
asked, already scooting toward Raine to make way for the
new arrivals. Raine saw Daff flinch and figured Aimee had
kicked her with the toe of one pointy pump. Daphne sent
Aimee a baleful glare, but did her best to stop slouching and
appear friendly as the men approached their table.

Raine tried to forget about Calder and his defection while
Mr. Clean and his friends discussed current events and re-
galed them with tales of their experiences in IT consulting. As
she nodded and smiled, she couldn't help but wonder if the
Bureau had ruined her for all men. This guy was nice and
probably made five times what Calder did. In a bad year. Still,

when he talked about the stress of missing a deadline, and someone's system not going live the week it was supposed to, and all the overtime he'd worked to fix the problem, she just couldn't help but think . . . *this guy is never going to be my hero.* If they got mugged leaving this bar, he'd probably wet his pants and hand over his wallet—and her—without protest.

She knew she wasn't being fair, but at least she was being honest with herself. And she refused to let him buy her another drink because it really didn't seem fair for him to foot the bill when she knew damn well that she wasn't interested in him.

Raine waited until there was a lull in the conversation to interrupt. "Hey, guys, I'm, uh, sorry to be a party pooper, but I've had a really long day. If I don't get going, they're going to find me curled up under this table tomorrow morning." She pushed her chair away from the table, being careful not to bump into the group of people standing behind her at the crowded bar.

"I'll walk you to your car," Mr. Clean, whose real name she couldn't quite recall, offered.

Raine smiled. She supposed now wasn't the right time to announce that she was perfectly capable of killing a man if the need arose. Naw, she'd let him be a gentleman. She appreciated the gesture, at least. "Thank you," she said, slipping her tan leather handbag over her shoulder before waving good-bye to Aimee and Daff, who actually appeared to be enjoying themselves.

Mr. Clean pulled open the glass door of the bar and motioned for Raine to precede him out into the warm night. Raine shivered a bit through the thin blouse she was wearing as her skin adjusted to the non-air-conditioned air.

"So, I apologize for boring you. I've been out of the dating scene for awhile and I think my conversational skills are a bit rusty."

Raine stifled a gasp and stopped on the sidewalk. "Oh, no. It's me who should apologize. I was . . . I really did have a long day and I'm afraid I wasn't paying attention to you. I should have just told my friends I was too tired to come out with them." Raine gave herself a mental kick for hurting this guy's feelings. She wished she could remember his name, at least. Bob? No. Rob? Mmm. Maybe.

"No, it's okay. I'd rather have you tell me the truth. It looks like I'm going to be doing this for a while longer, and it would be best if I knew that I was driving women *not* to drink." He laughed an endearing, self-deprecating laugh.

Raine winced. "No, really. Rob, right?" She waited until he nodded, then began again. "It's not you, Rob. I swear. To be honest . . . I recently resigned from the FBI and it's been, um, a really long time since I was in the dating scene myself. I think I'm just having trouble with the whole thought of it."

"Wow. You were in the FBI?"

Raine started walking again, hoping he wasn't going to ask her if she'd ever killed a man. That was FAQ #1. She preempted him by saying, "Yeah, and it didn't leave a lot of time for a social life. Plus, it's really hard on relationships. I mean, you can't just go out to a bar and tell someone about your day. It's like, 'Hi, nice to meet you. How was my day? Well, let's see. It started off with the interrogation of a hostile witness and ended with a drug raid. How about you?' That kind of information is a bit intimidating on a first date."

"I can imagine," Rob said with another genuine laugh. "No guy wants to date a woman who can kick his ass."

Raine laughed. Maybe this guy wasn't so bad after all. "Exactly. Now that I'm out of the Bureau, I plan to let myself go. I haven't worked out in almost a year. The fry guy at the local McDonald's knows my name. I spend all day in front of a computer. I can almost feel my muscles atrophying as we speak."

Rob put a hand on her arm and stopped, turning to face her. "You're really funny, you know. I'm just sorry we didn't meet under different circumstances."

"What do you mean?" Raine asked, frowning.

"I mean," Rob said, pulling a pistol from the pocket of his jacket and aiming it at her chest, "that I'm here to collect the last half of the kill money for Grady Thompson. Your message said to meet you here tonight and, although I don't usually like to meet my clients face-to-face, I made an exception in your case. After all, it's not like an ex-FBI agent who's hired two hits is going to turn *me* in, right?"

THIRTEEN

"SO, your friend seemed nice. Do you guys all work for the same company?" Aimee asked, licking the crystallized sugar that had fallen from the rim of her glass onto her bottom lip. Idly, she looked around the bar and wondered how many of these beautiful people would go home with strangers this evening.

"Bill and I do. But we don't know that other guy. Rob, I guess his name was? He came over and asked if we wanted to meet you and, well, of course we said sure. I mean, that's what we're all here for, right?"

Aimee's radar went on instant alert as she set her glass down on the cocktail napkin with a thud. "What do you mean, you don't know him? He said you all were friends."

The man closest to Aimee shrugged and looked at her as if she were about to go psycho on him. "Well, he lied then. I've never seen the guy before tonight."

Aimee turned and grabbed Daff's arm. "Did you bring your gun?"

Daphne looked at her friend strangely. "Of course."

Heads turned as both of the men at the table leaped up,

overturning their chairs. Bill had his hands up in the air even before Daff reached for her purse. Aimee grabbed for hers, too, but knew it was useless. It was a tiny, beaded crystal bag in the shape of a bow, outlined in red, and was barely big enough to hold her driver's license and a lipstick, much less a gun. She imagined Daff probably had a Colt .45 wrapped around her thigh as well as the 9mm in her purse.

"Wait a minute," the guy who had been talking to Aimee protested. "We're not into that sort of thing."

Aimee ignored the men as she pulled Daphne behind her through the bar. "Come on," she said as they burst out into the breezy night. "I have a feeling that Raine is in trouble."

"WHAT did you find in the motel room?" Calder asked, dreading the answer.

Jim Wilkins didn't turn his attention from Raine's VW, parked just across the aisle in the public parking lot. "Do you really want to know?"

Calder rubbed his throbbing temple with a thumb. "Yeah."

"We found three high-powered rifles, one of which I'm guessing was used to kill Grady Thompson. We also found several passports and a receipt for the deposit of five thousand dollars cash. There was also a laptop power cord, but no laptop."

"That all?"

Jim glanced out the driver's side window of the surveillance van. "There was an e-mail from Raine in the trash can, suggesting the assassin meet her at Chasey's tonight to collect the remainder of his fee."

Calder resisted the urge to slam his fist into the dashboard. "This is insane. Why does everyone believe Raine would be so stupid? This is the woman who broke into the FBI computers when she was seventeen. Do you really think she's going to go around arranging face-to-face meetings with assassins or e-mailing her intended victims telling them to watch out? Shit, if she wanted someone dead, she'd be a hell of a lot smarter about it than this."

"Well, that may be, but we seem to be gathering quite a lot of evidence to the contrary."

"It's all circumstantial and you know it."

"We have motive, we have opportunity, and we have your girlfriend meeting with an assassin. We were too late to catch her at the bar, but it looks like she changed the location of the meeting because she's leaving already." Wilkins nodded slightly as the lights of the VW flicked on and off again as Raine pushed the button on her keychain to unlock the doors remotely.

Calder's hand was on the doorknob when Wilkins's voice stopped him. "I certainly hope you're not planning to interfere with my investigation, Preston. That might be what the experts like to call a career limiting move."

The VW's backup lights winked at him flirtatiously as Raine put the car in reverse. Calder steeled himself and settled back into his seat. "If you lose her, I'll kill you myself," he said menacingly.

Wilkins remained silent as he followed Raine's car out of the parking garage and into the busy downtown Atlanta traffic.

THEY were a mile away from the bar when Wilkins's handheld radio crackled to life. "Wilkins, we need you back here. There's something you've got to see."

Wilkins looked over at Calder, who gave him a look that would have chilled a regular man's blood. Wilkins pressed the talk button on the radio. "No can do. I've got the subject in sight and must retain visual. Over."

"Uh, I don't know who you've got in your sights, but I can assure you that we've got our assassin right here, hanging by his balls. And I mean that literally." There was the unmistakable sound of a chuckle on the other end of the line.

Wilkins raised his eyebrow questioningly. Although this was the other man's case, Calder was the superior officer. Calder hesitated, then pulled his cell phone off his belt and dialed Raine's number. He couldn't trust that she was safe—and not on her way to meet an assassin—without talking to her himself.

She must have glanced at the number of the incoming call, because she answered with a chipper sounding, "Hi, Calder. What's up?"

"I understand you may have had some trouble tonight at Chasey's," he said, aware that Wilkins was listening to every word.

"Nothing my friends and I couldn't handle. But thanks for your concern. I know this isn't easy for you."

Calder closed his eyes and rubbed his aching forehead. "Nothing's ever easy with you, is it Raine?"

He heard the smile in her voice as she answered. "Honey, that's part of my charm." Then she hung up on him, leaving him shaking his head at the disconnected phone in his hand.

With a long-suffering sigh, Calder turned to Wilkins and nodded. Wilkins made a U-turn at the next light, heading back toward the bar. When they were about two blocks from the upscale watering hole, Wilkins's partner waved them down. Wilkins double-parked the van, flipping on the emergency flashers and ignoring the traffic snarl he'd just created.

One of the advantages of being an agent, Calder thought as he and Wilkins piled out of the vehicle—free parking, anywhere, anytime. Too bad the rest of the job sucked.

Then he stopped on the still-warm sidewalk, blinking as if the sight before him were a mirage.

"Somebody get me down from here," a thirty-something man with neatly trimmed brown hair screeched out of the left side of his mouth. The right side of his face was smashed up against a telephone pole, his head lashed to the pole by a nondescript blue-and-yellow striped tie. He was completely naked, his skin so white it nearly glowed in the moonlight shining overhead.

As the gathered crowd of FBI agents and several passersby looked on, the man slipped a fraction of an inch. His high-pitched scream raised the hairs on the back of Calder's neck.

When Calder looked up at the man's face again, he saw the glistening of tears on his cheeks. It took Calder a moment to realize that the trousers that had been tied around the man's hips hadn't been placed there to hide the man's naked ass from the gaping public, but rather to make sure that his genitals came in contact with the telephone pole.

The telephone pole that surely left a few splinters embedded in this guy's testicles every time he moved.

Calder cringed as the man slipped another inch and howled again.

"Jesus Christ," Calder ordered, taking charge of the situation even though this was technically not his case, "cut him down already."

CALDER was lying on the couch in her apartment when Raine got home after stopping at the ATM to deposit a much-needed check. He had changed from his spook-blue suit and starched white shirt into faded Levi's and a Def Leppard T-shirt. He'd taken off his once-white Nikes and placed them neatly under the coffee table along with his socks. She'd forgotten that about him, that he liked being barefoot. An easy thing to forget after almost a year apart, she supposed. More easily remembered were the bad things, although there really hadn't been much aside from his ultimate defection.

Calder mumbled something and rolled over on the couch, his arm flopping up to cover his eyes. Raine stood in the kitchen and watched him for a moment. His T-shirt clung to his broad chest and the flat muscles of his abdomen. His biceps flexed and relaxed as his arms settled into place. In his usual suit and tie, he looked big and intimidating, but in jeans and a T-shirt, he was even more so. The casual clothes made him seem more raw, closer to losing control of all the leashed power that she knew was bunched up inside of him.

She shivered and set her car keys down on the counter with a faint jingle. When she looked back to Calder, she saw him watching her.

Raine pulled her bottom lip into her mouth to moisten it. Then she cleared her throat. "What are you doing here?"

Calder stretched, catlike, before answering her. "I came to make sure you were all right."

"How did you get in?" she asked. "I don't recall giving you a key."

"Uh, refresher course: I'm FBI, remember?"

Raine gave him a half-smile. Yeah, okay, so gaining entry to one woman's apartment wasn't exactly something that required a lot of fancy training at Quantico.

He watched her come around the kitchen and into the living room, the heels of her knee-high boots making a clunking noise on the hardwood floor as she came toward him. Her legs were silky smooth above the boots and Calder had the sudden vision of her riding him, her leather boots on either side of his hips as she took him to the finish line. His cock went instantly rock hard.

"I like your boots," he said, shifting positions on the couch to give himself a little more room in his jeans.

Raine propped her hip against the arm of the chair opposite the couch, one of those sexy boots swinging back and forth right in front of him. From here, he could see almost all the way up her mid-thigh-high black skirt. Not that he was looking . . . but, hell, yes, he was looking. She had on a frilly, see-through sort of blouse over a black tank top. Raine wearing a staid blue pantsuit had been hard enough to resist. This new, high-heeled, short-skirted, sheer-bloused Raine was killing him.

"You still haven't answered me," she said, her voice barely penetrating the lust-induced fog in his brain. "Why are you here? I figured I'd seen the last of you this afternoon after I'd been brought in for questioning. We both know this sort of thing isn't good for your career."

"Fuck my career," Calder growled, pushing himself off the couch in one lithe movement.

Raine seemed surprised. Either that, or she thought that yelping like a puppy whose tail had just been stepped on was going to turn him on. Not that he needed much encouragement.

She stood up and took a step back, but Calder reached out to stop her. He looked down at his large hands on her hips. Tan fingers against black leather. He held her in place, taking a step forward to rub his erection against her stomach and groaning when she pressed back.

He moved one hand from her hips and slid it through her hair to cup the back of her head. Then he lowered his lips to hers, his mouth devouring hers. She sucked his tongue into her mouth and Calder groaned at the answering pull in his groin. He broke off the kiss, intending to wrest control back from her. His lips moved to the soft spot below her ear and he licked the skin there, then whispered her name in her ear, his breath hot and moist.

When Raine made to push his T-shirt up over his head, Calder growled. "Leave it. I want you first." Raine shrugged, but the look in her eyes was watchful, wary. Calder couldn't explain his sudden need to be in charge of their lovemaking—not to himself or to her. All he knew was he wanted to be the one calling the shots tonight.

He put his hands at her waist, slipping his fingers under the filmy blouse she wore. Slowly, he inched the fabric up, letting it tickle the bare skin of her arms as he tugged it free and tossed it onto the chair behind him. He pressed himself into her, his thigh between her legs, rubbing her sensitive skin, taunting her with all the layers of clothing between them.

Raine tried to rub against him, but he held her back, forcing her to move to his rhythm, making her wait for him.

Reaching around her back, Calder slowly unzipped her skirt, then slid his hands down her hips, pushing the leather down, down, down as he went. His hands encountered the tiniest triangle of fabric, and then nothing but bare skin. God, he loved her newfound penchant for thong panties.

Calder laid his forehead against Raine's and tried to rein in his labored breathing, kneading her naked skin all the while. Then his mouth returned to hers, her teeth nipping his tongue as he pushed into her.

Wanting to feel her skin against his, Calder hurriedly stripped out of his T-shirt and pulled her tank top over her head. He felt her nails running lightly up and down his back and he shivered, backing her up against the wall that divided kitchen from living room. He reached around and stopped her teasing hands, gathering both of her wrists in a tight grasp and raising them above her head.

He broke their kiss to look at her, backed against the wall with arms raised, her breasts moving slightly as she breathed in and out. Her hair wasn't long enough to cover the taut, rosy nipples that were puckering under his scrutiny, caressing the top of her shoulders instead. Calder put his free hand under her chin and raised her face so he could see her eyes. Her eyelids were half-closed, her normally light green eyes darkened with passion.

"Is this all right?" he asked, his voice husky. "I know I'm . . . pushing it. I just . . . need this so badly."

In answer, Raine pushed away from the wall and rubbed her naked breasts against his chest. Calder closed his eyes as a wave of lust broke over him. Then he bent down and lazily circled one of Raine's nipples with his tongue, wetting the sensitive skin and then blowing on it. Raine moaned and pulsed against his thigh, and Calder realized that he wanted to make her come just like that, with nothing but his tongue and the rough feel of his jeans on her soft skin.

He hooked the fingers of his free hand under the thin straps of fabric holding her panties up and tugged. The black silk fell around her boots. Then he pressed himself between her legs and pushed her back against the wall, so that she was nearly riding his thigh. His mouth went to her other breast, licking, blowing, sucking gently at first and then harder as her breathy moans became more and more desperate.

Raine's eyes were closed, her head resting against the wall, her creamy white skin laid bare.

Calder could hear her breath coming faster and faster and he knew she would fly apart right now if he touched her with his fingers, but just knowing that he could do it without even touching her was making his cock harder than it had ever been before. He felt her breathing change, nearly panting now, and he pressed his thigh into her, moving the denim up, up, up against her skin.

And suddenly, she was there, her breath hissing out in a strangled sort of scream as if she were trying to control it, but unable to do so completely. Her hands pushed against his fist and her entire body tensed, her back arching and her breast pressing into his mouth.

Calder didn't move until she nearly collapsed against him, and then he slowly lowered her arms, putting his own arms around her to caress the smooth skin of her back.

Her mouth nibbled along his collarbone as she stood there in his arms. When her mouth reached his neck, she raised her head, her green eyes almost black with spent passion.

It took a moment for the words she whispered to make any sense, so he just continued holding her and stroking her back as they sunk in. "Now, would you like to tell me what that was all about?" she asked.

FOURTEEN

MEGAN stood behind the last car in the row and shined the weak flashlight from side to side. There were four vehicles, including her mom's Pioneer, on the first floor of the metal box she was trapped inside of. Now the question was, was this the only floor? At one point during her search, she found herself giggling over the thought that this might be some sort of secret underground lab where the villains brought stolen cars to make them into weapons of mass destruction.

Once the hysterical bubble of laughter had dissipated, though, she began to wonder if this were just some sort of shipping container. That made a lot more sense, but was much less James Bond-ish than the whole secret lab idea, which was somewhat disappointing. Megan was starting to become just a bit attached to the thought that she could become a sort of female James Bond. Jane Bond? She could just see introducing herself as, "Bond. Jane Bond."

Megan coughed to cover another borderline-hysterical giggle and frowned sternly. "Okay, stop horsing around," she chided herself in her best grown-up voice.

She followed the pale beam of the flashlight over to the

side of the container, where she'd seen a ladder disappearing into the darkness overhead. Clutching the flashlight in one hand, she started climbing, stopping just before she emerged into the next level. If someone was watching the opening, she wanted to surprise them. Steadying her feet on the next rung, Megan stood up just far enough so her eyes cleared the ceiling. Cautiously, she raised the flashlight and shined it on the second floor.

"More cars," she whispered, seeing nothing but tires in the dim glow of her light. She turned back to the ladder to see how far up it went, and was relieved to see that it ended just above her head. Good. That meant she only needed enough courage to tackle this one floor.

Megan cautiously hauled herself up to the second floor, watching the darkness for any unexpected sign of movement. Then, having learned from her experience down below, she opened the door of the car in the back and turned on its head-lights to illuminate the rest of the vehicles.

Funny how the unknown wasn't quite as scary in the light.

Megan went through the car and found the usual assortment of half-empty potato chip bags and a warm soda or two. When she opened the front door of the next car in line, though, her breath froze in her lungs.

"Ohmigod, ohmigod," she said excitedly, reaching out to touch the silver plastic cradled in a black holder.

It was a cell phone. Her salvation. All she had to do was call 911. The police could tell where she was from the cell signal, couldn't they? And then they would come and get her. Not as exciting an ending as a James Bond/Charlie's Angels movie, but in a few hours, she'd be back home! Megan's hand flew to her chest, her heart feeling like it was beating a thousand times a minute. She was going home. The first thing she wanted to do was to eat about four boxes of macaroni and cheese. Then she'd guilt her mom into making her favorite chocolate cake with that coconut frosting.

And then . . . oh, then she'd snuggle in between her mom and dad on their big, comfy bed and they'd fall asleep watching reruns of "MASH" like they used to. Megan didn't even care if she was too old for that now. She'd even let Matthew sleep with them—as long as he stayed down at the foot of the bed.

Megan's hand trembled as she picked up the phone. Even if it wasn't charged, she could turn on the car's battery and that would make it work. She didn't even have to turn on the car itself, and didn't have to worry about killing herself from the fumes.

"Thank you, God," she whispered, closing her eyes as she pulled the phone toward her.

Her fingers shook as she flipped open the top of the thin, rectangular phone. She couldn't wait to talk to her family again. And to Emily. She even missed school.

She dialed 911 and hit SEND, and then pressed the phone to her ear, the plastic warm against her skin. She couldn't believe her luck in finding a phone. Her mom never left hers in the car, and, obviously, neither did the owners of the other vehicles she'd searched.

The phone made a funny blip sound and Megan pulled it away from her ear to look at the screen. She thought it had said it was half-charged, but maybe she was wrong. When she saw the words emblazoned across the small screen, she slowly slid to the floor, her sweats wiping a clean stripe through the dust covering the tan paint. No, this couldn't be happening.

She was going to go home, damn it! She was going to eat fattening foods and curl up with her family and watch TV. She was not going to spend another day trapped inside this airless container with no one to talk to, no food to eat, and nothing to do.

Megan nearly choked on the hiccupping sob that escaped her throat as tears started to flow down her cheeks.

"Damn you!" she screamed, holding the phone up in front of her face.

Tempted to throw the offending object against the wall, but knowing that the satisfaction of watching it splinter into a million pieces would make her feel better now but worse later, Megan tossed the phone back into the car and slammed the door. Her hopes had been shattered by two little words: *No signal.* Because of those words, there would be no easy rescue and she'd have to continue to be brave for God only knew how much longer.

Megan hiccupped again and drew her knees into her chest, looping her arms around her legs. Fear and hopelessness clawed at her like birds scratching for food. She might not get out of this alive. She hadn't found more than the odd half-empty drink or two, and very little food. Even worse, she had no idea how long she was going to be trapped in here. Two more days? Two more weeks? She didn't know.

That was the worst part.

"YOU know, it might be nice if you actually started keeping some food at your house," Calder complained, holding the door of the nearest McDonald's open for Raine.

She shrugged past him, still feeling a bit numb from the not one, but two mind-blowing orgasms she'd had with Calder before he'd asked if she was hungry. She'd suggested that perhaps she could do something to relieve his quite obvious erection, but he'd refused, telling her he'd rather just get something to eat. Raine was the first one to admit that McDonald's french fries were good, but were they better than sex? She didn't think so.

The front of the fast-food restaurant was empty, all of the various beeps and chirps echoing off the tile floor and sounding twice as loud as usual. The girl who had been wiping down the already clean counter and chatting with the kid in drive-thru looked like she planned to ignore them for the requisite amount of time, but she did a double take when her eyes lit on Calder's face. Raine smothered her laugh behind a fake cough and looked up to see him giving the girl his I-know-seven-hundred-ways-to-kill-a-person-so-if-you-don't-get-your-ass-over-here-and-take-my-order-right-now-I'll-show-you-number-three-fifty-two look.

The teenager scurried behind a register and listened intently while Calder told her what they wanted. Raine saw her hands shake when she held them out for Calder's proffered twenty.

"Has anyone ever told you that you excel at intimidation?

You must have gotten an A in that course at Quantico," she said after the girl rushed away to grab the last of the fries before her buddy in drive-thru could snag them.

Calder just looked at her, his eyes dark and flat and angry.

Well, hell, she'd be angry too if she was walking around with a raging hard-on like he was. Raine took a step closer, brushing against him. She figured he'd jump back away from her, but instead he put an arm around her shoulders and held her right where she was. She could feel his erection through the soft material of her loose sweatpants, but what really bothered her was the tenderness with which he pushed a lock of hair behind her ears and the softness of the kiss he placed on top of her head.

The teenager came back and nearly threw their food and drinks on the tray before pushing it across the counter toward them. Calder picked up the tray in one hand, his other arm still around Raine's shoulders. They found a booth at the back of the deserted restaurant and Raine slid in, expecting Calder to take a seat across from her. Instead, he nudged her over with his hip as he slid in next to her.

Raine divvied up their food before squeezing a ketchup puddle onto the paper lining of the now-empty tray and dredging two fries through the mess. Calder had unwrapped the paper around a portion of his Quarter Pounder and took a bite, then set it back down on a pile of napkins as if he weren't really hungry. Raine ate another handful of fries as the silence lengthened.

"Do you plan to tell me what's going on, or do I just get to guess?" she asked finally, looking at him out of the corner of her eyes.

Calder pushed away his half-eaten hamburger and reached for the iced tea he'd ordered. His arm was up along the back of the booth, the tips of his fingers lightly touching her through her T-shirt. He took a sip of his drink. Sighed. Took another sip.

Raine swallowed her fries and turned a half-turn to face him. "I thought you were through with me. Today, after I got done being questioned, I mean. You looked right through me as if we'd never met. I know . . ." She paused, ate a couple more fries, began again. "I know you thought you wanted me back. But now, with history repeating itself, you would be better off without me. Is that what tonight was? Your way of saying good-bye, good luck, and you'll never have sex this good again? Because, you know, you didn't need to do that. I already know that what we have—in bed, at least—is the best I'll probably ever get."

She swiped at the tears that had gathered in her eyes. Shit. For someone who professed to hate crying, she sure was doing a lot of it lately.

Calder turned and pulled her toward him, so close that she was nearly sitting on his lap. "Jesus, Raine, you're killing me. Tonight wasn't good-bye. Tonight was . . ." He sighed, ran a hand across his eyes as if the lights overhead were blinding him. "Tonight was me trying to control the only thing I seem to be able to control right now. You could go to jail for this, you know? And there's not a fucking thing I can do about it."

Raine reached out and touched his cheek, letting her hand slide across his whisker-roughened skin. She scooted even closer, her thigh on top of his. "Maybe tonight should be good-bye," she suggested softly. "At least until this mess has worked itself out. Being with me, well, I know it reflects badly on you. It won't be long before they start questioning you about information you may have leaked to me about the Thompson case since I resigned. I know how important your career is to you, Calder. I don't want to be the reason it ends. I don't think either one of us could live with it if I was."

Calder slammed his fist down on the table, making her—and their food—jump. "Damn it, don't you think I know that? I stayed away from you for eleven long months and do you know why? I kept telling myself that it was because I was giving you time to forgive me, but that's a fucking lie. It's because I'm a coward. I wanted to make sure that it was safe for me, safe for my career, when I came back. Jesus, Raine, I'm such a coward."

She didn't know what to say. Calder sat there with his head bowed, his thick dark hair falling forward, and waited for . . . what? Forgiveness? Could she forgive him for walking out on her to save his career? Could he forgive himself? And now what? Now that the nightmare had begun again, what was she supposed to do? Let him come over for sex because—let's face it—it was pretty incredible when they were together, and then pretend it didn't hurt when he walked away to keep his reputation intact?

No. There was no way she would do that. She was no saint, sacrificing herself to save the man she loved.

She knew how important his career was to him, and she even gave him enough credit to realize that what he felt for her was almost as important to him. But it was that "almost" that made the decision for her. It was that "almost" that had kept him away for eleven months. It was that "almost" that told her what she needed to do.

She slid her hands into his hair and pushed his head up so she could see his eyes. She nearly flinched from the pain she saw there, but forced herself to do what needed to be done.

"I deserve better than this, Calder. My life doesn't have a revolving door that you can walk through whenever you think it's safe to be with me. Love doesn't work that way. Now, if you'll excuse me, I'd like to be alone."

Raine let her hands drop and turned back toward the food on the table. She had no interest in eating, but she had to do something, so she reached for a lukewarm french fry and forced herself to start chewing.

"I'll take you home," Calder said, his voice cold and hard as if he were interrogating a hostile witness.

"No, thanks," Raine said without looking at him. "I am perfectly capable of taking care of myself."

Calder hesitated, but short of dragging her out of the booth—which he could have done if he'd been really determined, but not without a scene—he was out of options. Raine felt his eyes on her for a long time, but she refused to do anything to acknowledge that the man she loved was leaving her for the second time in a year.

FIFTEEN

RAINE dragged herself out of bed on Monday morning, feeling as though she hadn't gotten more than an hour's worth of sleep. A lousy way to feel on the day you'd decided to take your life back, she thought, staring at her red-rimmed eyes in the mirror above the bathroom sink.

She was done being a victim. She'd spent all day yesterday moping around her apartment and feeling sorry for herself, but now her self-pity had morphed into anger. It pissed her off that she was being set up again and that anger spurred her into action. Today she was going to wrest control of her life back from the forces that kept trying to take it away from her. Today she was going to start her own investigation into Grady Thompson's murder. Today she was going to find out just what the hell was going on with her one and only case at Partners In Crime. The company was her future and she'd be damned if she just sat back and let this latest fiasco interfere with that.

And today, when the FBI came to arrest her, maybe she wouldn't just be sitting around waiting for them to fuck up her life.

Raine stripped out of her pj's, tossing them across the floor with a little more force than was necessary as she stepped into the shower. She didn't take much time with her morning routine, anxious to start moving ahead with her new plan of action, which didn't include any extra time for primping . . . or for wallowing in self-pity. Forgoing her favorite high-heeled boots and short skirt for a pair of Keds and worn blue jeans, Raine grabbed her car keys and her laptop and stuffed them in an already-full tote bag. She took one last look around her apartment, making certain she hadn't forgotten anything vital, and then pulled the door shut behind her.

She had the feeling that when she returned, her apartment wouldn't be the same. Not if the FBI managed to obtain the search warrant she was pretty sure they were after.

Raine dashed across the street toward her VW, watching to see if she was being followed. Not that it mattered. She had nothing to hide.

As she sped toward the interstate, she kept one eye on the rearview mirror and another on the traffic ahead. Damn, it felt good to be working again. Even with the Thompson murder hanging over her head, she felt more energized than she had in months. She may not have been making a difference in anybody's life by trying to figure out what, if anything, was going on with Hope Enslar, but at least she wasn't hiding away in her apartment with nobody to talk to but her computers.

She changed lanes and glanced at her speedometer, making sure she stayed within the speed limit. When the digital clock on the dashboard rolled to the next minute, Raine cursed. She had forgotten all about her brother, who was probably halfway to her apartment by now.

Without taking her eyes from the road, she rummaged in her tote bag to find her cell phone. She cycled through her digital address book, pressing SEND when she came to Neall's home number.

"Please be late," she muttered into the receiver, hoping he hadn't already left since she didn't have his cell number.

He picked up on the fifth ring, sounding out of breath. "Robey," he answered.

"Hey, it's Raine," she said, swiftly changing lanes when a

red Porsche came behind her from out of nowhere and flashed his lights. Where did this asshole think he was? On the Autobahn?

"I'm on my way over. I'm just running a little late," Neall said, sounding defensive.

"No, don't bother going to my apartment. There's been a change of plans."

"But I can be there in fifteen minutes—" Neal started to protest.

"No, what I meant was that I'm not home, so it doesn't make sense for you to meet me there. I decided to do a little legwork this morning instead. But, listen, there are a couple things you could do to help me if you're still interested in lending a hand."

"Sure. Just tell me what you want me to do."

"Okay, first, I'd like you to set up some tracers on Hope Enslar. She's the head of R&D at Jackson Motor Company here in Atlanta. I trust you can find her social security number, address, birth date, and all that."

"With my eyes closed," Neall muttered as Raine continued.

"If she applies for credit, opens a bank account in the Cayman Islands, books a sudden trip to Switzerland, or registers her dog with Animal Control, I want to know about it."

"Easy enough. What else?" Neall asked.

Raine chewed on the inside of her cheek. What she really wanted was some information on Thompson's assassin, the mysterious Rob who had suffered from a sudden case of the splinters on Saturday night. But did she really want to let her brother in on that? It wasn't that she didn't trust him, it was just that . . . well, she didn't know why she was balking exactly. Perhaps because what happened with the Thompson case was so important to her future. While she appreciated Neall's offer of assistance, especially with their history of polite estrangement, she just didn't feel comfortable opening up her entire life to him just yet. It made her feel too vulnerable. But she had no such qualms on the Enslar case probably because, as she'd said the other night, it wasn't like this was a matter of life or death.

Raine cleared her throat, "Next, I'd like you to see what

you can dig up on Hope's father. He was head of R&D for JMC back in the seventies and early eighties. I doubt you're going to find much, but it can't hurt to look."

"Anything else?"

"That should do it. Why don't we plan to get together tomorrow afternoon and compare notes? I can meet you at your place."

"All right. What time?"

"Three o'clock? Does that work for you?"

"Yeah, sure. But, hey, you never did tell me why you had to cancel on me. Are you breaking into somebody's house or something?"

"No," Raine answered, taking the exit for the Jackson Motors plant. "I'm going to install a keystroke logger on Ms. Enslar's computer. And then," Raine paused, looking over her shoulder as she eased her car into the right lane. "And then I think it's time I paid a visit to Hope's father."

"THIS is bullshit and you know it," Calder accused, planting his six-foot-one-inch self in the doorway of Wilkins's small office. "Raine didn't arrange the hit on Thompson, and rifling through her underwear drawer isn't going to prove otherwise."

To his credit, Wilkins remained impassive under Calder's dark glare. "If you're so convinced we're not going to find anything, why are you worried?"

"I'm just trying to spare someone I care about the nightmare of having her apartment ransacked. She's been through enough this past year." Sounding defeated, Calder plopped down in the chrome-and-plastic chair across from Wilkins's desk. He clasped his hands between his knees and shook his head with disgust. "This is the second time she's been framed and I can't seem to get anyone to concede that we should be focusing our investigation elsewhere. Or, at the very least, to consider any other scenarios."

Wilkins leaned back in his chair, propping one shoe up on an opened drawer and swinging the other in time to some silent music that must be playing in his head. "Tell me this,

Preston, why is it that you've devoted your entire career to upholding a system that you seem to have no faith in?"

Calder's eyes narrowed on his colleague's face. "What the hell do you mean by that?"

"I mean just what I said. You've spent—what? Twelve? Fifteen years in the criminal justice system? How could you have wasted so much of your life on a system you believe sends innocent people to jail for murders they didn't commit? Do you think I have such a hard-on for nailing someone for the Thompson killing that I'm not going to do my job and thoroughly investigate all angles of this case? Do you think I'm going to manufacture evidence that doesn't exist just so that the defense attorneys can get up in front of a courtroom and make a joke out of me and the Bureau in front of a jury? Yes, we have an e-mail from Raine to our assassin, and we have a random meeting between said-assassin and Raine at a local watering hole. Does that mean that I'm ready to throw her in jail? No. Does it mean that I want to have an expert scour her computer for more evidence? Yes. Now why don't you just leave me alone and let me do my job. I can assure you, I am not interested in railroading your girlfriend into prison so that I can stamp CLOSED on this file."

Calder grimaced at the gray carpeting underneath his feet. "I'm being an asshole, aren't I?"

Wilkins didn't say anything for so long that Calder looked up just to make sure the other man hadn't fallen asleep or something. "I think you're just trying to protect someone you care about, and that's admirable. The thing is, though, if she didn't commit this crime, she doesn't need your protection. And if she did do it, there's absolutely nothing you can do to keep her safe."

Calder squeezed his eyes shut, Wilkins's words echoing through his head. "Nothing you can do to keep her safe." That was the inescapable truth, wasn't it? He wanted to get Raine as far away from this mess as he could, send her off to some deserted island somewhere where she'd never be touched by murderers and rapists and child molesters.

Jesus. Calder pinched the bridge of his nose. Why hadn't

he picked some nursery school teacher or advertising executive to fall in love with? Why had he, instead, fallen for a woman who actually sought out criminals for a living? He needed to have his fucking head examined.

"Look, man," Wilkins said, coming around his desk and laying a conciliatory hand on Calder's shoulder, "I know this must be hard for you, but you have to trust me to do my job. Now, if you'd like to come along on our little panty raid"—this said with a mocking raise of his eyebrow to needle Calder about his underwear comment earlier—"you're welcome to join us. I can assure you, however, that I'm much more interested in Raine's hard drives than the labels on her bras."

RAINE absently pushed the strap of her pink satin bra a bit further down her shoulder, making sure that no color was visible through her faded Star Trek T-shirt. She cursed herself for not remembering to wear plain white cotton. Female techies as a general rule weren't big on ultra-feminine lingerie. Or anything feminine, for that matter. Like their male counterparts, they tended to favor drab clothing, science fiction, and above all their computers. They never complained about their long days because, truth be told, they enjoyed spending twenty hours a day staring at their monitors. Getting paid just made it all the sweeter.

They were more comfortable chatting online than in person, and they couldn't understand why the general populace didn't understand the finer points of the argument on the Unix versus Windows operating system debate.

Pulling the bangs of her drab brown wig over her eyebrows, Raine waved her magnetic keycard over the reader that guarded the entrance to JMC's research and development department. The indicator light flashed green and Raine pulled open the door. She stopped at the first cubicle. No use trying to pretend she knew where she was going when she didn't.

"Hi," she said to the back of a short-haired man who sat facing the walls of his cube. "I'm Karen Michaels from the IT help desk. Hope Enslar called in a problem with her computer a few hours ago. Could you tell me where she sits?"

The man swung around and looked at her through thick glasses. "Yeah, uh, she's over there. First office on the right," he said, waving his arm briefly before turning back to whatever it was he had been doing.

"Thanks," Raine said, taking off in the direction he'd indicated.

As she pushed open the door, Raine noticed that Hope's office was larger than the others she passed. Nothing so egalitarian here as identical offices, no matter a person's rank. Hope's office was spacious enough to hold not only a large desk that faced a wall of windows overlooking the row of cubicles in the hall but also contained a round table with several chairs surrounding it. There was a credenza behind the desk, flanked by two bookshelves filled with three-ring binders and lots of hardcovers with titles that didn't give much insight into the books' contents.

But Raine's attention was focused on Hope's desk. Or rather, on the laptop on Hope's desk. Raine observed that it was a newer model Dell as she looked outside to see if anyone was watching her. It was plugged into a docking station, making it easy for the user to take her laptop home at night without having to plug and unplug all the various attachments like the keyboard, mouse, network cable, and printer.

Raine moved around to the front of Hope's desk, swearing silently when she noticed that Hope had set her screensaver to password-protect her computer if she was away for a certain length of time.

Raine shrugged as she sat down in the fancy leather chair behind Hope's desk. Oh well, password protection was just a minor nuisance. Raine's first order of business after entering JMC this afternoon was to find an empty desk and hack into JMC's network. She'd found the relatively isolated cubicle of one Stephanie Yamamoto, turned on her computer, and went to work. After four minutes, she'd discovered that JMC used the standard first initial/last name username convention. And after another three minutes spent searching Ms. Yamamoto's drawers, Raine had found the Post-it used to scribble the ever-changing and, thus, impossible to memorize, passwords Stephanie was currently using. Raine wondered if "Sammy0806" was a combination of Stephanie's kid's name and birth date, hubby's name and wedding date, or dog's name and PIN. People's passwords, she'd found, almost invariably meant something to the user. But even then, they tended to write them down since they had to change them so frequently and often forgot which one they had used last. When Raine was signed on as Stephanie, she opened the woman's e-mail account, trying not to be nosy and peek at the string of messages in her inbox. Still, Raine found it fascinating how much you could learn about a person from her e-mail, so it was hard not to snoop.

There were several opened messages from a Sam Wilde—presumably the Sammy of the password fame—whose signature line indicated he was the assistant to the CEO. Raine couldn't stop herself from clicking on the last one, sent three days ago and already marked as read by Ms. Yamamoto. She looked over her shoulder and then, convinced that no one had noticed her intrusion, proceeded to read an incredibly hot note from Mr. Wilde to Ms. Yamamoto.

Whew! Raine fanned her suddenly flushed cheeks. Didn't these two know that companies routinely spied on their employees, even going so far as to filter incoming and outgoing messages on several "hot words," including one of the more popular ones: *sex?* Raine hoped for Ms. Yamamoto's sake that JMC wasn't quite up to that level of snooping. If they were, she'd bet that this supposedly private affair between Sam and Stephanie was garnering a lot of very public attention in JMC's IT department.

Her curiosity satisfied, Raine opened the meeting schedule function of Stephanie's e-mail program. She selected a new meeting request and entered Hope Enslar's name in the first line. When she tabbed to the next line, through the miracle of modern technology, she was able to see Hope's schedule for the rest of the day. Her calendar was blocked off from 11 A.M. to 12:30 P.M. and then again from 2 to 3 P.M. Raine glanced at her watch. It was twelve-fifteen, which didn't leave her enough time to make it to R&D and do what needed to be done. Instead, she'd have to wait until Hope's two o'clock meeting started.

Hmm. An hour and forty-five minutes. What was she going to do for an hour and forty-five minutes? She clicked on one or two more messages from Sam, some hot and some just the typical complaints about work from one employee to another. She had to get away from Stephanie Yamamoto's e-mail. If she didn't, she knew herself well enough to know she'd end up reading all of the letters from Sam Wilde just out of sheer curiosity. And what was that saying? Curiosity killed the cat?

"Yeah, but satisfaction brought him back," Raine muttered under her breath as she clicked on the X to close the e-mail program and then shut down Stephanie's computer.

Well, cats and torrid love notes aside, she had nearly two hours to kill. She supposed that now was as good a time as any to pay a visit to Hope Enslar's father.

RAINE wasn't sure what she had expected to find at Norman Enslar's house, but the two-story colonial in this upscale neighborhood had revealed nothing besides a man in a broken-down body and his brawny caregiver. From where she stood, just outside the master bedroom near another doorway in case she had to make a quick getaway, Raine heard the rustle of newspaper and the even tones of the man at Mr. Enslar's side. She could see Hope's father lying in the king-size bed, his thin chest moving up and down under the blanket covering his body.

What an awful existence, she thought.

Just then, Mr. Enslar's leg twitched and his nurse looked up. He patted Norman's arm comfortingly. "Are you thirsty?" he asked, leaning over to pick up a glass of water with a straw sticking out the top. Whether Mr. Enslar was thirsty or not, the water was brought to his lips. Too far away to hear anything more than the faint rustle of the paper as it crinkled in the nurse's lap, Raine couldn't tell if he drank or not. When the man sat back, returning the glass to the nightstand as he relaxed, Raine was surprised to find Mr. Enslar staring straight at her. She held her breath, her weight balanced on the balls of her feet, waiting for him to sound the alarm. Anything, even another jerk of his toes, might make the nurse look her way.

But Mr. Enslar merely closed his eyes. No, wait. He didn't close both of his eyes. He just closed one eye, and then opened it again slowly, as if it cost him a lot of effort to do even such a small maneuver.

Raine smiled, but didn't chance a wave. Then, keeping her eye on the pair in the bedroom, she slowly, silently, made her way back down the stairs and out of the house.

SIXTEEN

SO now here she was, back at JMC ensconced in Hope Enslar's office, surreptitiously searching Hope's desk for a clue as to her password. She knew from a test she'd just performed using Stephanie Yamamoto's username and incorrect passwords that the network administrators had set the system to permanently lock a user out after five failed attempts to log on. This meant that someone trying to hack into their network only had five tries to get it right before they had to move on to a different user. If a legitimate user had simply mistyped his password five times, someone from IT was called to reset the user's account. While she appreciated the safety measure from the standpoint of one who did security consulting, this made Raine's task of unlocking Hope's computer a bit more difficult, especially since she didn't find any stray Post-its lying around with passwords scribbled on them.

Okay, so here's where the hacker's job really got creative. Raine sat back in the padded leather executive chair and looked around Hope's office. Most often, she could find a clue about someone's password by the pictures on her desk or something posted nearby. She knew Hope didn't have any children, so that possibility was out. Kids' names and birth dates and husbands' names and year of marriage were the most frequently used passwords for women. For men, it was sports teams and their own date of birth or star athletes with their team number. But Hope was a childless, unmarried woman, so all of those possibilities were out. Raine looked for a picture of a pet—the next most frequently used password for women—but didn't see even a goldfish among the papers on Hope's all-business corkboard.

So that left Hope's father Norman Enslar, seemingly the only thing in Hope's life that meant something to her besides work. Raine figured her number one choice should be Norman's name and some variation of his birthday, either the month and day or the year. Unfortunately, she didn't have that information handy. But she knew who might.

Keeping one eye on the activity outside Hope's office, Raine picked up the telephone perched on the edge of the desk. She pressed 9 for an outside line and then dialed her brother's number. This time, he answered on the second ring.

"Neall, it's Raine," she said, keeping her voice down so as to not attract any attention.

"What's up?"

"Have you had a chance to get any information on Hope's father? Specifically, I'm looking for his date of birth."

"Trying to crack a password, huh?" Neall asked.

Raine grinned despite herself. "How'd you guess?"

"I know a thing or two about computers."

"This would be so much easier if Hope had a child," Raine said.

"Well, hold on. I think I've got Mr. Enslar's birthday here somewhere." Raine heard the clacking of computer keys as Neall searched his notes. "Yeah, here we go. December 7, 1941. Man, this guy was born under some unlucky star, wasn't he?"

"No kidding," Raine muttered, helping herself to a piece of notepaper that had FROM THE DESK OF HOPE ENSLAR emblazoned across the top. She wrote down Norman's birthday, then asked, "Is there anything else you've found out that might help me here? Any nieces or nephews I should know about? Any ex-husbands around? Oh, where and when did Hope graduate?"

Neall's fingers clacked on his keyboard again as he looked for that last bit of information. "Negative on the nieces, nephews, or ex-husbands. Our Hope is pretty much a one-man woman, and that man is her daddy." He clicked a few more keys and recited Hope's educational history, and then said, "There's really nothing else I can tell you, sis. Sorry I couldn't be more help."

Raine tapped her fingers on the edge of Hope's desk. "That's all right. Hopefully, this will be enough. I'll see you tomorrow."

She had five chances to get this right. She wrote her first and second guesses on the slip of notepaper in front of her: Norman41 and Norman1207. Three and four would be Hope's high school and college names and years of gradua-tion. She left the slot for number five blank, hoping she wouldn't have to get that far.

Turning to the keyboard, she typed in the first password, crossed her fingers for luck, and hit ENTER. It took about ten seconds for the network to reject her. Damn. She repeated the process on the next three choices, only to be met with the same result. Raine stared at the blank line she'd drawn for her fifth guess and chewed on her bottom lip. What else in Hope's life was so significant that she'd use it as her pass-word? It occurred to Raine then that Hope might be one of the only people in the universe who actually used random words as her password—a tactic that made hacking in this manner virtually impossible, but which also made it virtu-ally impossible for a person to recall their password the day after they'd chosen it. No, the odds were that Hope had cho-sen something that she could remember.

Raine frowned, trying to think of what she should use as her final try. She leaned back in Hope's chair, scanning the office one last time for any clues. Her eyes lit on the cork-board to her right. Reaching out, she flipped through the var-ious graphs, memos, and assorted Dilbert cartoons, trying to find something that might be of use. She lifted a cartoon pok-ing fun at loud people who shouted into their speakerphones and saw a yellowed piece of newspaper. She had to stand up to get close enough to read the small print, but when she did, she was surprised to find that it was an article about Mr. Enslar's accident. Raine knew all the details about the accident. The Pronto that was JMC's answer to the cheap but well-built Hondas and Mazdas that were flooding the American market had a critical design flaw that, when hit in a certain way, caused the gas tank to explode. Mr. Enslar, who had been on the Pronto's design team, had shown his support of the vehicle by buying one for himself, a decision that changed both his and his daughter's lives irrevocably.

Raine pushed aside a memo and looked at the date on the newspaper clipping. July 17, 1984.

In the blank spot on the notepaper in front of her, Raine wrote: Pronto1984.

This time, she didn't bother crossing her fingers after typing in the password. She hit ENTER and, in less than ten seconds, she was in.

HOPE Enslar never went anywhere without her cell phone. She liked knowing she could always be reached, even though she couldn't recall the last time anyone had called her on her cell. As she sat in the conference room, waiting for the hourlong HR-mandated performance review training to end, she found herself staring at the silent phone on the table next to her blank notepad and wishing it would ring.

Performance reviews. *Ugh.* These things had to be the bane of every manager's existence. Why couldn't employees just figure out for themselves how well or poorly they were doing based on the raises she doled out? Everyone knew the average percentage. This year it was a paltry three percent because of the faltering economy and the relative glut of SUVs on the market so it didn't take a rocket scientist to realize that if you got five percent you were doing a great job, and if you got one percent, you'd better tell your mother, sister, and best friend to stop calling and get your ass back in gear or you might just lose your job when the next round of layoffs hit.

But no, HR had complicated forms that had to be filled

out, and you had to document how even your star performers could improve. It seemed to her like the perfect way for HR to make sure *they* never got laid off.

Suddenly, a miracle occurred. Right after the HR Director finished explaining that they had changed their rating system from 1–5 to 1.5–5 because "giving a 1 is simply too hurtful to the employee," Hope's cell phone started to jingle merrily. As a joke to herself, she had downloaded the tune to "Girls Just Wanna Have Fun," and the peppy song had her stifling a smirk as she grabbed her belongings and headed for the door with an apologetic wave to the HR team.

She glanced at the number displayed on her phone's screen, but didn't recognize it. "Hello," she answered, after hitting the TALK button.

"Ms. Enslar? This is Chris Robbins from Atlanta Emergency Services. We're on our way to Atlanta Memorial Hospital with your father's nurse and he asked us to call to let you know that he had to leave your father alone."

"Oh, no," Hope said, sorry that she had ever wished her phone would ring. "Is Randy all right? What's happened?"

"It's nothing to worry about, Ms. Enslar. Randy slipped while giving your father a bath and it looks like his leg is broken. Your father is fine, but a bit shaken, as you might imagine."

"Yes. I . . . thank you. I'll cancel the rest of my meetings and be home right away. Please tell Randy not to worry. I'll take care of my father."

"I will. Good-bye, Ms. Enslar."

"Good-bye." Hope slipped her phone into the pocket of her white jacket and hurried toward her office to get her purse and her laptop so she could leave. "Poor Randy," she murmured under her breath as she rounded the corridor leading to R&D. A broken leg. That had to hurt. Then, selfishly, she hoped he hadn't slipped while he was carrying her father. The last thing Daddy needed was a fall, on top of everything else.

Hope waved her pass card over the reader, frowning when it remained a solid red. She tried again, slower this time, and the light turned green. Pulling open the heavy door, she stepped into the department and cut across the maze of cubicles in the middle of the floor on her way to her office.

RAINE pulled the disk from her pocket and slid it into the laptop's disk drive. She moved the keystroke logging program she'd brought from the disk to Hope's hard drive, then opened the startup script file and inserted code to instruct the program to begin when the computer started up. She could have just placed it in Hope's startup folder, but that made it easier for another computer professional to spot. Not that most IT professionals didn't know how to open an initialization file and edit it, too, but this just hid her logger a little deeper in the structure of Hope's computer.

The logger would stealthily record every keystroke Hope made, revealing to Raine everything that Hope did on her computer. It would capture the content of any e-mail Hope sent, every URL she typed in, every memo she wrote. And hopefully, it would give Raine some clue as to why Norman Enslar had gone through the painstaking process of sending a letter to the FBI about his daughter. If not, Raine was about two days away from telling Calder that the goose chase was over. It was about time she got back to business development and worked on landing herself a real client. A real client who didn't have the underlying motive of sleeping with her and breaking her heart again, that is.

"Who are you and what are you doing to my computer?"

Shit. Was it past three o'clock already? Had she been staring off into space and thinking about Calder for *that* long?

Raine forced her heartbeat to slow. The key to successful infiltration was acting like you had every right to be there, she reminded herself. That did not include blushing and stammering when you were caught.

As she looked up at Hope, who was standing in the doorway watching her suspiciously, Raine's gaze passed over the clock on Hope's desk. No, it wasn't past three. As a matter of fact, it was only two twenty-eight. Hope should still be in her meeting.

But in life, "should" didn't count for much.

"I'm Karen Michaels," Raine said, rising from Hope's chair and holding out her hand in greeting. "I just joined the IT group this week."

Hope came forward and shook her hand, and Raine saw her studying the badge around her neck intently. The picture showed a woman with drab brown hair and brown eyes (thank God for the invention of colored contacts), with the same forced smile that all badge pictures had. Raine knew it looked just like her.

"Nice to meet you," Hope said politely, stepping back.

Raine prayed that she'd closed and saved the startup file she'd been working on, but couldn't risk chancing a look back at Hope's screen to make sure she'd done so. She had to stall long enough for the computer to go back into screensaver mode. Otherwise, Hope would know that she had been on her computer. Of course, the disk she had left sitting in Hope's disk drive might be a dead giveaway, too, Raine thought, giving herself a virtual slap upside the head for not taking it out as soon as she'd finished installing the keystroke logger.

"So," Raine began, "how long have you worked at JMC? It seems like a great company."

She saw Hope's eyes slide to the clock, her impatience warring with business etiquette.

"I started here as an intern in college," Hope answered. Then she made as if to cut the conversation short by saying, "I'm sorry, but I'm in a bit of a rush. Could you come back another time to finish whatever it was you were doing?"

"Oh, well, that won't be necessary. I was just checking out a complaint from another user. He called the help desk and said he was having trouble sending you a meeting request. We thought it might be a problem with your network cable, so I came on down to check it out." Raine didn't move from behind Hope's desk. She hadn't seen the telltale flicker that would indicate the computer had switched back to the login screen.

Hope pulled her coat off the hook behind the door and draped it across her arm. "Did you fix the problem, then?"

"Yes. It was a loose cable, just like we thought." Finally, Raine saw the light shift out of the corner of her eye and stepped out from behind Hope's desk. "You should be good to go," she said, using one of her most detested phrases of American slang.

"Thanks," Hope said absently as she walked to her desk, shut the top of her laptop, and released it from the docking station.

"No problem." Raine headed to the door as quickly as she could without making her retreat seem too obvious. Hope's voice stopped her just as she reached the doorway and thought she was home free.

"By the way," Hope began, sounding more suspicious than curious, "who was it that was trying to send me a meeting request? I'll have to make sure to call and let him know that everything's fixed now."

Raine pasted a smile on her face and turned back toward Hope, who was retrieving her purse from her bottom left desk drawer. "It was Sam Wilde, the CEO's assistant. He was trying to set up a meeting with all corporate officers the week of Memorial Day, but he had some difficulty being able to see when you might be available. He shouldn't have any trouble now."

"Oh. Okay, thanks." Apparently satisfied, Hope closed her desk drawer and turned her back on Raine, dismissing her as effectively as if she'd slammed the door in her face.

MEGAN had no idea if it was day or night. Her watch said that it was almost three o'clock, but, since the clock wasn't digital, she didn't know if that was A.M. or P.M. Stretching out on the backseat, she shrugged. What did it matter? She had been trapped in this metal box for days, her food supply consisting of a handful of cereal and crackers she'd managed to scrounge up. And to make matters worse, she was bored.

Bored, bored, bored.

This was even worse than end-of-summer-break boredom. At least during summer, she could call Emily and they could talk about how bored they were together. Megan sat up and pushed her backpack out of the way with her foot. The contents shifted, and her trig book slid out through the unzipped top. Megan reached for the book, flipping it open to a chapter on factoring polynomials. Ugh. She was so bored she was almost considering reading her math book to distract herself.

Megan stood up, hunching her shoulders so she wouldn't hit the ceiling of the SUV. She scolded herself for leaving the dome light on when she dozed off. She had no idea how long it would take to drain the battery, but she knew she had to make it last as long as possible. Nothing would be worse than being in here without any light.

"Yeah, except for being in here without any water," she mumbled to herself, unlocking the doors of the SUV with the button on the dashboard.

She still had three more cars to go through upstairs. After having her hopes dashed with the cell phone, she had just wanted to climb back into her mother's SUV and sleep off her disappointment. So she had.

Megan stepped out of the Pioneer, raising her arms above her head as she did. One thing was for sure, she had certainly had time to catch up on her sleep these past few days. Now she was rested and relaxed, but that just made the boredom all that much worse to bear. She felt more alert and energetic than she had in months, but had no outlet for this newfound well of strength. If she were stuck in here for another day, she'd start running laps around the cars just to give herself something to do.

She climbed the ladder to the second level and decided to start on the front car and work her way back. By the time she made it to the second-to-last car, her frustration with the situation was getting the better of her. She kicked the front tire of a new sedan and frowned as her big toe started to throb.

Wait a minute. She squinted up at the car ahead of her, the letters JMC in blue-and-white letters across one corner of the trunk. Her hand fell away from the door of the sedan and she walked around the back to see the same familiar blue-and-white JMC on this car. It occurred to her then that *all* of the cars in the container were JMCs, all used but fairly new, like her mother's. Most likely, all had been stolen, just like her mom's Pioneer.

Megan took a step away from the sedan. These cars were all stolen. And now, now they were probably on their way to someplace like Mexico or Cuba or something, somewhere where there was a market for stolen American cars. Probably some crazy rebel army wanted a fleet of vehicles to win some kind of war with a neighboring government. Hadn't she seen a movie a few months ago where rebels were driving Jeeps through the jungle, killing each other with machine guns and having giant snakes drop out of the trees on top of them?

Megan shivered and put her arms around her waist.

Even worse, hadn't a couple of American girls wandered out into the jungle despite some cute cop-type guy telling them it was dangerous? Yes, and the rebels caught them and sold them as slaves, only the one girl, the brunette one—the blonde girls were always the first to die in the movies—managed to escape and went back to find the cop guy to help her avenge her friend's murder.

Megan fought off a wave of panic that threatened to choke her.

She didn't want to be sold into slavery. She didn't want to get raped or hit across the face by some hard-hearted rebel guerrilla wearing camouflage and holding a machine gun. And most of all, she didn't want some giant man-eating snake dropping out of the skies onto her head.

In order to avoid getting captured, she was going to have to outsmart the rebels. But how?

Megan pushed her bangs out of her eyes with the back of one hand. Well, she didn't exactly know how she was going to escape. Now that she realized what sort of horror Silver Eyes and Shorty had planned for her, though, she knew she had more to worry about than what she was going to eat for the next few days. There wasn't going to be a rescue team waiting for her when this container was finally opened.

She was more likely to be facing a firing squad instead.

SEVENTEEN

CALDER stood in Raine's kitchen and watched a guy with a dark blue FBI windbreaker walk out the door carrying a computer hard drive. Wilkins and his team had actually done a pretty good job of being thorough without leaving behind the destruction Calder had seen at some search sites. He didn't know if the team was being courteous because Raine used to be one of them or if Wilkins had done it out of respect for him. Calder guessed it was the former.

As much as he wanted to cast Wilkins as the bad guy in this, what the other man had said earlier was true. Wilkins was just doing his job. Right now, Raine was their only lead in the Thompson killing, and they had to conduct a search to make sure they didn't find any more evidence linking her to the assassin.

Still, he wished he could spare her all this. He refused to admit that somewhere, way back in some dark place in his own mind, a small part of him was afraid that Wilkins's team might find what they were looking for. It was the same fear that had him holding his breath for months after Jeffrey Allen's murder. Whether this fear stemmed from the tiniest whisper of doubt about Raine's innocence or the worry that whoever was framing her had gotten smarter than last time and had done a better job of planting evidence for the authorities to find, he didn't know.

"Hey Shawn. Be careful with that, will you? That computer cost me nearly three grand." Calder heard Raine's footsteps in the hallway and scowled at the nonchalant way she greeted the agent who had confiscated her computer. Didn't she realize what could happen here? She could end up in prison; an ex-FBI agent surrounded by hundreds of hardened criminals who would like nothing more than the chance to get their revenge on the justice system. Calder rubbed a hand across his forehead. There was no way he could protect her if she went to prison.

"What are you doing here?" Raine asked, hefting two plastic grocery bags up onto the kitchen counter.

Calder was relieved to note that she was dressed casually today. No high-heeled, fuck-me-against-the-wall boots, see-through blouses, or short skirts. Instead, she was wearing worn blue jeans and an old T-shirt and tennis shoes without socks.

She grabbed two cans of soup from the first grocery bag and raised up on her tiptoes to place the cans on the top shelf of her pantry, and Bugs Bunny's feet appeared beneath the hem of her jeans. The feet disappeared when she had both heels planted firmly on the ground again.

"I, uh, came to make sure you were all right. I mean, the guys have searched your place pretty well, and I was afraid you might be, uh . . . traumatized or something."

Raine shot him a look from under her eyebrows that told him exactly what she thought of his noble gesture.

"Look, Calder, I can handle this without you. I've done it once before, remember? I was alone then, and I managed just fine. Although I guess you would have no way of knowing that, since you weren't around." She grabbed a twelve-pack of Coke and shoved it in the fridge with more force than was necessary.

Calder smiled wryly and clutched his chest. "Direct hit. Ouch."

Raine sighed then, her shoulders slumping as she closed

the refrigerator door and leaned against it, crossing her arms over her chest and turning to face him. "I don't want to fight with you. I don't want to *anything* with you. My apartment's been ransacked and the FBI has confiscated my computers—which are the way I make my living, I might add—and, lucky me, I'm going to have to spend the rest of the night cleaning up the mess. I don't have the energy for you right now. Why don't you just go away? Please."

Calder felt his own shoulders slumping as he watched her. He put a hand on his neck and rubbed his own tired muscles. In addition to his own heavy caseload, he had appointed himself the unofficial overseer of Wilkins's investigation of Raine, too.

"I can't do it," he admitted after a long pause where the only sound was the occasional clomping of heavy feet in the back of Raine's apartment. "I know all the reasons I should stay away but I just can't leave. Not again."

Raine closed her eyes. "Don't you get it, Calder? I want you to go."

"I know, but—"

Whatever he was going to say next was cut off when Wilkins stormed out of Raine's bedroom, a dark look on his face. He had several slips of paper in his left hand and a dark blue velvet bag in his right. "Did you know about these?" he snarled in Calder's direction.

Calder remained leaning against the counter but felt his stomach drop to his feet. "I don't know. What are the 'these' in question?" he asked mildly.

Wilkins held up the velvet bag. "This is a shitload of really expensive jewelry. And this"—he waved the pieces of paper in front of Calder's face—"*this* is a bunch of receipts from a local pawnshop. The last one is dated two weeks ago. And would you like to know how much it was for?"

Calder felt as if someone was squeezing his chest with a steel vise. His ribs ached with the effort it took him to speak. "Ten thousand dollars."

"Exactly!" Wilkins shouted, slamming the receipts down on the counter with disgust. "The exact amount of our assassin's fee to kill Thompson. In cold, hard cash."

Calder tried to ease a breath into his sore lungs. "I thought you never took any of the jewels your father stole," he said softly, turning to Raine.

Her green eyes regarded him coolly, impassively almost, across the small expanse of linoleum separating them. She looked away, and then back again, and Calder saw that he was mistaken. There was nothing at all impassive in her eyes. As a matter of fact, she looked positively murderous.

"That's right," she said, not even bothering to glance at Wilkins, who was nearly shaking with anger at Calder's side. Then she unwound her arms from around herself and pulled open the door of the fridge, taking out a chilled Coke and popping it open before she continued. "I never took anything from my father's estate. But I did inherit a few things from my mother when she died. Or didn't you consider that my socialite mama would have a small fortune of her own?"

With that, she winked at Wilkins, smiled coldly at Calder, and raised her soda in a mocking salute.

SOMETHING was wrong.

Hope looked up from the desk in her home office and felt somewhat comforted by the light burning in her father's bedroom. She could even see Randy's form silhouetted in the window as he took care of a few final tasks before he went next door to his own bedroom. At least nothing was wrong there.

No, it was something else. Something that she didn't quite understand yet. Something that had to do with the prank call she'd received earlier that day telling her that Randy had fallen, when in fact, he'd been home with her father the whole time. She'd come racing in, worried that her father might be hurt, only to find him lying in bed with Randy in the chair next to him, watching his favorite soap.

There were other things, too. Small, niggling things that disrupted the normal routine of her life. Hope narrowed her eyes. If she were into all that New Age crap, she might label it as a disruption of her aura, but all she really knew was that something didn't feel right and the very vagueness of it disturbed her.

Her laptop beeped and Hope shook her head in an attempt to shake off the sense of gloom that had descended upon her this evening. But when she looked back at her computer screen, her gloom only deepened. "Non-system disk or disk error," it read. She popped the black plastic disk out of her disk drive and turned it over. She didn't recall using a disk lately. Most of the files she worked with were too large to fit on a disk. She slid it back in the drive and scanned it, only to find that it was empty. She pulled the disk back out and slapped it down on the desk next to her.

"I don't have time for this," she muttered. And it was the truth. She had an operation in Miami to set up and she didn't have time to waste staring out the window, worrying about nameless, faceless goblins on blank computer disks.

As the light in her father's bedroom went out, she turned her attention back to her computer, where the query she had just run had delivered its results. She'd wanted to know how many new JMCs had been bought by residents of Miami in the past eighteen months. It had been awhile since she'd set up an operation in Miami, so she was delighted to find that the pool of available vehicles was much larger than she'd expected.

She opened her web browser and typed in the URL for the operation's website, then keyed in her username and password. Next, she clicked the tab labeled ADMIN and selected the ARCHIVE PREVIOUS RECORDS button. With the op in Boston completed with no complications, she figured it was safe to remove the records from the live site. When the team was assembled in Miami, she didn't want to have to worry about them having to slog through useless information to find their targets. Although, she had to admit that the website she'd built for the operation was pretty much foolproof. With the latest enhancements, her car theft ring was more efficient even than operations at the JMC plant itself.

Hope was unable to stifle a pleased smile at her own

handiwork. She loved technology and all that it could do for people who knew how to harness its power.

With another mouse click, she uploaded the information from her query onto the website. When her team was in the field, all they'd have to do is log onto the website, enter their current address, and wait for the system to return a list of potential targets. Since the website was directly linked with JMC's satellite tracking system, her team knew exactly where each vehicle was located and how long it had been at its current location.

Commercial parking lots were the first locations hit, and airports were a virtual gold mine. All those vehicles just sitting there unattended, ripe for the plucking. The easiest marks were the vehicles where the owners placed their parking tickets on their dashboards instead of taking the ticket with them. That just made it that much easier to drive out of the lot, and all it cost her team was the price tag on the parking ticket.

When the thief located the vehicle he wanted to steal, all he had to do was to select it from the list and click the UNLOCK button on the website. That sent a message to Sat-Trac that the owner of the vehicle had locked himself out of the car, so SatTrac sent a signal to the chip embedded in the car's computer to unlock the doors. Once safely inside, the thief clicked a second button to disable the tracking system. Then he'd use the VIN to find the vehicle's key from the set Hope would send prior to the operation. When the vehicle was parked in the garage that had been set up for the op, its license plates were stripped, registration replaced with a fake document, and the tracking system permanently destroyed following instructions from the one person who had been integral in designing the tracking system: the head of JMC's R&D department, Hope Enslar. Once the system had gone live, operations were transferred to a newly created department under another executive's control, but since Hope and her team were involved in any major overhauls to the SatTrac system, she was kept well aware of any changes that might impact her own side operation.

Finally, the vehicles were driven to the nearest shipping

port, put on cargo containers, and shipped to wherever demand was the greatest. The entire operation was running so much smoother now that it was fully computerized. She never could have envisioned it working this way when she'd set up the theft ring a decade ago. Back then, her business was conducted via fax and telephone and it could take up to a week to fulfill the backlog of orders. Now, with the same manpower, they could steal twice as many cars in just one night—and with a lot less risk.

Hope surfed back to the home page and ran several tests to make sure her data had uploaded without any problems. Then, because she was still feeling somewhat unnerved by the sense of foreboding she'd felt earlier, she tested her data again, just in case.

EIGHTEEN

"**AS** I told you the last three times you asked, I pawned some of my mother's jewelry to invest in assets for the company I've started with two of my former colleagues at the Bureau. Our accountant can verify this investment, as well as the purpose for which these funds were used. I believe the Sony desktop you have in your custody was purchased with some of the funds. The rest was used for website development, salaries, letterhead, and business cards, if I'm not mistaken. Starting up a business is expensive, as you might imagine." Raine calmly slid back in the uncomfortable chair Wilkins had waved her into two hours ago in the interrogation room of the Atlanta office of the FBI. She was all too familiar with the process of questioning a suspect and figured she'd be lucky to get out of here before tomorrow morning. Once again, she'd had to blow off meeting with her brother on the Enslar case. Only this time she'd had little choice in the matter, even though Wilkins had assured her that her cooperation in his investigation was purely voluntary at this point.

Right. She knew if she didn't cooperate, he'd get a warrant for her arrest. And spending the night in jail would be far worse than being stuck in this sterile interrogation room for hours, so she was doing her best to stay calm while she answered the same questions over and over again.

"And what about the e-mail from you to Thompson's assassin, detailing the payment terms and where you two were going to meet?"

"Were you able to recover Rob's computer? If so, did you open the e-mail and check the Internet headers on it? You keep insisting that the message came from me, but does the IP address match with any of the computers you found in my apartment?"

Wilkins slammed his hands down on the table in front of Raine, making both her and her Coke jump. "I don't know what you're talking about."

Raine narrowed her eyes and leaned forward. "Well, a jury will have it explained to them by the expert witness my defense attorney hires, so you'd better learn real fast. It's incredibly easy for spammers and hackers to send e-mail messages that appear to be from someone you know, but which contain a virus or spam or even just a bogus message like the one someone sent to that assassin that was supposedly from me."

"I don't believe that it could be that easy. If it were, why don't more people manipulate the system?"

"Because most people wouldn't have any reason to do so, that's why."

"That can't—"

Wilkins was interrupted when a large man with the darkest skin Raine had ever seen opened the door to the interrogation room and asked the agent for a moment of his time. Raine watched him leave, biting her lower lip as the door swung closed behind him. She refused to glance over at the wall of mirrors, knowing that she was being observed. Briefly, she wondered if Calder was there, then told herself she shouldn't care. She'd meant what she'd said last night. If she were the reason his career suffered, neither of them could move past it. Last year, before all hell had broken loose, he had taken her to meet his family. Women were noticeably absent from the

Preston household—probably because the Preston men hadn't met enough female law enforcement officers to round out their group of cops.

Calder's grandfather, father, and brothers were all police officers of one sort or another. She remembered raising her eyebrows and remarking to Calder's father how proud he must be of his boys as introductions were made. She was only being the tiniest bit facetious when she'd said it.

Not that being in law enforcement was a bad thing. It was just odd to her that it seemed to be the only acceptable form of employment for the Preston brood.

But seeing how deep-rooted that "to serve and protect" mentality was in Calder's family had made her realize that his need to be a lawman ran far deeper than any feelings he could ever have for her. It was simply too important to him, to his family, and to his own sense of self-worth. She would never make him choose between her or his career in large part because she knew which one had to win for him to stay sane.

"Okay, what is this, some kind of joke?" Wilkins slammed back into the room, and even though Raine had been expecting his ire, her head still jerked around with surprise.

She schooled her features into the best impassive mask she could manage. "I have no idea what—"

"Cut the act," Wilkins said, moving toward her menacingly. He tossed a handful of papers down on the table in front of her, put his fists on the table, and fixed her with an angry glare. "How were you able to send e-mails to my boss that look like they're from me?"

"I told you, it's easy for someone with good computer skills to send mail that looks like it's from somebody else. I had the feeling that you wouldn't believe me, so I had to prove it. This seemed like the most effective way."

Wilkins snorted and waved a hand at the pile of papers he'd thrown on the table. "You sent pictures of me having sex with barnyard animals. That's not funny."

Raine coughed to cover a laugh. Well, *she* thought it was funny. "I'm sorry," she said, trying to sound apologetic but not quite succeeding.

"Sure you are." Wilkins gathered up the e-mails, glanced

at them, and then threw them in the wastebasket under the table with a disgusted shake of his head. "All right. So I'll concede that hijacking someone's e-mail address may not be as difficult as I previously believed. And you can bet that I'll be contacting your accountant for a full report on your cash flow. But what I still don't get is that if someone else sent that message to Thompson, how the hell could he be so sure that you'd be at Chasey's that night?"

Raine absently toyed with the hem of her T-shirt. "I can't help you there. Maybe one of my e-mails to my business partners was intercepted. Or someone managed to hack into one of our electronic calendars. I just don't know. It's not like we were guarding the information aside from using an ordinary firewall."

"Mmm," was Wilkins's only reply.

Raine folded her arms across the top of the table, shivering in the cold room. "Look, I did not hire a hit on Grady Thompson. I had no access to his file after I left the Bureau. How could I have known the time and date he was going to be arrested?"

Wilkins pulled out the chair across from her and sat down, leaning back and crossing his ankle over his knee as if he had nothing better to do than spend all afternoon chatting with her. "See, that's the thing," he said, steepling his fingers together at chest level. "Besides coming to drop off those delightfully detailed e-mails about my heretofore undisclosed poultry fetish, my boss also wanted to let me in on a little secret of yours. Would you like to know what it is?"

Raine grimaced and shivered again, wishing she had thought to grab a sweatshirt before letting Wilkins drag her down to the FBI offices to undergo yet another round of "voluntary" questioning. "I'm not sure I do."

"Well, I'll tell you anyway." Wilkins regarded her calmly over the tips of his fingers. "Our technicians found a copy of Thompson's file on one of the computers we took from your apartment. So, it appears that you're not quite as uninformed as you might like me to believe."

* * *

"THE massive manhunt for fifteen-year-old Megan Mulroney wound down today as the obviously emotional officer in charge of the hunt, Lieutenant Kevin O'Reilly, said the Boston Police Department could no longer justify the amount of manpower that had previously been dedicated to the search. However, Lieutenant O'Reilly assured the girl's parents that he, personally, would not rest until the case was solved.

"Ms. Mulroney has been missing since last Thursday, when both the teen and the JMC Pioneer her mother had parked outside a local grocery store disappeared."

At Norman Enslar's bedside, Randy looked up to check on whether his patient was still awake. It seemed that lately more and more, Norman was prone to drifting off while Randy read to him. And there was just no use trying to entertain a sleeping man, so he'd rather save the newspaper for when Norman was awake.

Randy did his best to keep Norman's mind occupied when he was there. He had no way of knowing how Norman felt about being trapped inside a useless body, but he knew how *he* would feel. He would feel like swallowing the entire bottle of Valium on the nightstand and washing it down with a bottle of Scotch. If that didn't kill him, he'd find some other way. Still, he respected Norman's refusal to give up and wondered how much of his strength came from his daughter. Being childless himself, Randy couldn't imagine how difficult it must have been for Norman to watch Hope grow up without being able to participate in her life.

Randy hoped the small things he did helped to make Norman's life more bearable.

When he looked up from the paper, he expected to see Norman's eyes closed or, if not, to see the other man blinking up at the ceiling like usual. Instead, Norman was crying. But instead of looking sad, he looked . . . frustrated, angry almost.

Randy dropped the paper and leaped up out of his chair to find something to wipe Norman's eyes. "What's wrong?" he asked, becoming more alarmed when Norman's body started jerking uncontrollably under the covers. "Norman, are you all right? Are you having a seizure?"

Randy knew that Norman couldn't tell him what was

wrong, of course, but he still found himself reflexively talking to the older man. He reached for the blood pressure cuff in the top drawer of Norman's nightstand while muttering soothing platitudes about how everything was going to be just fine. Norman's body had stopped jerking, but he was still crying.

"Your blood pressure is normal." Randy slipped the cuff off of Norman's arm and shined a light into his eyes to check his pupils. Nothing seemed wrong there, either. Debating whether or not he should call 911, Randy stood back and frowned. If something was wrong internally, there was no way Randy would be able to tell. Up until just a moment ago, however, everything had seemed just fine. It was almost as if Norman was having a temper tantrum, not a seizure.

He wasn't going to chance making the wrong decision. Instead, he picked up the phone beside Norman's bed and dialed Hope Enslar's office number. She answered on the first ring, sounding panicked.

"Randy, what is it?"

Randy figured she must have caller ID to know it was him even before he said a word. "Ms. Enslar, it's your dad." *Well, duh, why else would he be calling?* Randy thought, rolling his eyes at himself. "I mean, of course it's your dad. He just had a strange . . . um, episode, I guess you could call it. He seems fine now. I checked his vital signs and everything is normal. I just wasn't sure if you wanted me to call for an ambulance. I don't think that's necessary, but I don't want to make that call without talking it over with you."

He could hear Hope's displeased frown even through the phone lines and he knew, after yesterday's prank call and now this, that she must be more than a little frustrated. After all, she had an important job, not one she could just keep walking away from every afternoon. Still, her reply was polite, if a bit on the chilly side. "You're sure you've checked everything? His colostomy bag isn't clogged or anything?"

Randy double-checked the line just in case. "No, it's fine. His BP is in the normal range, his pupils are reactive, and his temperature is a perfect 98.6. I don't know what else could be wrong."

"Okay. I'm coming home. It'll just take me a few minutes to reschedule the conference call I had for this afternoon. I should be there within the next twenty minutes. Call me on my cell if anything changes."

"Will do. I'm sorry to have to bother you, Ms. Enslar," Randy said, knowing this wasn't his fault but feeling guilty anyway.

"No, I'm sorry, Randy. You were right to call me and I appreciate it. I don't know what my father—or I—would do without you."

Randy was so surprised by the unexpected praise that he just mumbled a garbled "thanks" before hanging up. The warm glow that settled in his chest lasted until he heard Hope's key in the front door. Heck, he thought, it was probably going to last all night. Amazing what effect a few kind words could have on a person.

Hope came into the room and sent a distracted "hello" his way as she made a beeline for her father's side. Gently, she brushed away a lock of hair that had fallen across her father's forehead.

"Are you okay, Daddy?" she whispered, turning his wrist around so she could check his pulse. His arm jerked when she touched him, making Hope frown with worry. She watched as his eyes cast wildly about the room, then came to a stop near where Randy was standing. He stared fixedly at Randy's feet. Hope glanced over at Randy. Was he the problem? Had he been abusing her father all along? Was that why her father was so upset?

Randy reached down to pick up the newspaper that had fallen on the floor and folded it neatly before putting it on the table next to his chair. Hope saw her father's eyes flutter, following Randy's every move.

Oh, God. That was it. This is what she got for not watching the security tapes, for trusting Randy so implicitly with the care of her father.

Hope tried to keep her breathing calm and even while she turned to Randy. "Would you leave my father and I alone now? I think maybe he just needs some quiet time. I'll make sure he gets his dinner if you'd like to take the night off."

Randy blinked several times before responding. "Have I done something wrong here?" he asked. "Because it sounds like you're dismissing me."

Just in case her hunch about Randy was wrong, Hope didn't want to alienate the man who had seemingly provided such good care for her father for several years. "No, you haven't done anything wrong. I just figured that since I'm here, and since I'm going to be too worried about my father to leave him tonight, you might as well take advantage of the opportunity and get some free time for yourself. But you're certainly welcome to stay here, of course."

Randy watched her for several long seconds before taking a step back toward the door. "All right," he said. "I think I'll drive out to Fayetteville and visit my brother. I haven't seen him in ages."

Hope nodded and reached across the bed to grab the thermometer Randy had left on top of the covers. Randy's next words made her pause in what she was doing.

"But if you do decide to fire me, I hope you would at least do the courtesy of doing so to my face. I think after all these years of taking care of your father, you owe me that."

Hope turned the thermometer over and checked the temperature, lightly tapping it on her palm. By the time she turned to answer, Randy had already left. She waited until she heard the garage door opening before making her way downstairs, her keys nestled in her palm. She walked down the hall and through the elegant gourmet kitchen that had never been used to make anything more complicated than a protein milkshake, and stopped in front of a door that was always kept locked.

She selected a gold-colored key from her keychain and put it in the lock. The door swung open easily and a wave of chill air wafted out to greet her. With a shiver, Hope stepped into the small room that she'd paid to have equipped with all the latest monitoring equipment. With a few taps of the mouse, she was watching herself come into her father's bedroom on the screen in front of her. She clicked the button to make the footage jump back in time, figuring she'd start an hour before Randy had called and then go back further if necessary.

Hoping she wasn't going to be forced to watch Randy abusing her father in some way, Hope seated herself in the chair in front of the computer monitor and watched an afternoon in her father's life go by.

After fifteen minutes, she had an even greater appreciation for Randy than before. God, this was dull. Her father lying helpless and unmoving in his bed. Randy giving him some water. Randy pointing to the TV set, watching her father's face, presumably searching for some interest on the older man's part. Randy sitting down, picking up the newspaper and reading.

And then, all of a sudden, her father was jerking violently in his bed.

Randy threw down the paper as he reacted to the emergency thoroughly and professionally. Randy wiped her father's eyes, looked at the telephone, obviously not sure what to do next. He called her at her office and then sat down next to Dad on the bed, checking his pulse for the third time, worry and concern evident in everything he did.

Hope backed up the footage and watched it again. And again.

She found no clue as to what had set her father off. Randy had done nothing besides read a newspaper to an invalid.

Wearily, Hope rested her chin on her hand. The only thing that was clear to her right now was that Randy deserved a raise for the care he was providing her father. Other than that, she didn't—

Wait a minute.

Hope played the footage again, in slow motion this time, leaning forward so that her nose was almost touching the computer screen and studying her father's face intently. When Randy had started reading the paper, her father's demeanor was completely relaxed. His shoulders were back against the bed, his eyes half-closed. Hope stopped the action on the next frame. Her father's shoulders had jerked off the bed, his neck tense and his legs stiff.

Maybe it wasn't something Randy had done to her father that had upset him; perhaps it was something Randy had read to him, instead. She replayed the tape, turning up the sound and listening to Randy reading the story about that missing girl in Boston. But why would that upset her father?

Maybe it was something on the back page of the paper that her father had seen while Randy was reading the front page. She'd have to go look at it herself to see.

Hope returned the monitoring system to its normal operation and backed out of the room, closing and locking the door behind her before she headed upstairs. She was relieved to find her father asleep when she returned to his room. She almost never left him alone but she didn't want to risk upsetting him again if he saw her reading the paper, so she quietly snagged the paper from the table and headed into the next room to see what could have possibly set him off.

She scoured the back page, looking for anything that might have bothered her father—maybe another car accident like the one he'd been in so long ago—but there was nothing that reasonably could have set him off. Maybe there was something in that story Randy was reading after all. Hope flipped the front section of the paper over. Tiny lines furrowed across her forehead when she read the story about the missing girl in Boston.

"The poor thing," Hope murmured, imagining how awful it must be for the teen's parents to have lost their daughter.

She started the second paragraph and had to read the sentence twice because her eyes had become fixed on the make of the Mulroney's car. Hope's heart took off like a rabbit knowing it's been spied by a nearby hawk. She counted backward, trying to remember the exact date of the Boston operation.

Her hands went cold as she was gripped by a sudden sense of dread.

Hope closed her eyes. "Please, God. Let it be a coincidence," she prayed, whispering the words.

Setting the paper beside her on the couch in the upstairs sitting room, Hope tried rubbing some warmth into her hands. Her team couldn't be involved in the disappearance of the missing teen, could they? She wasn't as confident as she once might have been, since she'd long been removed from the non-management-related duties of the organization she had started so many years ago. They were still a small group—less than twenty, including the (mostly) guys who actually stole the vehicles—but Hope had little or no contact with all but her ops manager, a frighteningly efficient man named Victor Kincaid. Before she raised her concerns with Victor, she'd do a little research of her own.

Tiptoeing past her father's room, Hope silently made her way downstairs and out of the house. She ran toward her own driveway where her car was parked. She'd been in such a hurry to get to her father's side that she'd left her laptop in the front seat, never once worrying that someone might come by and steal it. Her little neighborhood was pretty much crime free.

Hope shouldered her laptop bag and headed back to her father's house. It only took a few minutes for her to get hooked into JMC's network, and Hope was glad that she'd paid extra to have her father's home wired for the latest technology, even though she knew he'd never be able to use it.

She logged into the sales system and, leaning over to look at the newspaper article so she spelled the name right, typed the Mulroneys' name into her computer. It took a few minutes for the system to spit out the information she needed, and Hope used the time to read the rest of the article about the missing teen. Finally, the sales information showed up on her screen, and Hope wrote down the VINs of the two Pioneers sold to the Mulroneys in Boston before closing out of the sales system.

"We love repeat customers," she muttered.

Next, she clicked on her web browser, frowning at the relative slowness of her laptop today. She'd noticed it earlier but hadn't given it much thought.

She didn't have time to think about it now, either.

After Hope pulled up the website for the theft ring, she clicked the button that would allow her to search archived records. When a box popped up asking for the VIN to search for, Hope typed in the first number she'd retrieved from the sales system. She hit ENTER and waited, silently praying for the machine to respond with a NO RECORDS FOUND message.

Her prayer was not answered.

She didn't have to bother entering the second VIN. She clicked the link that had appeared on her screen and the details of the theft—details such as the time the Pioneer arrived at the garage for stripping and the exact moment it was driven into the cargo container that would take the vehicle to its new owner—appeared. Hope opened the spreadsheet where she had tracked the resale information for that particular shipment and searched for the Pioneer's VIN.

Venezuela. That's where the SUV was headed.

But what in the world had happened to that poor girl who had, through some sick twist of fate, been in the right place at the wrong time? Hope wondered as she stared at her computer screen with growing horror.

NINETEEN

MEGAN hit the jackpot on the last car.

When she'd first started searching the vehicles, she had tried to find out who owned the vehicles. She didn't know why, but it seemed that she owed that much, at least, to the people who had ridden, eaten, fought, or had sex in them. It turned out, though, that the information in the cars was bogus. At least it was with her mother's Pioneer, who had a registration and expired insurance cards under a fake name in the glove compartment.

She supposed that made sense. The thieves wouldn't want to take the chance that maybe they'd get stopped by the police, who might run a check and discover the car had been reported missing. She didn't know why they hadn't totally stripped the cars of everything, but she was glad they hadn't. The books she'd found in the sedan behind her mother's SUV had alleviated a little of her boredom, although, aside from a handful of paperback novels, they were mostly bed-time stories for a two-year-old. And at least the meager stash of leftover food she'd managed to accumulate was better than nothing.

Megan's stomach growled at the thought of food. She'd finished off her last Pop-tart and all the Cheez-Its that had fallen behind the baby's car seat. What she wouldn't give for a box of mac' and cheese right now. Megan swallowed.

"Stop thinking about food," she ordered herself sternly, opening the front door of the sporty convertible on the second floor that she hadn't yet searched. She slid into the leather driver's seat and couldn't stop the "ooh" that came from the depths of her I-get-to-drive-next-year-and-I-want-a-cool-car-like-this soul.

What was it about sports cars that made you instinctively put your hands on the steering wheel and start making *vroom-vroom* noises in your head? Megan wondered as she did just that. Next, she laid her arm on the top of the door and pretended to give an I'm-too-cool-to-even-bother-looking-at-you-in-your-minivan look at an imaginary car. Man, she wished she could drive this baby.

Megan sighed. There was no way her parents would ever buy her a car like this. She wasn't even sure they were going to buy her one at all. She'd been dropping hints since the day after her last birthday, but so far they hadn't said a thing besides, "We'll see." Even if they did get her a car, she knew it would be something that was—number one, safe; and number two, practical. Ick. Safe and practical. The two most hated words in the teenage vocabulary. Well, except for maybe *homework* and *chores*. Those two were pretty bad, too.

Longingly, she ran a hand across the leather seat one last time. Then she pulled the lever to open the trunk, got out of the car, and looked into the miniscule backseat to see if the owner—she'd decided to call him Antonio after the cute senior who had been born in Spain but moved next door at the end of last year when his parents got divorced and his American mother moved back home—had left her anything to eat back there. Unfortunately, he hadn't.

Megan put a hand to her stomach to stop it from growling and looked dubiously at the miniscule trunk.

"Not likely that Antonio has groceries for four back there," she said, rounding the end of the car. Figuring she'd never know if she didn't look, Megan crossed her fingers and lifted up the lid of the trunk.

She hit the jackpot.

Antonio must have been planning one heck of a party, because his trunk was crammed full of grocery bags.

"Yes. Yes. Yes, yes, yes," Megan sang, punching her fist in the air and jumping up and down with glee. Then she bent down and hugged the bags. When she stood up straight again, she discovered that she was crying. Turning away from the groceries, Megan wrapped her arms around herself and leaned against the bumper of the convertible, sobbing with relief.

She hadn't realized until that moment how truly spoiled she was. Whenever she was hungry, she could find something to eat. Her mom bought snacks and made sure to keep Megan's backpack full of goodies in case she got hungry before crew or between classes at school. Either Mom or Dad would make dinner every night. The freezer was stocked with all her favorites—Eggo waffles, hash browns, ice cream. And she always had money in her pocket, just in case.

Megan hiccupped, thinking of those commercials about starving children that she and Emily had made jokes about when they'd come on the TV. Those kids were really starving, and here she was, crying because she hadn't had a real meal in a few days.

Megan wiped her eyes. When she got back home, she was going to start sending half of her allowance to those poor kids. Nobody should ever have to go to bed hungry.

With that resolved, Megan decided to haul the groceries down to her mother's SUV since she had come to think of the SUV as her base camp. She planned to take her time going through each grocery bag, in large part because it would help alleviate her boredom for a while. She still needed a plan for what to do when the cars were delivered to the Mexican rebels. She'd already decided they were headed to Mexico, mostly because she didn't know enough about any other foreign countries to pick an alternative. But that could wait.

She had a meal to eat first.

* * *

CALDER refused to admit that he was working late in order to be in the office when Wilkins was through interrogating Raine. Instead, he blamed his heavy workload—a legitimate excuse since there were always more crimes to be solved than there were agents to solve them—for his still being at his desk at nine that night when a call was patched through to his office.

He answered the phone with a terse, "Preston," his mind still occupied with the case he was researching.

The man on the other end of the line introduced himself as Lee Henderson, the police chief of a small town up in northwestern North Carolina. "We've got ourselves a child abduction case and we sure could use a bit of federal help," he said, sounding calm and unhurried in the manner of a true Southerner.

Calder flipped the notebook on his desk to a clean page. "We'll give you whatever you need. Can you fill me in on the details?"

"Sure can. I got a call from a judge here in town a couple hours ago. Seems his little girl told him she was spending the night at a friend's house, but when the judge called over to check on her, the friend had no idea what he was talking about."

"How old is the girl? What's her name?"

"She's almost thirteen, but looks about twenty. Her daddy says she's going through some sort of phase where she's wearin' a faceful of makeup and talkin' back and dressin' like a . . . well, you know what I mean."

Calder grunted. Yeah, he knew all too well what Henderson meant.

"Girl's name is Brittany Monroe. Father is Judge Thomas Monroe, who works over in Asheville. The judge is a single father. Lost his pretty young wife to cancer about three years back."

"Poor bastard," Calder muttered.

"Yeah. Seems Judge Monroe is having a bit of a hard

time raising his kids on his own. Brittany is the oldest of his three girls and he said she's been givin' him fits since last September."

"So, my question is, what happened in September?"

"Now, see, that was my first question, too," Henderson said, sounding pleased with himself. "Seems the judge remembered right clearly the day little Brittany changed. He said the girls had been limpin' along okay since their mother died. Things could have been better, but they could have been worse, too."

Calder tapped his pen on the edge of his desk, trying to curb his impatience at the molasses-dripping-from-a-spoon pace of this tale.

"So it's Labor Day weekend and the judge has a little more time off work than usual. He'd been leaving the girls home alone while he worked last summer, figuring at twelve, ten, and nine, they were old enough to stay out of trouble. He assumed they all hung out together and kept an eye on each other while he was gone, but being home for four days, he realized that his assumption was not correct. Seems Miss Brittany was spending an awful lot of time down the road with a neighbor who had moved into town 'bout a year back."

Calder rubbed his forehead and shook his head. "Let me guess. This neighbor was a man, probably about the same age as the judge, had a good rapport with all the neighborhood kids. Nicest guy on the block. Always happy to look after people's children if they had to run out for a spell."

"Bull's-eye. All except the age part. Our guy is younger—about twenty-four. When he moved into the neighborhood, he told everyone he had come from Atlanta, was recently divorced, and had kids of his own that he missed something fierce."

"So nobody would suspect his interest in their children."

"Most likely."

Calder closed his eyes. He didn't even need to hear the rest of the story to know what had changed in young Brittany's life last summer. Child molestation by a family member or friend was all too common a tale in Calder's line of work. The guy had probably managed to keep Brittany quiet by either threatening to hurt her little sisters if she told, or by convincing her that her entire family hated her and that he was the only one who really loved her.

"So, let me guess. Judge Monroe realizes his daughter's spending way too much time alone with a man twice her age and he starts to get suspicious. He tells Brittany that she is no longer allowed to go down the street on her unsupervised visits, and Brittany rebels."

"You got it," Henderson agreed. "Fast forward to now. The judge catches Brittany in a lie and suspects that she's been sneaking off to the neighbor's house all this time. He goes down the street to retrieve his daughter and have it out with the neighbor, but the house is empty. The guy's car is gone and the judge realizes it's even worse than he suspected."

"So he calls you to find his daughter and catch this bastard."

"Yep. Which I do, only I'm probably thirty minutes too late. That's where you come in."

Ah, Calder thought, the point at last.

"Brittany's abductor, John Moss, bought two one-way tickets to Miami on Greyhound. From there, I assume he'll take off for Mexico or the Caribbean."

"Shit," Calder cursed, rubbing his forehead again. "If he makes it out of the States, we'll probably never see Brittany again."

"Well, the bus we're pretty sure they're on makes a stop in Atlanta. I'm on my way there right now, but I'm afraid I might be too late. I was hoping you could round up a few of your colleagues, head on down to the bus station, and take a look around for me."

"You got it," Calder said, scribbling down the names and numbers of the agents he'd call in on his way to the bus station. "How about pictures? You got anything on Brittany or Moss you can send?"

"I'll have my assistant e-mail copies to you right now. Should be to you in less than a minute. Thanks for your help. I owe you one."

"Always happy to assist, especially since you've already

done all the legwork," Calder said after exchanging cell numbers with Henderson. "I'll be at the station in fifteen or twenty minutes with three of my best agents. We're gonna nail this bastard."

"Hoo-yah," Lee Henderson responded, leading Calder to believe that the small-town cop might have done a stint in the military. Then Henderson hung up, leaving Calder to wait impatiently for the pictures to appear in his inbox. He used the time to call the two men and one woman he'd picked as his takedown team. His explanation of the situation was much less detailed than Henderson's—a one-sentence directive to meet him outside the downtown Greyhound station to arrest a child abductor. That was all his team needed.

Calder printed copies of the pictures as soon as he received the e-mail from Henderson's assistant and, grabbing them off the copier, he ran out of his office and out into the night.

This was one case the bad guys were not going to win.

HOPE turned right onto Jonesboro Road, looking at the directions she'd printed off from Mapquest to determine her next move. Left at Constitution.

She had picked someplace neutral to meet Victor Kincaid, the man who had run the operation in Boston last week. The coffee shop out near Turner Field was central to them both and had the added advantage of being a place Hope would never frequent in her daily life. There would be no risk that anyone would recognize her.

Hope put a hand to her chest, as if that would slow her racing heart.

She had to know what had happened in Boston and she didn't want to chance talking about it over the phone. She knew she was being paranoid, but lately there had just been too many disruptions in her normally dull, routine life for her not to be suspicious.

With a frown, Hope took the next turn, slowing her car on the nearly deserted street. What if . . . what if these so-called disruptions were related? Hope's eyes narrowed in the darkness as she pulled her car over to the curb in front of the poorly lit diner. That prank call about her father. The IT person she'd found in her office yesterday. The blank disk in her disk drive. The team of security people who had been sniffing around the plant that night she'd been unable to sleep and had gone to the office to get some research materials she needed. Four surprising events in a life that was normally predictable. Two out of the four events had even come with plausible explanations. But what if those plausible explanations were lies? What if they were just cover stories to make her less suspicious? What if she were being watched? What if—as she had done with her father's nurses—someone had planted surveillance equipment in her office? But how would anyone know about her involvement with the car theft ring in the first place? Maybe someone on the ops team had alerted the cops? But why? They were all paid very well for what they did. And who did they really hurt? Nameless, faceless insurance companies were the only ones who really suffered from the losses. And even they were able to pad their rates to recoup the lost cash. So, yes, consumers paid a tiny bit more in their insurance premiums to fund it, but surely that wasn't the type of moral dilemma that would send a wealthy member of the team to the police, was it?

Hope crossed her arms over her steering wheel and laid her head down. God, she was scared. Maybe it was time for her to hand this whole thing over to someone else.

Her revenge against JMC had never brought her the sense of satisfaction she was seeking. Not really. Her father was still a helpless invalid. She had still lost her youth at seventeen. Revenge hadn't changed any of that. Yes, it had made her rich, but, if she were being honest with herself, she had to admit that her salary and stock options at JMC alone would have done that.

She knew it was foolish, but she had never contemplated what she would do if she got caught. The operation had run too smoothly for too long, and she had become complacent. Now, faced with the fear that she had been found out, Hope couldn't stop shivering. What would her father do without her? What would she do without him, without the safe little life she had built around herself all these years?

Hope gasped and grabbed the steering wheel when a knock sounded on the passenger-side window. She looked up into a pair of nearly colorless eyes.

"Oh, it's you," she said, rolling down the window. "Look, I'm a little freaked out and I'm really not in the mood to eat. Do you mind if we drive around for awhile instead?"

"Not at all," Victor said smoothly, opening the door when Hope clicked the button to unlock it.

Hope pulled away from the curb, watching in her rearview mirror to make sure she wasn't being followed. This whole thing was making her paranoid.

They drove in silence for a few minutes as Hope tried to get her bearings since she wasn't all that familiar with this part of town and didn't want to chance ending up in a part of town where a shiny new luxury car was sure to be noticed.

"So," she said after a while, breaking the silence, "it's been a long time since we've talked in person. How did things go in Boston?"

Victor slid a sidelong glance at her but didn't seem surprised that she was asking about their last operation. "We handled things. We always do."

"What does that mean, you 'handled' things? What things did you have to handle?"

"Why don't you ask the question you really want to ask?" Victor countered, his voice as cool and calm as if they were talking about the weather.

"What about that girl?" Hope whispered, wanting more than anything for Victor's answer to be, *What girl?*

"We handled it. I don't think you really want to know the details."

Hope closed her eyes for a long moment, not caring that she was careening down the road, unable to see. She'd known it, of course. From the minute she'd seen the match come up on her computer earlier, she'd known that the missing teen was connected to the car theft ring's operation. But still, she'd hoped for a miracle. She didn't quite know what she'd thought Victor was going to say that would explain the girl's disappearance. Maybe, "Yes, we accidentally abducted her in her mother's car and we locked her in a basement with plenty of food and water. We were just waiting a while to call and tip off the cops."

Right.

She looked over at Victor, who was watching her with his flat, lifeless eyes.

Hope felt every hair on her body tingle and licked her suddenly dry lips. "What—" Her voice cracked, so she stopped, and then began again. "What did you do with her? I need to know."

Victor laughed a humorless laugh. "We didn't kill her, if that's what you're asking."

Startled, Hope turned to look at him. "You didn't? Oh, thank God."

"Brakes," Victor commanded.

Hope instinctively obeyed, turning her attention back to the road just in time to avoid rear-ending the car in front of them. She let out a relieved sigh, then laughed, shaking her head. "I was so worried that . . . Well, never mind. So where is she then?"

Victor seemed amused by her reaction but Hope didn't care. So what if he had been making fun of her, trying to get her to believe the teen was dead because of them? As long as the girl was okay, Victor could mock her as much as he wanted.

"We didn't kill her, but she most likely won't survive the trip."

It took several seconds for Hope to understand what Victor was saying. When she did, all traces of relief drained out of her body. "What do you mean? What trip?"

Victor's gaze was steady on Hope's profile as she clutched the steering wheel and stared straight ahead. "The trip to Venezuela in the back of her mother's SUV," he answered. "And even if she does manage to survive the boat ride, I doubt she'll be up for the drug runners, crocodiles, spiders, and snakes she'll have to face when she gets released into the jungle."

"No," Hope breathed.

"Look," Victor was beginning to sound annoyed at her line of questioning, "what we do out there on those ops can get dangerous. We all know it. Well, maybe everyone but you knows it," he amended. "You sit in your pristine office upgrading our website or cutting paychecks, with no understanding of the potential danger involved."

"I understand the danger. It's just . . . it's just that we've never faced this before."

Victor's voice became more gentle. "Yes, we've been very fortunate. But when something like this happens, you find yourself having to make some tough decisions. I can honestly say that I regret having to do what I did with that girl. The bottom line, though, was that it was either her or me, and I haven't survived this long without a strong sense of self-preservation. I did what had to be done."

Hope thought about that for a long moment. Would she have done the same thing in Victor's place?

If she were faced with going to jail and losing everything she had worked so hard for over the years, could she have slammed the door on another person's life?

Probably.

Hope shuddered with the implication of that truth. What an awful thing to know about oneself.

But now that she recognized that about herself, she knew what her next step had to be. She looked briefly at the ruthless man in the seat next to her before turning her eyes back to the road. "I think someone may be on to us," she said, before detailing the suspicious events that had her looking over her shoulder this evening.

"All right," Victor said after a short silence. "Let's start with the first event. You say you interrupted three people who told the gate guard they were in your department and then told you that they were with a security firm. Did you happen to get the name of the firm?"

Hope started nodding even before Victor finished. She reached behind her seat with one arm and pulled her purse onto her lap. "Yes, I still have the business card from the woman who did most of the talking." She fished around for a moment, then pulled the card from a pocket of her purse. "Her story checked out with the head of security, but I still thought it was odd. I mean, why say they were from my department? Why not engineering or IT or something? Unless they needed access to R&D . . ." Her voice trailed off.

Victor glanced at the card before pocketing it. "I'll check it out. But let's make one thing clear first."

Hope turned to look at him as the silence lengthened. "What's that?" she asked finally.

"If there's anything suspicious about this Raine Robey . . ."

"Yes?" Hope said, holding her breath.

"It's either her or you. You're going to have to tell me which one you choose."

Suddenly cold, Hope reached out to inch the heater on. Warm air instantly breathed over her feet and Hope felt goosebumps rise on her arms. She turned the car back down the street where the diner was located and stopped when she had come full-circle.

"I choose me," she said quietly, unable to meet her own eyes in the rearview mirror. "I choose me."

TWENTY

"SO, have you finally come to the conclusion that you don't have enough evidence to convict me?" Raine asked as Jim Wilkins reentered the interrogation room.

"No. I think that with the evidence we have, it would be fairly easy to railroad you into prison." Wilkins leaned against the wall of the room near the door, crossing his arms across his chest and eyeing her impassively.

Raine quashed the first flutterings of fear in her gut. Wilkins was right. They had enough evidence, circumstantial as it may be, to arrest her for arranging the hit on Grady Thompson. She might have been able to explain the jewelry she'd pawned a few weeks before the assassination and the bogus e-mail that she had supposedly sent, but even she didn't have an excuse for why Thompson's file was on her computer. She had no idea how it had gotten there. As someone who held herself out as an expert in network security, it was unlikely a jury would believe her system had been breached. Even she didn't believe that. She had all the safeguards in place: a first-class firewall, continual virus scans, e-mail filters. There was no way a hacker had broken into her system and installed that file on her hard drive. That meant that either someone in the Bureau was gunning for her and had planted the evidence on her computer or . . . . hell, she didn't know what the alternative was.

All she knew was that she had not cracked the FBI's computers to get a copy of the Thompson file. But all a jury would need to hear was that she *could* have.

"I didn't do it," she said quietly, the words echoing in the bare room with its dull gray walls.

Wilkins watched her for a few more seconds. Then he unfurled his arms and pushed himself away from the wall. "I believe you. That's why I'm releasing you. Go home and get some sleep."

With that, Wilkins opened the door and waited while his words penetrated the fog of Raine's exhausted brain. She had been in the interrogation room with no breaks aside from the occasional short trip to the ladies' room for the past thirteen hours. She'd been questioned by no less than four FBI agents, all asking the same questions over and over again—a repeat of the nightmare she had suffered through eleven months ago, complete with watching the man she loved walk out of her life for a second time.

Raine slowly stood up and walked to the door, half-expecting Wilkins to slam it in her face and yell "Gotcha" from the other side.

Raine's eyes narrowed. Gotcha. Wasn't that e-mail address the same as the one used by whoever had sent her that awful time bomb message? That entire incident had slipped her mind with everything else that had been going on. She knew it was probably futile, but maybe the Bureau could run a trace on the message and come up with some evidence as to the real culprit behind the murders.

"I got a threatening e-mail from someone calling himself gotcha@partnersincrime.us about a week ago. I think it's from whoever it was who framed me. It should be on the computer you confiscated. The sender attached a sound file of a gunshot. It was the first time I'd heard that noise in almost a year and it really freaked me out. I knew it was probably futile to try to trace the sender and, to be honest, I have spent the last eleven months doing everything I could to erase the memory of what happened the day Jeffrey Allen was murdered. Maybe . . ." Raine stopped and rubbed her chin thoughtfully. "Maybe the attached file carried more than just the sound of a gunshot. Maybe it contained the code to install the Thompson file on my computer, too. Could you have your experts look into it?" Raine didn't add that she had made a backup of her hard drive and taken it with her before the cops came and cleaned out her apartment so she'd be looking at the suspicious e-mail, as well. Better to keep that information to herself for now, lest Wilkins realize that she still had a laptop they hadn't commandeered.

Wilkins nodded. "Okay. We'll see what we can find out. In the meantime, let me know if you plan to take any long trips in the near future. We may still need to call you in for further questioning."

Relieved that she was going home and not to jail, Raine hurried out the door and down the hallway, followed by the agent, who escorted her down to her car in the parking garage. Raine was fairly confident in her ability to stave off a stalker or rapist, but she decided a police escort to her car in the deserted garage made some sense. Confidence was one thing, foolhardiness another.

She made a quick call to Aimee to let her and Daff know that she'd been released, then refused Aimee's offer of dinner. Her ordeal had left her wanting nothing more than to go home alone and lick her wounds. Raine rolled her window down as she drove through the streets of downtown Atlanta on her way back to her apartment. She considered turning the radio on and triumphantly blasting her relief at being released, but she didn't feel so triumphant. As a matter of fact, she felt rather melancholy instead.

No, she wasn't being charged for a crime she didn't commit. But she was no better off now than she had been a week ago. Her only case was going nowhere, her lover had chosen his career over her, and someone was trying to frame her for murder again.

Raine knew she was lucky that a levelheaded agent like Wilkins had been assigned her case. She'd known enough cowboys in the Bureau who would have been only too happy to do as Wilkins suggested—railroad her through the justice system on circumstantial evidence just to say they'd closed the case.

Raine pushed a hand through her hair and tilted her head to let the warm night air wash over her. May in Atlanta was still fairly pleasant, without the humidity that would come when summer began in earnest. Still, that was a small price to pay for the mild winters here. She thought of the years she'd spent hunting white-collar criminals in frigid Chicago, with the wind whipping off of the lake and turning her ears blue. That was where she and Calder had met. He'd headed up the computer crimes division in the office when she had transferred in. As with any workplace, office romances in the FBI were officially frowned upon. But with so many unmarried agents living, eating, and breathing their jobs, after-hours trysts were more the rule than the exception. Still, when it was clear that she and Calder had a relationship that was more than just a fling to fill the time between one workday and the next, Raine had transferred out from under Calder's direct supervision and only worked computer crimes when someone in his division directly requested her assistance.

God, she missed her old job.

The adrenaline high she got when breaking a case was like nothing else she'd ever known. It had made her more sympathetic to drug addicts, who craved that high above all else. She supposed that was what she missed most of all. As an agent, her life was exciting.

As a computer network specialist, her life was . . . dull.

She hoped that as Partners In Crime matured and they got more cases, things would get exciting again. Although having someone frame her for murder was certainly livening up her life, tracking Hope Enslar was turning out to be a real bore.

Raine rolled up her window as she approached her apartment building. Usually it was fairly difficult to find parking on the street, but tonight was an exception. As if it had been saved for her, an open spot sat right across from her building. Raine eased her VW into the spot, making sure to leave plenty of space between her and car in front of her. There was nothing worse than getting blocked in by some jerk who didn't pay attention to the space between parked cars.

Raine pushed open her door and stepped out into the night. She debated whether or not to leave her laptop in its hiding place under the spare tire in the back, but decided she might as well get it now as have to trundle out here in her pj's tomorrow morning to get it. Besides, with car theft being what it was, it was always better to bring valuables inside than leave them in a car on the city streets.

Tugging up the hatchback, Raine leaned in to move the cover off the spare tire.

Suddenly, the tiny hairs on the back of her neck prickled.

Raine jerked up just in time to see a short man emerge from behind the trunk of the car behind her. Instinctively, she dove into her car and pulled the hatchback closed behind her, pressing the lock button on her keychain to lock herself safely inside.

Lying down on her back, she kicked out the thin pressboard that covered the back area from prying eyes, then launched herself over the backseat.

One of her instructors at Quantico had a phrase she loved to drill into her students' heads: A car was a two-thousand-pound weapon. Raine heard those words in her head now as she lunged between the driver and passenger seats and fumbled to get her key in the ignition with shaking hands. She had just managed to get it in when she heard her locks pop.

Raine cursed, thinking she had accidentally pushed the wrong button on her keychain and opened the doors herself. She pushed the door lock button again and cranked on the ignition.

The locks popped open again, only this time she wasn't fast enough to get them locked again before a tall man jerked open the passenger door and hurled himself inside. Raine gunned the accelerator, cranking the steering wheel to the left to avoid slamming into the car in front of her.

That was the last thing she remembered before the man in the passenger seat jabbed a needle in her arm and her world went dark.

* * *

THEY almost missed her.

The picture Calder handed out showed a bored-looking preteen, obviously annoyed at being forced to join in the fun of a backyard barbecue. She wore a pair of tiny black shorts and a neon pink tank top with PRINCESS spelled out in sequins across her budding breasts. Henderson was right when he said Brittany Monroe looked older than twelve, but it wasn't just the makeup she wore that caused it. It was something in her eyes that said she might still be a little girl according to her birth certificate, but was no longer a child in her heart.

Calder sat on the hard bench in the Greyhound station watching the crowd while trying to make it appear that he was doing no more than just waiting for his bus to board. He put his arm around the shoulders of the pregnant woman next to him.

"See anything yet?" he asked, leaning over to speak directly in her ear.

"Nope. Everyone boarding the bus to Miami checks out so far. I wish we could just search every bus for that poor little girl." Shari Wilkins rubbed her stomach, obviously thinking how awful this must be for "that poor little girl's" parent.

"I'm sorry." Calder reached out and put a hand over Shari's, an instinctive gesture that—had anyone been paying attention—would have seemed perfectly natural coming from the father of the baby.

Shari was, aside from being Jim Wilkins's wife, a good friend of Calder's since before she'd even met her husband, a top-notch FBI agent, and a master at surveillance. That's why Calder had asked her to come along tonight. That, and he knew that, since Wilkins was still at the office interrogating Raine, Shari was home alone tonight anyway. He hadn't given any thought to what it might put his fellow agent through emotionally. Calder didn't know how any agent could be exposed to the horrors of what man did to his fellow man and still contemplate having children. They knew all too well what dangers lurked around every corner.

"It's okay," Shari said, squeezing his hand and then letting hers drop. "I guess you just never get over wanting to right all the wrongs in this world."

Calder laughed and shook his head. "Naw, it sort of comes with the badge." He was silent for a moment, still watching the crowd. "There's a woman coming your way with a baby in her arms and a girl in a ponytail beside her. The girl looks too young to be Brittany, but there's something about the woman that seems . . . I don't know. Off."

"Got 'em," Shari said, shifting in her seat and grimacing as if she were in pain.

"You okay? I thought you still had two more months to go before you deliver. God, please don't tell me you're going into labor. I knew I shouldn't have called you so late. Your husband is going to kill me," Calder groaned.

Shari settled back, managing to poke him in the ribs. Hard. "Jesus, what is it with you guys? A pregnant woman gets a gas bubble and you're ready to put her on twenty-four-hour bed rest. Give me a break. In two months, I'm gonna pass something the size of a small watermelon out of a tube as wide as a cigar. I think I can handle sitting on my ass for two hours watching for bad guys, don't you?"

"Sorry," Calder muttered sheepishly. Okay, so he'd admit that his protective streak sometimes was a bit . . . wide. What could he say? It had been in his blood for generations.

"Okay, the whole family's going into the ladies' room. I think it's time for me to tinkle." With that, Shari heaved herself, belly first, off the bench and followed the woman into the bathroom.

Calder sat on the bench, his gaze fixed on the bathrooms, waiting for Shari to come out and tell him that his hunch was wrong. As he waited, a young boy walked into the men's room, the ends of his short hair sticking out of a baseball cap. Calder saw the boy come out a few minutes later and walk toward his family—a man, woman, and another young boy. A few minutes later, Shari came out of the bathroom with the young girl who had gone in with her mother. Calder watched as Shari patted the girl's arm, then gave her a little wave as she made a beeline back to the bench.

"Okay, you were right about the woman," she said, leaning into Calder's chest as if resting on him. "It's our guy. You'd think he'd be smart enough to pee sitting down if he's trying to pose as a woman." She sounded disgusted, but Calder was glad for the man's mistake. That meant they were one step closer to finding the girl he'd abducted.

"What about the girl?" he asked.

"The one who went into the bathroom with him?" Shari asked, watching the ladies' room door intently.

Calder nodded.

"She's just a kid he met on the bus from Marietta. She's meeting her older sister here and they're going on to Alabama, so she's safe."

The phony mother/child abductor came out of the ladies' room, adjusting the sling across her chest that held what was supposed to be a newborn.

"I've got him," Shari said, watching the man shuffle across the room and stop to stare outside the windows at the loading area where several dozen buses on-loaded and off-loaded passengers.

"Where's Brittany?" Calder muttered under his breath, his eyes scanning the crowd to see if anyone was making a move toward the windows. But no one was paying any attention to the guy. God, what if he had already figured out he'd been made and sent Brittany ahead on another bus? Even with four agents covering the busy station, it was possible that—

Hold on.

The boy he'd seen go into the men's room earlier turned slightly so that his back was to Calder. Calder watched as the boy's hand crept up to his shoulder. His thumb slipped under the neckline of his T-shirt and then, in an unconscious gesture, he hitched his bra strap back up on his shoulder and let his hand fall back to his side.

Now, Calder might not have any young sons or nephews yet, but he was pretty sure that boys weren't wearing bras nowadays.

He willed the boy to turn around again so he could get a look at his face and got his wish when the boarding for the next bus to Miami was called. The boy turned and looked toward the door and Calder caught sight of his face. The eyes were gray and the look in them, pure Brittany. Annoyed, angry, *knowing*. It had to be her.

God, please let it be her, Calder prayed silently as the family started moving toward the door with Brittany following.

He spoke into the tiny mouthpiece attached to the collar of his worn jacket. "I've got Brittany and Shari's got Moss. Let's split into our teams and take them into custody."

Calder didn't wait to hear back from the other two agents before helping Shari to rise and, putting an arm across her shoulders to complete the picture of the loving couple, said, "I'm gonna stop her before she gets on the bus."

"Got it."

Shari and Calder melted into the thin crowd making its way outside. Moss remained motionless near the bank of windows and Calder felt a drop of sweat slide between his shoulder blades. He was pretty certain they'd ID'd Moss correctly, but what if he was wrong about Brittany? What if that movement on the boy's part was to scratch a mosquito bite instead of tugging up an errant bra strap? What if Moss had already got Brittany on another bus, headed somewhere they weren't expected? He could have already made arrangements to meet the girl anywhere. It would be easy for him to get off the bus at its first stop and hop on a plane or rent a car to meet her.

At the doorway, Shari made a big show out of looking in her purse for something and then pushing Calder ahead while she went back to the bench they'd been sitting on earlier to retrieve her lost item. Calder knew that Moss would be in Federal custody within seconds.

Now he had to get Brittany.

He picked up his pace, skirting the crowd to catch up to the family she was traveling with. He saw the other agent on his team standing near the bus being loaded for Miami, looking as if he were just taking the last drags on his cig before boarding the bus.

Calder caught up with the family and, sending a silent

apology for what he was about to do, surreptitiously stuck his foot in the young father's path and jostled him just as he started to lose his balance. The man fell forward onto the pavement, the bus tickets that he had clutched in his hand scattering across the concrete.

The man's wife stopped and pulled her young son out of the crowd. The other boy followed.

Calder moved forward as his colleague dropped his cigarette and started toward him.

"I'm so sorry," he said, holding his hand out to the man on the ground while keeping all his attention focused on Brittany. Impatient, she put her hands on her hips in a move that was all girl. Then, sensing that her body language wasn't right, she stuffed her hands into the front pockets of her jeans and tried to act like she wasn't annoyed at the delay.

Calder wondered if this poor girl knew what sort of life was ahead of her if she got on that bus with Moss. Probably not. He had probably promised the girl all the love, affection, stuffed animals, and ice cream she wanted.

Yeah, right. Most likely, Moss planned to take her somewhere where young prostitutes brought a high price and turn her into his own personal whore. By the time she was fifteen, she'd be of no use to him any longer and he'd leave her in some miserable, stinking town with nothing to do but continue to turn tricks to survive.

Calder helped the man up off the pavement, saying, "Are you all right?"

The man good-naturedly rubbed at his chafed palms. "Yeah, I'm fine."

With his backup agent standing less than a foot from Brittany, Calder decided not to tiptoe around the question he most needed answered. He glanced toward the windows and saw Shari putting handcuffs on Moss. "Look," he began, reaching into the pocket of his jacket to flash the man his FBI credentials, "I'm a federal agent on the trail of a child molester. Is this your son?"

The man's jaw dropped and, instinctively, he stepped back. Before he could utter an answer, however, Brittany herself provided the evidence Calder was looking for by turning to run. He clamped his hand on her arm before she got one step away.

Calder raised his eyebrows questioningly to the man across from him, wanting confirmation that he wasn't nabbing this guy's son—a son who had pretty sharp fingernails for a boy, Calder noticed, as she dug them into his hand, trying to get free.

"No. He's not our son. We just . . . felt kinda sorry for him because he was traveling all alone," the mother answered, since her husband was still staring at Calder in shock. "I mean, what kind of parent sends their kid by himself all the way from Atlanta to Miami? Don't they read the papers?"

Calder gave Brittany's arm a firm squeeze and said, "Stop that. Now," in his best I'm-a-federal-agent-don't-fuck-with-me voice. In response, Brittany tried to kick him, but he foiled her by holding her at arm's length so her shorter legs couldn't reach him. He turned his attention to the couple in front of him. "Yeah, it can be an ugly world out there. You all have a good trip to Florida. I'll take care of this one from here."

With that, Calder turned and gently pushed Brittany ahead of him into the Greyhound station where Shari and her team were waiting with the girl's abductor. As he pulled open the door, he heard John Moss moaning. Then Moss started shaking and suddenly slumped against the agent standing behind him, who instinctively caught him before he fell to the ground. The incredibly lifelike rubber baby that had been slung across his chest dropped to the floor and bounced while the agents surrounding Moss looked on.

"I'm having a heart attack," Moss moaned, his eyes rolling back in his head.

Calder kept a firm hold of Brittany's arm, keeping her from running to her abductor's side. She started sobbing, clawing at his hand to make him let her go.

"Please don't make me have to handcuff you, Brittany," he said quietly, trying to calm her down.

"He's going to die. Somebody help him. Don't let him die," Brittany pleaded.

Calder stepped in front of the girl, blocking her view of Moss. "He's going to be fine. Agent Wilkins—she's the pregnant one—used to be a nurse. She knows what to do in a medical emergency. Now, I need you to calm down so that Agent Wilkins can focus on helping Mr. Moss. Can you do that for me?"

Brittany seemed to look at him for the first time, blinking up at him with indecision in her eyes. Calder felt a shudder pass through her body before she nodded.

Shari was leaning over Moss's prone form, laying the back of her hand on his forehead like a mother taking her child's temperature. She looked up at Calder and shook her head almost imperceptibly to indicate that Moss was faking it.

"Okay, Brittany, we need to clear the area so that Mr. Moss can get the medical attention he needs"—which was none, Calder said silently to himself—"so I need you to come with me."

Brittany looked past him to her neighbor, still lying motionless on the floor. Her obvious concern for the man who had taken her innocence made Calder want to throw something—preferably something sharp—right into the black heart of the man lying on the floor. He knew it would take years of therapy for this poor kid to feel normal again . . . *if* she ever did. Most likely, she would always feel as if she were to blame for what had happened to her.

Brittany nodded, and her whole body seemed to relax. Calder loosened his grip just a bit as they started toward the door.

Just as they reached the front door of the bus station, it was flung open. A red-haired, ruddy-faced man dashed in, nearly running into Calder.

"Preston?" he asked, out of breath.

"Yeah?" Calder answered suspiciously.

"I'm Lee Henderson." The police officer handed Calder his ID, then looked around the room. "Looks like you've got things under control."

"Yes, we do. I was just taking Ms. Monroe down to the office—"

Before Calder could explain the situation, the front door

burst open again, this time to admit a beefy man with a broad chest and a head of thick, black-and-silver hair. He had a gun drawn and was pointing it at Calder's head.

"Daddy," Brittany gasped.

"Judge Monroe? What are you doing here?" Lee Henderson asked.

"Move back," Brittany's father ordered authoritatively, keeping his back to the wall so none of Calder's teammates could move into position and disarm him.

Shit. This was not good.

Calder was wearing a bulletproof vest under his jacket and polo shirt, but that wasn't going to help him if the judge aimed for his head. Of course, he could miss—hitting a relatively small target like a person's head was much more difficult than Hollywood made it seem, even at close range. But Calder really didn't want to take that chance. Instead, he did as Judge Monroe ordered, calmly taking a step backward, pushing Brittany behind him protectively. He raised his free hand in supplication. "Okay. I'm moving. Just stay calm."

Thomas Monroe laughed chillingly. "Don't worry. I'm calm. *Deadly* calm, you might say." He sidled over to where Moss was being held, keeping his gun trained on Calder the entire time. When he was within pointblank range of Shari Wilkins, he lunged, wrapping his arm around her throat and shoving the barrel of his pistol against her temple.

Calder's jaw clenched as he took a step toward his friend and fellow agent. She motioned for him to stop just as the judge tightened his grip around her throat.

"Stay where you are," the judge ordered. "I don't want to kill her, but I will if I have to."

With a glance to the agent closest to him, Calder gave up custody of Brittany so he could deal with this new crisis. He berated himself for not telling the team to hustle Moss out of here, phony medical emergency or no. Instead, he had been trying to do what he could so Brittany wouldn't be traumatized any more than she was already by having to watch her abductor—who she most likely had been convinced was the only person in her life who loved her—being hauled out of the bus station by his balls, if necessary.

This is what he got for trying to be sensitive.

"Judge Monroe, you don't want to do this. We need to question your daughter, but you can rest assured that we'll take good care of her. Come on now, put down the gun."

Judge Monroe looked at Calder, his gray eyes the same color as his daughter's, but filled with cold loathing instead of hot anger. "I don't think so. Tell him to get up," he said, jerking his head toward John Moss, who had scuttled, crablike, against the legs of Shari's backup the moment Judge Monroe had entered the bus station.

Calder didn't see any choice but to nod at the agent Moss was trying to hide behind. The agent, an ex-Marine who had a good hundred pounds on Moss—all of it muscle—grabbed the scruff of the child molester's neck and hauled him up into a standing position.

"Now all of you, step away from him."

It didn't take a genius to realize what Thomas Monroe had in mind. He had already passed judgment on John Moss, and now he planned to be the man's executioner.

"Judge," Calder said quietly but forcefully, "you need to take a moment and think about what you're doing here. Your little girls have already lost their mother. If you go through with this, they'll lose their father, too. Do you really want to do that to them? You know what life in the foster care system is like. You probably see kids like that in your courtroom every day."

Calder saw the judge flinch, the first crack in his facade since he'd burst into the bus station. Calder kept at him. "Strangers are never going to care for your girls the way you could."

Judge Monroe blinked and his mask cracked open a little wider. "The girls will be raised by my sister, their godmother. She'll be a better parent to them than I ever was. I failed them, don't you see? I can't live with myself knowing that I didn't keep my girls safe."

"No parent can keep his children safe all the time. All it takes is one minute when your back is turned for tragedy to strike. But everything is going to be all right now. We'll get Brittany lots of counseling and there are plenty of parenting classes out there for you, too, Judge. Your family can recover from this," Calder assured him, relieved to see the judge's expression start to waver.

"Besides, Daddy, you know what killing John will do to your career. You might even lose that job you love so much more than you love your own children."

Calder grimaced as Brittany's vitriolic accusation rang through the tense bus station. These were not the words of a twelve-year-old girl, but those planted by a pedophile trying to lure his next victim into his sick trap.

So that's how Moss had convinced Brittany her father didn't love her, by using his job against him.

The agent holding Brittany clapped a hand over her mouth, but before Calder had a chance to undo the damage she'd done, Judge Monroe had slipped his mask of hatred back on. His gray eyes had gone cold and lifeless again as he started to speak.

"My job was to protect my child and I failed. For that, I am more sorry than you'll ever know." Then, without warning of what he was about to do, Judge Monroe shoved Shari aside, took aim at Moss's heart, and fired. Calder heard Brittany's muffled scream behind him as Shari Wilkins drew her gun on Thomas Monroe, followed by every other agent in the room.

Moss lay on the floor, moaning, now needing medical attention for real.

"Mr. Monroe, drop your weapon," Shari ordered.

Instead, the man turned his gun on the female agent. Calder's blood froze in his veins. Whereas before, he had been fairly certain the judge was just using Shari for cover so he could get to Moss, now there was no reason for him to be pointing a gun at the agent except to kill her. Did he believe the authorities were somehow to blame for his daughter's abduction?

"I know you don't want to kill me," Shari continued, as Calder's mind raced through possible scenarios. He could push Shari out of the way and take a bullet himself. He had no doubt that Monroe could get at least get one shot off before the other agents killed him. He'd take that chance, but what if he pushed too hard and injured Shari or jeopardized her baby? No, he couldn't risk that.

Keeping his gun trained on Judge Monroe, Calder took a step forward, trying to draw the other man's fire. He couldn't risk shoving Shari away, but maybe he could get Monroe to shift his attention in another way. "A jury might be lenient on you about shooting the man who harmed your daughter, but they're not going to be so understanding if you kill a federal officer."

"I don't care. I'm going to shoot her," the judge said, the barrel of his gun shaking as he kept it pointed at Shari's chest.

"No, you're not. You want us to shoot you. We call that suicide by cop, you know. It happens a lot more often than you might think," Shari said gently. "Put the gun down, Mr. Monroe. You don't really want to die, do you?"

She kept talking, her voice low and soothing. "You'll never see your kids again, never have a chance to see them graduate from high school or get married or have children of their own." Shari rubbed her own distended stomach with one hand. "I know I can't wait to see this little one grow up."

At that, Judge Monroe started to cry. Big wet tears trickled down his face as the gun he was holding lowered inch by slow inch. "I can remember my babies being born like it happened yesterday. They say that first babies come out the slowest, but not Brittany. She pushed out into the world less than two hours after her mama's water broke. Our doctor never even had time to get to the hospital, so she was delivered by the doctor on duty that day. She came out bawling and hungry. Her mama's milk hadn't come in yet so we had to start her on the bottle instead. But she was just amazing. So tiny. And perfect. I just couldn't believe that her mom and I had made this perfect little human being, you know? It was the most beautiful moment of my life."

The judge turned his gun in his palm so the barrel was facing away from Shari Wilkins and reached out to hand it to the agent, who nodded as she took it.

The other two agents waited inside for the ambulance that

would take John Moss to the hospital, and Calder and Shari led the now-handcuffed Judge Monroe and his tearful daughter out of the bus station.

When Monroe was safely ensconced in the back of Shari's car, Calder turned to her and asked, "How did you know he wouldn't shoot you?"

Shari closed the door of her Bureau vehicle. "I couldn't be certain, of course. But when he first grabbed me, before he shot Moss, he whispered something to me that made me believe he didn't mean me any harm."

"Yeah, what was that?" Calder asked.

"He said he was sorry," Shari answered, rubbing the side of her stomach absently.

TWENTY-ONE

MEGAN woke with a start and stared out into utter darkness, wondering why she couldn't see the nightlight that was always plugged into the outlet in the corner of her bedroom. She rolled over . . . and fell off the narrow bench seat of her mother's SUV.

Blinking away the dullness that had settled in her brain, Megan swallowed past her swollen tongue. Ugh. She felt awful.

She steadied herself with two hands on the seat and pushed up off the floor, feeling around the floor for the flashlight she could have sworn she'd left lying right next to her. A sudden flicker of memory from the night before seared into her brain. Or was it the morning before? Megan had lost all sense of time after being stuck in this container for so long. She had been shining the flashlight upward from her chin, watching herself in the mirror as she giggled and made spooky, ghost story–type sounds.

Why had she thought that was funny?

Megan found the flashlight under the driver's seat and flicked it off and then on again. Damn it. She'd left it on and now the batteries were dead. There was something strange covering the end of the flashlight and Megan grimaced, wondering what it was, but unable to see in the darkness inside the SUV.

She reached up to turn on the dome light and found that she'd left that on as well.

Great. The Pioneer's battery was dead, too.

Megan slumped down on the floor, surrounded by the evidence of her one-man party. Among the other things she'd found in the convertible had been a stash of beer and wine. After a couple of beers, Megan's curiosity got the better of her. She'd never tried wine before. Determined not to be defeated by the fact that she didn't have a corkscrew, Megan used a pen from her backpack to push the cork inside the bottle instead.

She hadn't liked the first drink, but she kept drinking, trying to figure out what it was that made adults like the stuff so much. When over half the bottle was gone, she was starting to think that wine wasn't so bad after all.

She tore a chunk of cheese off the block she'd been nibbling on and reached for a cracker. She took a bite, savoring the creamy texture of the cheese and the salty crunch of the cracker, and then washed it down with a chug from the bottle of wine.

Megan had burped and said "Excuse me" to the empty car, and then started giggling.

She had taken another drink of wine and looked out over the smorgasbord of goodies from the convertible. Salami and cheese. Crackers and little spicy beans. Chips and salsa. Some lettuce and tomatoes, plus baby carrots, celery, and red peppers with a bottle of ranch dip. Megan had set aside the packages of raw meat and some sour cream that smelled funny. If she got desperate, she would eat those, too, but for the moment she had decided to stick with the stuff that she knew wouldn't make her sick.

The box of jumbo-sized ribbed condoms she'd found in the bottom of one of the bags had gone into her backpack.

Later, after several more sips of wine, she'd taken one condom out of the box, ripped open the foil package, and studied the thing. She'd never been this close to one before. Megan knew her lack of sexual experience was because she was the type of girl that boys thought of as a friend, not a girlfriend. At five-feet-nine-inches tall, with a solid, athletic build, she towered over most of the guys her age. She probably outweighed them, too, but she tried hard not to think about that. She knew plenty of girls who were so obsessed with their weight that they refused to eat for days at a time or else ate whatever they wanted and threw up afterward. After lunch at school, you could stand in the girls' bathroom and look at the position of the feet under the stalls to figure out who was bulimic. Megan thought it was sad that probably six out of ten stalls had feet facing the wrong way.

She was lucky because her mom had been big, too. She'd shown Megan pictures of herself back when she was Megan's age and she stood out like a hulking giant among her petite classmates. Since Megan thought her mom was one of the prettiest mothers she knew, it was hard to think of her as an awkward teenager who felt too big for her own skin sometimes just like Megan did.

"Just wait until college. Boys start to get smarter—and bigger—after high school," her mom would say whenever Megan came home crying because the boy she liked was interested in the tiny Heather Allison or Tiffany Jones-types instead.

So, Megan was resigned to the fact that this was probably the closest she was going to get to a condom until she went off to college. She had unrolled it onto the end of the flashlight, wondering if a guy's penis was as hard as this when he was having sex. She hoped not because that might really hurt. She had also wondered if it got this big. The condom easily fit over the end of the flashlight so they must get this big, Megan thought. But that didn't seem like it could be right. Even the heaviest-duty tampons were only about one-fourth the size of this. Did that mean that they didn't make tampons for women whose vaginas were big enough to accommodate the size of a jumbo-sized penis?

Feeling sleepy, Megan had dropped the flashlight on the floor and curled up on the bench seat of her mother's car.

When she got back home, she'd ask her mom about all this, she thought as she drifted off to a dreamless sleep.

Now fully awake, Megan scowled at the mess on the floor of the Pioneer.

"That was really stupid," she admonished herself. "What if the rebel guerillas had broken in while you were asleep? You would have been too drunk to even put up a fight."

Angry with herself for not thinking about this possibility last night, Megan started gathering up the remains of her feast. She'd been careful not to eat too much, at least, separating the groceries into neat piles to last her for at least seven more days. After that, she'd have to think about eating the raw meat, even knowing those extra days without refrigeration would make it that much riskier. Still, she'd tried to force herself to eat some of the chicken before and it had made her gag.

No use eating something that was just going to make you throw up, Megan figured. If she was still stuck here a week from now, she'd be desperate enough to try starting a fire and cooking the meat first. Right now, though, she was still too scared of what a fire might do in this closed-in area to chance it.

Megan set the grocery bags outside the SUV near the rear tire and walked to the sedan behind her mother's SUV to turn on the headlights so she could see. Then she went back to the Pioneer and pulled her notebook and a mechanical pencil out of her backpack. She flipped to the page where she had started to plan what she was going to do to survive.

Her list had stopped after item number two, which was rationing her supplies, and Megan was surprised to realize that, after several days stuck in here, a real plan had actually formed in her brain.

She smiled wryly at her list as she wrote, "Dump out wine and beer," for item number three.

Then she neatly penciled in the rest of her list.

4. Move upstairs to "safe" vehicle (if rebels know you're here, they'll search Mom's car first) with full gas tank—question: Do all cars have keys in glove compartment??

5. Figure out where all controls are on the safe car so you can make a quick getaway (windshield wipers, etc.)
6. Use lights from other vehicles to keep safe car's batteries from dying
7. Rig warning system to door of container
8. Clean up evidence that you're here, just in case rebels aren't expecting you
9. Start exercising so you'll be ready to outrun the rebels if necessary

Megan chewed on the end of her pencil, her teeth clicking against the metal clip as she reread her list. She liked number nine the best. It sounded just like something James Bond would do.

NINETEEN paces. That's what it took to make it from his couch to the French doors leading outside and back.

Nineteen lousy steps, back and forth. Back and forth.

Calder had left his office after two grueling hours of questioning Brittany Monroe. The girl had given them more than enough to put the seriously injured but not dead John Moss away for a very long time, including where he kept his video equipment and the tapes he'd made of himself and Brittany. And himself and lots of other little girls, too, Calder guessed.

He'd actually been surprised that Brittany folded so easily. Most victims in her shoes would have taken some time to see that the ones who sexually abused and abducted them were not the ones who loved them. Calder suspected that Brittany had begun to question that notion from the time Moss started showing interest in the girl across the aisle from him, more than halfway through the bus ride to Atlanta.

With her head hanging, she admitted that she never believed her father cared that much about her until he showed up at the Greyhound station to stop her from leaving. It was then she realized that John had been lying to her all along.

So she talked and talked, for two long hours, giving the

details of her relationship with Moss until at last she fell asleep, exhausted, sitting up in her chair.

By then, having realized he hadn't heard or seen anything of Raine, Calder debated whether he should go to her apartment to tell her what a fool he had been or let her sleep. Trying to be noble, he decided to let her sleep, but he was not so lucky. Wired from the arrest, his mind tripping over itself as one thought after another raced around in his brain, Calder couldn't sit still.

So he paced.

And paced.

Calder stopped near the French doors and stared out into the black night. Clouds covered the moon and the stars, shrouding the world with inky darkness. Judge Monroe's words had stayed with him all night, echoing inside his head. "It was my job to keep my child safe and I failed."

Calder put out a hand and touched the cool glass of the door in front of him. He identified with how the judge felt, even though he couldn't rationally condone the judge's act of vigilante justice. Deep down, though, Calder knew he'd do the same thing if faced with a similar situation. It was his job to protect those he loved, and the law be damned.

The only thing he'd do differently is that he'd have made sure to kill Moss, not just injure him as the judge had done.

Finally, his brain settled on one thought: He had lied to Raine.

Yes, he had broken up with her because he was a coward. But it wasn't his career he was so frightened of losing, it was Raine herself. When she had been implicated in Jeffrey Allen's murder, he hadn't turned from her because he was afraid of how her actions might reflect on him, he had run because he knew he couldn't protect her and that scared the shit out of him.

Even worse, it suddenly occurred to him that he had wanted her to resign from the FBI. His own refusal to back her up with her superiors had nothing to do with his own belief that anyone was capable of murder if pushed too far. No, he had wanted her out of the Bureau, where she faced danger every day, and locked away somewhere safe where no one could ever hurt her.

Calder rested his forehead on the glass and closed his eyes. God help him, love had turned him into an overprotective male-chauvinist pig. Now, the question was, what was he going to do about it? Stop loving Raine?

Calder snorted. Right. Like that was really an option. He'd tried that one for nearly a year, until the loneliness had nearly torn him apart and he'd ached to see her again. Hell, he'd even fabricated a case out of that old man's letter just to have a reason to talk to her again. And with her back in trouble over the Thompson assassination, he had let her down again.

He was such an asshole.

Calder slammed his fist against the wooden part of the French door, glad for the pain that took his mind off his self-flagellation. He may be a coward and an asshole and all the other names he was calling himself, but he wasn't going to let one more hour slip by letting Raine think so, too.

Grabbing his keys and his wallet from the coffee table, he headed toward the front door, determined to set things right with the woman he loved.

TWENTY-TWO

"WHERE the hell is she?" Calder asked as soon as Aimee yanked the door open, wearing a red silk robe that hung open to reveal a matching nightgown.

"I presume the 'she' to whom you are referring is Raine?" Aimee asked, raising one eyebrow at him quizzically. She didn't seem surprised to see him standing on her porch, his hair standing on end like a madman, at three o'clock in the morning.

Calder pushed past her into the living room, glancing at the couch and praying he'd find Raine sleeping soundly there, but the couch was empty. "I went to her apartment and she's not there. Her car was gone, too."

"Have you tried her on her cell phone?" Aimee asked, still sounding unconcerned.

"Yes. She's not answering."

At that, Aimee frowned. "She always answers her cell."

"I know. Why do you think I'm so worried?" Calder started pacing again, noting absently that Aimee's living room was twenty-four paces around. "Where could she be? Why isn't she answering her phone?"

Aimee speared him with a level look. "She called me a few hours ago to say that Wilkins was done questioning her and that she was on her way home. I'm sure that's where she is. Have you considered that maybe she's just not answering calls from you?"

"Yes," Calder answered abruptly, stalking over to Aimee's cordless phone and thrusting the receiver at her. "Will you call her? I have to know she's safe."

Aimee dialed her friend's phone. On the fourth ring, Raine's voicemail picked up and Aimee left a message that Calder was here and they were concerned because she wasn't answering.

She and Calder looked at each other over the couch. Aimee was the first to look away. Tightening the belt on her robe, she started toward the kitchen, saying over her shoulder, "I'm going to make some coffee. I'll be right back."

Calder continued pacing, willing Aimee's phone to ring, hoping Raine was just avoiding his calls and not out there somewhere in danger. Besides Aimee and Daphne, who did Raine know in Atlanta? More importantly, who did she know here who would keep her out past 3 A.M.?

"Have you tried calling her brother?" Daphne asked from the bottom step of the staircase leading upstairs. Obviously, Aimee was concerned enough about Raine to have roused her housemate—a fact that did not comfort Calder at all.

"No, I didn't think about that. They're not exactly close."

"True, but Neall offered Raine an olive branch and I think she's eager to improve their relationship. Now that both of their parents are gone, they only have each other. Maybe she's over at Neall's house, catching up on old times," Daphne suggested.

Calder picked up the phone. "Do you have his number?"

"No, but if you call the Bureau, I'm sure you could get it."

Calder grunted and called the number for the Atlanta FBI office. Daphne didn't seem to like him much. Then again, she didn't seem to like anyone very much, aside from Raine and Aimee.

Neall sounded groggy when he answered the phone, not

surprisingly since he had probably been woken from a dead sleep. "Yeah?" he asked.

"Robey? It's Calder Preston. I'm calling for Raine. Is she there?"

"Why the hell would she be here?" Neall asked grumpily. "Man, it's three A.M."

"I know. I'm sorry. I just . . . I can't find your sister and it's not like her to disappear in the middle of the night. If she's doing anything at three o'clock in the morning, it usually involves sitting in front of her computer."

Neall was starting to sound a bit more awake when he responded, "Look, Preston, I know this is an option you may not want to consider, but did you ever think that maybe my big sister might be, uh—how do I say this—having a sleepover with somebody else?"

Yeah, he'd considered it. For about a nanosecond, and then he'd rejected the idea out of hand. There was no way Raine was with another man. Calder refused to believe otherwise.

"Yeah, well, I'm sorry, but she's not here," Neall said after a long, awkward silence. "Is there anything I can do?"

"If she contacts you, will you let her know that I'm looking for her?"

"Absolutely. I'm sorry." Neall paused, clearing his throat. "You know, sometimes women just like to do this kind of thing to torture us, to make sure we know who's holding the power in the relationship, if you know what I mean."

Calder silently shook his head. If there was one thing Raine wasn't, it was a game player. When she was mad at him, she fumed openly, banging things around to show her displeasure. She was not the type to give him the silent treatment, nor would she disappear like this just to punish him. Besides, she hadn't known that he was going to show up at her door tonight. As far as she was concerned, their relationship was over.

But one thing Neall had said rang true. If Raine had wanted to torture him, she had found the best way to do it.

Calder hung up the phone and turned to Daphne and Aimee, who had changed out of her slinky nightwear and into a sensible pair of jeans and an oversized T-shirt. Aimee handed him a steaming mug of coffee and sat down on the couch. Daphne hauled a heavy dining room chair from the other room, turned it around and straddled it, resting her arms along the back.

"What'd he say?" she asked.

"Nothing. Just that Raine wasn't there."

"Is he coming over?"

Calder frowned. "No. He suggested that Raine might be doing this just to, uh, punish me."

Aimee set her own coffee cup down on the table in front of her. "No way. Raine wouldn't do that. Besides, if she had, she'd be over here," she said with a laugh.

"I agree," Daphne said. "So, what do we do to find her? I don't suppose the Bureau installed a GPS tracking device on her car after this latest fiasco?"

"I don't think so, but I'll call Wilkins to make sure," Calder said.

"You sure you want to do that?" Aimee asked as Calder reached for the phone.

"Why not?" Calder was already dialing Wilkins's home number.

"Because someone could accuse you of interfering in an official investigation for personal reasons, that's why. That sort of thing isn't good for your career," Daphne said, her voice dripping with sarcasm.

Calder eyed the redhead levelly but didn't respond immediately, mostly because he didn't think, "Fuck you," was the appropriate thing to say. After a calming breath, Calder finished punching in Wilkins's number and said, "Look, Daphne, I made a mistake before by letting Raine go. But I'm here now and I love her, and I'm not going to let her down again. So could you cut me some slack? I'm sorry I'm not Superman, okay?"

Daphne didn't have time to slice him with another of her barbs because Jim Wilkins picked up the other end of the line with a sleepy, "Hullo?"

"Wilkins, it's Preston. I—"

Before Calder could get any further in his explanation, Wilkins, sounding completely wide-awake now, started shouting into the phone. "You've got some goddamn nerve calling me, you asshole! Do you realize that you put my wife's life in jeopardy tonight? She could have been killed. And you're the one who called her in on the case. What were you thinking? No, be quiet Shari, this is between me and—" Wilkins's voice stopped abruptly.

"Calder, I am so sorry," Shari Wilkins said, sounding horrified. "Jim had no right to lay into you like that. I could have asked to be assigned to light duty during my pregnancy but I chose not to. As bad as it was tonight, I think it would have been worse without me. I knew Judge Monroe wasn't going to hurt me, but I'm not sure he would have been so conflicted about hurting another man. Not after what Moss had done to his daughter."

Calder was a little worried about how Shari had managed to get the phone away from her husband. He could just imagine Wilkins writhing on the floor right now, clutching his balls. "It's okay, Shari. I understand how your husband feels. I . . . well, I'd feel the same way if I were him."

He heard Shari let out an exasperated sigh. "You guys are such jerks. Do you think that because you're loaded with testosterone, you're the only ones who worry? How the hell do you think *I* feel when Jim goes out on a bust? You think I'm not scared just because he's a big strong man?"

She didn't sound particularly complimentary with that last phrase, so Calder just kept his mouth shut as she continued her rant.

"Do you know what I would do to someone who threatened any one of my family members? I'd rip their goddamned eyes out and shove them down their throats."

"Shari—" Calder tried to interrupt, the visual image she'd just given him making him blink.

"No, you listen to me. Both of you," she said, her voice muffled as if she'd turned her head to the side. "Are you listening?"

"Yes," Calder answered, feeling like a naughty first grader.

He heard a muffled reply through the receiver and assumed that Jim had answered likewise.

"Good. Then let me tell you something that I want you to

try to get through your thick, Neanderthal skulls. You. Are. Not. Responsible. For. Me. Got it? I am an educated, intelligent, FBI-trained woman. The fact that I have indoor plumbing and you don't does not make me in any way less capable than you. I appreciate your concern and I love you for it"—Calder assumed this last was directed at Jim and not him—"but I am not willing to live in a gilded cage for anyone. Now, if you'll excuse me, all this excitement has roused the baby, who is jumping up and down on my bladder. Play nice," she finished her lecture, handing the phone to Jim.

The silence dragged on several seconds too long before Calder coughed. "You still pissed?" he asked.

"Yeah," Jim answered.

"Okay. I don't blame you. But right now, I need some information. Raine's missing—"

"What?" Jim yelled, then lowered his voice lest Shari be alerted that trouble was brewing here. "No way. I told her she was not to go anywhere without telling me. Shit. Doesn't she realize that I'm the only one keeping her ass out of jail? If Jarvis decides to bring her in for questioning again and she's disappeared, he's going to insist we get a warrant for her arrest."

"I don't think she went voluntarily," Calder said quietly.

"Huh?"

"I know Raine. She doesn't just go wandering the city at this time of morning, especially not without her cell phone. That's why I called you. I wondered if maybe you guys had installed a tracking device on her car to aid in your investigation."

"No. With the assassin in custody, we didn't feel it was necessary."

Calder squeezed the bridge of his nose between his thumb and forefinger. "Well, I had to try. Sorry to wake you. And tell Shari . . . um, never mind."

"Yeah. You, too." With that, Jim disconnected the call.

Calder turned to Aimee and Daphne and shook his head, even though he pretty much figured they already knew it was a bust.

"Well, I say we go back to Raine's place and wait for her there," Daphne said, getting up from her chair and dragging it back to the adjoining dining room. "It's not like I'm going to get any sleep now."

"I think someone should wait here in case she tries to call," Aimee said.

"Okay. I'll go to Raine's and—" Calder broke off when his cell phone started ringing. *Please, let it be her,* he found himself silently praying. But when he looked at the number displayed on the screen, he saw that it was the Atlanta Bureau's main number.

"Preston," he said, answering the call.

"Calder, it's Alex." Calder's boss sounded as if he, too, was having trouble sleeping.

"Yes?" Calder said, impatient to get off the phone and get back to Raine's apartment.

"I'm afraid I have some bad news."

Calder rubbed his forehead. Was there any other type of news that was delivered at 3 A.M.? "What is it? Did Moss die?" he asked, knowing that it would be tougher for Judge Monroe to get a light sentence if Moss died.

"No." Alex stopped and cleared his throat. "I'm afraid that Brittany has . . . um, I don't know quite how to say this."

"Damn it, no. Don't tell me that she tried to commit suicide," Calder said, his free hand fisting at his side. All too often, victims of child abuse blamed themselves for being preyed upon and acted on those feelings of self-hatred before they could get help.

"No. Brittany's fine. She just . . . I hate to tell you this, but she just accused you of flirting with her when you escorted her to your office."

"What?" Calder yanked his phone away from his ear and stared at it as if it had just grown teeth and tried to bite him. There was no way—no way!—he had been flirting with that twelve-year-old girl. The very thought of it made him shudder with disgust.

He put the phone back to his ear in time to hear Alex say, ". . . nonsense, of course, but we'll have to go through the motions of a formal inquiry."

"This can't be happening," Calder muttered, slumping down on Aimee's couch as she and Daphne watched him curiously from across the room. Suddenly, it occurred to him that all his present troubles were being heaped upon him by members of the so-called fairer sex.

This is almost enough to make a guy swear off women for good, Calder thought as he ended the call. Then he pictured Raine the way she looked, sitting in the booth at McDonald's with hurt and a tender sort of protectiveness shining from her eyes as she told him to go.

Yeah, he wasn't quite ready to give up on women just yet. At least not the one he loved so fiercely that his heart ached with it.

"YOU killed a federal officer?" Hope Enslar nearly dropped the cup of hot tea she was holding.

Victor watched her with his curiously expressionless silver eyes. She had told him to investigate Raine Robey and do whatever he felt was necessary if he'd found out anything suspicious, but . . . Well, okay, she really wasn't surprised.

Subconsciously, she had known something wasn't right ever since the night she'd found that woman and her cohorts in the hall outside R&D. Still, to have Victor sitting in her kitchen calmly explaining that he had taken care of her "problem" as matter-of-factly as if he were discussing the extermination of some vermin that had infested her lawn made her uneasy.

"Number one, I did not kill anyone," Victor corrected coolly. "Ms. Robey is simply taking the long way to Alaska. Her condition when she arrives at her intended destination is not my responsibility."

Hope shivered, wondering if a jury would buy his line of reasoning.

"Number two, she was not, at the time of her . . . vacation, shall we say? . . . a federal agent. She was merely a private citizen who had formerly worked for the FBI. Now, as for the colleagues who were with Ms. Robey that night, unless you can get me a copy of the security video, I'm at a bit of a loss for what to do next. I figure the best course of action is to just be alert to anything unusual that may happen in the next few days. If Ms. Robey's colleagues surface, we can deal with them then."

Hope absently nodded her agreement, quelling a wave of dread that rolled through her stomach. *Please,* she thought as she showed Victor to the door, *please, let this be the end of this nightmare.*

TWENTY-THREE

"I'LL never wish for a more exciting life again," Raine promised, groggily opening one eye to stare at the gray carpeting squashed against her cheek. Her tongue felt as if it had swollen to three times its usual size. She swallowed, but that just pushed her tongue against the back of her throat and made her gag. Opening her mouth, she tried to suck in a breath, but the air was hot and stuffy and heavy inside the car, and all that did was make her lungs hurt.

Raine licked her dry lips and rolled onto her back. Gingerly, she tried moving her legs and felt an answering twinge at her wrists. Great, the two assholes who'd attacked her had tied her ankles and wrists together behind her back.

"Somebody must watch the bad guy network on TV," she muttered thickly.

Well, fortunately, she was a member of the good guy network, so getting out of the restraints was more a nuisance than anything else, even with her still-fuzzy brain. Raine sat up in the hatchback of her VW and rubbed her left wrist, wondering just where the hell she was. It was dark and the only noise she could hear was a low, throbbing hum. The floor of the VW was vibrating, as if the engine was on, but Raine didn't think that was it. It was a bigger vibration than what would be produced by just a car's engine.

Raine lifted up the latch of the hatchback and the car's dome light went on. She looked down at her watch and tried to remember what day it had been when Wilkins released her. It was 2:14 P.M. Thursday now, according to the digital readout on her watch. Let's see, it had been . . . what? Tuesday night? No, Wednesday morning, early. She'd been out for over thirty-six hours, and she was still dizzy from the effects of whatever drug they'd given her. Even worse, she was so thirsty she'd even drink a Pepsi right now if one magically appeared in front of her.

She swung her feet to the floor, keeping one hand on the car frame to steady herself. Cautiously, she stood up and walked around the VW, pulled open the driver's side door, and hit the headlights to see where she was, but all around her was orange steel. It appeared as if she were inside some sort of metal container like she'd seen at shipyards.

Raine heard the whistle of a train just then, the noise faint through the thick walls of the container. Well, that solved the mystery of the vibration and the familiar swaying. She was on a train.

Raine grabbed the flashlight she kept in the glove compartment and set out to explore the seemingly empty cargo container. Still feeling somewhat faint, she had to keep a hand on the side of the container to stop herself from falling.

It didn't take her long to give a cursory once-over to the bottom floor. Forcing herself to take it slowly, she shoved the flashlight down the waistband of her jeans and tackled the metal rungs leading to a second floor. By the time she reached the top of the ladder, she was panting from exertion. Raine pulled herself up onto the floor of the next level and lay there, sucking stale air in and out of her aching lungs while her pulse slowed.

She may have let herself become a bit lazy over the past eleven months, but climbing one flight of stairs normally didn't leave her shaking and exhausted. She flopped onto her back and stared up into the darkness.

She was alone. With no food and no water, on a train headed for God—and the conductor—only knew where.

Raine felt tears welling up in her eyes. Well, wasn't this a metaphor for her life? Trapped by her dwindling finances, deserted by the man she loved, her life careening down a path of someone else's choosing.

Raine gave in to a bout of self-pity and let the tears drip out of the corners of her eyes and into her hair. Her sniffles echoed loudly in the empty container, ricocheting off the steel walls, bouncing down from the ceiling and hitting her again.

She missed her father. He was the one person in her life who had truly understood her. Not only that, but he encouraged her to push herself and didn't pass judgment on her need for adventure. Yes, so maybe he had romanticized his code of honor among thieves, making her believe that it was possible to enjoy the thrill of breaking the rules while professing to cause no harm, but his encouragement had paid off. She'd used her computer skills to great advantage over the years, catching criminals much worse than her father had ever been.

Raine swiped at her tear-soaked eyes and forced herself to get up off the floor. Self-pity wasn't going to get her out of here.

She took a deep, shuddering breath and walked slowly around the second floor, shining her flashlight in every corner to make certain she didn't miss anything that might help her escape. As she made her way back down the ladder, though, Raine knew that all she had to work with was whatever was in her own car.

She looked around, hoping some brilliant plan would strike like lightning in a summer storm, but nothing did. Briefly, she wondered if the acid in her car battery would dissolve steel.

"Yeah, but how the hell am I going to get the acid out of the battery?" she muttered to herself. MacGyver, she wasn't. Her training at Quantico had covered lots of topics—wiretapping, bomb-making, and firearms to mention a few—but never once had they covered automotive maintenance.

She could use her car as a battering ram to try to open the door of the container, but that was pretty risky. She could easily be killed in the resulting explosion or overcome by toxic fumes.

Raine decided to search her car for anything that might help get her out of here. Starting at the hatchback, she pulled her laptop out of its hiding place under the spare tire. If she were able to connect to the Internet she could have sent an e-mail to Daff or Aimee, but, unfortunately, she wasn't set up for satellite transmissions. It wasn't often that she needed to check e-mail from her car. Besides, she doubted the signal would make it through the walls of the container since, as she discovered when she pulled her cell phone from her purse, which her kidnappers had thoughtfully left stuffed under the driver's seat, she couldn't get a cell signal in here, either.

Okay. So what did she have to work with? A laptop, a cell phone, and a jack. Great.

Raine sat down on the hood of her car and nibbled at her thumbnail. Hadn't she read about a bunch of Chinese who had stowed away in a cargo container bound for L.A.? They'd nearly died from the sweltering heat inside the container. Their trip to sunny California was ill-timed at the height of the summer season, but they'd managed to punch a fist-sized hole in the seal of the container and took turns gasping in breaths of fresh air. After weeks at sea in cramped quarters, the authorities who discovered the nearly dead men had deemed the container a hazardous waste site and had taken hours to decontaminate it.

Raine didn't plan to be in here that long. Her greatest threat was lack of water. She'd already been in here for a day and a half, and she'd drunk sparingly for half a day before that since she'd been stuck in an interrogation room with half a dozen of the Bureau's finest looking on. Plus, it was so damn stuffy in here that she was sweating—not perspiring, but sweating—profusely, which just exacerbated her thirst.

If she could make a small hole in the container's seal, though, she might be able to hang her cell phone outside and get a strong enough signal to make a call. She'd recently bought a camera phone, and hopefully, she'd be able to capture enough of the passing scenery for Aimee or Daff—who also had the new phones, thanks to Raine's infusion of capital into the business—to recognize where she was. If not . . . well, if not then maybe they'd have to call in some of their old friends from the Bureau to put a locator trace on her cell.

"THIS is bullshit and you know it," Calder said, eyeing his boss from across his desk.

"We've reviewed the tapes of the interview you did with the girl and find no evidence of wrongdoing. But she says that your inappropriate behavior began in your car. Why didn't you ask Agent Wilkins to take the girl?"

Calder leaned forward, his right knee jiggling agitatedly. He didn't have time for this, not with Raine still missing. He'd put a trace on her cell at four o'clock yesterday morning and spent last night sitting inside her apartment with her hostile friend Daphne looking as if she'd like to stab him in the neck with a butter knife the minute he closed his eyes.

He hadn't slept in days, and now he was being accused of flirting with a twelve-year-old, and Raine had disappeared without a trace.

What a fucking pooch screw, as his dad would say.

"I didn't have Shari take the girl in because she seemed to have a better rapport with Judge Monroe than anyone else on the team and, in his agitated state, I felt that she should stay with him. The daughter seemed to calm down after Moss was taken away and I didn't see any need to call in the assistance of another agent to take her back to the office. Since we all arrived at the scene in our own vehicles, it would have complicated the logistics unnecessarily to have another agent leave his car at the Greyhound station just to make the twenty-minute ride back here with me. Miss Monroe was in the backseat of my car the entire time I was driving and I never said anything inappropriate to her. You know this kind of crap happens all the time."

Alex Jarvis seemed to take up all the extra space in Calder's small office. "Yes, it does. That's why you'd think you'd know better than to ride alone with a female sexual-assault victim."

Calder surreptitiously clicked the button on his computer to refresh the trace on Raine's cell phone, an action he'd performed at least twenty times in the last ten minutes. "I shouldn't have to protect myself from those I'm trying to protect," he muttered.

"This is the reality of law enforcement, Preston. It's not always as easy as the good guys versus the bad guys."

Calder's tenuous hold on his temper snapped as he suddenly realized that this was exactly how Raine must have felt after being accused of Jeffrey Allen's murder. Every day, he risked his life to get scumbags like John Moss off the streets and this was the kind of shit he had to put up with? He slammed his hand down on top of his jiggling right knee to make it stop and glared at his boss across his desk. "Look, I made a judgment call. If you don't trust my judgment, then maybe it's time you consider firing me."

Calder clicked the REFRESH button on his computer again, then jerked to attention when, instead of the "no signal found" response he'd received since yesterday morning, he got a latitude/longitude reading instead. His phone rang at the same instant that he clicked the button to see the location on a map.

He looked at the caller ID on his phone and picked up, answering with a terse, "She's in Arizona. What the hell's she doing there?"

"I don't know," Aimee answered. "She called Daff, but all we're getting is picture feed. She isn't talking."

"Okay. I'll be right there." Calder hung up the phone and grabbed his laptop. "I've got to go. Raine's in danger," he said to Alex, pushing back his chair.

Alex looked at him steadily for a moment, his dark eyes hiding whatever he was feeling. "I'll grant you a short leave of absence due to a family emergency. I expect you to be available for questioning in the Monroe case, however. Do you understand?"

Calder understood exactly. His boss was doing his best to salvage Calder's career.

"Yeah, I understand," Calder said quietly. "Thank you."

Alex just nodded as Calder yanked open the door to his office, nearly tripping on a basket someone had left on the floor outside. Calder reached down and picked it up, his cheeks flaming with anger when he realized what the basket contained.

"For your new girlfriend," the card read in neat, block letters. Inside the basket were Barbie and Ken dolls, plus a bag of Hershey's Kisses and some balloons.

"Very funny, you assholes," Calder yelled. None of the agents in the office would look him in the eye as he shot the room a disgusted glare. Ripping off the card, he thrust the basket back toward Alex. "Here, why don't you give this to your kids. But I'd check the candy first if I were you. Knowing these jerks, you'll find a razor blade in it."

TWENTY-FOUR

"WHY isn't she talking to you?" Calder asked, clasping his hands behind his back to stop himself from driving a fist into the wall with frustration. It was, indeed, Raine's number that showed up on the screen of Daphne's cell phone, but ever since she'd called, all they heard on the other end was silence.

"Obviously, because she can't," Daphne answered without taking her eyes off the screen.

"What is your problem, Daphne?" Calder stopped pacing to glare at the redhead.

"You're the problem, Preston. You can't keep showing up in Raine's life when it's convenient for you. She deserves someone who loves her enough to stick it out during the hard times."

Calder was surprised by the calm tone of Daphne's voice. He had expected her to respond in anger, but her quietly uttered words had even more impact than if she had yelled them.

Balancing himself on the arm of the couch, he reined in his own anger. "I know she does. That's why I'm here. I realized two days ago that I love her too much to let her go again."

Daphne's eyes flickered to him and then back to her cell's video screen, but before she could say anything else, Aimee interrupted. "You two need to bury this animosity right now. We've got to focus all of our energy on finding Raine. When we do, you're welcome to get back in the ring and go another ten rounds for all I care, but for now, knock it off."

Calder was getting a little tired of being treated like a recalcitrant child, but figured it wouldn't make things any better if he pointed out that Daphne was the one who'd started it. Besides, he agreed that their focus should be on finding Raine, not on fighting among themselves.

He raised his hands, palms up in surrender and said, "You're right. Look, I'm going to go out and get my laptop and see if I can get the phone company to tap this phone call and send the image Raine's transmitting to me, too. That way, we'll have a larger picture to analyze."

"Good thinking," Aimee said.

Daphne just grunted, but Calder took that as a sign of approval, or at least of acceptance that he was here to stay. He'd met Daphne before, briefly, when he and Raine had been together in Chicago, but he didn't remember her being so . . . hard-edged. Of course, a woman's friends were never hard on her boyfriend when the relationship was going well. It was during the rocky patches that they turned on the guy, eager to agree about what an asshole he was for leaving the toilet seat up or not calling at the exact time he said he would.

He knew that wasn't fair, though. His crimes against their relationship were vastly worst than that. He could only imagine the support Daff and Aimee had been pressed upon to provide when Raine moved out of his life. He, at least, had work to bury himself in. Raine had had nothing but her friends.

Calder grabbed his laptop from the passenger seat of his car and walked back to the house, neatly shoving his emotional turmoil into a mental compartment and locking the door behind it. Later, he could reexamine his feelings of guilt for abandoning Raine. For now, he had work to do.

Within minutes, he had a mirror image of the video being

transmitted from Raine's phone to Daphne's up on his computer screen. Aimee pulled up a chair next to him at the dining room table and peered at the footage. So far, all they'd seen was mile after mile of seemingly endless desert. Calder had called his counterpart at the FBI office in Phoenix to ask for assistance, but the woman who answered the phone told him that they didn't have the manpower to spare if he couldn't give her more specific information as to Raine's whereabouts. The coordinates he'd gotten from the traced call put her on or near Interstate 10, along with hundreds of other travelers.

"Okay, let's start brainstorming some possibilities," Calder said, taking a notepad of yellow lined paper out of his laptop bag. "She's obviously traveling at a fairly fast clip on some sort of ground transport—a car, a semi, or a train."

"Or a bus," Aimee added.

"Well, that narrows it down," Daphne muttered, earning her a frown from Aimee.

"We're assuming that Raine is with her cell phone. Is that a safe assumption?" Aimee asked.

"I think we have to go with that. Who else would have called Daphne's number? And why would they be feeding us this information?"

"Maybe to throw us off track," Daphne suggested.

"That could be, but it's our only lead. Even if it's a dead end, we have nothing better to go on," Calder said.

"I agree," Aimee added. "If it's a red herring, we might be able to find some evidence as to Raine's whereabouts if we find her phone."

"Okay, so we know that her phone, at least, is on a bus, train, car, or semi. The terrain she's passing by is too close for a plane and I think we can safely rule out a boat. Let's try to narrow down our options. If she's traveling on a bus, car, or semi, we should see some glimpses of pavement or other vehicles."

"Wait a minute," Daphne interrupted as a dark shape appeared on the edge of her screen. She squinted at it, then gave up and moved to stand behind Calder. As the shape got closer to Raine's phone, its image became clearer. It was a train, barreling down fast on the phone.

"I think we have our answer," Aimee said.

"Yeah, unless she's in a car that's on a road paralleling a set of railroad tracks," Calder said skeptically.

Just then, the image blurred and then, suddenly, the screen went black.

"Fuck," Calder cursed, frantically grabbing up Daphne's phone in the hopes that only he had lost the connection. But Daphne's screen was the same inky black as his, making him curse again.

They waited, staring at his computer screen to see if the images would come back online.

Calder switched to his call tracing program and hit RE-FRESH, but the reading didn't change, which meant that either Raine had stopped or she'd lost her phone. *If she's still alive.*

Calder shoved the thought away. She had to be alive. He would accept nothing else.

"All right, I'm going to get on the phone with the railroads and see what trains they'd expect to see in the Phoenix area at this time of day."

"I'll call the Phoenix P.D. and see if they can get an officer to check out the tracks where Raine dropped her phone," Daphne volunteered.

"And I'll go make some coffee," Aimee said. "I'm guessing we're all going to be up pretty late again."

SHE'D lost her phone and she was dying of thirst. Literally.

Raine had checked over her car three times, trying to find anything she could drink. She'd even dipped her finger into the wiper fluid well, hoping that someone at the Jiffy Lube had filled it up with plain water instead of soap, but no luck.

She wished her superhero training had covered escaping from a locked cargo container. Funny, she thought, sitting in the driver's seat of her VW and staring into the darkness, how the books she'd read always portrayed FBI agents as nearly invincible. She didn't feel invincible.

"Maybe that's because you're not an agent anymore," she said wistfully.

Maybe that was it. Maybe it was the badge that had made her feel so powerful, not the sixteen weeks of training she'd received at the FBI Academy. She didn't know what good her badge would have done her in this situation, though. Unless the new badges came equipped with laser-beams that could slice through steel.

Raine laid her head back on the headrest and closed her eyes.

She wondered if anyone had missed her yet. Aimee and Daff weren't expecting to see her until tomorrow night, when they'd planned to meet at Aimee's for a going-away party. Aimee was leaving on Saturday morning for San Antonio to start her case with McConnell Aviation and Daff was headed up to New York on Sunday for a meeting on Monday with her brother's publisher. Funny, she'd signed Partners In Crime's first client and she was also the first one to start her case. Made sense, she supposed.

Her mind wandered over the sparse facts of the Enslar case: the crippled father, his successful daughter, the missing Pioneer up in Boston.

And then, perhaps because her woozy mind was more imaginative than her lucid one, it occurred to Raine that the missing teen could be in the same situation Raine herself was in. Megan had been sleeping in her mother's Pioneer when it was stolen and the thieves could have driven the SUV, with Megan in it, into a container just like this one and shipped her somewhere. That would explain the disappearance of both the girl and the car.

Of course, her theory could be nothing more than an elaborate plot brought about by thirst and the aftereffects of the drugs in her system.

"Why would thieves steal one car and ship it somewhere, though?" she asked herself.

Raine shook her head, trying to clear it as she stared at her windshield wipers. Whether her theory was right or not, she'd never be able to share it with anyone if she didn't get out of this damn metal box.

But what could she do? She'd already tried to enlarge the hole in the container's seal, but it was no use. No matter how big the hole, she wasn't thin enough to slip through the gap. But the thought of just sitting here waiting to die wasn't acceptable either.

Raine chewed on the inside of her cheek, but try as she might, she couldn't think of what to do.

She'd already tried turning on the engine to see if any exhaust was visible. If it was, she could back the car up and gouge another hole in the seal at exhaust pipe level to try to signal someone that something was wrong back here. Unfortunately, her car was running fine and the exhaust coming out of the pipe was warm, but completely colorless.

Next, she thought about trying to soak pieces of her car's carpeting with gasoline and setting them on fire outside the container, but she didn't have any matches and her cigarette lighter had been replaced with a cell phone charger instead.

In a few more hours, she knew she was going to have to try the one thing she'd hesitated doing earlier—ramming her car into the door of the container to see if it would budge. The problem was, she would have to be close enough to the car to release the emergency brake when she did it, so that meant she couldn't hide upstairs. It would be dangerous. Even without an explosion, car parts would be flying around at high speed and there was nowhere Raine could hide for protection.

No, she would give Daff and Aimee a few more hours to find her before she made one last-ditch effort to save herself . . . or die trying.

TWENTY-FIVE

MEGAN knew the instant that things changed. She had become so accustomed to the soothing hum beneath her that when it stopped, her head jerked up from the book that she had been reading.

Her parents would be astounded at the enthusiasm with which she had thrown herself into books after days and days of abject boredom. In the stack of library books she'd found, she'd discovered a bunch of paperback novels. She had never realized that reading could be so fun. It was like getting to go on an adventure without actually having to experience the same discomforts that Megan had become all too familiar with during her ordeal.

Because she didn't want to run down the battery of her getaway car, Megan used the dome lights of the other vehicles in the container to read. So far, the batteries of four out of the eight vehicles were dead. When number six died, she'd have to quit reading.

Fortunately, in between books she had practiced what she was going to do when the rebels opened the container, so Megan was on her feet running as soon as the vibration stopped. She had picked her safe car very carefully. She needed a vehicle that was small enough to be fast and get good gas mileage but still be safe. It had to have a full tank of gas, plenty of oil, and have a place where she could hide if she needed to.

She hated having to cross Antonio's convertible off her list, but she knew that, even with the top up, it wasn't as safe as one of the more practical cars. Plus, when she looked at the gas gauge, she'd discovered that it only had half a tank left. In the end, she'd decided on a dark blue two-door with backseats that folded down to expand the capacity of the trunk. It was the first car on the first floor, three cars behind her mother's SUV. She had scraped together everything that might be used as a weapon or for survival once she escaped and loaded it all into the trunk, leaving herself just enough room to hide.

At first, she'd thought a car on the second level would be safer, but then she tried to anticipate which cars the rebels would unload first and decided they'd probably move the first floor out and then start on the second. Besides, she figured it would be easier to escape from the first floor if something happened because she wouldn't have to get the car down to ground level before making her getaway.

Now, with something going on outside the container, Megan figured it was time to put her plan into action.

She tossed the book she'd been reading into the trunk of the blue car and wiggled backward into her hiding place. She'd carefully rigged a piece of the twine Silver Eyes had tied her up with to the backseat of the car so that she could pull it nearly shut behind her. Then she'd propped a screwdriver she'd found in one of the cars in the gap to make sure she didn't close herself in.

During one of her many practice runs, she'd made sure she knew how to escape, both by kicking the backseat in front of her to ensure that it would open if the screwdriver got displaced and she accidentally shut herself in and by finding the trunk release.

There was no way these bastards were going to keep her trapped in here forever.

It quickly became stuffy in the trunk, even worse than it had been before. Megan wiped the sweat off her upper lip and tried not to breathe too deeply. After what she figured was about a week in the same clothes, she didn't smell too good—and she smelled even worse in the close quarters of the trunk of her safe car.

Megan rested her chin on her hands and watched the keys to the car dangle in front of her eyes. When it was time for her to make her getaway, she didn't want to have to worry about where the keys were, so she'd tied them to the string she used to close herself inside the trunk and then tied a pocketknife she'd found in someone's glove compartment right below them.

She waited for something to happen, for the guerillas or *someone* to jerk open the door of the container, but for what seemed like hours, it was silent. Megan felt her eyelids grow heavy in the hot confines of the trunk, but didn't allow herself to open the gap any wider. She wished she could read her book again. She had been at a good part when the vibration stopped and she wanted to know how the heroine managed to save the world from an unscrupulous—a word she'd learned while reading the book—nuclear arms dealer. But it was too dark in the trunk to see much of anything. So instead, she visualized what she was going to do when her car was offloaded from the container. She'd wait a few minutes and let the rebels go back for the next car and then, with the keys in her hand, she'd stealthily—another new word learned while reading—creep out of the trunk and into the driver's seat. Then she'd floor the accelerator with all her might and get the hell out of there.

She stifled a yawn and closed her eyes, telling herself she could visualize the scene much better that way. Just as Megan started to doze off, she was jerked awake by the sound of a metallic screech.

"Ow," she yelped as her head whacked the side of the car.

Suddenly, the car tilted forward and Megan slid against the back of the seat in front of her. Before she could stop herself, she was halfway out of the trunk. A faint memory stirred in her brain. Back when her mother's car had first been stolen, the container had moved like this, and it had only gotten worse.

If she managed to get herself back into the trunk, she could end up getting smacked by something sharp that she'd stowed back there.

No, it would be better if she buckled herself in.

Megan let herself slide all the way out of the trunk just as the container shifted backward. She used that momentum to shut the seat so that none of her supplies could fall out. With her feet braced on the back of the passenger seat, she held herself in place and grabbed for the seatbelt. She knew the container had to stay relatively stable or the vehicles inside would crash into one another. Still, she felt safer being buckled in as the container wobbled around.

Anticipation that her ordeal was nearing an end made Megan feel like yelling, but she didn't dare. She couldn't wait to see her family again, to sleep in her own room and talk on the phone with Emily and go to school every day. She couldn't believe that she actually missed school, but she did. It gave her life purpose, kept her moving ahead, and gave her a sense of accomplishment with every test she passed, every semester that ended.

Even more, she realized how valuable knowledge was. If she knew more about chemistry, she might have figured out what chemicals she had in here that would burn through metal and get her out. If she knew more about geography, she might be able to recognize where she was when the container door opened. If she'd paid more attention to her foreign languages, she might be able to find someone to help her even in a strange land.

That was the key to James Bond, and even to Charlie's Angels. They knew stuff, useful stuff that helped get them out of binds. It was that knowledge, even more than their strength or powerful guns or great hair, that saved them.

Megan wanted that knowledge now, too. And as soon as she got back home, she was going to throw herself into her studies with a fervor her teachers had never seen. At least, not from her.

Megan bounced up and back down again on the seat and

then waited for the next jolt to occur. Instead, there was only silence and a strange lack of movement that made her shiver. Hurriedly, she unbuckled her seatbelt and repositioned herself in the trunk to wait for the rebels to appear.

And she waited. And waited. And waited. And, finally, she slept.

IT was time.

Raine blinked, her eyelids long unaccustomed to any moisture. It was like sandpaper running along a piece of glass, harsh grains of sand scoring the surface.

She resisted the urge to rub her eyes, knowing it would just make it worse. A dry, hacking cough racked her lungs and abraded her sore throat.

God, what she wouldn't give for a six-pack of Coke.

Raine forced herself to stop thinking about fluids. *That way lay madness.*

She refused to voice the thought. She had neither the energy nor the oxygen to spare. Breathing had become more and more difficult and she tried not to waste the effort unnecessarily.

Pushing her back against the warm metal of the container, Raine eased herself up off the floor and walked to the open driver's side door of her VW. A few hours ago when she still felt she had some strength left in her, she had rigged it all up. First, she had tried to break off the door, knowing it would be easier for her to yank on the parking brake and get out of the way without having to worry about getting smacked by the open door of the car. An added benefit was that she could use the door as a shield to hide behind when she sent the VW careening toward the opening of the container.

It had taken nearly all her strength, but she had done it.

Next, she pushed the car all the way to the back of the container so it would have the maximum amount of distance to gather speed. Then she rigged her jack under the seat and against the gas pedal so that when she turned the ignition, the engine would get plenty of gas.

Finally, she took off her shirt and tore it into strips. With two strips, she tied the steering wheel in place, looping one around the rearview mirror and another around a hole where the driver's side door used to be attached. Then, deciding that she might not have the mental edge needed to get out of the way of the tires after she released the parking brake, Raine tied the remaining strips of her shirt together, tied one end to the pull-handle of the parking brake and neatly laid the rest of her makeshift rope in a straight line to the door that was propped at an angle against the wall of the container.

Now, with her eyes so dry she could hardly keep them open, her lips cracked and swollen, and her lungs burning, Raine knew she had to take this chance. Staying trapped in here any longer would only mean certain death.

She figured this crazy scheme decreased her chance of death to only about 95 percent.

Raine slid her hand along the hood of her car, trying to keep her balance as the train swayed from one side to another. As she turned the key in the ignition and heard the car's engine rev, she tried not to think of anyone she knew and loved. That was too melancholy and made her want to start crying again, which she discovered was impossible in her state of dehydration.

Unfortunately, much as she might want to keep her mind off her loved ones, her brain had ideas of its own. *Poor Neall,* she thought.*When I'm gone, he won't have any family left.*

She was glad that Daff would still have Aimee for a friend. Raine could feel her friend's humanity slipping further and further away, and she knew that Aimee sensed it, too. Daff's brother, Brooks, might buy her lie that because she no longer haunted Ground Zero she was healing, but Aimee knew better and she wouldn't let Daff go, no matter how hard she tried to push her friend away.

And Calder? How long would it take him to forget about her? How long until he found a woman who would never do anything to interfere with his career? Who would never even consider rubbing elbows with child molesters, rapists, and terrorists. Who would never hand him the terrible choice she had handed him over a plastic table and a couple of Big Macs: Your career or me, pick one.

God, how she wished he had chosen her. Selfish as she knew that was, it was how she felt. Even knowing how important his job was to him, she had silently hoped he'd be waiting outside after she'd told him to leave.

She had lied to him. She had told him she would never make him choose, but that's what she had been doing. Only, he had picked the wrong answer. Now she was going to die here, all alone.

Raine closed her eyes as she tugged the gearshift down into reverse with her foot on the brake. If the parking brake didn't hold . . . well, Raine was prepared to stay with the car if the parking brake didn't hold. It was her only chance.

Slowly, she eased up on the brake and let out a sigh of relief when the car remained in place.

She climbed out of the car, careful not to bump the rigging she'd prepared, and took up her position behind the door propped against the corner of the container. She'd stowed her laptop and flashlight there, and took a seat beside them, picking up the end of the tattered rope she'd tied together.

Yes, it was time.

Raine pulled in an aching breath, peered around the edge of the door, and yanked. Her head thwacked the wall of the container, bouncing off of it like some character in a cartoon, as the rope broke. She would have cried tears of pain if she'd had any left in her. Instead, she didn't even bother to rub her throbbing skull as she crawled out from behind her makeshift shelter.

The VW sat mocking her with its shiny new paint job and big, bright eyes, its engine revving merrily.

Okay then, let's do this the hard way.

Raine scooted along the floor on her hands and knees until she reached the car. Pulling herself up into a crouch, she reached out with her right hand and grabbed the parking brake's release handle.

All right. Give it a tug and dive for cover.

Without waiting for her brain to protest, she did just that, pulling on the brake as she tried to get out of the way of the car's path.

But she wasn't fast enough. As the car zoomed toward her, Raine threw herself backward. The left front tire ran over her right foot and Raine screamed and scrabbled toward her shelter.

Before she could get undercover, the sickening sound of metal against metal and the smell of leaking acid hit her like a wave as the VW rammed the door of the cargo container. Something hard and heavy smashed into her thigh as she dove behind the door and curled herself into a ball, trying to protect her head.

When the first explosion sounded, all she could think was, *I hope Calder misses me when I'm gone.*

TWENTY-SIX

"I am a federal officer, and I'm ordering you to stop that train," Calder said, nearly shouting in his frustration to get this bureaucratic asshole to do what he was told.

"Do you have a warrant to search the train?" the fortyish-looking man asked.

Did everyone in America know about proper search and seizure procedure these days? Damn cop shows.

Calder rounded the man's desk menacingly. "No. I didn't have time to get a warrant. A woman's life is in danger. You need to stop the train."

"Look, I would if I could. But it's my job on the line if I do what you ask without the proper documentation. We've got crews waiting in L.A. to offload the cargo and get it rerouted onto trucks and other trains. If this train is late, we're paying all those guys to stand around with nothing to do. Like I said, without a search warrant, I can't stop this train."

Calder turned to look out the window at the empty tracks behind the man's desk. According to the railroad employee, the train Calder prayed Raine was on was still about ten minutes from this small waystation. They were only an hour from L.A., but what were the chances that he'd have any better luck there? He'd meet the same resistance in L.A. trying to get someone to let him search the train while they were offloading its cargo.

He flipped open his phone and dialed Aimee's number. "Any luck with the warrants?" he asked.

"Not yet. I—"

"Oh, shit!" the man next to him yelled, leaping up out of his chair.

"What?" Calder asked, anxiously turning back toward the window in the man's office.

"The conductor just tripped the fire signal," the man answered, stabbing several buttons on a panel in front of him.

"I've gotta go," Calder said, abruptly ending his call to Aimee. "Where are they?"

"Still about eight miles back. The fire department should already be on their way."

"Come with me," Calder ordered, and this time the man obeyed. They raced outside and jumped in Calder's rental car, with Calder silently making simultaneous deals with both God and the devil to keep Raine safe.

"Take a left," the railroad employee said as Calder spun the car out of the driveway.

In minutes, they could see the train, its brakes laboring under the effort to slow thousands of tons of steel, lumber, and other freight to a stop.

"It'll take them a bit longer to come to a complete stop," the railroad employee said, but Calder kept driving, headed toward the smoking cargo container three cars from the caboose. There were no signs yet of any fire or rescue vehicles, and Calder ruthlessly crushed the fear that they would be too late. He knew that Raine was in that container as surely as if she had come out waving a white flag.

He drove his car up over the grassy bank leading up to the railroad tracks and wasted barely a second shoving it in park before leaping out to race to the now-stopped train.

Smoke oozed out of the cargo container from every tiny hole and crevice as Calder ran around to the back of the flatbed car. The door of the container was slightly askew, and thick, gray fumes poured from the narrow gap. Calder slammed his fist against the metal and yelled, "Raine, where are you?"

He tried peering into the container, but got a lungful of smoke for his trouble. The bottom of the container hit him at about gut level and it was hard to see through the smoke pouring out. Coughing, Calder frantically tugged on the door of the container, searching for a handle of some sort when it wouldn't budge. When his probing fingers encountered a lock, he cursed, but didn't stop yanking on the door.

"Raine," he called again, banging on the door with his free hand. "Raine, are you in there?"

The squeal of sirens sounded in the distance as Calder stood outside the container, frustrated by his inability to help save her. What if the entire cargo inside the container was on fire? Raine would be in there, burning alive while he stood outside banging and yelling, unable to do anything more.

"No!" he yelled. "You're not going to die. Not today. Not while I'm alive. Do you hear me, Raine? You're not going to die today."

Calder gasped when a hand suddenly appeared from the gap between the door of the container and the floor. He crouched down, trying to see through the thick smoke as he grabbed Raine's hand.

The sirens grew louder, but Calder ignored them, pressing closer to the container and reaching up to feel along Raine's wrist up to her elbow. He couldn't get his hand past that because the gap in the seal was too narrow.

Please, he prayed, *please let her be all right.*

And then, faintly but clearly, through the thick smoke choking his lungs and burning his eyes, he heard her say, "Did you miss me?"

CALDER sat on the hard vinyl chair next to Raine's bed and watched her sleep. She looked a lot better than when the fire department had cut her out of the cargo container, her eyes red-rimmed and swollen, her hair hanging limp and lifeless around her shoulders, her pale skin covered with soot and bruises.

He brushed a lock of hair away from her forehead, wishing he could forever erase that awful picture of her from his mind. Leaning forward, he rested his elbows on his knees and stared at the bland linoleum under his feet.

She had almost died.

If the train had made it to L.A., the container she was trapped in was to have been loaded on another train headed up to Anchorage, while other containers were headed to cities all across the country. Since he had no idea which cargo shipment to look in, the task of finding her before her body shut down due to dehydration would have been nearly impossible. Not that that would have stopped him from trying.

"Bet you wish I was a librarian."

Calder raised his head to find Raine looking at him, her mouth curved up in a slight smile. He reached out to take her hand, his fingers intertwining with hers. "Yeah," he admitted sheepishly. "I guess I do."

"I feel the same way about you."

Calder frowned. "What?"

Raine's smile widened, but then she winced, making Calder reach for the lip balm on the nightstand next to her bed. Her lips were dry and cracked and he dipped a finger into the tub of oily goo and smoothed it gently over her mouth. She leaned her cheek into his hand when he was done, closing her eyes tiredly.

"You think you've cornered the market on feeling protective of the people you care about?" she asked.

"Of course not. I just . . ." He shrugged, not comfortable with this line of questioning. "I suppose I never thought about how you felt when I was on an op. I supposed you knew I could take care of myself, so you wouldn't worry."

She laughed, her breath tickling his palm. "Are you implying that I can't take care of myself?"

Calder looked at the tubes sticking out of her arm and the bruise on her forehead and resisted the urge to climb into bed with her and wrap her so tightly in his embrace that she would have trouble breathing. Instead, he curled his fingers into her face, caressing her cheekbone and rubbing his thumb along her jaw. "Well, you *are* the one wearing the backless gown, aren't you?"

"I was hoping you might find it sexy."

Calder felt a sudden intense pressure behind his eyes and knew he had to get out of here. How could she joke around like this? Didn't she know how close she had been to dying?

How would he have lived without her? How could he have gone on, day after day, with his heart buried six feet underground? And she was fucking *joking* about it.

"Look," he said, pulling his hand out from underneath her head, "I shouldn't be here. You need your rest and the only reason the nurses let me stay was because I told them I needed to ask you some questions. I'll see you tomorrow morning. The doctor said she should be able to release you around nine."

Gathering his suit jacket from the back of the chair, Calder stood up to leave.

"You're not invincible either, you know," Raine said quietly, and he turned to find her watching him with her cool green eyes. "What happened to me tonight could just as easily have happened to you. You may be a hero, but you're not immortal."

Calder walked to the door of her room and, without looking back, he muttered, "Hell, Raine, I'm not even a hero."

Then he left, closing the door behind him with a soft click.

TWENTY-SEVEN

"WOMEN going through labor aren't even kept in the hospital this long," Raine complained, restlessly shoving the thin hospital blanket down to the foot of her bed.

"The doctor hasn't signed your release papers yet," Calder said impassively from beside her, not bothering to look up from the latest edition of *Cosmo*. "Is it true that all I have to do to get you to be my eternal love slave is to give you a backrub every now and then when I don't want sex? That seems counterintuitive."

"We're women. Logic is foreign to us," Raine said, her voice dripping with sarcasm.

Calder had shown up this morning in a surprisingly cheerful mood. He had picked up a discarded stack of magazines from the nurses' station and was proceeding to work his way down the stack, from *People* to *Good Housekeeping* and now on to *Cosmo*. He didn't even seem to care that the doctor was almost an hour late.

Raine, on the other hand, was sick and tired of confinement. After being trapped in that cargo container, she wanted to get outside and see the sky . . . and get back to work on both the Enslar case and on finding out who had set up the hits on Jeffrey Allen and Grady Thompson and framed her for it. She had a hunch that whoever had trapped her inside that container had something to do with one of these cases, and she'd had enough of playing the victim. Now it was time to go on the attack.

"You could at least give me the clothes you brought so I can get changed," she cajoled. "That way, we can leave as soon as the doctor comes."

"I don't trust you," Calder said. Then added, "Besides, I've got to finish this magazine. There's this quiz about what your sexual fantasies say about you. What do you think mine will say?"

"That you're a controlling jerk who thinks women belong in boring, safe jobs because you don't think they can take care of themselves?" Raine suggested sweetly.

Calder took a pen out of his jacket pocket, made some notes on the magazine, and then looked up at her with surprise. "Well, imagine that. That's exactly what the experts say, too."

Raine nearly growled with frustration. She wanted out of here. Now.

Finally, the door swung open and the shockingly young woman who was Raine's doctor entered the room. "Good morning," she said cheerfully.

Raine grunted, and impatiently answered the woman's questions about how she was feeling. After several minutes of poking, prodding, and chart notating, the doctor nodded her satisfaction and told Raine she could go.

Calder thanked the doctor and handed Raine the plastic bag containing the clothes he'd bought for her that morning.

"Did you bring my laptop?" Raine asked as she scooted off the bed and stood up, holding the back of her hospital gown together behind her. No matter that Calder had seen her naked butt before, there was something just plain sick and wrong about letting her gown gape open like that.

"Yes, it's out in the car. I downloaded your e-mail last night in my hotel room. Man, you get a lot of messages."

"Yeah, hackers love e-mail," Raine called from the

bathroom, not bothering to close the door as she pulled on the black nylon thong panties Calder had so thoughtfully provided. Okay, so maybe he was an overprotective jerk, but he wasn't all bad.

"I saw a few from your brother, Neall. Are you two still getting along?"

Raine pulled a brightly patterned floral skirt out of the bag and snapped off the tag. Calder had bought a black, V-neck blouse to go with the skirt, plus a pair of low-heeled black sandals. She was impressed that he hadn't gone for jeans and a T-shirt. Really impressed. She pulled the blouse on over the black bra he'd bought and Raine stifled a giggle when she thought of him going up to a salesclerk and saying, "I need to buy a bra for a woman. She's about so big," and cupping his palms to demonstrate her small but adequately sized breasts.

Pulling a hand through her hair to straighten it, Raine responded to Calder's question about her relationship with Neall. "We're doing fine. I doubt we'll ever be close, but I appreciate his help on the Enslar case."

"Why are you two so distant? I mean, I know you grew up in different households, but you *are* family."

Raine slipped her feet into the sandals Calder had bought and wished she'd thought to ask him to buy her some make-up while he was out shopping. A bit of foundation would have been nice to cover the purplish bruise on her forehead.

Oh well, there was nothing she could do about it now. She glanced in the mirror to make sure her rear view looked okay and then stepped back into the hospital room, where Calder had stood and was putting on his jacket to leave.

"I don't know why, exactly. Our visits typically overlapped a few weeks on either side. I would go to Mother's house in June and Neall wouldn't leave for Dad's house until July, then I'd come home in August and Neall wouldn't go back to France until September, but we just never seemed to hit it off. He always seemed . . . I don't know. Jealous, I guess. Maybe because I was older than him. Everything he tried, I'd already done. It didn't help that we had many of the same interests. I loved computers from the minute Dad introduced me to them, but by the time Neall got exposed to them, I was already way ahead of him. It was like he was always racing to catch up to me."

"Hmm. I can understand that. I suppose my younger brothers probably feel the same way."

Raine lightly punched his arm as they walked down the hall toward the exit. "Yeah, well, you probably treated them the same way you do me, so I'll bet they resented the hell out of you. Tell me, did you take on *their* bullies, too?"

Calder's steps faltered as he started coughing uncontrollably.

Raine looked at him, alarmed. "Are you all right? Are you suffering some aftereffects of smoke inhalation? Should I get the doctor?"

Calder raised one hand to stop her from summoning a crash cart and then choked out one last cough. "No, I'm fine. You just surprised me with your observation. I never realized that I did that."

"Did what?" Raine asked, having forgotten what she'd said in the anticipation of having to do an emergency tracheotomy.

The glass doors leading outside *whooshed* open and a slight breeze rushed in to greet them. Raine took a deep breath of fresh air and marveled at the sensation of sunshine bouncing off the pavement and warming her feet through her sandals. God, it felt good to be free again.

"I protected my brothers all the way through school. Even when I was in college, I'd make a point of showing up after their classes the first week of school to make sure nobody picked on them."

"See," Raine said cheerfully, her mood considerably lighter now that she was no longer cooped up, "you *are* an overprotective jerk."

She grabbed Calder's hand and stopped him on the sidewalk, smiling. He brooded back, his eyebrows drawing together as he frowned. "I'm not a jerk," he protested.

Raine lifted her free hand and wrapped it around his neck, pulling his forehead down to hers. "I know you're not," she said softly, kissing him on the mouth. "What I want to know is, while you were busy keeping everyone else safe, who was protecting you?"

Calder wrapped his arms around her back and pulled her so close that Raine could feel his chest rising and falling with each breath that he took. "I've always been able to take care of myself. It's the rest of you I'm not so sure about."

With that, he kissed her, his lips achingly gentle, as if he were worried that he might hurt her.

"THOSE HR meetings are such a waste of time," the head of IT muttered as he and Hope Enslar walked out of the conference room together.

"I know. Like we don't know that discrimination is illegal," Hope agreed. "Hey, I meant to call the help desk later but maybe you could help me."

"Sure. What's up?"

"My computer's been running a little slow lately. I wondered if maybe someone in your department could take a look at it."

"No problem. We may need to defrag your hard drive or optimize your paging file."

"Uh . . . okay," Hope said, which she figured sounded better than, "huh?" She might be an excellent web designer, but she'd never cared much for the more technical aspects of computers.

"I'll send somebody by to take a look at it."

"Great, thanks." Hope waved at the IT manager before turning down the hallway that led to R&D. Within half an hour, a jeans-clad techie was sitting behind her desk, muttering to himself as he clicked her mouse from one task to the next. Hope sat at the round table over by the bank of windows and realized how dependent she was on technology when she found herself with nothing to do. Everything she did nowadays required a computer. Weird.

"Well, here's the problem," the help desk guy said, making Hope look up from the table she'd been blankly staring at for the last five minutes.

She got up and went to stand behind the man sitting in her chair. She expected the answer to be evident on her screen, but all she saw was a black window with a bunch of undecipherable text on it.

"What is it?" she asked finally.

"Did you know that someone's been recording your every keystroke?"

Hope's mouth dropped open, but she shut it immediately when she realized she must look ridiculous. "No. I didn't."

"It looks like this program was installed"—he typed in a command and hit ENTER—"on Monday at two twenty-eight P.M."

"This isn't something that JMC's doing company-wide, is it?" Hope asked, feeling every thud of her heart as she contemplated what this meant.

"No. There are companies that employ the use of spyware to keep tabs on their employees, but I refuse to work for them. I figure if an employee is spending so much time surfing the Net that he's not able to perform his job, his supervisor should fire him. If he's accomplishing his goals and still has time to goof off . . . well, I guess he's entitled to a little downtime, you know?"

Hope nodded, even though she didn't quite agree. "Can you tell who installed it? And what exactly does it do? I mean, so it records my keystrokes and then what?"

The IT guy leaned back in her chair as he continued scrolling through the text on her screen. "I can't tell who installed it, but I can tell you what it does. Whenever you type something, the program records what you've typed in a file that is open, but that you can't see. This particular program is set up to e-mail that log file every half hour whenever you're connected to the Internet. This type of program can be used by hackers who want to find out your passwords. For example, if you have an online brokerage account and you go to the site to sell some stock, what you type in as your username and password are recorded by the program. The hackers could then log into your account after you leave the site and wreak all sorts of havoc using the information you just unwittingly provided to them. That's just one example, of course."

At the mention of usernames and passwords, Hope felt herself becoming faint and had to lean against her credenza for support. She swallowed several times and took deep breaths, trying to keep herself from passing out.

When had she gone in and checked on the Mulroney's SUV? If it was after this program had been installed, whoever had installed it had access to the car theft website.

And had they seen her search for that missing teenager's SUV? If so, they would no doubt put two and two together and bring her in for questioning. What would she say to them? That she had merely been trying to help in the investigation? If so, why hadn't she come forward earlier to offer her assistance? And what if they discovered that the signal to disable the Mulroney's vehicle had been sent from her website?

But wait. She could explain all of this away. She could say that she was researching car theft statistics in conjunction with the nationwide survey that had just been released, and that it was only out of curiosity that she later checked the Mulroney's VIN to see if it turned up in her data. She could say she didn't offer to assist with the investigation because she had no information aside from what police already knew. All her records told her was that the tracking system on the SUV was disabled during the timeframe the police knew the Pioneer had gone missing, and that the vehicle's last known location was the grocery store parking lot.

The only thing that could hurt her would be if the spyware program had seen the sales information in her spreadsheet showing that the Pioneer was on its way to Venezuela.

"Can this program capture a picture of programs I've opened? Like if I opened a Word document someone sent me. Would the hacker who installed this program on my machine be able to see what the document said?"

The IT guy shook his head. "No. There are other programs that can do that, but whoever installed this seemed more interested in just capturing your keystrokes."

Hope felt her pulse slow. That was a relief. Since all of the information about the car theft ring resided on her laptop, if her computer was suddenly destroyed, there would be no way to link her with the disappearance of the Mulroney's vehicle.

The only thing that could trip her up now was if, by some miracle, Megan Mulroney survived that trip and was able to get to the authorities. Hope didn't believe that Victor and his team had left no evidence behind when they'd stolen the vehicles. It was impossible for them to drive a vehicle and not leave behind some clue such as hair or fingerprints. And if Victor was identified, Hope knew he'd take her down with him.

Despite Victor's assurances that the teen would either be dead from lack of water or would perish in the harsh South American jungle, Hope couldn't just trust fate on such an important matter.

But what could she do? She couldn't just call up the Venezuelan buyer and tell him to kill the girl if she had managed to survive the trip. What if the buyer was not sympathetic to her plight? After all, there was a big difference between buying stolen vehicles and murdering an innocent kid.

Hope also knew she couldn't call Victor to take care of this for her. He would just insist that she not break with her routine in case the Feds were watching. Or worse, he'd tell her to pack up and head for Mexico, which she couldn't do. She couldn't leave her father. He didn't have anyone else but her.

No, she was going to have to take care of that missing teen on her own.

"Are you okay?"

Hope realized that the IT guy was staring at her strangely, probably because she'd gone into a trance there for a while. She shook her head. "No. As a matter of fact, I'm not feeling very well. Could you uninstall that program for me so I can take my laptop and go home?"

"No problem," the techie answered.

In less than three minutes, he was finished. Hope stopped him just as she was about to leave.

"By the way," she asked, "were you able to tell where the recorded data was being sent?"

"Yeah. It was being e-mailed to <u>rainerobey@ partnersincrime.us.</u>"

TWENTY-EIGHT

"I knew it!" Raine screeched from the back bedroom of her apartment, causing both her brother and Calder to come running from the living room, where they were sorting through the thousands of lines of logged keystrokes that had been e-mailed to Raine from Hope Enslar's computer.

"What?" asked Calder, who was first to reach the room.

"That e-mail I got, the one with the gunshot sound file? It *does* contain the Thompson file. That's how the creep who framed me planted that evidence. I knew it."

Neall leaned against the doorframe. "Well, what good does that do you? It's not like you can trace the sender."

Raine swiveled back to look at her laptop. "Yeah, but it's nice to know that I was right."

"You're lucky that Wilkins got assigned to this case," Neall said. "Not a lot of agents would have released you with this kind of evidence against you."

"I know."

"Although, if Wilkins had held you, you would have been in a nice, safe jail cell instead of out getting kidnapped," Calder argued.

"I hardly think the words 'nice' and 'safe' can be used in conjunction with jail," Raine said dryly.

Calder crouched down and wrapped his strong arms around the back of her chair, encircling her chest in a tight hug. "I'm glad you're safe now," he whispered, nuzzling her hair out of the way to plant a kiss on the sensitive skin below her ear.

"Me, too." Raine reached up and laid her arms over his. His forearms and biceps were huge, easily twice the size of hers. As much as she hated to admit it, it gave her feminine heart a thrill to know that he was bigger and stronger than her. She wondered how many hundreds of thousands more years it would take to breed that sort of response out of the human race. Nowadays, even the top brass at the FBI realized that it wasn't brawn that made for a superior agent, it was brains.

Well, that and a hell of a lot of firearms training, Raine added.

In any event, she knew that big and strong wasn't as important in civilized society as smart and rich, but she couldn't dismiss the instinctive pull of attraction she felt for this man. And it wasn't his superior investigative techniques that made her stomach go all fluttery when he was around.

She looked up just then and caught Neall watching them intently. Uncomfortable with his scrutiny, she cleared her throat, dropped her hands from Calder's arms, and twisted around in her chair. Calder stood up, leaning against the edge of her desk while he gently massaged her shoulders.

Raine was about to start purring when she realized he was doing that love slave thing he had read about in *Cosmo* to her. Still, even knowing he had an ulterior motive, it felt too good to make him stop. Instead, she leaned back and let him continue.

"So, have you found anything yet that might link Hope Enslar to the missing girl in Boston?" she asked.

"Yes. The program captured her logging in to the JMC server and querying a program about the Mulroneys. Then she went to a website that no longer seems to exist on the Web and typed in the VIN of the missing Pioneer. I'm working to recover that website from the server where it was stored, but I'm not having much luck," Neall said.

Raine tilted her head to look at Calder. "Is this enough to bring her in for questioning?"

Calder was already shaking his head. "No way. That's too loose a connection for anyone to take seriously. All she'd have to say is that she read about the missing teen in her local paper and checked JMC's records out of curiosity."

"And the deleted website?"

"Without knowing what sort of site it is, we have nothing to go on."

"Okay, then I guess we just keep digging," Raine said, her shoulders slumping with defeat. "I have to tell you, though, after having been locked in a container myself for a few days, I think the chances that Megan is still alive are pretty slim. Unless she found water, she would have died from dehydration by now."

Calder rested his hands on the back of Raine's chair and crossed his ankles out in front of him. "I wish we knew where to start looking. Even if we were certain the Pioneer got loaded into a cargo container, it could be anywhere by now. And not just within the U.S. Those things get shipped all over the world."

"Well, unless you find anything in the last few e-mails from Hope's computer, I'd say we're out of leads," Raine said dispiritedly.

"Yeah, let's just pray she screws up soon," Calder said, giving Raine's shoulder one last squeeze before making his way back to his computer.

MEGAN stared down at her last bottle of water and struggled to hold back her tears. The temperature inside the trunk had steadily increased throughout the past few hours, until she felt like a human cinnamon roll. She had stubbornly refused to open that last bottle of water, though, knowing that as soon as she did, the clock would start ticking down the hours until she died. With the cap still tightly closed on that bottle, she could live indefinitely.

But she was so thirsty.

Sweat dripped off her constantly, soaking her bra and panties. She had stripped out of her T-shirt and sweats long ago, keeping them close so she could pull them on in a hurry when the container was opened.

What if they never opened it, though?

Megan squeezed her eyes shut. No, they had to open it sometime. Why bother to steal all these cars if someone didn't want them?

Maybe they were storing them somewhere, like out in the middle of the desert, for a few months or even a year so nobody would be suspicious when the stolen vehicles turned up again?

"No, that isn't going to happen," she said aloud.

This was just like what her crew instructor always said. The minute you believe you're beaten, you've lost the race.

She wasn't ready to believe she was beaten. Not yet.

Megan took the last bottle of water and pushed it to the dark recesses of the trunk where she couldn't see it anymore. Having to look at it was like putting a diet pill in front of an anorexic. She might be able to resist for a little while, but the compulsion to take what she so desperately craved would overcome her eventually.

Megan forced her breathing to slow, trying to conserve her energy.

She would need everything she had—mentally and physically—when they finally opened the door of the container and let her out.

RAINE groggily picked up the telephone beside her bed on the fifth ring. Before she could answer, the voice on the other end of the line shouted, "Caracas."

"Yeah, and mariachi to you, too." Raine's voice was muffled by the pillow she had her face planted in.

"Raine, wake up. Hope Enslar's booked herself on a flight

.o Caracas that leaves this afternoon. My sweepers picked it
up and alerted me the second she paid for the ticket with her
American Express. We've got to get packed. I've already
booked tickets for the same flight."

"Who is it?" Calder grumbled beside her.

Raine yawned and forced herself to get out of bed. "It's
Neall. I'll take it in the other room."

Calder mumbled something incoherent and rolled over
into the warm spot she had just vacated, hogging virtually the
entire bed with his big body and long, tanned limbs. Raine
was tempted to stand there and stare at him for a while, but
she managed to pull herself away with the promise that the
sooner she got this conversation over with, the sooner she
could get back into bed with Calder.

She padded on bare feet out to the kitchen and pulled open
the refrigerator door. Since Calder had seemingly moved in
yesterday—without discussing it with her, she'd like to add—
he'd stocked her fridge with all manner of healthy food
choices like lettuce and milk and bread and she even thought
she saw a package of boneless, skinless chicken breasts back
there somewhere.

Ugh.

She pushed aside the lowfat milk and grabbed a Coke.

"Sorry about that. So what were you saying? Hope's going to Caracas?"

"Yeah, and I don't think it's a coincidence. The logging
program stopped sending us information yesterday afternoon, and now Hope's booked herself on a last-minute flight
to South America. I think she's going to try to disappear now
that she knows we're on to her."

*Or maybe Raine's hunch had been right and Hope was
going down to Venezuela to make sure the trip down to
Caracas in a cargo container had killed Megan Mulroney.*

"Okay. Give me the flight details again." Raine grabbed a
pen with Bugs Bunny's head on top out of the holder that
looked like two rabbit's feet and wrote down the information
Neall read to her. "And you said you booked two tickets?"

"Yeah, I figured you and I could go down and see what
this is all about."

Raine wondered if she should get Daff and Aimee involved, but quickly dismissed the idea. Aimee had probably already left for San Antonio and Daff was leaving tomorrow on her own op. Besides, this was a job that she and Neall should reasonably be able to handle.

"Great work, Neall. Why don't you swing by on your way to the airport and pick me up."

"Will do, sis. See you in a few."

Raine hung up the phone and took the receiver with her back to the bedroom where Calder was sleeping. She slipped back under the sheets, pushing against him to make him move over. Instead, he rolled a few inches to the side and draped himself over her, his skin hot against hers.

"What was that about?" he asked sleepily.

"It was Neall. We're leaving for Venezuela in a few hours to follow Hope Enslar."

"Hmm." Calder nuzzled her neck, trailing a line of kisses from one side of her shoulders to the other. Then, suddenly, he jolted upright, taking the covers and his own warmth with him. "What the hell did you just say?"

"Give me back the blanket. I'm cold," Raine protested.

"You're going to South America? Today? And you just drop it on me as if you were going to the mall with Aimee and Daff?"

Raine felt her temper start to rise, and her temperature right along with it. "You hired me to do a job and that's what I'm doing."

"I hired you for a case I thought was total bull . . ." He stopped then, obviously realizing what he had been just about to admit.

Raine glared at him from across the bed. "I know. A case you thought was total bullshit, so I'd never be in any danger. Well, it looks like maybe you were wrong and a teenager's life could be at risk."

"Then give me some time to go to the Bureau and convince them of that."

"We don't *have* time. Hope is our only link to Megan Mulroney. If we let her get on that plane without us, it's likely that she'll disappear. By the time you meet with your boss and—by some miracle—convince him to open an official investigation based on what, in truth, amounts to no more than a hunch, it will be too late. Hope could be anywhere in South America by then."

The skin on Calder's neck turned a mottled shade of red, and Raine knew he wanted to tell her she was wrong but couldn't. They both knew that what she'd said was the truth.

"I can't just hide here in my safe little apartment while a potential kidnapper goes free. I would think that you, of all people, would understand," Raine said, running a frustrated hand through her bed-head messy hair.

"I do understand," Calder shouted, then added quietly, "I just don't want you to get hurt."

Well, didn't that just take all the wind out of her sails?

Raine closed her eyes and shook her head. "Living with you is impossible, did you know that?"

Calder sighed. "I know. It's hell, isn't it?"

Raine reached out and put her arms around his big, warm body. "Yeah. Look, I have to go. You know that. Remember, I got the same training from Uncle Sam that you did. I can take care of myself. Besides, Neall will be with me. That should comfort you. Or does he need to pass some sort of testosterone test before you'll feel better?"

Calder buried his head in her neck. "I can't help it, Raine. I love you."

"I know, but you're going to have to figure out a way to deal with this because I've decided I can't live my life playing it safe. I'm just not wired that way. After this case is over, I'm going to start calling up my old friends from the Bureau and actively asking for cases they can't tackle. It's only going to get worse for you from here."

As Raine held Calder tight, she felt his shoulders start to shake.

She wasn't certain if he was laughing or crying. She wasn't even sure she wanted to know.

RAINE was right. He needed to figure out a way to come to terms with the life she had chosen. He knew he could no more live a quiet, safe life than she could. As she'd said, he just wasn't wired that way. The sense of fulfillment that came from tracking a criminal and bringing him to justice couldn't be equaled in the business world. Sentencing him to a life behind a desk would be like sentencing him to die a slow death.

The truth was, he loved Raine just the way she was. Part of her attraction was that she, like him, thrived on a life lived on the edge. So how could he want her to change? Even more important, *why* would he want her to change?

Calder pulled his suitcase out of the trunk of his car and then started toward the airport terminal.

As he approached the check-in counter, his cell phone rang.

"Great, this is just what I need," he mumbled when the Atlanta FBI's main number flashed across the screen.

"Preston," he answered, sliding his ID across the counter to the ticket agent. Then he covered up the mouthpiece and said, "I'm on the two P.M. flight to Caracas."

"Calder, it's Alex. You need to come in for questioning on the Brittany Monroe case."

"I can't." Calder slipped his Bureau credentials out of his wallet and handed them and his boarding pass to the TSA agent manning the security line.

Alex was silent for a moment. When he finally spoke, his voice was low and menacing. "What do you mean, you can't? Don't you realize your career might be on the line here?"

Calder hoisted his suitcase up onto the conveyor belt leading to the X-ray machine and, for good measure, slipped off the black loafers he'd put on that morning as part of his disguise. Then he said, "Just a second," and tossed the phone into the bucket with his shoes. He passed through the metal detector and impatiently waited on the other side for his luggage to be cleared. After several advances and retractions, his carry-on bag rolled out, followed by his shoes and cell phone.

Holding the phone to his ear, he slipped on his left shoe and then his right.

"You still there?" he asked.

"Yeah. What the hell was that?"

"Airport security."

"Why are you at the airport? I told you, you need to get down here right now. Wait a minute, Wilkins is pitching a fit outside my office. Hold on."

Calder walked toward the gate where the flight to Caracas would board. When he was within sight of the gate, he slowed to a stop and took a seat across the wide hallway, his gaze searching for Raine. He found her immediately, her head covered by a big straw hat. She was wearing a garishly bright Hawaiian shirt and jeans, along with the ubiquitous American standby of white tennis shoes and socks. Her brother sat beside her, with a nearly identical costume.

As Calder watched, Raine grinned at a toddler across the aisle whose harried-looking father was doing his best to keep the little girl from careening into people's legs.

Yeah, good luck trying to hold her back. Calder silently commiserated with the young father before turning his attention back to his phone call.

"Preston, where the hell are you?" Jim Wilkins shouted in his ear.

Calder grimaced down at the phone in his hand. "Good morning to you. How's your wife?"

"You leave Shari out of this. She's . . . shit, she went into labor yesterday. Two months early. This is all your fault, Preston. You should never have called her in on the Monroe case."

Calder felt the tension squeezing his skull and pressed two fingers just above his left eye to relieve the pressure. "I'm sorry."

"Yeah, well, you're going to be even sorrier if you don't tell me where your girlfriend is. I've been trying to get a hold of her for hours but she won't return my calls. Where is she? I told her to check in with me if she leaves the area. I have some more questions for her on the Thompson case and I want to talk with her right now."

"Why is everyone so impatient this morning?" Calder asked, watching the grinning toddler evade her father's grasp and go barreling toward Raine's knees. Raine laughed and put her hands out to keep the little girl from crashing into her kneecaps. "I have no idea where Raine is," he added. "I left her at her apartment this morning."

"I don't believe you."

"Calder, listen to me," Alex's deep voice chimed in—obviously his boss had put him on speakerphone. "You do not want to add obstruction of justice charges to the rest of the crap you're gonna be facing. Tell Wilkins where Raine is and get your ass back here on the double. Your leave is officially over."

Calder sat and looked at Raine for a long time as she smiled at the toddler's father and dangled a set of plastic keys in front of the little girl playfully. Nobody else in the waiting area paid her any attention—a female tourist playing with someone else's kid to occupy the time until the plane boarded was not such an unusual sight. Calder knew part of it was an act. Hiding in plain sight, they called it; making yourself the object of attention so your subject would never expect you were following him.

But the other part was, she was a genuinely decent person who truly believed in that "to serve and to protect" oath they'd taken and was willing to do anything, including risking her life, to keep others safe.

With a laugh, Raine pushed the toddler back toward her father and swept a watchful gaze over the waiting area. She looked past him, not registering any surprise that he was there. She must have known he wouldn't let her go without him. Either that, or his disguise was even better than he'd thought.

He cleared his throat and slipped a pair of dark sunglasses over his eyes.

"When I get back into town, I'll submit my formal resignation, Alex. Until then, I'm afraid I'm going to have to decline your requests to come in for questioning or to reveal the whereabouts of the woman I plan to marry. Raine didn't hire those hits on Allen or Thompson and you both know it. Somebody's setting her up and it's time the Bureau stopped looking for a scapegoat and started investigating these cases in earnest. As for me, I would no more flirt with a twelve-year-old girl than cut off my own dick." Calder winced at the very idea of that one.

"I'm sick of these Bureau witch hunts. It's bad enough that I spend my days with thieves and murderers, I shouldn't have to put up with this bullshit in addition. You want to keep good agents, maybe you should learn to trust them a little bit more."

With that, Calder turned off his cell phone and slipped it into his pocket.

Raine had said she couldn't force him to choose between her and his career, but that didn't mean he couldn't make that choice of his own free will.

"Well," he muttered under his breath, walking toward the gate as the flight to Caracas began to board. "If you can't beat 'em, join 'em."

TWENTY-NINE

MEGAN refused to cry as she broke the seal on the last bottle of water.

She'd waited until the container was on the move again, assuming that's what the loud vibration and gentle swaying had signified. It meant more days would pass before the container was opened and she could escape. She hadn't had a drink in twenty-four hours and she couldn't stand it any longer.

Taking care not to spill one precious drop, she lifted the bottle to her lips and took a small sip. She let the water roll around on her tongue for a long time before swallowing, as if by doing so, she could make this final bottle last longer.

At least it didn't seem to be getting any warmer inside the container, she thought, rolling over onto her back after putting the cap back on the bottle. It was still stiflingly hot, but not unbearable.

With the container moving, Megan felt okay in getting out of her hiding space in the trunk and lying in the backseat of her safe car with all the windows open. Unlike before, when all around her had been dark, tiny speckles of light penetrated the metal walls of the container. She looked around now, trying to find a hole large enough for her to see out of. That was probably the worst part, not knowing where she was or what was going to happen next.

Hating the feeling of helplessness that was threatening to overwhelm her, Megan decided to go upstairs and see if there were any larger holes in the walls of the container up there. She debated whether to put on her sweats and shirt again, and decided to compromise by pulling on just her T-shirt.

She climbed the ladder slowly and cautiously, taking care to grip each rung firmly before hauling herself up. She had not survived this long only to hurt herself in a fall that she could have avoided by being careful.

Holding on to a joist in the wall, Megan stood on the second level and looked around. Her eyes had long become accustomed to the dark inside the container, much like they did at night when her nightlight burned out.

Slowly, she walked around the perimeter of her cell, lifting her gaze from floor to ceiling and back again. She rounded the front vehicle and looked down, noticing a strange light shining off the toe of her tennis shoe.

Crouching down, Megan felt along the wall until she found a hole no bigger than the tip of her pinkie just above the spot where the floor met the wall. Megan laid down on the floor and tried to position her head so she could see outside. She smashed her face into the floor, nearly desperate enough that she'd be willing to break her own cheekbones in order to get a glimpse of the outside world after being trapped so long in the dark.

Had the hole been another fraction of an inch lower, she might have had to do just that.

As it was, the hole was so small that she found it hard to make out all that she was seeing. At first, it seemed as if she were looking at some sort of cake with layers of green, light brown, darker brown and black, topped with a frosting of blue smeared with white. Suddenly, a piece of the light brown layer moved.

"It's an animal," Megan gasped, pulling away from the wall and blinking several times to clear her vision. That meant she wasn't in some enclosed area where someone might see if she tried to make the hole bigger. There was a screwdriver down in the trunk of her safe car. She could use that to chip away at the metal.

She was going to be able to see outside.

Megan leaped up off the floor and raced toward the ladder, but went sprawling to the ground when the truck lurched to a sudden stop. Instinctively, her hands went out to break her fall. Her left wrist made a sickening crunch when she landed on it awkwardly and with all her weight.

She groaned as pain radiated up her arm, then abruptly sucked in her breath when she heard a clanging near the door of the container.

No! After all this time, someone was opening the container, but she couldn't get down to her safe car. What was she going to do?

Megan didn't have time to come up with an elaborate escape plan because just at that moment, the container door flew open, letting in harsh shards of light. Blinded after so long in the darkness, she blinked again and again, trying to take in as much as she could.

The outline of a semi was directly in front of her. The layers she had seen through the pinhole became strikingly clear. Grass, some dryish-looking mud, tan-colored cows with pronounced shoulder blades and U-shaped horns, mountains in the distance, topped by a cloud-streaked blue sky. Were they in Texas? That was the only place Megan knew where cattle were raised on enormous ranches. Had her over-imaginative mind simply leaped to the worst conclusion after seeing one too many action/adventure movies?

Then she heard voices. Men's voices. Raised as if they were arguing. She couldn't make out what they were saying because they were talking too fast. Megan wasn't even sure they were speaking English.

Suddenly, a shot was fired from somewhere nearby. Cradling her injured wrist, Megan scrambled under the nearest vehicle. She was guessing they weren't in Texas.

Was it the rebels? Did they know she was in here? Is that why they were shooting?

Think, Megan, think. You can't just lie here and let them take you without a fight.

Pain clouded her thoughts, but Megan tried to ignore it. Just like when she was rowing and her shoulders screamed in aching protest, she pushed the pain away in order to do what she had to do. In a race, she did it because she couldn't let her teammates down. Now, she was in the most serious race of her life and it was herself that she couldn't let down. Her very life depended on it.

Footsteps sounded on the floor below her, thick-soled boots echoing against metal. More yelling, in a language she couldn't understand, floated up to the second floor.

Megan glanced behind her. There were four vehicles up here—two sedans, the convertible, and another SUV like her mother's. Megan squinted, trying to remember if any vehicle was low on gas and which ones had dead batteries. The SUV probably wouldn't go as fast as the convertible, and it wouldn't get as many miles to the gallon, but it would give her a better place to hide.

Her decision made, Megan slid out from under the car she had hidden below, keeping her gaze trained on the ladder leading down to the first floor as she moved. The floor of the container was hot on her bare legs, and Megan wished she'd put on her sweats. She felt too exposed wearing only her T-shirt, tennis shoes, and panties.

She got up into a crouch and scrabbled backward toward the SUV. When she heard footsteps on the ladder, she turned and raced to the back of the container. She only had a few seconds before they discovered her.

Megan dashed around the side of the SUV. She couldn't open the trunk, which faced the open end of the container and was in full view of anyone climbing up the ladder. Instead, she would have to get inside the SUV first and then slide into the back.

As quietly as possible, she lifted the door handle on the passenger side of the SUV. The seal made a whooshing noise as she pulled open the door. Megan prayed that the rebels hadn't heard it over the sound of their own footsteps and the yelling from down below. With the door open just enough for her to crawl inside, Megan heard someone coming toward her. She didn't waste another second worrying. Instead, she dragged herself inside the vehicle and pulled the door closed behind her with her uninjured hand. She didn't bother latching it all the way, too afraid that it would make noise and give her away.

As the rebel came closer, Megan looked around desperately for a place to hide. She couldn't risk diving over the backseat into the trunk area with him so close.

Lying down on the floor, Megan flattened her back against the wall of the SUV, letting her legs slide into the cut-out area around the door that served as a step to get up into the vehicle. The only way the rebel could see her was if he got right up next to the passenger windows and peered straight down.

Or if another rebel looked in from the driver's side of the vehicle.

Megan's heart stopped as a man stepped into view. He headed toward the front of the container, his dark hair neatly cropped under a tan hat. His uniform had sweat stains under the armpits, and a machine gun was cradled under his right arm. He yelled something to the man on the passenger side of the SUV and started to turn around. Megan dove between the two bench seats in the back of the vehicle and curled herself into the smallest ball possible, holding her breath.

Her heart was making up for lost time now, beating so hard she was afraid it was going to dislodge itself from her chest and end up where her appendix had once been.

When the door of the SUV was flung open, Megan knew that she was about to die. Because if the rebels didn't kill her, her racing heart and the lack of oxygen to her brain would.

"SO. How was your flight?"

Hope adjusted the earpiece in her ear and grimaced out the window at the mountains in the distance. So much for not letting Victor in on her plan to take care of Megan Mulroney herself. "Uneventful," she answered shortly.

"I thought you were going to continue with your usual

routine. You know, lay low. Don't do anything suspicious?"

"I couldn't leave this to chance. What if the girl's not dead? What if our buyer on this end of the line turns us in? You may be able to just pack up your life and move on if our scheme is discovered, but I can't do that. My father can't travel and I can't leave him."

"You don't have to explain yourself to me. You're the boss," Victor said mildly.

Suspicious, Hope narrowed her eyes. Victor wasn't one to just accept her decisions without question. "Are you saying that you agree with me?"

Victor paused for a moment before answering. "I'm saying that it's too late to change things now, so you might as well do what you went down there for. You know where the vehicles are being offloaded, right? Are you on schedule to be there before the buyer gets to the site?"

"Yes. I have all the information right here." Hope patted the briefcase beside her, as if Victor could see what she was doing. "And I should make it there hours before the buyer shows up. That will give me plenty of time to clean up any evidence Megan might have left behind. I'm crossing the Orinoco River right now."

"Good. Then I guess I'll see you when you get back."

"Okay. I'll give you a call about the Miami job when I get back to the States."

Victor muttered something appropriate and hung up, leaving Hope feeling somewhat relieved. She had hoped he wouldn't find out about this trip at all, but somehow, in the back of her mind, she had suspected he would. There was something about him, something that made Hope think he had connections in more places than even she knew. When he did find out, she'd expected him to blow up, to rail at her for being stupid or for taking matters into her own hands against his advice. For some reason, she was glad that he had realized this was just something she had to do.

Flipping up the volume on her radio, Hope smiled at the cheery pop song that blasted from her speakers. Maybe this would turn out all right after all.

From three cars back, Victor watched Hope Enslar's head

bob up and down in her rental car as if she were a teenager rocking out to the latest hit. His odd silver eyes hidden behind a pair of dark sunglasses, he continued to watch as she passed a slower moving vehicle. The short, olive-skinned man in the passenger seat beside him mumbled something in his sleep and rolled over to face the door.

Why hadn't Hope listened to him? If she had, he wouldn't have to kill her.

THIRTY

NINE hours after their plane touched down in Caracas, Raine started to get impatient. They'd driven all night past mile after mile of soaring mountains, flat grassy plains, and had crossed the mighty Orinoco River—a river famous for both its freshwater crocodile and for the fact that at certain times of the year, along certain routes, it flowed opposite its normal direction.

Still, as beautiful as the countryside was—even in the moonlight—Raine wanted to get out of the rental car and *do* something. Not to mention that she really had to pee.

"Damn it, where is she going?" Raine wondered aloud as she glanced over at Calder in the front seat. They hadn't changed out of their disguises, with Raine and Neall still dressed as the quintessential American tourists. Calder, however, looked more like the scores of handsome Venezuelan men Raine had seen at the airport than a tourist. He had slicked back his hair and was wearing a pair of tailored black slacks and a stylishly silky shirt.

The only problem with his disguise was that Raine had a hard time not staring at him. The clingy material of his shirt outlined the well-defined muscles of his chest and his taut abdomen. His thick, dark hair curled slightly around his ears and tickled the back of his neck, taunting Raine to reach out and twirl one errant lock around her finger.

But she didn't, focusing instead on keeping far enough behind Hope Enslar's rental car to avoid being spotted, yet close enough not to lose her subject. So far, tailing Hope had been mind-numbingly easy. As an agent, Raine had learned to be prepared for changes in plans and the unpredictable behavior of her subjects. Indeed, a large part of the adrenaline rush she enjoyed so much came from that anticipation of the unexpected. That was one reason why she was able to understand her father's inability to stop stealing. The excitement of not knowing what might happen next, of having to be alert for any sudden changes, fueled the addiction to continue in his high-risk occupation.

And, of course, the lucrative nature of jewel theft didn't hurt, either.

"What's so funny?" Neall asked from the backseat, making Raine realize that she'd been smiling at the thought of their father and his nontraditional occupation.

"I was just thinking about Dad," she answered. "He probably would have made a great FBI agent if he'd ever gone legit."

Neall snorted. "Oh, yeah, I can just imagine him on a drug raid with his fancy clothes and elaborate plans. He'd get blown away by the first shit-for-brains dealer he tried to sweet talk. Or rob."

Raine frowned at the vehemence of her brother's words, but bit back the defense that was on the tip of her tongue. There was no point in arguing about it. Besides, Raine was willing to admit that she probably romanticized their father's criminal activities a bit more than she should. "Maybe so. I just meant he'd probably get off on the adrenaline rush of the job."

"Right. Like there's a lot of adrenaline involved in tailing a suspect or being on a stakeout."

Raine laughed at that and raised her hands in surrender. "Okay, you got me there. Some parts of the job are downright bo-ring. Like driving nonstop all through the night, tailing someone who doesn't so much as neglect to use her turn signal when changing lanes."

"Or doing document analysis," Calder added with a grimace. "Do you remember that case where we had to sift through nine thousand job applications trying to find a handwriting match to our unsub?"

"You're right. That beats even the worst surveillance op," Neall agreed.

"Finally. We've got some action." Raine gripped the steering wheel tighter and sped up as the green car in front of them signaled a right turn off the two-lane highway. Following cautiously, Raine piloted their own car down a dirt road, doing her best not to alert Hope to their presence.

It was Calder's job to keep track of where they were traveling. A few miles back, he'd wondered aloud if Hope had plans to cross into Colombia, since they were nearing the border. Several open-air trucks hung with green tenting had passed them as they continued south and west toward the port town of Puerto Ayacucho, their beds filled with camouflage-outfitted young men armed with machine guns. The Venezuelans were serious about keeping Colombian drugs out of their country, and Raine had read that carrying an ounce of marijuana was considered just as serious as a kilo of cocaine by Venezuelan courts.

Fortunately, neither should be a problem, Raine thought as she slowed the car near what appeared to be a clearing.

She hadn't noticed how thick the jungle around them had become until now. In the misty light of pre-dawn, she saw hanging moss draped over tree limbs like the melted clocks in a Dali painting. Ferns and other broad-leafed plants that Raine didn't recognize grew out of the dead trees that had fallen to the forest floor and encroached on the dirt road as if threatening to take back what was once theirs.

"We should continue on foot," Calder suggested, voicing Raine's thought.

"Somebody needs to stay with the car," Neall said.

"Any volunteers?" Raine asked, knowing she'd rather be in the middle of the action than baby-sitting a ton of steel, or whatever the hell it was that cars were made out of nowadays.

"I'll stay," Neall surprised her by offering.

"Great." Raine put the car in park and eagerly hopped out of the vehicle, the warm moist air of early morning enveloping her in a sloppy hug. She unbuttoned the brightly patterned shirt she was wearing over a gray T-shirt and tossed it into the backseat. Her blond hair was already pulled into a ponytail to keep it out of her eyes and off the nape of her neck. Although temperatures in Venezuela hovered around eighty degrees, the humidity added a heaviness to the air and caused a line of perspiration to form on her upper lip.

Calder changed into a pair of tan cargo pants and a thin, long-sleeved shirt and swapped his black loafers for a pair of sturdy boots. He was in the process of tying the laces when Raine rounded the back of the Jeep.

"Got your gun?" she asked, pushing the clip into the Heckler 9mm Neall had had no trouble buying outside the Caracas airport while Raine watched Hope and Calder took care of renting a car.

"Of course," Calder answered, straightening from his crouch. He looked every inch the warrior he was, his impassive eyes giving away nothing—not fear, not excitement, not any one of the emotions Raine knew he must be feeling.

She clamped down on her own exhilaration at the thought that she was getting ready to see some action again after so long away. At that moment she realized just how much she'd allowed the asshole who'd framed her to take from her. By not fighting back, she thought she'd been taking a stand against letting him manipulate her life. Instead, she'd become exactly what he'd intended—a victim. She'd hidden in her apartment with her computers for months, and would probably still be hiding if Calder hadn't forced her out with the Enslar case.

Raine tilted her face toward the sky, letting the warm morning breeze caress her. It felt so freeing to be back fighting crime again, to know that what she did really mattered.

"Thank you for not suggesting that I be the one to stay with the car," she said without looking at Calder.

"You're welcome," he responded, zipping several items into one of the many pockets of his pants. Then he took a step toward her and kissed her fleetingly on her upturned nose. "It wasn't easy."

Raine grinned. "I'm sure it wasn't."

Calder grinned back and kissed her again before saying, "Let's go." Then, with a wave to Neall, who had remained in the backseat, he headed off into the jungle.

THEY hadn't killed her.

Megan had been too scared to open her eyes and watch what was happening, so all she knew was that the man with the machine gun had hollered something at the man who had opened the door of the SUV and he slammed the door and walked away. She sat on the floor, the carpeting making her rear end itch beneath her underwear, hugging her knees to her chest and not daring to move.

Their footsteps retreated and, within minutes, the container door closed and Megan was lost in the darkness again.

She started shivering uncontrollably despite the hot, sticky air inside the container. The vibration and sense of movement began again almost immediately and Megan welcomed the familiar rocking. Being faced with the reality of men hunting her with machine guns was a lot scarier than she had expected.

In the movies, you always knew the good guys would win. Megan had not considered until this moment that the real life James Bonds and Charlie's Angels were injured and even killed in the line of duty.

Megan hugged herself tighter, wincing when her left wrist banged against her knee. She didn't think it was broken—not that she knew how to tell—but it sure did hurt.

She took a deep breath and leaned back against the wall of the SUV. The fear that she might die would only make things worse. She needed to believe that she could beat these guys or she'd just sit up here being scared and shivering like a frightened rabbit.

And that, she supposed, was the key. Real-life heroes were

probably just as scared as she was now, but they did what they had to do despite their fear.

"That's what I'm going to do, too," she muttered, pushing herself up off the floor. She had a good plan for escape and she was not going to let herself be caught off guard again. Bored, hot, tired, sticky, afraid—none of that was going to distract her again. She would sit in the trunk of her safe car and wait for days if she had to, getting out only to stretch her legs occasionally and go to the bathroom.

Carefully, she hauled herself back down to the first level, making sure to keep her weight off her injured wrist. She did a couple of stretches and laps around the container, and then crawled into the trunk from the backseat. Then she took one quick drink from her bottle of water and settled in to wait. After awhile, she felt herself start to doze off and welcomed the oblivion that sleep provided.

Megan didn't know how long the truck had been stopped when she awoke again, but glanced at her watch and realized that she had slept for a good eight hours. Her right leg was cramping from being wedged in one place for so long and her left wrist still ached, but it didn't hurt as bad as it had before. With a stretch, Megan rolled over and pulled her legs under her. The seat in front of her was wedged open just a crack so she could see a tiny slice of what was happening in the container.

It was dark and eerily quiet, as if even the air around her seemed to be waiting in taut anticipation for something to happen. Without knowing quite why she did it, Megan grabbed the car keys tied to the rope in front of her.

Then, with no loud voices or anything to warn her, the door of the container was jerked open. The hinges protested with a metallic squeal. There was a commotion outside and some more sounds of metal scraping against metal, and then Megan watched as a slim woman wearing a pair of neatly pressed gray slacks and a sleeveless white blouse walked by the safe car and headed purposefully toward the front of the container. She didn't bother looking into any of the other vehicles as she passed, stopping instead at the back of Megan's mother's SUV and grabbing the back door latch.

In that instant, Megan knew this woman was looking for her. Her first thought was, *Thank God. It's not the rebels.*

She started to climb out of her hiding place, but then hesitated.

How did this woman know where to find her? She wasn't dressed in a police uniform, not that that necessarily meant anything. Maybe she was undercover and had her ID in her wallet.

Megan's eyes narrowed on the seat in front of her.

Maybe she'd wait just a minute and see what the woman did when she discovered Megan wasn't still trapped in the back of her mom's Pioneer. A week ago, she would never have been so suspicious, but now she knew how deadly one mistake could be.

The back door of the SUV opened wide to reveal an empty trunk, and the woman in the gray slacks slowly turned around and looked at the rest of the cars in the cargo container. She didn't say anything, didn't yell Megan's name or say that she was the police and that it was safe for her to come out or anything.

Instead, she walked to the side of the SUV and cautiously peered in.

The woman didn't move like someone who was trying to rescue a missing person. As a matter of fact, when she turned, Megan saw the gun she had leveled at the Pioneer.

This woman was not here to save her. She was here to finish the job Silver Eyes had started.

Megan waited patiently in the trunk until the woman rounded the front of the SUV and was as far away from the container's entrance as possible. She couldn't wait to see if the woman would go upstairs first. If she searched the first floor before going upstairs, Megan would get caught before she had a chance to get away.

When the woman was at the front of the container, Megan made her move. Cutting the keys off the rope, she lurched out of the trunk and dove for the front seat, praying that there was a ramp for her to back down. She couldn't take the time to check. Besides, she didn't have any options left. If she ran outside, the woman would surely shoot her and Megan didn't have anything to protect herself with. She didn't think hiding behind a bunch of cows like the ones she'd seen before was going to save her.

Megan saw the woman's startled surprise through the windshield of her mother's car as she shoved the key in the ignition of her safe car.

She gunned the engine, slammed the car in reverse, and looked in the rearview mirror.

Yes! There was a ramp leading to the ground.

Megan desperately searched for an escape route as she backed the car down the ramp. The woman ran toward her, but stopped about halfway down the container and aimed her gun at Megan's chest. Megan ducked below the dashboard and kept her foot on the gas.

The car hit the grassy earth at the same time the woman fired off a shot. Megan didn't know if she'd been hit, but didn't slow down to find out.

She raised her head just enough so she could see above the dashboard. The terrain here was very different than what she'd seen before. There were no open plains with docile cows and tall mountains in the distance. Instead, she was in a small, grassy clearing surrounded on all sides by dense forest.

Megan turned the car around and headed in a straight line away from the cargo container.

THIRTY-ONE

"I can't breathe past all these bugs." Raine coughed, swatting at her face.

"I read about Venezuela on the way down. I hate to tell you this, but these blackflies aren't even the worst of what you'd encounter in the jungle."

Raine shuddered and put a hand over her mouth to keep the flies out when she talked. "I don't want to know about it. Let's just see if Hope leads us to Megan and then get out of here. I don't mind fighting criminals in the concrete jungle, but this is way out of my league."

Calder nodded, seeming perfectly at home in the hot, humid, bug-infested forest they were traipsing through. Raine tried to mimic his flies-are-my-friends stance. He didn't even bother trying to swat them away, just breathed calmly in and out through his nose while keeping his eyes trained ahead. She succeeded for a moment, but then one fly crawled up her nose and she snorted and shook her head and shivered all at once. Then she reminded herself that a girl's life could be on the line here. That was much worse than inhaling a fly or two.

The thought calmed her, made her feel more centered. She

didn't even flinch when the damn things started biting her.

A gunshot pierced the quiet just as she and Calder reached the clearing up ahead. Raine saw a car spinning around on the grass below a semi with a cargo container loaded on the back. Another shot was fired from inside the container as the car on the ground headed toward them.

"We can't risk crossing the clearing with the shooter in the back of the truck. She'll pick us off like—"

"Don't say flies," Raine interrupted.

The car bore down on them while they remained hidden just inside the tree line. Raine squinted to get a good look at the driver. She was a young woman with wild eyes and dirty, matted brown hair. She had on a filthy once-white T-shirt and gripped the steering wheel with grimy fingers.

She didn't look much like the picture of the clean and healthy teenager Calder had received from the Boston P.D., but then again, those pictures didn't take into account what the girl would look like after being locked up in a cargo container without running water for so long. Raine knew firsthand that it wasn't easy to stay clean under those circumstances.

"It's Megan. She's alive," Raine shouted to Calder, racing after the teen after adding a whoop of joy.

Calder debated waiting for the shooter to emerge, but figured saving the girl was more important right now. He and Raine reached the rented Jeep at the same time. Calder threw open the driver's side door and cranked on the ignition, barely waiting for Raine to get inside before wheeling the Jeep into a U-turn and heading after Megan.

"What's happening?" Neall yelled from the backseat, closing the lid on his laptop.

"We found Megan. Someone, presumably Hope Enslar, was shooting at her."

Calder paused at the junction of the dirt road and the highway, slamming his fist on the steering wheel when he spotted Megan heading south.

"No, don't go south. Go north," Calder muttered, wishing he had a way to contact the girl. According to his guidebook, to the south lay nothing but sparsely populated settlements, dense jungle, and the end of the paved road. They'd had to stop in and register with the National Guard about twenty miles north of Puerto Ayacucho and had been warned that the areas south of this were frequent hotbeds of violence between border guards and drug runners, not to mention the jungle filled with malaria-carrying mosquitoes, deadly snakes, spiders, piranhas, and crocodiles.

He sped up, trying to catch the smaller vehicle before Megan got any deeper into the wilderness. The speedometer was nearing one hundred when he finally got close enough behind her for her to see his face in the rearview mirror.

Calder grabbed his wallet out of one zippered pocket of his pants and tossed it to Raine. "Could you get my badge out of there?" he asked.

She pulled out his Bureau credentials and handed them to him, and Calder held up the side with the badge on it, hoping that he was close enough for Megan to see that he was one of the good guys.

Megan shook her head as if to say that she didn't believe him.

Calder held up one hand, palm out, and eased up on the accelerator. "Okay, we'll do it your way," he muttered. "I'm going to bet you don't know this road ends in about thirty miles."

"Poor kid," Raine said, shaking her head. "She's got to be terrified. I know I was after just being locked up for a few days. She probably doesn't think she can trust anyone."

"Yeah. But whether she knows it or not, we're gonna keep her safe."

Raine looked over at him, and Calder saw her start to smile, despite the circumstances. "Yeah, you're right, *we* are."

All traces of a smile disappeared, however, when Megan sped up again, obviously deciding she could outrun them. Calder had to floor it just to keep the smaller vehicle in sight. The speedometer topped a hundred, then a hundred and ten, a hundred-fifteen. Calder was afraid to slow down, afraid to lose Megan again after they'd just found her. What would the sheltered teen do out here in the middle of the jungle where most likely none of the natives spoke English? She might end up a target of kidnappers or even worse.

No, he couldn't let her get away. It was just too dangerous.

The road curved up ahead and Calder tapped the brakes, then watched as Megan, just ahead of him, tried to slow down just a few seconds too late. Her back tires squealed on the pavement and Calder watched in horror as she lost control of her vehicle.

He wrestled to keep the Jeep from hitting Megan as her car spun into the oncoming lane, then swerved to avoid landing in the soft shoulder of the road. The sickening crunch of glass breaking and metal twisting came from behind them as Calder safely eased the Jeep to a halt twenty yards ahead.

Raine's feet hit the ground just as Calder put the Jeep in park. He was right behind her as they ran back to Megan's wrecked car. The driver's side door hung open and there was a smear of fresh blood on the windshield, but Megan was already gone.

Raine started off into the jungle, but Neall grabbed her. "Here," he said, holding out a lightweight backpack, "take this. I packed water, bug spray, some first aid supplies, that kind of stuff. You don't know what you're going to need out there."

"Thanks," Raine said, looping her arms through the straps of the pack.

"I'll stay here in case she doubles back," Neall said.

"Keep your eye out for Hope," Calder warned. "She has a gun and she wants Megan dead."

"Will do. You guys be safe." Neall stood back as Calder and Raine entered the jungle, watching them go with cool green eyes.

"MEGAN, we're with the FBI. We're here to help you," Raine shouted into the dense forest. Plants with stalks as thick as Calder's biceps littered the ground and strange-sounding birds screamed from overhead as they thrashed through the dense jungle with its canopy of intertwining tree limbs. Raine pushed a branch away from her face and instantly felt a stinging sensation, as if someone had jabbed her with a cattle prod.

She shook her hand and screamed involuntarily at the inch-long ant clinging to the back of her hand. Wiping it against her pants, she dislodged it with a long shudder.

"Megan, come on. This is no place for us. I just got bit by an ant that's bigger than my cat back in Atlanta."

"You don't have a cat," Calder muttered, turning around to frown at her.

"Yeah, and I'm not with the FBI, either. So sue me." She looked around to see if she could spot any movement in the jungle. "Megan, I don't know what you want us to do to prove that we're your friends, but we've been tracking the people who stole your mom's car and that's how we found you. We just want to get you home safely."

Raine stayed quiet and still for a long moment hoping Megan would show herself, but the teen remained hidden.

Calder took up the cajoling. "We know you were hurt back there. We have first aid supplies and some fresh water. You've got to be thirsty after being in that container for so long. You're really smart to have figured out how to survive. I'll bet you can't wait to get home and tell people how you did it. You're going to be everyone's hero after this."

Still nothing except the faint *whoosh* of wind through the trees and the occasional screech of an unfamiliar bird.

Raine turned to Calder. "Okay, we know she was bleeding. Let's start looking for tracks."

Calder nodded and they fanned out from the last spot of blood they'd seen on a vine hanging from one of the trees that choked out the sunlight from up above.

"Here," Calder shouted from over to her left. Raine followed and they fanned out again, each of them finding some clue that kept them moving deeper into the jungle.

The sound of the wind rushing through the leaves got louder the deeper they got into the forest, and Raine began to wonder if it was the wind after all. Maybe there was some giant bug camp up ahead, with all manner of flying insects laying in wait for them. She was no more phobic about bugs than the next person, but she wasn't quite accustomed to having a swarm of flies around her head at all times, biting every bit of exposed skin. She found herself following Calder a bit closer, the dead tree limbs and dry brush of the jungle floor crackling under her feet.

They followed the trail of blood, the forest floor becoming

softer and more sponge-like with every step. Then suddenly, they stepped out of the forest and nearly fell into a murky river.

Raine looked up and then down the bank of the river, dense with bright green foliage, and saw Megan about twenty yards downstream, standing at the edge of the forest as if trying to decide whether or not to jump in the river. Raine held up both her hands as if to show she wasn't hiding anything and yelled, "Don't do it. We don't know what's in there."

The girl looked as if she might jump just to defy the order. Raine looked down into the river, but couldn't see anything but yellowish-brown water.

"What *is* in there?" she asked quietly.

"You don't want to know," Calder answered quietly back. Then, louder, he shouted, "Megan, this is the Orinoco River. We're in Venezuela. In South America. There are piranhas in the Orinoco. I read that in my guidebook on the flight down here from Atlanta. I have the book with me right here." Calder slowly unzipped one of the pockets on the leg of his cargo pants and pulled out a guidebook with a picture of palm trees and an ornate building on the front. Raine was beginning to wish she'd thought to wear a similar pair of pants. Her jeans were much less useful, and were leaching up the water from the soggy ground beneath her feet.

Calder quickly flipped through the book, and then set it, spine up, on a broken tree stump and backed away. "I opened it to the section on the part of the country we're in right now. Now, we're going to back away so you can come read it, okay? It says you have to be careful about jumping into the river if you're bleeding, because piranhas are attracted by the scent of blood."

"You're not lying, are you?" Raine asked under her breath.

Calder took several steps away from the riverbank. "No," he answered. "And I didn't even mention the Orinoco crocodiles or more aggressive caiman that might want to take a bite of her."

Raine shuddered. "I miss the city."

They backed up a good twenty-five feet and stood waiting, praying for Megan to reappear.

* * *

MEGAN watched the man and woman disappear into the forest, poised on the balls of her feet to leap into the river until she saw them emerge farther upstream. The book lay open from where the man had left it, gleaming white against the dull browns and lush greens all around her.

Could she trust them?

And where was the third person she'd seen in their Jeep when they'd been following her? Was this just a trap to lure her away from the river so the remaining man could grab her?

But then, what if they weren't lying? What if she jumped in the river and was eaten alive by a pack of hungry piranhas? When she'd imagined her escape from the container, she had only planned on having to evade human predators. Man-eating fish had never once entered her imagination. Nor had the swarming flies that were buzzing around her head, threatening to drive her crazy.

She had to see what the man's guidebook said. If the other man jumped out and tried to catch her, then she'd know they were lying and would leap into the river.

Megan cautiously took a step forward, her tennis shoes making a sucking noise as they sank into the dark mud at the edge of the river. Swiping at the flies to get them away from her face, she took another step toward the guidebook. A rock up ahead on her right glistened wetly in the bright sunshine and Megan idly wondered what made it shine like that.

She was five feet away from the rock when she froze.

Don't scream. Don't scream. Don't scream.

The giant snake snoozing on top of the rock that jutted out in the water hadn't moved, its dark, moist coils looping over and over on top of itself. Its underbelly was a bright gold, its head bigger than Megan's two fists put together. The thickest part of its body was larger around than Megan's thigh though not, she thought, stifling a near-hysterical giggle, wider than her hips.

A song she'd learned in kindergarten—one so totally inappropriate right now—flashed into her head.

*I'm being swallowed by a boa constrictor. I'm being
swallowed by a boa constrictor. I'm being swallowed
by a boa constrictor, and I don't like it very much.
Oh no, oh no, he's up to my toe. He's up to my toe.
Oh gee, oh gee, he's up to my knee. He's up to my knee.*

Megan felt her breath coming in tiny, panicked bursts.
She stood, frozen with shock, knowing the worst thing she
could do would be to run or do anything to startle the snake.
Rationally, that is.

Irrationally, that song kept playing in her head.

*Oh fiddle, oh fiddle, he's up to my middle. He's up to
my middle.
Oh heck, oh heck, he's up to my neck. He's up to my
neck.*

Without her brain sending her legs the signal, they decided
to move on their own, picking her feet up out of the mud and
clambering desperately backward, away from the giant snake.
Not watching where she was going, Megan's foot landed on a
tree trunk, bared of its bark by who knew how many years of
exposure. The limb was slippery and Megan's slimy, mud-
caked tennis shoe slid down over it, and her arms windmilled
in the air as she fought to keep her balance.

Her hand hit the surface of the water as she desperately
fought to stay upright and she sent a shower of water onto
the snake. It opened its eyes and looked right at her as she
flailed in the shallow water. It started uncoiling from the
rock, moving into the river headfirst in her direction.

*Oh dread, oh dread, he's up to my head. He's up to
my . . . gulp.*

The song ended.
The snake slithered toward her.
And Megan screamed.

THIRTY-TWO

HOPE saw the smoking wreck up ahead, the car's radiator hissing more steam into the already steamy jungle. She craned her neck as she passed a Jeep stopped on the other side of the road.

Probably just some Good Samaritan who had stopped to help.

She slowed her car and swung around on the highway, easing in behind the smashed car. Unbuckling her seat belt, she decided to leave the keys in the ignition in case she had to make a quick getaway. If Megan identified her, she might have to shoot her and get out of here—fast. Hope slid a light-weight lab coat over her shoulders and pocketed her gun before stepping out of the car.

The man sitting alone in the backseat of the Jeep opened his door the same time she did, and Hope kept her hand in her pocket, wrapped around the butt of her gun.

"What happened here?" she asked casually as the man loped across the highway.

"Are you Hope Enslar?" the man asked, his voice low and urgent.

Hope yanked her gun out of her pocket and stepped back until her hips were against the warm metal of her rental car. "Who are you?"

The man held his hands up in the air as if she were trying to rob him. "I'm your savior," he said, just as a car came screeching around the bend, tires screaming in protest as they tried to keep their grip on the road. The car careened to a stop a few yards beyond the Jeep and the driver hastily backed up until he was directly across from the wreck.

Hope was astounded when Victor and his second-in-command, a short, swarthy man named Tony, stepped out into the road.

Keeping her gun trained on the stranger's chest, Hope frowned at Victor and Tony. "What are you doing here? I thought you were back in Atlanta when you called me?"

"When I discovered you'd booked a flight down here, I decided to come, too. I figured you might need the help."

Hope shrugged defensively. "I was doing okay."

Victor raised one eyebrow at her mockingly. "Yeah, that's what it looks like. Who are you?" he asked, turning to the man who was still holding his hands in the air in front of Hope.

"Look, we don't have a lot of time here," the man said urgently. "They could come back at any second. You want Megan and I want Raine and Calder, so I say we join forces. I planted some drugs on Raine and the border guards around here are serious about punishing people for that kind of shit. I've manufactured plenty of evidence against them. All I need is about half an hour of online time to get it uploaded properly."

"I think you should just kill him," Victor said, leaning against the car next to Hope and crossing his arms over his chest.

"No, look, this solves all of our problems," the man protested. "If we can get the border guards on our side, we'll have help in tracking Megan down. Plus, if the guards kill Calder and Raine, none of us have to fear any repercussions. They'll be the murderers, not us. We can all go back to our happy little lives in the States and never have to worry about this coming back to bite us."

"Why didn't you just go to the authorities alone?" Hope asked.

"I needed someone to keep an eye on Calder and Raine. If they showed up at the cops' headquarters while I was here . . ." The man's voice trailed off before he cleared his voice and continued. "Well, I just couldn't take that chance. But now that I'm not alone, I don't have to worry. If you guys stay here"—he nodded toward Victor and Tony, who had pulled out his own gun and had it aimed at the other man's heart—"and make sure Calder and Raine don't make it out of the jungle before we're ready, Hope and I can go down and make our case with the local police. What do you say?"

Beside Hope, Victor clenched and relaxed his jaw while she ran over the merits of the man's plan. The man made some sense. She was especially intrigued by the thought that the local police would be responsible for removing all of her problems. She could go back to her life in Atlanta and she wouldn't even have to shut down the car theft ring. As she saw it, there was only one question: Why was this man trying to kill the people who were after her?

"Who are you?" she asked, cocking her head to one side and waving away the bugs buzzing around her face.

"I'm Raine's brother, Neall Robey," he answered. Then, in a chillingly calm voice, he added, "And I want my sister dead."

"STAY calm," Calder shouted as he crashed through the thick underbrush at the river's edge. Chances were, the snake would slither away. Megan was large and noisy, and most likely it would be frightened off.

Still, he would have shot at it if he hadn't been afraid of either hitting Megan or having the bullet ricochet off the rock in front of her. Movies always made it seem so easy to hit the exact target you were shooting for. Good guys routinely shot guns out of the bad guys' hands or aimed at their knees to stop them from running. The truth wasn't quite so elegant. Calder never aimed a gun at anyone he didn't intend to kill. And with the anaconda so close to Megan, he just couldn't take the chance.

Instead, he pulled a vicious-looking knife out of a snapped pocket of his pants and ran toward the teen, who had fallen backward and was up to her chest in the water.

"No, no, no. Get away from me," she sobbed, trying to scramble away in the mud.

When Calder was still ten feet away she screamed again, the horror-filled anguish in her voice raising goosebumps on his arms. He hacked through the tree limbs that seemed to delight in coming back and slapping him in the face when he pushed them away and finally emerged in the river next to Megan.

Her skin had gone a deathly pale, her eyes so wide from shock that the brown irises were ringed with white.

Raine dropped the backpack Neall had given her and jumped into the water next to him and grabbed Megan's arm. "Come on. Let's get you out of here. Everything's going to be okay," she said, obviously trying to calm the teen.

Megan's teeth started to chatter as if she were chilled, which was impossible in the tepid water and tropical air. "It b-b-bit me," she managed to stutter out through lips that were taking on a bluish hue.

"Oh, shit," Calder swore. "Where did it get you?"

"L-leg," Megan stammered.

Calder reached down into the murky water and grabbed Megan under the armpits, trying to pull her out of the water. Something bumped against his calf and he tried not to think about what sorts of creatures were swimming around down there. He was almost glad the water was too muddy to see what lay beneath the surface.

Megan's body barely budged, even with him tugging with all his might. Calder looked over his shoulder at Raine.

"Give me your knife," Raine said from behind him.

"I'll do it," he argued, glad they both understood what was keeping Megan in the water.

"No, you're stronger than me. You need to keep her from going under."

Calder didn't have time to argue. He felt an enormous

force pulling on Megan and he lurched backward as the anaconda tried to jerk Megan underwater. Turning to the side, he showed Raine the knife that was still clutched in his right hand. She took it from him and swallowed visibly before starting toward Megan's trapped feet.

Gripping the handle so hard her knuckles turned white, Raine reached down into the water to feel around for the enormous snake. Her fingers brushed against its cool skin a second before it lashed out, hitting her at knee level with a force that sent her flying into the water. She held the knife tightly, refusing to let it go. Without it, they'd have no defense against the snake.

Raine struggled to her feet, shoving the wet hair that had come loose from her ponytail out of her eyes. She eyed the river, waiting for part of the snake's body to break the churning surface so she could strike.

Calder grunted from the strain of holding Megan back, and Raine finally saw a glossy brown coil emerge from below. She lunged at it, stabbing sharply downward and across in order to inflict the maximum amount of damage. Her first strike missed, and so did her second, but on the third try, she managed to sink the knife into the snake's soft flesh. The serrated edge of the blade ripped an ugly red gash through the gold skin.

Raine didn't know whether she'd killed the snake or not, but it loosened its grip on Megan enough for Calder to be able to drag her ashore, with Raine close at his heels. Once they were back on solid ground, Calder propped Megan against the thick trunk of a tree and crouched down to look into her glassy eyes.

Raine stood nearby, her hands on her knees, trying to calm her labored breathing.

"Megan, I want you to listen to me," Calder said, reaching out to put his hands on her shoulders. "I know you're frightened—hell, *I'm* still shaking—but you're going to be all right. You just need to stay calm. That snake that bit you back there, it's an anaconda and it's not poisonous. You're okay now. Do you understand?"

Megan's teeth were chattering as Raine sat down beside

her on the forest floor and wrapped an arm around the girl's shoulders.

"You've been so brave," Raine said. "Your parents are going to be so proud of you."

At that, Megan started to cry. Deep, wet sobs shook her body and Raine turned and held the girl tightly to her chest. She couldn't even imagine the ordeal this poor kid had been through.

As she rocked Megan and whispered comforting words to her, Raine looked up at Calder, who was frowning in the direction of the river while he picked up the knife Raine had dropped a few feet away.

"We're going to get you out of here, Megan," he said, his voice laced with such steely resolve that even Raine was comforted.

Megan's sobs had quieted to hiccupping gasps of indrawn breath. Raine gave her a final squeeze and scooted back to give her some room. Calder held out a hand to help her up, and then turned to Megan.

His outstretched hand was large and tanned, and Megan's looked small and fragile in comparison as she put her hand in his. As he pulled her up off the jungle floor, Raine watched his jaw tighten, his dark eyes intense and serious. Then quietly, almost too low for her to hear what he said, he made his vow to Megan. "I will do anything to get you home safely. Anything."

It was at that moment, standing in this humid jungle with flies biting and buzzing angrily around her head, dripping mud and snake guts, and fighting the urge to vomit, that Raine finally understood why she loved this man so fiercely . . . and why she had been so wrong to try to make him choose between her and his career.

What he did for a living wasn't just his job. It was who he was, deep inside his soul. He didn't fight crime for the same reasons she did—not for excitement or even atonement for the sins of others. He did it because he had been born to protect others. It was as simple as that.

It went against everything in him to see her embrace danger as she did. No wonder he hadn't put up a fight when the

Bureau tried to oust her. He embraced her skills with computers, encouraging her to go after white-collar criminals, but when her job had put her face-to-face with a cold-blooded killer, he had been all too happy to let his superiors remove her from danger.

Calder had already started back through the jungle and Raine trotted to catch up with him. "You know," she said, ducking to avoid hitting a low-hung branch, "we make a great team. Maybe you would consider joining Partners In Crime with me?" She reached up on tiptoes to plant a kiss on his startled mouth and then winked at him. "You're a pretty handy guy to have around when a girl's got to battle monsters."

With that, she gently tapped his cheek and then disappeared into the jungle.

NEALL was impressed by how easily Hope Enslar had slipped into her role as his partner in the FBI. She kept the National Guard captain distracted by outlining the Bureau's case against Raine, Calder, and Megan while Neall was busy uploading the evidence he'd manufactured. The National Guard station was surprisingly modern, with several computers and copy machines off to one side of the busy squad room lined with desks. Hope sat in the captain's office, watching through the glass as Neall clicked one link after another, ostensibly bringing up case files on the alleged drug traffickers.

He couldn't believe how well this had all come together.

When he'd discovered that Hope was coming to South America, he hadn't been able to contain his excitement. Before that, he wasn't sure exactly what he was going to do to get rid of his sister. His second attempt to frame her for murder hadn't seemed to work any better than the first.

But this . . . this was perfect.

Venezuela had harsh penalties against drug traffickers. Neall even hoped that the officers who found Raine and Calder were the types to mete out their own brand of justice. If not . . . Neall shrugged. If not, what did it matter? He'd planted enough evidence to prove that they were so deep in the drug trade that they'd be thrown into some backwater jail for the rest of their lives.

That was enough punishment to satisfy Neall.

Really, it wasn't even punishment he was after. No, all he really wanted was to get his sister out of his life for good. After thirty-one years of living in her shadow, he'd had enough.

Up until a year ago, it seemed that Raine could do no wrong.

She was their father's favorite. He had told the story of how she'd hacked into the FBI's computers as a teenager so many times that Neall wanted to bash the son of a bitch's face in. Even within the Bureau, his sister's computer prowess was legend. It seemed that whatever Neall did, his sister had done before . . . and done better, according to his colleagues. All of that was bad enough, but when she'd announced that she thought Calder was "the one" almost a year ago, Neall had had enough.

Even without the Bureau's current "don't ask, don't tell" policy, Neall would have kept his sexual preferences a secret. His father, a notorious womanizer, would have even more reason to shun his only son if he'd known Neall was gay. And he knew that many of the men he worked so closely with would harass him if they knew. Hell, many of them didn't even want to work with women—being on a stakeout with a "homo" would be considered even worse.

So he had invented a string of girlfriends over the years who conveniently broke up with him just before any major social events that would have required their presence. And he never let on that his feelings for some of his coworkers were not always one hundred percent professional. It had never been much of a hardship, though. He had an active social life that no one at work knew about, but that was fine with him. That is, until he met Calder.

Neall had worked with Calder years before the other man transferred to Chicago and met Raine. Calder was in San Francisco at the time, working on a bank fraud case. He had requested Neall's assistance as a junior agent to help organize and analyze the millions of bank transactions they had to sift through. Neall had come up with an easier way to slice the data—a method that probably saved the team working the case hundreds of manhours. To show his appreciation, Calder had taken the team out to dinner after the case was solved, and he affectionately clapped Neall on the back and announced to the rest of the agents that Neall was a godsend. Despite the fact that he knew Calder wasn't gay, Neall had fallen for him that night.

That unrequited love was a bad enough burden to bear, but when Calder had later transferred to Chicago and rumors started flying about his relationship with Neall's sister, Neall had been filled with fury.

Raine had everything Neall coveted: their father's affection, professional respect, and now, the man that Neall loved.

Raine's hints about a pending engagement had been the last straw. Neall could no longer contain his rage, so he figured out a way to take everything away from her. And it had worked beautifully. With Jeffrey Allen's murder, Raine had lost her job and Calder's affection. For once, Raine was not the world's darling.

He would have left it at that if Calder hadn't come back into Raine's life. But he had. Neall used his own formidable computer skills to put an automated watch on his sister's telephone. He'd been alerted the first time Calder had called his sister, and Neall knew that it wouldn't be long before Raine had it all again. He'd had to stop it, and figured the best way would be to sabotage one of Raine's former cases. Surely, with two assassinations linked to her, the Bureau would feel they had enough evidence for a conviction. As usual, however, his sister managed to escape even that unscathed.

So when he'd had the chance to get her down to Venezuela, where it wouldn't be so easy for her to prove her innocence, Neall had grabbed the opportunity. He hadn't planned for Calder to get entangled in the snare, had figured that with the second smear on Raine's record, Calder would leave his sister once and for all. Instead, he pulled an Arnold Schwarzenegger and came back.

Somehow, though, it seemed fitting that Calder would be taken down with his sister. Neall hadn't intended that to happen, but now he saw that it was the only way.

Besides, if Neall couldn't have him, wasn't it nice to know that no one could?

"Do you have the case files up now?" Hope Enslar asked from behind him, startling him.

Neall coughed and half-turned to face Hope and the police captain. "Yes. It's all right here." He waved at the screen and stood up to let the officer take a look.

Neall winked at Hope as the captain took his time paging through the lengthy rap sheets Neall had compiled for Raine and Calder. Megan Mulroney's file was much thinner, but still contained charges of drug possession and selling narcotics.

After a lengthy pause, the captain pushed back the chair and stood. In perfect textbook English, he thanked Hope and Neall for the information, and then added, "I can assure you my men will be searching for these criminals within the hour. The Venezuelan government treats very harshly those involved in the illegal drug trade."

Neall hid a smile as he said good-bye to the officer. Then he and Hope left the police station, exchanging congratulatory grins as they climbed in the Jeep and headed back toward the jungle.

THIRTY-THREE

"I can't wait to get out of here," Megan said, traipsing between Calder and Raine, who had introduced themselves as they started the trek back toward the highway. With a shudder, she tried to forget how it had felt to have that snake coil itself around her ankles and try to drag her underwater. She didn't think she'd ever forget, though.

"You were really awesome back there." She glanced back at Raine and felt a rush of gratitude for the woman who had saved her life. Raine was blond and not nearly as stocky as Megan, but not thin, either. She had this air of authority around her, like she knew she could handle anything. And she had, not even freaking out when that giant snake attacked her. Megan knew if it had been her, she would have gone screaming into the jungle rather than jump in the water to save someone like that. But not Raine. She'd grabbed that knife from Calder and kicked some serious anaconda ass.

"I was scared to death," Raine admitted with a sheepish grin.

"No way! You didn't seem scared at all."

Raine shook her head and ducked under a tree branch.

"Are you kidding? The wildest animal I've ever seen before is my downstairs neighbor's rabid Chihuahua. I was terrified."

"Me, too."

"Yeah, well you had every right to be."

They picked their way carefully across the forest floor, trying to avoid disturbing anything else that might want to kill them. Calder led the way through the nearly impenetrable jungle, occasionally glancing at a compass that he'd tucked into yet another pocket of his cargo pants. Sunlight speared the ground every few feet from holes in the leafy canopy overhead, and wherever it hit, steam rose from the ground.

If she hadn't spent the last week trapped in a cargo container, Megan probably would have thought the jungle was quiet. Instead, her ears seemed attuned to every noise that broke the silence: the sharp cries of a bird, the crunch of leaves beneath their feet, the scratch of a twig against her sweats, the buzz of the flies that swarmed around them.

Megan squinted through the trees when she heard a sound from off to her left that seemed out of place.

Raine noticed her hesitation and frowned, putting a hand on Megan's arm and leaning forward to speak directly in her ear. "What is it?"

"I don't know. I just thought I heard something over there." She jerked her chin to indicate where she thought the noise had come from.

Calder, too, had stopped, peering into the foliage surrounding them. "Could be Hope," he said.

"Only if Neall didn't stop her," Raine answered. She and Calder exchanged a look that Megan didn't understand.

She presumed Hope was the woman who had shot at her when she drove out of the cargo container and that Neall was the guy who had been in the backseat of the Jeep that had been following her. That meant Neall was a good guy like Raine and Calder, and Hope was the bad guy. So if it *was* Hope here in the forest, that meant she'd probably hurt Neall to get past him. Okay. Now Megan understood that look that had passed between Raine and Calder.

Before she had any more time to ponder that, she heard more scuffling off to her left and then, suddenly, a rotted tree trunk next to her exploded at the same time a loud blast shattered the air.

She saw a flash of tan through the leaves and a man shouted, *"¡Parren! ¡Policia!"*

Megan winced as Calder grabbed her arm and yanked her with him as he started back toward the river.

She wanted to fight him, to scream that there was no way—NO WAY!—she was going back there, but as another gunshot ripped past them and sent a fern ·flying, she saw Raine running up ahead and shook off Calder's hand, picking up her pace. If Raine could go back to the river, knowing what dangers lay hidden in its depths, so could she.

Who needs James Bond when you've got a real-life hero to emulate? Megan thought, leaping over a fallen tree with Calder at her heels.

"WE'RE going to have to steal their boat," Raine whispered to Calder, who was crouched down next to her on the jungle floor, looking from the group of five people gathered around a campfire to the wooden canoe-like boat lying ashore several yards away.

"We can't leave them stranded," Calder argued.

"Nobody's shooting at *them,*" Raine insisted. "They'll find their way to safety without having to travel as fast or as far as we need to. I don't know about you, but I'm not going to surrender to a bunch of cops who introduce themselves *after* they've already started shooting. You said this river marks the border between Venezuela and Colombia. If we can find a town on the other side, maybe we'll be able to get some help. It's too wide here to swim across, even if Megan wasn't terrified to get in the water."

"We can't endanger these strangers just to save ourselves."

He had that stubborn set to his jaw that told Raine he wasn't going to budge. She thought about taking Megan and the canoe and just leaving Mr. Morality here to fend for himself, but she couldn't do it. Mostly because she knew he was right. Plus, she needed him. And, oh yeah, she supposed the fact that she loved the stubborn jerk didn't help.

"Then what do you suggest . . ." Raine stopped talking as a buzzing noise sounded in her ear. She waved her hand, assuming it was yet another flying insect intent on having her for lunch, but the noise just got louder. Suddenly, another boat, larger than the one beached up ahead, came around a bend in the river and headed toward the other rafters camped near the shore.

The second group beached their boat, tying it loosely to a tree limb hanging over the tea-colored waters of the Orinoco. They sloshed out, loudly, laughing and slapping one another on the back. Raine guessed that none of them had started their day by wrestling with a giant anaconda.

"Okay, now can we take their boat?" she whispered.

Calder nodded. "I'll meet you and Megan down by the river in one minute."

Raine turned to Megan, who was crouched down in a thicket of brush, intently watching the campers as they ate lunch and swapped stories of their journey. She backed quietly into the jungle, waving for Megan to follow. Within moments, they were crawling along the water's edge toward the smaller of the two boats beached on a tiny strip of mud.

They couldn't just jump into the boat, start the engine and roar off. The larger boat would catch up with them in no time. Instead, they'd have to get far enough away from the camp that the campers would either not hear the engine start, or would be too far behind to catch them.

Raine looked down into the murky water and wrapped her arms around her middle, swallowing the fear that threatened to choke off her air supply with its cold fingers.

"Get in the bottom of the boat and lie down," she whispered, handing Megan the backpack Neall had given her and giving her a small push toward the smaller boat, which lay just downstream of its larger counterpart. Megan looked back at her briefly, but then got down on all fours, scurried out to the boat as quickly as she could with mud sucking at her every step, and then pulled herself up and over the side.

Had anyone from the camp been watching closely, they would have seen a flash of her dirty white T-shirt as she rolled into the boat. Raine cautiously inched her hand out to untie the rope from the tree limb that moored the boat in place. At any second, she expected someone in the camp to raise the alarm, but she managed to get the boat untied before anyone noticed anything amiss.

Trying to quiet her active imagination, Raine kept hold of the rope as she slipped noiselessly into the tepid water. The bow of the boat bumped her right between her shoulder blades, following her like a pet dog on a leash as she led it downstream, away from the vacationers' camp.

She struggled to keep the boat close to shore until Calder caught up with them, her feet blindly seeking purchase at the bottom of the murky river. Something brushed against her ankle and, in a moment of instinctive panic, Raine jerked her feet up out of the mud. Caught in the strong current, the boat started dragging her out into the middle of the river before she could regain her footing.

Raine wrapped the rope around her left arm and struck out toward the riverbank, paddling as quietly as possible to remain undetected by the campers upstream. She finally managed to get her footing again in the soft mud and decided to stay still for a moment to give Calder the chance to catch up. She couldn't wait to get out of this damn river and into the relative safety of the boat.

With a shudder, Raine vowed that when this was all over, she'd never set foot in any body of water besides a crystal clear swimming pool ever again.

When Calder appeared at the edge of the jungle, Raine pushed the boat closer to him, indicating with her free hand that he should slide in and get down. He nodded silently and eased into the river, holding a dull green pack aloft to keep it dry. After tossing the pack into the boat, he eased up and over the side near the bow.

Raine kept a hold of the rope as she took a step away from the shallows at the edge of the river. She heard a splash behind them but ignored it, figuring it was just a tree limb or piece of fruit dropping into the water.

"Get in the boat. Now," she heard Calder order urgently as his head appeared above the bow.

She didn't turn to look and see what sort of danger lurked behind her, she didn't tell Calder to stop bossing her around, and she didn't hesitate to grab the edge of the boat with both hands and kick up out of the water with all her might. Calder grabbed her under her armpits and hauled her aboard amid a flurry of flailing arms and splashing. He collapsed into the bottom of the boat with her on top of him and crushed her to his chest with his eyes tightly shut.

Raine lay in the boat, dripping and panting and staring at the exposed skin at the base of Calder's neck half an inch from her nose. He shuddered beneath her, his whole body jerking with the force of it.

"Another anaconda?" she asked almost conversationally as Calder opened his eyes and squeezed her again, convulsively.

He shook his head and then let her go, getting up into a half-sitting position. He scanned the surface of the river, then nudged her shoulder to indicate something sticking up out of the water about ten feet away.

Eyes, the same greenish-gray as its scaly snout, watched them assessingly.

"He looks pissed," Raine commented, idly smoothing her wet jeans over her thighs with her palms. She picked at a loose thread near the seam. Then she looked back at the crocodile, the tip of its tail a good fourteen feet from its nostrils, hung her head over the side of the canoe, and violently threw up.

"STEP away from the boat," Neall said, pointing his .45 at the group gathered around the large hollowed-out boat with a black outboard engine attached to its stern.

"Look here, you can't take our canoe. We've already lost one boat today. We need this one to get back to the main camp."

Neall calmly squeezed the trigger and the man—presumably the group's leader—yelped with surprised shock as the bullet hit the ground in front of him, sending bits of mud and dead leaves skittering up to splatter his pants.

Hope stood shoulder to shoulder with Neall, her gun aimed at the shorter man next to the supposed leader. Tony and Victor were already in the process of untying the boat from its moorings, having spotted their quarry floating down the river about twenty minutes ago and determined to follow them via the faster water route. Keeping them in sight on foot was too difficult. With no real riverbank to follow, they had to dart in and out of the jungle, tripping over fallen trees and getting caught in the muck at every turn.

Though they were outnumbered by the campers, Neall's obvious willingness to shoot anyone who tried to fight them kept them back. Darting a glance behind her, Hope saw that Victor was already sitting in the front of the canoe, holding the boat in place with a long pole while Tony worked in the back to get the outboard started. When the motor buzzed to life, Hope warily took a step backward toward the boat.

Neall remained where he was, his pistol sweeping the crowd, waiting for someone to step forward or make any sort of threatening move. There was no doubt in Hope's mind that he would kill anyone who did.

Keeping her own gun pointed toward the camp, she gingerly squished through the mud, ruining her favorite gray leather loafers. She tried to kick the worst of the mud off as she took a seat on the narrow slat at the middle of the boat, but it was no use.

"Come on," Victor said, straining to keep the boat from drifting out into the river.

Neall backed to the canoe and put a hip up on the side. Then, giving it a push off, he said, "Gun it," before toppling back into the boat at the same time Tony eased the engine into gear.

Hope looked back to see the campers stomping the ground as the boat pulled away and, for the first time since this whole nightmare had been set into motion, she felt a faint twinge of guilt. What would happen to those people? Would they be able to find their way back to their camp without a boat? What if they all died?

Victor had made it seem so simple before. It was either her or Raine. Her or Megan. That choice seemed so easy, and in the heat of battle, it *was* easy. She had no problem shooting at Megan when the teen had stolen that car and tried to run from her. Her adrenaline had been pumping, egging her on. But now that she couldn't blame her actions on simple instinct, it made it more difficult to swallow that she was only doing what she had to do to survive.

"You all right?" Neall asked, struggling to sit up as the wobbly boat rocked from side to side with his every movement.

"I'm fine," Hope answered automatically, while Victor ordered Neall to sit still. She looked up ahead, to the muddy brown water lined on both sides with foliage so thick it was impossible to see what might be lurking beyond. She missed her house, missed her father and her quiet life. "I just want this all to be over," she said, banging her shoes against the bottom of the boat one more time in an attempt to loosen the mud clinging to their surface.

THIRTY-FOUR

"I'M starving," said Raine. "I would trade my right arm for a Big Mac right now."

Calder set the flashlight he'd stolen from the campers on the ground and sat down. After hauling the heavy canoe up onto the firmest ground they could find and covering it with branches to camouflage it, they'd found this small clearing and tried to make themselves as comfortable as possible for the night. Although he'd brought along some matches, he hesitated to make a fire, worried that the smoke would give away their position even surrounded by the darkness that was closing in on them for the night.

A loud screech from somewhere near them had Megan huddling closer to Raine. Calder didn't blame her.

"Let me see if there's any food in this pack," Calder said, riffling through the army green backpack he'd taken from the camp earlier. There had been several similar packs lying around the perimeter of the campground, so Calder hadn't felt too badly about taking one, figuring the other campers would share with their less fortunate traveler. He hoped they would, at any rate.

He pulled out a baggie full of some sort of trail mix from the pack and tossed it to Megan. "Here, try this."

"Maybe Neall packed something more interesting," Raine said hopefully, unzipping the top of Neall's lighter green pack. She rooted around for a minute, then started taking each item out of the pack one by one: A can of bug spray. Chlorine tablets to make safe drinking water. Two bottles of water. Sunscreen. A length of nylon rope. A packet of steel fishhooks and some fishing line. Band-Aids and a tube of antibacterial ointment. A kilo of cocaine. An extra pair of socks. A plastic tarp.

Raine's breathing stopped as she and Megan stared at the neat line of supplies laid out before them.

"Holy shit," Calder said, looking at the vacuum-packed brick of white powder Raine had pulled from the bottom of Neall's pack. It gleamed in the light from the flashlight, the plastic wrap catching the light.

"Is that what I think it is?" Megan asked, her brown eyes nearly as wide as they'd been that morning when the snake had tried to drown her.

"I'm going to assume so," Raine answered.

"How would you know what cocaine looks like?" Calder asked, frowning at the teen.

Megan blinked several times but didn't raise her gaze from the ground. "I watch movies. Everybody knows what cocaine looks like."

Calder sighed. "What's the world coming to?"

"Are you going to slit it open and take a taste of it? They always do that in the cop shows," Megan said knowingly, seemingly over her initial shock.

"Real cops aren't that stupid," Raine said.

"You never know what it really could be. What if it's rat poison? Or laced with some psychedelic drug that will blow the top of your head off?" Calder added.

"Never put anything in your mouth unless you know what it is."

Megan rolled her eyes at them both in typical I'm-a-teenager-and-I-know-it-all fashion.

"The bigger question," Raine said, reaching out to pick up

the rectangular package, "is why this was in the pack Neall gave me. It hasn't been out of our hands since the time he handed it to me this morning, so that only leaves two options. Either someone tampered with it at the airport in Caracas . . ."

Calder's gaze met Raine's across the clearing. He saw her clench her teeth and then relax, shaking her head before she voiced what they were both thinking.

"Or Neall planted it there himself and wanted me to get caught carrying it."

"Do you know why he'd do that?" Calder asked gently.

Raine looked down at the pristine white package in her hand and shook her head. "No," she answered. "But if he did, it's pretty clear he wants us dead."

HOPE jerked awake when a cacophony of screeching reached her ears. Pulling herself upright, she looked overhead, where the noise seemed to be coming from.

"What the hell is that?" Tony asked, looking around the jungle fearfully.

Before anyone could hazard a guess, a shower of leaves and screaming birds erupted from the canopy, chased by a swarm of white and reddish brown monkeys who were howling eerily as dawn broke.

Hope took a deep breath, thankful for the brief respite from the thousands of bugs that had flocked around her yesterday. At least when they'd been motoring downriver, the bugs hadn't been so bad. How anyone could live in this climate, she didn't know. As a matter of fact, she doubted anyone *did* live here. They hadn't passed so much as a single hut since starting down the river.

Beside her, Neall and Victor were sorting through several of the backpacks they'd taken from the campers yesterday before they'd stolen their boat. While Hope was still feeling a bit guilty over that, she was grateful when Neall tossed her some granola and a bottle of water from one of the packs. Leaning back against the fallen log she'd chosen for her resting spot, Hope dug out a handful of oats and chewed them slowly.

With a flash of blinding self-realization, it hit her that

although she would always choose what was in her own best interests, she didn't always have the guts to carry out that choice. Unlike Victor and Neall, who seemed totally nonconflicted about taking from others, or even killing others in order to get what they wanted, she couldn't seem to shake that tiny twinge of conscience that wasn't strong enough to make her refuse the food and drink, but left her feeling guilty as she ate.

"I'm filthy," Tony announced, interrupting her contemplation.

"Here, this guy was carrying some soap. Why don't you go down to the river and clean off?" Victor tossed a green-and-white striped bar of soap to the shorter man.

"You think it's safe?" Tony asked, obviously torn between fear and the desire to feel clean again.

Victor shrugged. "I guess so. Why would this guy be carrying soap if it wasn't?"

"That makes sense," Tony admitted grudgingly.

"Well, if you're going to do it, hurry up. I want to be back on the river in ten minutes," Victor said.

"Yeah, yeah, all right." Tony picked up a small towel that Neall had unearthed from one of the packs and thrashed through the brush on his way to the river.

Hope watched him go, wondering how someone so competent in one environment could be so fearful and incompetent in another. Tony was probably one of the best car thieves on her payroll. He was smart and resourceful and never panicked, according to Victor, who ought to know. Yet here in the jungle, he came off as silly and buffoonish.

She glanced out of the corners of her eyes at Neall Robey. Now, he seemed to be able to fit in anywhere. He was classically handsome, with high cheekbones, an aristocratic nose, and a strong jaw. His easy, take-charge manner at the police station yesterday had gone a long way toward convincing the captain that what he said was the truth, even before he'd shown the officer the evidence he'd planted. And here in the jungle, he gave off an air of confidence that Hope admired.

When she found herself wondering if he had a girlfriend,

Hope shook her head at her own folly. This was hardly the time or the place to—

An otherworldly scream pierced the air.

Hope looked up, expecting some sort of exotic animal to show itself.

Another scream rent the air, and this time both Victor and Neall leaped to their feet and followed the sound out of the jungle. Hope followed, lagging a bit behind out of a sense of self-preservation combined with sheer terror.

She stopped beside where Tony had hung his clothes on a low-lying branch on the riverbank. Tony stood about waist-deep in the water, his arms fumbling for something down around his legs. He let out another excruciating scream, his movements desperate.

"What the hell is wrong?" Victor yelled.

Tony took a step toward them and started screaming, "Get it out. Get it out!" Now his hips were out of the water and Hope stared with shocked fascination at his hands, wrapped around his penis and yanking as if he were trying to remove it from his body.

Hope had never known a man who didn't want to keep his genitals firmly attached to his body so she found the desperation with which Tony was tugging at himself highly odd.

"Oh, Jesus," Neall swore under his breath, loud enough that Victor turned to look at him.

"What?" Hope asked, her hand flying to her throat.

"The candiru. I forgot about the fucking candiru."

"What's that?" Victor asked as Tony let out another blood-curdling scream and dropped back into the water.

"A fish. Part of the catfish family. If you pee in the water, it follows the warm stream of urine and enters your body. Then it raises a set of spikes to keep itself lodged inside. I read about it in Calder's guidebook but forgot all about it till now."

Hope looked at Tony, who was clutching himself and moaning as if he wanted to die.

"How do we get it out?" Victor asked, his normally pale skin an ashen gray.

Neall closed his eyes and Hope saw him move his hands

over his own groin protectively. "You have to cut it off," he said.

"What? Stick a knife up there and cut it out?" Victor asked, turning an even sicklier shade of green.

Neall opened his eyes and Hope could see that even he was affected by this. "No. I mean there's no way to get him to a hospital in time. You have to cut his penis off."

The jungle started swirling around Hope's head as if she were a child on a merry-go-round. Individual leaves lost their distinction, all of it becoming one giant blur of bright green, and muddy brown mixed with blue sky. Then it all went black as, for the first time in her life, Hope fell to a dead faint on the jungle floor.

"I'M moving to Alaska," Megan announced as the canoe motored on and on through the worst heat of the day. This was like being in hell. Literally. The sun beat down on the top of her head mercilessly as she struggled to breathe in air that was so hot and thick that each breath threatened to choke her. Even being trapped inside that container hadn't been this bad.

Calder looked at the two women draped over the slats of the canoe and knew that if they didn't find a town on the other side of the river today, they were going to have to devise a plan B. He pulled out the guidebook he'd recovered yesterday morning after their battle with the anaconda, its pages damp and wavy, and traced the line of the Orinoco with the tip of one finger. As far as he could tell, they would hit some rapids today. The thought of going down a set of rapids didn't worry him much. He'd been whitewater rafting with friends up in Colorado a few times and figured they could handle it. He assumed this boat was designed to make it over the rapids, since the campers had been traveling downstream in it and he hadn't seen a takeout point yet.

He yawned and steered the boat closer to the center of the wide river.

After the rapids, they should only be about twenty miles from the major town of Puerto Ayacucho. Even though it was still in Venezuela, he knew they were going to have to take their chances and pull out of the river there. They were simply not equipped to go on like this, especially Megan, whose fair skin was turning a blistering red despite the sunscreen Raine had helped her slather on that morning and the plastic poncho she had draped over her shoulders.

No, he thought, yawning again in the sleep-inducing heat of the tropics, they were going to be out of this damned river by nightfall.

THIRTY-FIVE

VICTOR had left Tony in the jungle to die.

Hope listened to the steady drone of the motor, mesmerized by the thought that kept repeating itself in her head.

Before they shoved their boat away from the riverbank, Victor had yelled a promise that they would come back for him, but Hope knew it was a lie. He had left his colleague of who knew how many years moaning and desperate on the banks of the Orinoco River.

He hadn't even left him with a knife.

He'd said it was because he didn't want to give Tony a weapon in case he got desperate and tried to kill himself before they could come back to save him, but Hope suspected something different. She figured he hadn't left Tony a knife because they only had one and Victor was afraid they might need it for themselves.

She had pleaded with Victor to take Tony with them, but he had calmly told her that Tony would only slow them down.

"The sooner we catch Megan's boat, the sooner we can get back here and get Tony to the doctor," he'd said, refusing to listen to her argument that Tony wouldn't be in the way.

Neall had pulled her aside then, out of earshot of both Victor and Tony. "Look," he said, not unkindly, "Tony's probably not going to survive this, whether we take him with us or not. If we don't hurry and catch up with Raine and Calder, I can't guarantee what might happen. Yes, the National Guard is on the lookout for them, but they're not stupid. They had to have found the cocaine I planted in Raine's backpack by now. They know they're being hunted. Do you really want to see them make it back to the States? You know that would mean you could never go back. You'd probably be stuck here for the rest of your life. And you'll never see your father again."

In the end, Hope had stopped arguing, but she couldn't leave Tony like that, in pain and defenseless. While Victor had been distracted with starting the boat's motor, Hope had put a finger to her lips and tossed her gun into the jungle a few yards from where Tony sat. His soft brown eyes had been glossy with pain, but she thought she saw a flicker of gratitude in them as the motor roared to life and the boat sped away, leaving Tony behind.

Now, several hours later, Hope couldn't stop thinking about Tony and how cool Victor had seemed when he'd left his friend back there to die. She finally figured out that what disturbed her most was that he would have done the same thing if it had been her who had been injured. He would have left her there with no food, no water, and no way to defend herself.

Hope closed her eyes, but all she could see was Tony lying there against that tree. Only, suddenly, in her mind it wasn't Tony who was being abandoned.

It was her.

THE roar finally jolted Calder out of his half-asleep daze and he came fully awake in the time it took him to blink his eyes once.

His hand was still on the tiller, where it had been for hours, with the engine still humming away, despite the fact that the current didn't need any help. It was pulling them inexorably and quite quickly toward the roaring rapids up ahead.

And this roar was nothing like anything he'd ever heard before, a noise so deafening that it chilled his blood despite the unwavering heat from the sun overhead.

"Wake up," he shouted, prodding Raine with his foot.

Raine sat up, rubbing the sleep out of her eyes. "Sorry, I must have fallen asleep," she surmised unnecessarily. "What's that noise?"

"Rapids. We've got to get out of here. It sounds like Niagara Falls."

Raine turned wide green eyes on him. "You know, Preston, when I took this case, you never mentioned anything about giant snakes or crocodiles or going over freaking Niagara Falls in the equivalent of a barrel. I'm charging you double my hourly rate for this."

"Fine. I'll write you a check as soon as we get out of this mess. But for now, do you think you could get back here and help me?"

"Yeah, no problem." Raine knew it was wrong to be flip and sarcastic at a time like this, but she couldn't seem to help it. Fear sorta did that to a person.

She reached out and gently shook Megan's shoulder. Not that she felt it was absolutely necessary for the poor kid to be awake before she died, but . . .

Megan grumbled and stretched in the bottom of the boat as Raine made her way back to where Calder sat struggling to hold the motor across the current. The little boat skipped and danced across the surface of the river, going ten feet downstream for every one it gained on the riverbank.

"What now?" Megan yelled over the roar, sounding extremely grumpy.

"Ever been whitewater rafting?" Calder yelled back.

Megan looked back at them and shook her head as if this were all their fault instead of the other way around, but she didn't say anything besides, "What do you want me to do?"

"I'm trying to get us out of here. But if I can't . . . uh, hell, I'm not sure what we should do."

Raine thought about it for a minute, leaning all of her weight on the rudder to help Calder keep the canoe on a path toward the jungle. Right now, they couldn't see the rapids, could only hear the roar that kept getting louder and louder the closer they got. If it were like Niagara Falls—*and please, God, don't let it be that bad, she prayed*—what could they do to increase their chances of coming out of it alive?

Hmm.

They didn't have any lifejackets, just a backpack full of fairly ordinary camping supplies. Aside from the kilo of cocaine, which Raine had sprinkled over the river last night, she couldn't even think of anything that Neall left her that would float.

The only thing they had was this boat.

Raine squinted toward the bank of the river, which didn't look as if it were getting any closer. She nearly groaned when she saw something move. Then saw several somethings move, the sun glinting off the barrels of their machine guns.

She turned to Calder. "Looks like the welcoming party has arrived."

Calder looked behind him and swore.

"Do we chance them or the river?" he asked.

The bullets that peppered the water around them were answer enough for them both.

Raine let go of the tiller and grabbed the backpack from the bottom of the boat. She rummaged around inside until she found a length of nylon rope. "Grab that rope from the bow," she yelled to Megan. They were picking up speed now that they had stopped fighting the current. Several more bullets shattered the surface of the river, but they were too far away to be of any real concern.

Megan clumsily waddled to the front of the boat and tossed the heavy rope back to Raine. It wasn't as long as Raine would have liked, but then again, nothing had gone right since the minute they had set foot in this godforsaken jungle, so why start now?

She had no more time to curse fate, however. Instead, she grabbed Calder's knife out of one of his pockets and hastily cut the nylon cord into three lengths as he struggled to keep the canoe from spinning around in the current. There wasn't enough rope to tie each of them to the boat by their waists as Raine would have liked to do so she decided on the wrist instead. If nothing else, it would give them each something to hold onto while they drowned.

Shaking away that horrible thought, Raine slid Calder's knife back into his pocket, turned to Megan, and said, "Give me your wrist."

Megan held out her arm and let Raine lash her to the rope tied to the front of the canoe. Raine had no idea if this would make things better or worse for them. Tied like this, were they more likely to get hit by the boat and die than if they went down without being attached to the boat? She had no idea. Nothing in her previous experience had ever prepared her for this—except, whenever she saw those whitewater rafting movies, didn't the danger always seem worse when someone couldn't get back to the boat? At least like this, they might have something to help keep them afloat.

"That's what I hope anyway," Raine muttered under her breath as she finished tying Megan to the boat and started to do the same to Calder.

He waved her off. "Ladies first," he shouted.

Raine didn't waste time objecting, lashing herself to the rope as quickly as she could.

In front of her Megan was shivering, but Raine didn't have time to stop and comfort the girl. She did have time to grin, however, when Megan raised her free hand, made it into a fist, and shook it at the police who were too far away to see now, but were presumably still watching them from the riverbank.

"Jerks," Megan screamed above the roar of the waterfall that was just now coming into view.

It was even worse than Niagara Falls, with two enormous drops broken by a flat expanse of boulder-strewn plain. Raine's fingers fumbled on the nylon line, and then she frantically resumed trying to tie Calder to the rope attached to the boat. He put his hands over hers to still them and shook his head. It was no use.

In the split second before the river dumped them over the

vast waterfall, Calder grabbed her hand and held it tightly in his.

"I love you," he mouthed, not bothering to try to make himself heard over the roar of water crashing over the mammoth-sized boulders below.

As the bow of the boat tipped over the edge, Raine smiled and yelled, "I love you, too." Then she grabbed Megan's hand comfortingly, gripped Calder's hand as tight as she could, and let the river take her.

THIRTY-SIX

CALDER wrapped his free hand around the narrow slat that served as a seat as the canoe went over the waterfall. Not that he thought it would matter.

He watched it all happen in slow motion. The boat tipped nose-first out of the water and plunged downward. Raine and Megan had wrapped their legs around the slat in the middle of the boat, but were thrown forward with the force of gravity. Raine's hand was ripped out of his grasp and Calder grabbed his seat with both hands, trying to stay with the boat.

The upper falls emptied onto a flat plateau that also served as the basin for another, smaller waterfall that poured down from the left.

Great, Calder thought. *So if this waterfall doesn't pound us to death, that one will.*

The boat rammed into the rock plateau with such force that Calder was thrown from his seat. He struggled to keep his head above water as the river tried to push him under. When he finally managed to claw to the surface, he could see nothing but whitewater all around him, churning like the milk for a latte.

Calder attempted to turn onto his back, remembering the river position he'd been taught his first time out rafting. Feet in front, butt up, hands behind your head for protection, and just let the force of the water push you along.

Right. Easier said than done when the river was intent on flipping you around and dragging you under.

The plateau dumped the water from two arms of the same river through a narrow lower waterfall into a serene-looking blue lake. Mist rose from the bottom of the falls, and sunlight reflected off the airborne droplets, creating a rainbow-like effect.

It seems like much too beautiful a place to die, Calder thought, taking a deep gulp of air right before his body was pulled underwater and tossed like an insignificant limb over the edge of the second set of falls.

The force of the water drove him down deep into the lake. He tried to swim out of it, but the falls kept pushing him down, down, down until his lungs felt as if they were about to burst. The temptation to open his mouth and take a breath was nearly overwhelming, but Calder fought it. He kicked out, trying to get free of the force of the water pouring over the falls and hoping that he was swimming toward the surface of the lake. With all the silt churned up by the pounding water, it was impossible to see anything besides his own arms flailing wildly with the effort to find air.

Something whacked him on the back of the head—hard—and Calder fought the blackness encroaching on the edge of his consciousness.

You have to save Raine and Megan. The thought spurred him to fight harder to get out of the river's grasp.

And, finally, the river let him go.

Calder shot to the surface, gasping for breath as his head rose above the waterline. Spotting an outcropping of rocks well away from the pull of the falls, he lashed out in their direction, exhausted and past caring whether or not the police were waiting for him at the river's edge.

* * *

RAINE groggily pulled herself onto the jungle floor with her uninjured arm.

Perhaps tying herself to the boat had been a bad idea. She'd been fine until the bottom of the first set of falls, where the canoe hit the rocky bed of the first pool with such force that the boat splintered into a thousand pieces. That was when she realized that her weight was pulling Megan down. Desperate, she had clawed at the knot tying her to the tow rope and had freed herself. The rope—with Megan tied securely to it—was attached to a large plank of wood that Raine hoped would help the teen stay afloat as the entered the second waterfall.

Then she was too busy to think of anything at all as her right shoulder slammed into a partially submerged boulder. She must have blacked out from the excruciating pain because when she next opened her eyes, she found herself bobbing face up in a quiet cove overhung by thick, leafy trees.

She pulled herself ashore, wincing with pain. She'd never had a dislocated shoulder before, but she guessed that it was most likely what was wrong with her. Either that, or she'd struck the rock hard enough to break something, which was also a possibility.

Raine lay on the forest floor, listening to the wind tickle softly through the trees. The roar of the waterfall seemed far off, but she knew her mind was probably just dulling the sound. If she had been alone, she most likely would have closed her eyes and laid there for hours. It was so peaceful.

Well, peaceful aside from the wave after wave of pain shooting through her shoulder, she amended.

Still, the effort involved in making herself get up and start moving again would have been too great if not for the voice inside her head shouting, "Get up! Go find Calder and Megan."

She hated that voice.

Raine pulled herself into a sitting position by grabbing the trunk of a fallen tree and using it to hoist herself up.

Ugh. That hurt.

Her right arm hung limp at her side. Great. From what

he knew of dislocated shoulders—which was all from the
ethal Weapon movies—the only way to relocate them was
o pop the joint back into its socket using extreme force.

Raine leaned against the tree trunk and forced herself to
stand up. She looked from the arm lying useless at her side
o a sturdy-looking tree several feet away.

She let out a deep, long-suffering sigh. This was going to
aurt like hell.

Gathering all her strength, she squared off against the tree
ike a matador daring the bull to strike. Only, in this case, she
was the bull. She rushed the tree, throwing her shoulder into
at for the maximum effect.

The force of the blow left her gasping for air like a pira-
nha jerked out of the Orinoco.

Even worse, it hadn't worked. Her arm was still buzzing
with pain as if it had been attacked by hundreds of angry
wasps. She couldn't leave it like this. Every step was torture.

Raine looked at the length of nylon cord still tied to her
right wrist. Then she looked at the tree again as a plan
formed in her mind. She tied the rope tightly around the
trunk, right above a thick branch that looked as if it could
hold her weight. That effort alone made tears come to her
eyes, and Raine steeled herself for what was coming next.

With her arm secured in place, she closed her eyes, letting
the tears run unchecked down her cheeks. Stepping away from
the tree, she waited until her arm was taut and then, with an an-
guished scream that tore involuntarily from her lips, she pulled
her own legs out from under her and swung from the rope.

Her body hit the tree trunk with a thud that was followed
by a sickening pop.

Raine laid her cheek against the smooth bark of the tree
and closed her eyes for just a moment while the pain subsided. Then, knowing she may have just given away her position with her involuntary scream, she untied the cord from
around the tree and ran into the jungle.

THEY found Megan first.

From down below the rapids, Hope had kept her eyes on

the little boat as it tipped over the waterfall. She had tried to follow the boat's progress after that, but it had been impossible in all the churning water and now she knew why. The boat had split apart at some point during its journey downstream.

Fortunately, Megan popped up, young and healthy and already kicking toward shore as Hope spotted her. Hope had backed behind a thick bush and watched Megan swim to shore. Before she had gained her footing on the lake bed, Victor was standing before her, waving with his gun for her to get out of the water.

Megan hesitated, looking back toward the rapids as if contemplating whether she could swim back up them.

"Why doesn't he just shoot her?" Hope whispered crossly.

Beside her, Neall was already shaking his head. "We can use her for bait. To lure Calder and Raine out of hiding."

Hope grimaced, wishing Victor would just get it over with. When Megan looked at her, her brown eyes full of anger and determination, Hope turned away. She didn't want to start thinking of Megan as a person. Instead, she was simply an obstacle that had to be removed. That way, there would be no regrets.

Victor had chosen a stretch of waterfront ground that was relatively free of foliage as the place where they would get rid of Calder, Raine, and Megan once and for all. The river curved around right here, surrounding them with water on two sides. Behind them, the forest had retreated, leaving a good fifteen feet of nothing but low shrubs and making it impossible for Raine or Calder to spring a surprise attack.

Although she was sure that Raine and Calder had started out with guns, their ammunition would never have survived a soaking like the one they'd just had.

Victor held his own completely dry and perfectly operational gun to Megan's temple. The advantage of having the police on their side had been being waved down a few miles from the rapids and shown the overland route instead.

"Calder? Raine? I've got Megan," Victor shouted, swiveling the teen around as if to show her off.

Then, more quietly, he turned to Hope and said, "Get the knife out of my pack."

Hope grabbed the pack Victor had thrown to the ground and rummaged around until she found a hunting knife with a serrated blade. She held it out to him, but he shook his head.

"No, I've got to keep hold of her. I want you to cut her palm. Deep. I want lots of blood."

Megan gasped and tried to twist out of Victor's grasp, but he just tightened his grip around her neck as her eyes went wide. Hope refused to look at the girl as she grabbed for her thrashing hand. Holding tight to Megan's hand, Hope clenched her teeth and ran the blade over Megan's taut palm. The skin parted easily and Hope swallowed a wave of revulsion when she realized how fragile human beings really were. She put the knife back into the pack and stepped back away from the girl.

Keeping his eyes on the forest behind them, Victor grabbed the back of Megan's T-shirt and shoved her down to the ground on her knees.

"If you're out there, I want you to watch this," he yelled. Then, with his booted foot between Megan's shoulder blades, he pushed her arm into the water.

All was quiet for a moment, and Hope began to wonder what the hell Victor was trying to prove. Big deal, so Megan had a cut on her hand. That was no worse than the gun he'd held to her head.

Suddenly, the water around Megan's arm started to churn wildly.

Megan screamed and a shudder ripped through Hope's body at the sound of it, the air filled with horror and pain and fear. The teen rolled out from under Victor's foot, pulling her arm out of the water and beating it on the ground to loose the fish that still had a grip on her palm.

"These waters are filled with piranhas," Victor shouted, impassively watching Megan as she curled into a fetal position on the ground, sobbing and cradling her injured hand. "They'll leave you alone if you're not bleeding, but you won't last five minutes in the water with them if you are. If you don't come out, we'll cut the girl inch by inch and let the fish have at her until she's dead."

Hope felt her jaw go numb from clenching it so hard.

This was horrible. She had never intended it to go this far. A nice clean killing was one thing, but this . . . this sort of torture was more than she could bear.

"Victor, we—"

"All right. I'm here. Leave the girl alone," Calder announced, emerging from the jungle with his arms up in the air.

Hope watched as Neall leveled his gun at his former colleague. "Surprise," he said with a carefree grin, as if he were leaping out of a darkened room at a friend's birthday party.

"Actually, I'm not surprised at all. We found the drugs you planted on your sister and figured you had turned," Calder said impassively, crouching down to squeeze Megan's shoulder in comfort.

"Stay calm, Megan," he said quietly, before getting to his feet, standing in front of the girl protectively.

Hope noticed he didn't tell her that everything was going to be okay. No use lying to the kid, she supposed.

"Where's your girlfriend?" Victor asked.

Calder's blink was the only thing that gave away his pain. "Dead, I presume. She wouldn't let you assholes harm Megan if she were alive."

Neall and Victor exchanged glances. Hope saw Neall shrug, as if to say, "I have no idea if he's lying."

Victor nodded, then turned to Hope. "Kill her," he said, pointing to Megan with the barrel of his gun.

Hope started shaking and wrapped her arms around herself to make it stop. "W-w-what?"

"That night in the car, I asked what you wanted to do if I found out we had a chance of being discovered. You said that you'd choose yourself. Well, this is it. It's you or this kid. Us versus them. You put us all in danger by coming down here, and now I want you to realize you're in this mess as deep as we are. You can't sit on the sidelines yelling 'off with their heads' anymore. Kill her."

His words were all the more chilling for the way he said them—calmly and matter-of-factly, as if he were telling her he preferred milk in his tea, not sugar. Hope opened her mouth to tell him she couldn't do it, but her teeth were chattering so badly, she couldn't get the words out. She tightened her hold on her own arms and tried to calm down.

"No gun," she finally managed to croak out.

Victor cocked his head at her. "Really? Now there's something I didn't already know." This time his voice was laced with sarcasm, telling her he had either guessed she had tossed Tony her gun or he'd seen her do it. He reached into the waistband of his jeans, pulled out another pistol, and held the butt of it out to her. "Here. You can use Tony's."

Hope met his gaze, his eerie silver eyes as emotionless as a shark's. She shook her head and dropped her gaze to her feet. "I'm sorry. I can't do it."

"That's what I thought." Victor slipped the gun back into his waistband, turned and, without blinking, shot her.

Hope staggered backward and sat down on the soft ground, looking down at the red stain spreading over her gray blouse with surprise.

No. He couldn't have shot her. Maybe . . . maybe . . . Her mind was having some difficulty processing the truth. There must be some other explanation, she thought. But, for the life of her, she couldn't come up with one.

She felt air, wet and sticky and coppery-tasting, burbling up through her throat.

Wasn't that odd? Wet air.

Hope giggled but the sound came out as a cough instead, spattering her arms with bright red splotches. She coughed again, harder this time, and Neall stepped back as her blood speckled his jeans.

Soft moss caressed her cheek and Hope realized that she must have laid down on the ground. Her eyes were closed and all she could see was black all around her. Right before the darkness claimed her, Hope saw her father, lying in his bed with Randy quietly reading to him. When they both looked up at her, Hope saw the tears in their eyes; her father's touched with sadness and Randy's with regret. Suddenly, she realized that she could hear the words Randy was saying at her father's bedside.

He was reading her obituary.

THIRTY-SEVEN

"YOU bastard," Megan screamed, launching herself with surprising strength at the man who had just shot Hope.

Watching from just inside the tree line, Raine was caught off guard. She'd arrived at the clearing just in time to see Hope fall to the ground and was planning her own attack when Megan went for the man's gut.

Or rather, his groin.

Megan rammed her head into him with such fury that Raine was certain he would topple over from the pain. Instead, he brought his gun down on the back of Megan's head so hard that his hand bounced up in the air from the force of the blow.

Megan crumpled to the ground and the man drew back one booted foot to deliver a vicious kick to her face, and Raine knew she had to do something. Calder had a knife—at least Raine hoped he still had it after his ride down the rapids. She bent down and picked up a smooth stone from the jungle floor. Maybe if she could distract the man and her brother for a second, Calder could save Megan.

"Stop," she yelled, racing out of the forest, her arm ready

to hurl the rock at the man's head. She lobbed the stone and hit the ground, rolling as Neall fired off a shot in her direction.

The man ducked her ineffective missile and took a step toward her, but Megan reached out and wrapped a hand around his ankle, making him stumble. Raine heard Calder grunt and looked over to see him grappling with Neall, trying to keep Neall's gun pointed away from her and Megan. She didn't know if that meant he had lost his knife in the rapids or if he simply hadn't had time to pull it out of his pocket, but then he kicked something her way and she realized he had dropped it on the ground for her.

Raine lunged for the knife, her fingers curling around the steel handle.

Megan screamed as the man stepped on her injured hand, crushing it beneath his heel like a discarded cigarette butt. The man with the silver eyes laughed and cocked his gun, aiming it at Megan's chest.

Raine was too far away to reach him. He was going to shoot Megan before she could stop him. She grabbed the knife's blade between her thumb and forefinger, reached her arm back, and threw it as hard as she could at his chest, knowing she had to aim for the largest possible target.

At the same moment, Megan twisted under his heel, lashing out with her tennis shoe-clad feet. Her heel connected with his testicles and she shoved upward with all her might.

He started to double over, and then collapsed on top of Megan, who screamed and tried to push two-hundred-and-twenty-five pounds of dead weight off her chest. Raine ran over and grabbed the gun out of his hand, grunting with exertion as she and Megan managed to roll him over to make sure he was no longer a threat. The knife she'd thrown had lodged in the man's throat. Had Megan's kick come a split-second sooner, she would have missed him entirely.

"Megan was right. You were a bastard," Raine said, nudging the dead man away from the teen.

Raine looked around for Calder and found him standing at the river's edge, peering intently at the surface.

"Where's Neall?" she asked, coming up beside him and

reaching out to touch his hand just because she couldn't believe he was really real.

"He jumped in the river," Calder answered, sounding distant.

Raine frowned and bumped against him. Jeez, the least the guy could do was squeeze her hand back.

"Why didn't you go in after him?" Megan asked, also frowning as she looked at the calm blue surface of the water.

"He had blood on his jeans. The piranhas will probably get him."

Calder swayed a bit, knocking into Raine and nearly pushing her into the Orinoco. "Besides," he said, sitting down heavily on the moss, "I've been shot."

And then, without further ado, he passed out.

"REMIND me to tell Calder he needs to go on a diet when this is all over," Raine said, raising her arm to wipe the sweat off her brow with the back of her hand. The flies that had become the bane of her existence swarmed around her face, apparently enjoying the delectable feast of human perspiration.

Beside her, Megan raised the neck of her T-shirt to cover her mouth so she could get in a few gasping breaths without worrying about inhaling an insect. "He is heavy," she agreed. "How much farther do you think we'll have to go?"

Raine shook her head. "I'm sorry. I just don't know." She looked down at Calder, who lay between them on a bed of palm fronds that they'd lashed together, and Megan could tell that she was worried about how quiet he had become over the last hour. They had tried to be gentle when dragging him through the jungle in order to get back to the road and try to find help, but it was nearly impossible. There were too many fallen tree limbs and plants in their way to make this an easy ride.

Raine pushed a lock of Calder's hair off his forehead and gently wiped his face with a strip of cloth she'd cut from Silver Eyes' shirt before they'd headed back into the jungle. Megan had been a little creeped out by the businesslike way

Raine had removed the knife from the dead man's neck, wiped it on the ground to clean off the blood, and then calmly used it to cut his shirt into strips to bandage both Megan's injured hand and the gunshot wound on Calder's arm. It was only when Megan saw the tears silently dripping down the other woman's face as she gently smoothed Calder's brow that she realized Raine wasn't quite as cool and calm as she pretended to be.

Megan had squeezed Raine's shoulder then in a show of feminine support. "What can I do?" she'd asked.

Raine had handed her the knife and told her to see if she could cut down a few branches from the smallish palm trees lining the banks of the river. Megan had been filled with a sense of pride when she realized that Raine was treating her not like some useless kid, but as someone who could help save them all. Which was why, even as the pliant palm fronds resisted her efforts to cut them down, the razor-sharp edges of the leaves slicing dozens of gashes along her hands and arms, Megan didn't give up. When she'd finally managed to wrestle two good-sized branches to the ground, Raine had finished bandaging Calder and started lashing the two boughs together. Soon, they had a sort of stretcher they could haul behind them and, after they'd gathered up everything useful from the packs littering the clearing—including Silver Eyes' gun—they set off into the jungle.

For the first hour, the going was difficult but bearable. Calder was heavy, and his jerky movements sometimes threw them off balance, but they managed to keep going. By the second and third hours, Megan found herself going into a sort of trance, the dull ringing in her ears broken only occasionally by her own grunting or a curse from Raine when they encountered an obstacle that forced them to change their course.

She had stopped looking at her watch after hour three. Knowing how long they'd been trudging through the jungle wasn't helping keep her flagging spirits up. She could tell that dusk was approaching, the infrequent snatches of light that beamed down on them through the thick canopy overheard starting to fade as twilight dawned.

"I need a break," Megan said, nearly staggering to her

knees with exhaustion as she propped her side of the stretcher onto a fallen log.

Too tired to talk, Raine rummaged through the pack lying at Calder's feet and handed Megan a bottle of water. She took out another one for herself, but paused to give Calder a drink before taking a measured sip for herself.

Raine sat silently on the log for a while, her eyes closed as if she were napping. Megan sat beside Calder on the jungle floor and shut her own eyes. She would never complain about crew practice ever again. If she hadn't been in such good shape to begin with, she didn't think she'd ever have survived this ordeal.

Of course, she thought, propping one eye open briefly to look at Raine, maybe it wasn't so much a matter of physical toughness as mental determination that had helped her to keep going when others might have given up. While Raine wasn't fat, she certainly didn't strike Megan as being overly physically fit.

Hmm. An interesting point to ponder later when I'm not so tired.

Calder groaned quietly just then, a sound so faint Megan would have thought she'd imagined it if Raine hadn't immediately gotten up to fuss over him. It didn't take a genius to figure out that these two were in love.

She caught Raine's concerned frown as the other woman drew back.

"Is he . . ." Megan cleared her throat and took another sip of water. "Is he going to be all right?"

"Yes," Raine answered immediately, her voice husky and fierce. She swayed a bit on her feet as she stood up fully and took her place at the left side of the stretcher. "Can you keep going?"

Megan felt her own legs wobble as she pushed herself up off the ground. Seems she didn't need any further evidence of which was more powerful: physical strength or mental toughness. Just when she'd thought she couldn't go on another step, some force from deep inside kept her going. She trudged on, nearly blinded by exhaustion, keeping her eyes glued to the ground just in front of her, telling herself that all she had to do was to take one more step. And then one more.

"Oh my God," Raine said, halting so abruptly that Megan stumbled.

Megan had to force herself to raise her head. Her neck felt as if it wouldn't support the weight, and she found her head lolling to the side, her eyes unable to focus on anything more than five feet away. "What is it?" she asked dully.

Raine lifted her right arm and pointed ahead of her without saying another word.

Unsure of whether she could handle the disappointment of seeing what Raine was indicating—whether it be a bed of crocodiles or a snake pit or an impassable stretch of river or who knew what other obstacle that was going to be thrown in their path—Megan stood for a moment, taking deep breaths in an attempt to draw some of the inner strength she had expended into this nearly impenetrable jungle back inside her body. Then, with a mighty effort to hold back her tears, Megan looked up and saw what she first believed to be some sort of cruel illusion her traitorous mind had conjured up to torture her with.

It was a mansion. Here in the middle of nowhere. A golden-brown stucco building with a red tile roof that seemed to go on forever, guarded by a wrought iron gate with the letter S worked into the intricate pattern every ten feet or so.

Megan felt two hot salty tears slide down her cheeks. "Is it a mirage?" she whispered.

When Raine turned to her, her cheeks were wet, too. "Not unless we're both crazy," she answered. Then she reached out to clasp Megan's hand, squeezing her fingers with a surprising amount of strength. "Come on," she said. "I think we've just found Superman's secret hideaway."

THIRTY-EIGHT

One week later

"SO, I heard from Megan today," Raine said, turning down a stately, tree-lined street.

"Yeah?" Calder asked from the passenger seat, absently nursing his bandaged right arm. The shot had broken a bone in his wrist, making virtually all everyday tasks a royal pain in the ass. Driving, for example. And getting dressed. Fortunately, he had Raine to squire him around and put on his boxers for him. He was actually enjoying being taken care of. So much so that he had encouraged his doctor just that morning to keep the cast on as long as he liked.

He shifted in his seat so he could watch her, her blond hair golden in the sunshine streaming in the window. She smiled at a group of children playing tag on one of the well-manicured lawns, their screeching laughter loudly piercing the quiet.

God, he loved her.

Even if she had rescinded her offer for him to come work

with her when she'd found out that Alex refused to accept his resignation.

"You're too good an agent to give up without a fight. You've been found innocent of all charges of misconduct. The board found no evidence that you'd behaved inappropriately with Brittany Monroe. And, as for not turning Raine in . . . well, every member of the committee admitted they'd do the same if their loved ones were at risk." Then Alex had dangled a juicy case in front of him, sweetening the pot. That and Raine's insistence that she really didn't want him hovering over her all day had made the decision for him.

"She told me that she plans to join the FBI when she gets out of college," Raine said, interrupting Calder's thoughts of his own career.

"Really?"

"Yep. Said I'm her inspiration. Can you imagine that? Me, a role model." Raine chuckled, and Calder reached up to cup his left hand around her cheek.

"Yes," he said, "I can imagine that."

Raine leaned into his hand, smiling. "Well, I think Megan is pretty admirable, too. I told her to give me a call when she's done her stint with the government. I'd hire her any day."

"Hey, that's not fair," Calder protested, pretending to be offended. "You wouldn't give me a job."

Raine grinned as she pulled into the driveway of a beautiful two-story brick home and then stepped out of the car. "You've already got a job."

"Yeah. Besides, I've come to the conclusion that you don't really need me around to protect you."

Raine came around the car and gave his uninjured hand a brief squeeze. "I'll always need you," she said.

"Well, maybe I should come work for you so you can protect *me*. After all, I'm the one who got shot."

"And the one Megan and I had to drag out of the jungle," Raine added cheerfully.

Calder shook his head with disgust. It was embarrassing to think of yourself as the strong, invincible one, and then have your lover and a teenager have to save your ass by dragging you through a forest while you lay unconscious on a bed of lashed-together palm fronds. Fortunately, help hadn't been far away. Shep Stockton, a rich oil baron with a hankering for the "simple" life, had built his gazillion-dollar mansion right in the middle of the jungle. With a full-time doctor on staff, phone lines to the United States, and a good relationship with the Venezuelan National Guard, it was as if the man had just waved a magic wand and made all their problems go away.

"So, tell me again why you wanted to talk to Hope's father," Calder said, falling into step beside Raine as they made their way to the front door.

"I'm curious about that letter. The one that got this whole snowball started on its path downhill."

"What about it?"

"You'll see in a minute," Raine answered mysteriously, ringing the doorbell.

After a few minutes, a sandy-haired man wearing blue jeans and a clean but worn polo shirt answered the door. "Yes? Can I help you?" he asked.

"Randy Franklin?"

"Yes," the man answered with a frown.

"I'm Raine Robey. The one who was investigating your employer, Hope Enslar."

"Oh. Yes. Would you like to come in?"

Raine nodded and they followed Norman Enslar's nurse into a living room that looked as if it had been decorated by the staff at *Architectural Digest*. Randy offered them something to drink and then disappeared for a moment when Raine asked for a Coke. He returned carrying a bright red can of her favorite drink.

"So, what can I help you with?" he asked, settling himself on a chair across from the sofa.

"What prompted you to send that letter to the FBI?" Raine asked.

Calder expected the man to look puzzled and ask, "What letter?" Instead, he leaned forward and rested his elbows on his knees, looking at the ornate oriental carpet beneath his widespread knees.

"I have a criminal record," he announced instead, making Calder blink at the sudden change of subjects. "I had a drug problem when I was younger and . . . well, let's just say it screwed up my life for a long time."

"Yes?" Raine encouraged.

"So. Well, I noticed that every time after Hope left her father, he was upset. And I couldn't help wondering why that might be."

Calder shook his head, trying to figure out what Randy's former drug problem had to do with this.

"She has a room, down here off the kitchen," he added with a wave behind him. "She has a surveillance system—to make sure no one abuses her father, I guess. One day, I came back to find Mr. Enslar in tears and I had had enough. I picked the lock—a handy trick I learned during my wild youth—and I listened to her talk to him about what she'd done. About the car theft ring she'd set up and how it didn't hurt anyone except the insurance companies. To be honest, it just pissed me off that she could tell her father all this when she knew he couldn't do anything about it. I knew that he wanted to tell her that what she was doing was wrong, but he couldn't, and it frustrated him."

Calder nodded as realization dawned. "Ah. So you sent the letter to the FBI and pretended it was from Hope's father."

"Yes. Because I didn't think you'd take it seriously if it came from a former convict."

"Why didn't you give us more to go on?" Raine asked, taking a sip of her soda and then replacing the can on the glass-topped table.

"Because there's no way you would have believed that it came from Mr. Enslar if it was any longer. As it was, I was afraid you'd ask how he managed to get it mailed without someone else's help."

"That's why we're here now," Raine said. "It kept nagging at me that something was wrong. Mr. Enslar can barely move. Even if he did manage to write that letter, how did it leave this house without your or Hope's help? And if Hope mailed it, why wasn't she suspicious about her father sending a letter to the FBI?"

Randy looked up from the carpet and smiled sheepishly at her. "I'm glad you didn't let that stop you."

Raine smiled back, stood up, and held out her hand. "I am, too. A teenager with a promising future owes her life to you, Mr. Franklin. Thank you."

CALDER ran his hand down the line of Raine's naked thigh, careful to keep his injured wrist out of the way as she flopped down bonelessly on his chest. The ends of her hair tickled his nipples as she kissed him lightly, waiting for her breathing to return to normal.

Outside the bedroom, his house was quiet and dark and safe. Calder let the fingers of his uninjured hand slide up over Raine's hip and she raised her head to smile at him. "You're really good at that."

Calder grinned. "*We're* really good at that," he corrected.

Raine kissed the bottom of his chin and rolled off of his chest and onto the bed. Propping herself up against the pillows piled up at the headboard, she reached out and pulled the blankets up to cover them both.

Calder pushed himself up next to her, scooting toward the center of the bed until their thighs touched.

"Do you think the piranhas got him?" he asked.

Raine smiled a slow, cold smile at him. "Who are you talking about?"

Calder frowned. Wow, had the sex really been that good? "Your brother. Neall Robey?"

"There is no such person as Neall Robey. If you check the records, you'll find that Neall Robey never existed."

"Raine, you didn't," Calder said.

Raine leaned across the bed and grabbed hold of her laptop, which had been resting on the nightstand on Calder's side of the bed. She opened the top and it instantly sprang to life, painting her naked skin with a bluish glow. "Yes, I did. He framed me for murder. Twice. He tried to kill us, and would have killed Megan, too, if he could have. Now he can spend eternity in some third world dung heap, trying to convince the authorities that he is who he says he is."

Calder looked at her silently for a moment, then shook his head. "Remind me never to cross you," he said, pulling her closer and ignoring the hard edges of the laptop that jabbed into his stomach.

"I will," Raine said, closing the lid of her computer and pushing it down to the foot of the bed. She turned and wrapped her arms around his waist, resting her head on his chest. And then she added, "Every day for the rest of our lives."

Turn the page for a special preview of
Jacey Ford's next novel

I SPY

Coming soon from Berkley Sensation!

[As our] spies we must recruit men who are intelligent but appear stupid; who seem to be dull but are strong in heart; men who are agile, vigorous, hardy, and brave; well versed in lowly matters and able to endure hunger, cold, filth, and humiliation.

—Sun Tzu, *The Art of War*

"WE'VE had a breakthrough on the propulsion system for the MC-900 jetliner. Engineering is hopeful that we'll be able to step up production and get the jets to market a year before we anticipated. I don't think I have to tell you all that this could mean billions of dollars in increased revenue. If we win this race to the market, we just might be able to put Rockton Aeronautical out of business."

Aimee Devlin sat in a corner of McConnell Aerospace's boardroom in San Antonio and transcribed the speech Joe McConnell was giving to his executive team. As her fingers moved almost silently across the keyboard of her laptop, she studied the six men and two women seated around the well-polished table. Her employer was convinced that one of these eight people was a spy, and he was paying Aimee a hefty sum to ferret out the traitor.

As the tiny clock at the bottom right hand of her screen rolled over to one o'clock, Aimee stifled a smile. Damn, but she loved billable hours. Getting out of the FBI—where she figured her hourly rate was about half of minimum wage, given the long hours she put in—was the best thing she'd ever done.

"I'm going to need details of the production process and what's involved in stepping up the rollout in order to make sure we have proper financing in place," Horace Gardner, McConnell's new chief financial officer, said.

Without turning her head, Aimee typed what the CFO had said into her Word document, then sent an instant message to her boss: *Too eager for information?*

She saw Joe's gaze flutter to the computer beside him before he looked back up and nodded almost imperceptibly. He was paying her to be suspicious, to note anything that struck her as odd. And their new CFO, who had joined McConnell just before Joe began to suspect that someone within his organization was engaged in corporate espionage, was number one on Aimee's watch list. Something about the man seemed off, though Aimee couldn't put her finger on exactly what it was that bothered her about him. There was just something that made the tiny hairs on the back of her neck prickle whenever he was in the same room.

Her background check hadn't turned up anything out of the ordinary, which Aimee thought must be the perfect word to describe Race Gardner: ordinary. He had medium-length brown hair, brown eyes hidden behind thick, wire-rimmed glasses, and an unremarkable physique concealed by the equally unremarkable blue suits he wore nearly every day. His résumé showed a steady rise in job responsibilities, from controller to VP of finance, and then to CFO. He hadn't job-hopped, but hadn't remained stagnant in one position for too long, either. He'd ranked in the top twenty percent of his class at Duke and had just-above-average SAT scores, but nothing that really made him stand out.

Aimee wondered if it was this utter blandness that

tempted him to sell McConnell's secrets to their top competitor. Perhaps he'd been wooed by the excitement of it—an element of danger in his otherwise dull life.

"Janine, give Race everything he needs," Joe said, waving a hand in the direction of his chief operating officer, who bobbed her head in agreement. Then Joe stood up, signaling an end to the meeting.

Aimee remained seated in the shadows as the executive team filed out of the room. Joe made small talk with several people as they left, then stopped Race at the door and asked if he'd wait for a minute so they could talk. Aimee stayed motionless against the wall. Fading into the woodwork was her particular specialty, a skill she'd honed over the years to the point that even she was sometimes surprised by her ability to make herself invisible.

"How are this quarter's financials looking?" Joe asked when he and Race were seemingly alone.

Race sat back down at the mahogany table and set his yellow notepad in front of him. "Not so good," he replied. "Without the low-interest government loans that were available to us last year, our cost of borrowing has increased significantly at a time when our needs for funding are on the rise. Do you have a sense of whether Congress is going to approve another round of loans for the aerospace industry? Because, if not, we may be overreaching by trying to step up production of the MC-900. I know you don't want to hear this, but we may have to slow down this project."

"We can't do that. Getting our jet to the marketplace first is the only way we can beat Rockton and recoup our research and development costs on the MC-900. If we wait, that just gives them more time to catch up."

"I understand that," Race said, his voice as bland and unemotional as the rest of him.

A vein in Joe's forehead began to throb as he slammed a fist down on the table, making Race's pad of paper jump. "You may understand, but do you care? I built McConnell Aerospace from nothing forty years ago. I'm not about to watch it self-destruct because you think it's bad timing. Now, it's your job to figure out how to keep us adequately funded. If you can't do that, I'll find somebody who will."

Race straightened his pad of paper until the bottom was perfectly aligned with the edge of the table. "I didn't say that I couldn't find creative, low-cost funding opportunities. I simply asked if you had any idea if Congress was going to come through with an aid package as they have in the past."

Watching him from the corner where she sat, Aimee had to admit that she was impressed by Race's ability to remain calm in the face of Joe's anger. Of course, if he *were* the spy, Joe's belligerent behavior would probably help Race to justify selling classified information to Rockton. Aimee was constantly amazed at how criminals managed to convince themselves that what they were doing was somehow warranted, as if the world owed them something for every slight.

"I don't know what Congress is going to do," Joe said with a frustrated sigh as he pulled out a chair and sat down across from the CFO. "Our lobbyist is doing the best he can, but with the economy being what it is, the Democrats are screaming for an end to corporate aid so that money can be diverted into welfare and daycare assistance programs and the like. I think we have to move ahead with the assumption that there will be no low-interest loans available to us from the government."

Race made a note on his pad of paper and nodded, then stood up to leave. "I'll put some ideas together on paper so we can go over them at our meeting on Wednesday."

"All right," Joe said, not getting up as Race left.

When the door closed behind the CFO, Aimee felt a strange emptiness, as if all of the energy had left the room. *How odd,* she thought.

She set her laptop on the floor beside her and stood up to stretch. Remaining unnoticed for long periods of time often demanded that Aimee stay completely still, which wasn't as easy as one might think and often caused her muscles to ache.

Joe swiveled in his chair, looking surprised. "Oh, Aimee, I forgot you were still here."

Aimee laughed. "Good. That means I'm doing my job."

Joe chuckled and stood up as Aimee bent to retrieve her computer. "Well," he said. "The trap's been set."

"Yes," Aimee agreed. "Now we just have to wait and see if our rat takes the bait."

"WE'RE going to have to step up our operation. They've had a major breakthrough on the propulsion system," Race said into his cell phone, looking around the sunny courtyard outside the McConnell Aerospace headquarters to make certain no one was close enough to overhear his conversation. "Did you get a chance to check out the documents I sent on McConnell's new assistant?"

"Yes, and I found something you might be interested in," Race's partner on this operation, Jake Haven, said. "That diploma you sent is a fake, although it was a fairly good reproduction. Rogers University changed the design of their diplomas in 1987, the year after Ms. Devlin supposedly graduated. The diploma you gave me, with a 1986 graduation date, is the new design, which means that whoever forged the document was working off the wrong version."

Race rubbed his jaw and frowned. So it looked like his hunch about Aimee Devlin was correct. She was not who she appeared to be. "Did you find out anything else?"

"I still have more research to do, but the social security number you got from her personnel file is bogus. I ran her name through the computer and got her correct SSN, then traced that to a bank account opened in Atlanta a year ago. She's been making biweekly five-figure deposits into that account for the past three months. In cash."

"What kind of five figures are we talking about? Ten thousand?" It was difficult to believe that an executive assistant at a Fortune 100 company could make that kind of money, but Race had to admit that he wasn't exactly up on the latest pay scales for secretaries.

"No," Jake said. "More like twenty-five, thirty thousand. Man, if that's the going wage for support staff these days, we're in the wrong line of business."

"Yeah, being a spy ain't what it used to be," Race agreed dryly.

"So, did you get the surveillance equipment I left at the dead drop?" Jake asked.

"Yes." Their dead drop—a place where Jake could leave, or "drop" something at one time, only to have Race pick it up at some time later, making it so the men never had to meet face-to-face and risk blowing their cover—was a hollowed-out tree in the park where Race jogged every morning before work. "I'm going to plant a camera in Ms. Devlin's office tonight. As McConnell's assistant, she has access to classified information about the propulsion system—information I intend to uncover."

DURING her years at the Bureau, Aimee had learned to leave nothing to chance. She couldn't shadow Race Gardner twenty-four hours a day, so she was going to have to rely on technology to give her investigation an edge. She'd seen the lights go off in his office about an hour ago and had patiently waited to give him plenty of time to make a final trip to the men's room or stop to chat with one of his direct reports before leaving the office for the evening.

Clicking off the lights in her own office, Aimee set her briefcase down on the floor in the hall and turned to close and lock her door. Then she pulled a credit card out of her wallet and folded a small piece of Scotch tape over the edge, being careful to leave the ends loose. She slid the card through the crack between the door and its frame and quickly pulled it back out again. The tape stuck to the door and frame on the inside. If the door was opened, the tape would either break or would not adhere back to the door, and she'd be alerted that someone had broken in to her office.

Satisfied with her handiwork, Aimee picked up her briefcase and headed down the hall to the deserted finance department. She checked all the cubicles surrounding Race's office to be certain that there were no other employees lurking about. Finding no one, she hauled a chair over from one of the cubes, withdrew a small round flashlight from her

ourse, got up on the chair, and shined the light into the crack
between the door and the frame. She moved slowly, checking for a "trap" similar to the one she herself had just set.
Even so, she nearly missed it.

There, just above the lock, was—of all things—a piece of
Scotch tape stretched across the crack.

Aimee shook her head and snorted. She had thought her
tape idea was so clever, but it seemed she wasn't the only
one to have thought of using a standard office supply to
booby-trap a door. She shrugged. Well, at least he'd chosen
something she knew how to rerig.

She dragged the chair back to its cubicle, smoothing out
the telltale tracks in the carpet on her way back. Then she
got out her key ring and used the master key Joe McConnell
had given her to open Race's office door. The tape came free
from the doorframe, and Aimee made a mental note of
where Race had positioned it so she could put it back in exactly the same place.

Taking a moment to let her eyes adjust to the darkness,
Aimee looked around Race's office. It looked exactly the
same as always—boring and impersonal. Where Aimee had
pictures of herself with her best friends Daphne Donovan
and Raine Robey on her desk, Race had none. His bookshelf
was stocked with such thrilling titles as *Fundamentals of
Corporate Taxation*, *Strategies in Corporate Finance*, and
Investing Essentials Vol. 10. There were no pictures of a wife
and kids anywhere to be seen. He'd listed a woman as his
emergency contact in the application personnel made every
employee fill out, but Aimee didn't know if she was a sister,
a girlfriend, an ex-wife, or just a friend.

And it didn't really matter. She wasn't interested in dating the guy, she was interested in nailing him . . . in the
criminal justice sense, that is. Aimee certainly didn't think
of drab, dull Horace Gardner in *that* way. Though only her
closest friends knew it, Aimee possessed a wild streak and
was attracted to guys who promised fun and excitement—
preferably *wealthy* guys who promised fun and excitement.
Her own ambition to make a fortune had led her to learn
what she could from the FBI and then take that knowledge

out to the business world, where companies were willing to pay dearly to stop illegal activities that impacted their bottom lines.

Her eyes now adjusted to the darkness, Aimee swiftly took a dime-sized listening device out of the pocket of her suit jacket and planted it in the one personal item in Race's office—a Zen garden complete with a mini-rake and several smooth stones. Aimee pushed the bug deep into the sand and smoothed the surface with her thumb. Then she pulled a piece of tape from his dispenser, removed the old piece from the door, and left his office, shutting the door behind her. She did her credit card trick again, leaving the tape right where she'd found it.

As she headed back toward the elevators that would take her down to the parking garage, Aimee felt a conflicting array of emotions. On the one hand, she was pleased to have discovered the source of McConnell's security leak so quickly. That would only reflect well on Partners In Crime, Inc., the corporate services firm she, Daphne, and Raine had started six months ago. Still, it would have been nice to have the steady income for a while longer. While Aimee didn't mind scouring the streets for new business, making cold calls didn't exactly pay well.

"Aimee, what a surprise. I didn't expect you to be working so late."

Startled, Aimee gasped. What the hell was Race Gardner doing back? And, even more importantly, had he just seen her come out of his office?

Aimee put a hand to her heart as if that would help slow her racing pulse. "You scared me," she said, eyeing the man across from her.

He smiled benignly, but for the first time Aimee noticed something in the brown eyes he hid behind those thick glasses. Something different. Something . . . dangerous.

A shiver ran through her body. "Someone walking over your grave," as her mother would say.

"Well, I'm going to call it a night," Aimee said, suddenly aware that she and Race were alone in the deserted building. Not that she wasn't confident in her ability to protect herself

most situations, but she wasn't foolish enough to dismiss
the slight prickle of fear that raised goosebumps along her
arms.

"Why don't you wait a second and I'll walk you to your
car? I just need to get something out of my office." Race
paused for a second, then added, "It's dangerous to be alone
in a parking lot at this time of night."

Aimee forced herself not to shiver again at the slightly
menacing tone of Race's voice. She swallowed, reminding
herself that the guy was a harmless accountant. Even if he
were stealing corporate secrets, it wasn't like that made him
capable of violence.

Did it?

"Oh, don't worry about me. I work late all the time. And I
have pepper spray on my key chain," she bluffed. "Besides,
it's not that late. It's only eight-thirty."

Race studied her for a moment and Aimee was struck
again with the niggling sense that she was missing something crucial in her analysis of Race Gardner. Finally, after
what seemed like a long time but was probably only seconds, Race shrugged and started down the hall toward his
office.

"Okay, then. I'll see you tomorrow," he said, tossing the
words over his shoulder.

As she headed to the bank of elevators and pressed the
call button, Aimee let out the breath she'd been unconsciously holding. It was only as the elevator doors slid
closed that Aimee realized what was nagging at the back of
her mind. When Race had startled her out in the hallway, he
hadn't just emerged from the elevators. He'd been coming
from the direction of her office.